ACCEPTABLE

LOSSES

....

ACCEPTABLE

LOSSES

A NOVEL BY EDRA ZIESK

SOUTHERN METHODIST
UNIVERSITY PRESS
Dallas

This novel is a work of fiction. Names, characters, places, and incidents are either the product of the author's imagination or are used fictitiously.

Requests for permission to reproduce material from this work should be sent to:
   Rights and Permissions
   Southern Methodist University Press
   PO Box 750415
   Dallas, TX 75275-0415

Cover art: Edward Hopper, *Railroad Sunset*, 1929. Oil on canvas, 28¼ x 47¾ in. (71.8 x 121.3 cm.), Collection of Whitney Museum of American Art, Josephine N. Hopper Bequest, 70.1170. Photograph Copyright © 1996: Whitney Museum of American Art.

Design by Tom Dawson Graphic Design

LIBRARY OF CONGRESS CATALOGING-IN-PUBLICATION DATA
Ziesk, Edra.
   Acceptable losses : a novel / by Edra Ziesk. — 1st ed.
      p.   cm.
   ISBN 0-87074-412-7 (acid-free paper). — ISBN 0-87074-413-5
   (pbk. : acid-free paper)
   I. Title.
PS3576.I298A65   1996
813'.54—dc20   96-30701

Printed in the United States of America on acid-free paper
10 9 8 7 6 5 4 3 2 1

For Kika. For Ben.

PROLOGUE

....

The girl gets dressed in the gray light of the morning. Every morning begins like this: with the grayed mist that comes in off the ocean four blocks away and precedes whatever color the day will turn into. The house is silent and cool at this hour, her parents asleep in their room at the front of the house. The girl, Joellen, imagines they sleep on their backs, their hands folded, not touching.

There is cereal in the kitchen and fruit but there is not always milk. Her mother is not good at remembering milk or bread or butter or paper goods; sometimes they have paper towels in the bathroom lying over the spool meant for toilet paper, the toweling torn into strips like Civil War bandages.

Joellen pours cereal into a bowl then runs water on it. She eats, holding her lips away from her teeth. It is like eating wet cardboard. Still, it is a taste she is used to.

Joellen leaves the house and walks to and then down the highway which runs parallel to the beach, her feet kicking the ankle-high weeds at the side of the road. She watches the toes of her shoes, polished with wet. The walk to school is almost two miles. There is a school bus, a yellow van, that Joellen rides home but she likes the walk in the morning. When she arrives the sun has started to burn through the mist; it is the color, now, of cooked butter.

The public school that everyone goes to if they live in this town is a one-story building, L-shaped, like a sprawling ranch house, newish and roomy. Nobody's here yet. There are no teachers' cars in the parking lot, nobody out on the yellow and blue fiberglass swings or the gliders or on the ball field. Joellen walks on the side of the highway that is not the school side, past the large fenced fields and the barn and paddock of the horse farm where the dust is the color of band-aids and where there's a hot-walking machine and a sign that says Flats Boarded, Trained, Bred.

She hangs on the fence and watches the horses. They are lean and fleet even when they're not moving. After a time she begins to cluck for them. A horse approaches. His skin shudders in an ecstatic way under her hand and then he stands, his head raised, while she leans over the fence and speaks to him, her lips pressed to the side of his neck.

Her mother, Isabel, is afraid of these horses, or would be if she came here and saw them. Until Isabel told her this, Joellen did not think her mother was frightened by anything.

They were on the beach, a day of wind and big waves. Joellen shivered.

Cold, puss? Isabel said and tugged her so Joellen scooted across the foot or two of sand between them. Joellen was watching the waves, how they began to build far out and got bigger and bigger until, just before breaking, they seemed powerful enough to reach them, the waves' tongues flicking them into the water as if they were as small and feeble as ants.

Does anything scare you? Joellen asked, mesmerized by the waves. She knew water, waves, did not.

Where I grew up in Columbus, Ohio, Isabel said, we lived a block from a stable.

Joellen did not know this was in answer to her question. Sometimes she spoke and Isabel spoke but they did not speak about the same thing.

There were lots of stables in those days, Isabel said. There were rag men with horses. Fruit and vegetable men. Milk got delivered by a horse and wagon. I used to go stand at the stable sometimes. I liked watching the horses go in and out.

Joellen pictured this. Compared to watching the horses run at the horse farm, "go in and out" sounded monotonous.

This one day I had a fever. It must have come over me suddenly, I don't remember. I didn't have it, then I did. I was watching the horses, but they began to seem different. Huge. Their eyes rolled back in their heads. Their *teeth* . . . Isabel said, and looked away from the water, as if horses were galloping there. She said, I've been afraid of horses ever since.

They are spelling. A list of words is written out on the board, the capitals tall and authoritative, the small letters like a string of humbled children following behind. There is the tick of the teacher's pointer tapping its way like a blind person from letter to letter, and the teacher's voice – M, she says, M, she says, M. They are up to words that begin with M now, though it is only October. Rushing, as if the alphabet had to be gotten through by a particular date, like the liturgical calendar. They spend only one day, one span of forty-five minutes on each letter; that is all the time each letter gets.

But what about AVIATOR? Joellen thought when they moved on to B from the A's. What about ASSASSINATE? What about CELERY, what about CANTALOUPE, what about HIGHWIRE, HAYWIRE, HAVOC? Words had histories, they had near and sometimes distant relations: Band and Bandage, Meaning and Meaningless, Mother and Mothered and Motherly and Motherless. The omissions shocked Joellen, the wordy world shaved down. Once, driven by a kind of grief for the overlooked words, she waited for the classroom to empty at three, lingering over her knapsack and papers and books, and went up to the teacher and said, Some are missing. She meant to give examples but the words, the left out ones, crowded and pushed in her head and not one emerged.

Really? the teacher asked her. Now pay attention, I have a question for you, are you paying attention? Am I running this class, or are you?

Joellen spent her time now under the droning C-A-T-C-H and E-N-E-M-Y and F-U-R-T-H-E-R and F-A-R-T-H-E-R making her own list, goaded by panic at the words she knew but couldn't remember, at the words she did not know, trying to save as many as possible. She began sometimes at home, at night, hunting for words in the foods and colors and appliances around her, in the book she was reading, in her parents' conversation, but it didn't matter. There were always words she forgot, words that showed up too late.

The sun's heat, the way it blanks and opaques the windows, and the voice of the teacher make the air in the classroom feel warped, though because she is nine, and because she is not thinking of words that begin with W, Joellen would not put it this way. She feels muzzy and dazed, as though she is fractionally distanced from the things she is seeing and hearing.

Her desk is near a window – Joellen Stein – the last row, in the middle. If she stood (she will not stand) she could see the horse farm across the road, the fenced paddock and fields, the animals like splashes of mud on a carpet.

M-U-S-I-C, the teacher says, then the class, a pointer's tick behind her. M-U-L-T-I-P-L-Y.

MAGIC, Joellen thinks. She thinks MURDER. She thinks MAGNIFICENT.

There is a sound from the front of the room, like cellophane being pulled off a package, and there is a pause, the moment it takes for the class to realize that the noise is the PA system being turned on.

Fire drill, someone says.

Air raid, someone else says and Joellen pictures the classrooms emptied, the rows of children facing each other on the floor in the hall, backs to the cool tiled wall, hands on their heads, knees up, white triangles of underwear showing like pennants under girls' skirts. The air raid drills make Joellen's father angry. He says they are useless. He says they are worse, they make children so fearful. Joellen does not think of these things. She thinks that the halls are too crowded, that they smell, that there is not enough air. She thinks "air" raid is wrong.

Boys and girls, a voice says from the box that is fixed to the wall over the blackboard. It is the voice of the principal's secretary. It will be a message that somebody's mother has dropped off a sweater, a lunch; that somebody shouldn't forget to go to the dentist. They will not go out to the field behind the school or into the hall. They will not even get to stand up.

But the voice does not mention sweaters or lunches. The voice says, Mr. Harold, which is the principal's name, and then Mr. Harold – a mythical presence, like Oz – speaks out of the box. Joellen thinks she is paying attention but the feeling of being slightly removed from herself in the slow-moving thickness of the morning persists and she hears only linkless words, as though Mr. Harold is calling them out from a list: Crisis, he says, and Cuba, and Missiles, and Possible. He says Home and Dismissed and something else that begins with May God.

And then they are outside, the sun fierce off the line of yellow buses. The sky is vacant and vast, a benign dopey blue. Joellen sees the horses as she comes out the front door, before they disappear on the other side of the curtain of buses. She can see only two, standing near the fence. They do not move. Their forelocks hang into their eyes like bangs.

The bus lets her off at her corner. There are no people out. Joellen goes up the front steps and crosses the gloomy front porch and goes in the front door of their house. Their house – her mother's her father's hers – sits like a misfit, brick and stern, between its lighter, shingled neighbors.

Inside the house there is an unfamiliar sweetish smell, a smell like cooked plastic, that turns out to be the smell of the TV, turned on. The TV is not often allowed to be on in their house. This is the first odd thing.

Isabel is sitting on the couch, her face, her hands frosted in the light from the TV. This is the second.

Isabel is usually not here. When Joellen gets home from school at the usual time Isabel is out on the beach, hunting for pieces of colored glass that have been battered and smoothed by the ocean, or she is upstairs in her workroom where she turns the glass pieces into mosaics. There are clear jars filled with beach glass in this room, a separate jar for each color: the lilacs, the lavenders, the frosted whites, the root beers, the several greens. The jars have a faint flavored smell to Joellen, like candies.

Less often, Isabel is in the kitchen, her face pink with the heat of the stove and with effort, her colorless hair matted onto her forehead and neck so that she looks skinned from a distance. Isabel is large, she dwarfs objects, eggs and spoons look stunted and precarious in her hands. She is grim and furious when she cooks and she cooks in huge quantities as though she is saying – There! That will last for a month, for a year – but she does not freeze or preserve things. She sets it all out the first night – chickens and yams and stuffing and gravy and vegetables – and then for as many nights as there's anything left, the same food in the same serving dishes, the portions diminishing, the food going flaccid and gray. After a week or ten days or two weeks Leon, Joellen's father, smacks his hand down on the table and yells Enough! This food is inedible! Why can't we have normal dinners?

Isabel looks at Joellen still in the doorway. Do you want anything? Isabel asks.

Joellen wants her to be upstairs in her workroom. She wants to go down to the beach; to walk, separate but joined to her mother, looking for green or root beer or blue up ahead.

Isabel looks back at the TV. Bluish shadows crawl over her face.

And then Leon comes home, and this is the third odd thing, and there is a kind of shouting inside Joellen that is both silent and loud. He is not *supposed* to be home. He is *supposed* to be out, at one of the colleges in New York and Connecticut and in other parts of New Jersey where he teaches single biology classes. It is hard to find jobs, he says. He is lucky to have them, though he has to drive hours back and forth every day and it costs what he says is a fortune in gas money.

Joellen watches to see what Leon will do about Isabel and the TV. She expects him to rush over and kick out the plug. We are not a TV-watching family! she expects to hear Leon say, his voice shocked as if Isabel is in violation of some fundamental law agreed upon between them. A TV is something they have, like a telephone. Leon watches only the news; Joellen's allowed to watch only policed. She is not allowed to watch what everyone watches – The Three Stooges, Popeye. Leon thinks these shows are mindless, violent, warping.

But Leon does not even take off his coat. He sits down next to Isabel. He leans forward and watches.

Crisis, the heads and torsos of men on the TV say. Missile and Threat and Standoff and Crisis.

Sometimes Leon changes the channel. In the fractional moment between man and man Joellen feels hopeful. But it is always another man in a suit saying the same things; sometimes, from channel to channel, the words overlap.

Nothing is normal. Leon is home and it is still light out and then it is not and they have not had any dinner and they are still watching TV. Joellen does not sit on the couch or the chair that, with the TV, is all the furniture there is in the living room, the three things huddled together for company. She does not want to sit in the grayed light that seems to her faintly contaminated. I thought we were not a TV-watching family, she says, her voice stiff and prudish and unfamiliar to her.

Leon doesn't answer.

Isabel reaches out, strokes Joellen's hand, once, twice, over her knuckles. Just for tonight, Isabel says.

Hopefully, Leon says, then presses his thin lips together. His hair is thinning and straight and his lips are thin and his body is thin and rangy. There are moments when Joellen can see what he looked like young, and what he will look like old, but not what he looks like now.

Tonight's extraordinary, Isabel says and Joellen closes her eyes. She does not want things to be extraordinary. She wants things to be plain.

Will we be here tomorrow, Joellen thinks, meaning not here, in front of the TV; not here, in this room; meaning PRESENT, meaning alive. But it is too big, an almost infinite question. Instead she asks, Will there be school?

Isabel reaches for her, pulls Joellen into the deep V between her large legs. They are the weight, the cool creamy color of marble.

I don't know sweets, she says into the top of Joellen's head. Hope so.

Joellen feels her mother's lips move against her scalp the way her own lips move when she presses them into the necks of the horses.

We'll say yes, Isabel says, but Joellen hears the hesitation before the word, her mother considering.

Tomorrow is N, is what Joellen turns her mind to, and she begins to hunt for N words. There is the Couch and the Chair. There is the TV, the Floors (which are Wood) and the Windows. There are Pants here and Shirts, Shoes, Hair, Hands. There are Buttons and Tubes and Isabel's two Legs and two Breasts, and there is Crisis and Missiles, but no N words that she can think of. Only No, cousin of Not, child of Normal, of Nothing.

PART I

CHAPTER 1

....

After his father left, Joe Handy's mother got worse and
then better. In the first days of his father's absence she sat drinking in the living
room with the lights off, her pink robe wrapped around her, her hair a dyed color
somewhere between platinum and silver, her white thigh looming where the robe
splayed open. When Joe came in the first day if he did not know, or did not yet
believe his father had taken off again, the sight and smell of his mother – spilled
booze, the dirty-carpet smell of the robe – told him.

She stayed drunk for weeks, then it ended. She went back to living her life.
Went to work steady – she was a receptionist at a beauty parlor; she drank less,
looked better, three months, six months, and that's when his father came home,
like wherever he was he'd gotten word she was doing okay and it's what he'd been
waiting for.

When he came home, Joe's father started out better, then he got worse, so
it seemed like the first days or weeks of his parents' reunion were the only times
they were on the same level, before they started falling off opposite sides of a
mountain.

His father came home smoothed out and with cash in his pocket – what
seemed like reams. It would be there, sprayed over the bed and sometimes the floor,
as though his parents had tossed it up and rolled around in it: Clyde and Bonnie.
No one knew how his father came by the money, or at least Joe never heard. It
wasn't work, his father was not one for steady employment, though he told good
stories about looking for and losing or quitting jobs, stories that made them all
laugh except his brother Gene. Joe could not ask his father where the money came
from, and his mother did not talk much at these times, only stood at the stove in
the kitchen and smiled, flirting with all of them, her face pink and shining, her eyes
flicking between the door and the stove and the door again.

Joe did ask Gene once: Where you think he gets it all? That money? his eyes
on Gene's hands lacing up black high tops. Gene was almost five years older, tall
and big also, and his size and his bulk, different from Joe's and from their father's,
made Joe sometimes shy in Gene's presence.

Gene didn't look up or stop lacing. Don't know, don't care, he said.

You don't think he, I don't know . . . Where could he get it? Joe said. He was thinking "bank robbery," which scared him but made him also vaguely proud.

Gene looked up at him. You got something that interests me you wanta talk about Joe? This doesn't interest me.

Those times just before and just after his father returned were the times Joe waited for without knowing he was waiting, but he waited for the other times too. The night when a dish broke, a glass got hurled, when noise swelled up and filled and burst out of the too-small, flimsy house.

The fighting began when his father announced, or his mother did, her voice scornful and cold, that he wasn't looking for work, that he didn't mean to, that he was just drinking up the money they did have. Maybe he'd ask her for money – A few bucks to tide me over. There's a few things I need.

Things! his mother said. I can name two: a brown paper bag and a bottle – but it was less about drinking that they fought than about where he went, who he drank with.

After he'd been home a month or two, clean months when they both worked and ate cooked meals and got up and washed in the mornings, Joe's father went back to the gas station where he spent his days with eight or ten other idle men leaning against the sun-heated hoods of parked cars, passing around bottles and cigarettes.

The gas station had no name, no sign, except for an old one that once said ATLAS BATTERIES, but that had lost its A and its T. Las Bat-ter-ies, Joe called it with an Iberian accent, like it was an island nation someplace whose name it was important to say right.

The gas station was owned by Claude Freemont, but nobody called it Freemont's, nobody but Joe called it Las Batteries, it was just "the gas station," the way some men said "The War." There was another gas station in town, the Last Gas Before Highway, the town's southernmost boundary. Nobody used it but summer weekenders, mostly boys in their early twenties and the girls who came with or on account of them, pouring in Friday nights blaring their car radios and whooping and trying to drink more beers than anyone else had, ever, and lived. Sunday nights they lined up at the Last Gas, wearing no shoes and cutoffs, their bare feet stuck out their car windows. Bennies, everyone called them, the sandy and drunk and rutting boys, though no one remembered who'd started that name or what it referred to.

Everyone hated the bennies, talked about the damage they did to the town and the houses they rented, though it was a shore town, it was their business most people relied on. But nobody hated them as much as the men at the gas station, and nobody talked about them more. Nobody had more time.

The men talked about other things too, though not about any one thing as much as the bennies. They snapped on each other and laughed. They listened for phrases or preferences or complaints from each other and used them for nicknames: Paint and Stogie and Big Daddy and My Man and Ringer or Ring-o and Bud and Miller and Vino and Scrapheap and Hoop and Cowboy and Stretch or Tiny and Abe and George and Twink and Sexy and Pappy and Gimp. Some of the names stuck, some changed. Joe's father Rusty was Bantam or Rooster or Red because he had boxed in his young years – semi-pro, he said; could've done better – on a circuit that took him from one small town to another, to bouts held in barns or garages at ten or eleven or midnight. They had the same grimed smell of blood and men's sweat and the same vicious and scratchy excitement as cock fights.

It was the talking the men did, all day every day and then they came back and started up again the next morning, that Joe's mother could not understand or live with. There were times when she stood in the kitchen, her arms crossed tight on her chest, and asked Rusty – What is it you all find to *say* all day long?

Rusty always told her. He went into detail, what this one said and what that one answered, and she felt better at first because it was *nothing* they talked about, nothing important or secret or interesting, even. But after a while she stopped picking over each word and remembered the quickness and color of Rusty's face and the way his hands flew when he talked of the men and she went back in her head over all the days and hours their life together added up to and tried to recall one single time when he'd looked like that, talking to her.

Joe's sitting out on the front step – a cracked concrete slab separated by two inches of air from the ones in front of the next-door houses. The houses are so close together you could sneeze or cough and not know if it was you or your neighbor; you could stick an arm out your dining room window and take a piece of plastic fruit off the dining table next door. It was supposed to be a summer community when it was built: a crescent of houses, a crescent of road around a man-made lake, but the lake never got dug and was still just a heap of dirt, pinkish and rutted. Borderline families lived here.

It's eleven o'clock. The light's clear and lemony, the wind's coming in off the water a mile away. Joe can smell the slight sourness of the salt and he puts his tongue out to taste it. He's waiting for LuAnne, his mother, to call him for breakfast. She does not often cook in the morning, but last night she said she was going to; laughed and said it'd be tomato juice and blueberry pancakes, red, white and blue for Memorial Day.

Joe's hungry, but breakfast is only half what he's waiting for. He wants the money LuAnne said she would give him to spend at the Fireman's Fair where he's been every day since it opened, but only to look. He's twelve, he doesn't have money of his own to spend, and he can't ask his father, who he knows is busted.

Joe's alone, then he's not: he feels someone behind him, the slight increase in weight or heat or pressure of the air at his back.

Hot out? his mother asks. Joe doesn't answer, waiting for some clue in her breathing, her voice, to her mood. If he says a wrong thing, she will not give him money.

Joe?

What.

You seen him this morning? Joe hears the faint click as she stands behind him, biting her nails.

Who? Joe says, though he knows she means his father, not Gene, and he thinks suddenly how no one ever asks where Gene is.

Joe turns on the step and sees, through the smoky mesh of the screen door, the faint pink of his mother's bathrobe, the dull silvered light off her hair. He says, Gene still here? though he knows Gene's at work, at the Last Gas, a job Rusty never mentions.

Go get him, his mother says. Go down there and tell him I need him. It's not something she's planned, just an idea she says as it comes to her; she might only be saying – Get me cigarettes, Joe. Get me an iced Coke – and Joe says to her, Ma. The Fair!

LuAnne, who's begun to walk back towards the kitchen, throws her weight forward, hits the door so it sings, then catches it on the rebound with her foot and what Joe's looking at now is the wild pink fur of her slipper.

I didn't hear, she says, her voice still pleasant so it doesn't go with the uncombed-looking slipper or the heave of the door.

You got a *job* to go to, son? You got some *occupation* I don't know about? Cause that's fine with me, see, you won't hear a peep out of me, I could use help gettin' food on this table. Now, unless you got some *job*, I'd appreciate it if you'd get your tight little Indian butt offa that step. She says Indian because Joe's hair is lank and black and flops over his forehead and because his eyes are near-black and, she says, don't show what he's thinking, like his father's. But she doesn't mean it as praise.

The gas station's maybe a half mile from their house. The closer Joe gets, the slower he walks. He does not want to go there; stand with his feet at the yellow curved line that lets you know where the road ends and the station begins. He does not want to see the men curled like large dogs over the hoods of the cars; smell, closer up, the stench of piss, old and new and sun-heated, that got so bad sometimes the men themselves couldn't stand it and made faces and fanned at the air and pointed at one another saying, I'd know the smell of *that* piss anywhere! There was nothing here that made him proud of his father.

Joe stands on the road side of the curved yellow line and waits for Rusty to look up and see him. He stands a long time because he's at some distance from where the men are but he will not cross the line: it's a promise he's made to himself. The men's movements are small from this distance, and blurred: a leg goes up on a bumper, a hand passes a brown paper bag. Joe feels his muscles beginning to twitch with the effort of holding himself perfectly still, but he does not mind this; likes the command he has over himself.

Then Rusty sees him and waves, his arm a long arc, but Joe will not move; will not move even when Rusty calls to him – Joe boy! Bring yourself back here! He holds out, making his father come to him.

You here for me? Rusty calls, on his way, slightly breathless.

She sent me, Joe says. Says she needs you. He feels eased after he says it.

You know why? Rusty says, and the way Joe hears it makes it seem he's about to be told some meaningful thing about his parents' marriage.

Why? he says.

Rusty smiles, his sharp nose and thin lips spreading and softening, then rebounding to sharpness. Why she wants me, he says.

Needs's all she told me, Joe says.

Rusty sighs, he waves at the men, then he tells Joe, Come on then.

They walk across the gas station as though this is the way they'd been heading. Rusty's shoes drag and stub on the paving and Joe looks down at them – slim shoes, black and low cut, a good leather, though they're filmed with dust now like worn Sunday shoes, handed down.

They walk down an alley and across the train tracks and past the stores of downtown and when they come out at the highway across from the marina Rusty says, Be outta school in a minute. Bet you got some big plans! and he winks.

Joe wants to say – opens his mouth and almost does say – How do you mean? because it's the kind of thing someone who does not expect to be here for the ending of school or the summer might say, but then he closes his mouth again biting the inside of his cheek, and that sharp and then lingering pain trips off another, a growling ache deep inside him, and he rubs his fist under his ribs.

You hungry? Rusty says, and Joe thinks – that must be what I am, and remembers that he didn't have any breakfast.

Okay, Rusty says. Let's go take care of business.

You got money? Joe says, then is instantly sorry. There are certain words he tries to keep from his father: money and leaving and family and father, whose great single weight could tip Rusty one way or the other, and Joe makes himself chew at the sore place inside his cheek.

But Rusty laughs; says, Don't you worry about it, baby boy. Believe it or not, I manage. I always got something tucked into my shoe for the necessaries. Just don't be tellin' LuAnne!

They are walking in the direction of the park where the Fireman's Fair is. You been here yet? Rusty says, lifting his chin at the Fair banner strung across the highway.

Joe shrugs and says, Sort of.

Sort of, Rusty says and puts his hand on Joe's shoulder and steers him across the four-lane, two-way highway. Sun glares off the asphalt and it streaks off the passing cars, so it's only the pressure of Rusty's hand on Joe's shoulder that saves him from stepping right out into traffic, and he feels what he never feels: a loosening of his own vigilance.

Rusty buys them each corn dogs; Joe watches him take money out of his pocket and pay and take the two dogs in his hands, and they walk through the Fair eating them, though Joe's only barely aware that he's eating: with each bite, the taste's a surprise.

They walk up the Midway, past rides and shies and booths of clairvoyants hung with black curtains painted with Zodiac symbols in bright scabbing colors. The booths have a tired generic feel. They lack the specific eagerness Joe saw in them the other times he'd been here, with no money.

On their second pass down the Midway Rusty stops at a booth where there are wooden milk bottles stacked up in pyramids and baskets of taped, chewed-looking baseballs and where stuffed rabbits and squirrels and pandas and dogs in the unreal colors of fruit-flavored sodas hang on the walls and ceiling of the booth. Joe's mother has a collection of animals like these that she keeps in a glass cabinet in the dining room though they are faded, their colors grayed down by dirt.

Used to be, I was pretty good at this, Rusty says, his eyes on the largest stuffed animal prizes hanging from the struts of the booth's canvas awning. What do you think, should I take me a shot, Joe? Rusty hands over his dollar, and takes the three balls the man in the booth hands out from his apron.

Rusty picks up one ball, holds it up with three fingers and he begins to turn it in a slow, delicate way, his thumb lightly stroking its taped sides. Watching him, Joe can barely see the ball rotate. Rusty's arm comes down finally, slowly. He stands still for a moment, the ball in his left hand – he is left handed – his right hand cupping his left, then he winds up, he pitches. Joe sees Rusty's shoulder pop and extend, the elbow, the following wrist, the ball leaves his hand, the hand stays extended, the fingers empty, curved downwards. It occurs in slow motion; the ball takes its time, sure of its own weight and of the thrust and intention behind it, then the pins shatter out – an explosion – though their noise is an ordinary one, like a toppled tower of blocks.

Joe blinks. The man in the booth says, What'll it be? and pulls two small sawdust-stuffed animals, stiff and immobile, from under the counter.

My wife likes them big ones, Rusty says.

The man looks amused. Big ones take three, he says.

Then I'll do three, Rusty says, and Joe wants to yell Stop! Stop! because Rusty seems suddenly open to failure or loss; to pain Joe can already feel for him. But he does not speak, he stands still and watches his father repeat the same deliberate motions – the almost invisible turn, turn, turn of the ball; the set and the windup. And he watches his father pitch again, the same flattened-out muscles, the snap of the shirt fabric over his back, and before the ball even hits Joe knows it's going to – 80, 90, 100 miles an hour he will say for the years and years he keeps telling this story.

A winner, a winner, the barker calls out in a slow lackadaisical way. He picks up the ball Rusty's just thrown and rubs his thumb over the tape and looks up at Rusty who laughs and leans over the counter and says to him, Don't you worry. It's still there. Secret's safe with me.

Rusty throws the third ball and knocks out a third pile of pins and this time the man doesn't call out. He just looks at Rusty, one eye half shut and suspicious.

We'll take that blue dog there, Rusty says and he points to a large dog the color of toilet bowl cleaner. The man needs a ladder to get it and while they're waiting, Rusty moves so his mouth's close to Joe's ear and he says to him – It's a racket. It's fixed. That tape? They put little pieces of lead underneath so the balls pitch all nuts. You just need to feel around for 'em, he says and holds his hand up again, the palm cupped, the fingers curved and Joe holds his hand the same way.

Compensate, Rusty says. Just take your time. Don't let 'em push you. You remember that, Joe. Compensate. Remember it was me who told you, and he leans in to take the blue dog from the barker.

Now that's fine, Rusty says, holding the dog out in front of him. You think this'll get your mother to forgive me? and he laughs.

I tell you what Joe, his father says, still looking right at the blue dog. I got an idea. Do this for me. Take this on home, give it to her.

What about you? Joe says. I'm supposed to be bringin' *you* home, not some blue dog. I'm . . .

Shhhh, Rusty says. Just to soften her up. Let her see it and keep it a bit, then I'll come waltzing in. She won't be so mad at me after a while. He winks as he hands the blue dog to Joe, then lays his hand on Joe's head, the palm scooped, the fingers spanned.

Take her that dog, he says. Say I'm on my way.

Joe doesn't look up, his head bowed under the weight of his father's hand. His eyes are on his father's delicate black shoes with their thin skim of dust. He sees them move, kicking and slapping at the dust of the Midway, and he holds the blue dog to his chest.

The dog's color runs when it comes up against dampness. Joe's palms and chest are turning the color the dog is. That blue: it will never come out of his shirt.

CHAPTER 2

Joe walks slowly home, holding the blue dog up to his chest. When it gets too heavy he holds it by an ear, the dog's flat seat bumping down the sidewalk behind him. The house is dark, LuAnne does not turn on lights during the day, but Joe thinks maybe she's gone too, and he pictures Gene and himself living here on their own. They are both in the kitchen eating cereal for breakfast. They are both standing up, wearing green jackets, he doesn't know why.

A noise from inside, the sound of a dish sliding over a dish, brings him back to the hot day, the sidewalk, the blue dog. He picks up the dog and goes in.

It's so dark inside, Joe can't see. He keeps his eyes open and watches the varied opacities in the room, dark shifting on dark; he thinks: this is what it's like to go blind.

Dishes smack in the kitchen. LuAnne knows someone is there, she's waiting to see how long it takes before she is noticed, tapping off seconds against the inside of the sink with a fingernail, the taps tiny and furious.

Ma? Joe calls.

LuAnne leans on the sink and looks out the window at the twin window of the house next door, though there is nothing to see: the window has a shade down, behind the shade that house is dark. The women who live in these houses smile at each other outside but they swaddle their windows in shades and blinds and lined drapes.

When enough time has passed in her own estimation, LuAnne leaves the kitchen, moves the two steps it takes to get to the living room. She is buoyant with anger, ready to say what she's been thinking all the hours she's waited – What if I was *sick*? What if I was *dying*? She has come, almost, to believe this.

Her eyes are focused front, at the height where she expects to meet Rusty's face, but there is nothing at that height; her eyes shoot straight back to the windows. Then something looms at her.

Here, Joe says, and shoves the blue dog at his mother. He told me to give you this. Said he'll be home later – and when he can feel that the dog has found LuAnne, that she has it, he lets go. His arms are suddenly light, and as he turns and runs out of the house – he is out the door with the sound of her voice, loud and thinned out behind him – Where? Joe? Jooooe! – they lift on their own, light as air.

CHAPTER 3

....

After his mother receives the blue dog from Joe's hands – when he has passed it, felt the release of its weight, pried open his cramped, knotted fingers – he runs. He pushes on the screen door which is light to him after the weight of the dog, and his mother's voice wheels behind him, the same as the sound the door makes, the same as the sound of the still air parted by the velocity of his moving body.

He runs till he sees the curved yellow line that marks off the road from the gas station, the yellow line like clown's lips, the yellow levitating above the blacktop, and he steps over the line, shuddering off the voice in his head that says Stop!, answering the voice by the forward thrust of his body.

He keeps his eyes on the cluster of men, watches their faces begin to resolve into features; keeps, as he nears them, only one face in his sight so that he will not know for this step, or this step, or the next that his father is not among them. He keeps his eyes on a face that is the pink of canned ham, that looks back at him and says, finally, What you want here, boy? Speak up!

My father, Joe says. Rusty Handy.

Joe, right? another man says. You his young one?

Joe turns towards this voice. He has to turn his whole body and in the process of turning, in the second before his eyes get to where his body is, he thinks this other man, slight, pale, silvery, is his father. The thought's in his body; before he can stop it he half-lunges towards the slight man, stops himself, nearly falls. There is laughter – the ham-colored man begins it – that comes also from the rest of the men except for the slight man. Joe looks straight at him, asks, He here?

Somebody shrugs – Joe sees it as a blur in the side of his vision, but he doesn't turn towards it. He waits for the slight man to speak.

Not since early, the slight man tells him, his voice an apology.

Not since he went off, the shrugging man says.

That was you, right? the slight man says. His eyes haven't moved off Joe; when Joe looks back at him it is like they're the only two here. This morning? the man says.

Joe nods to answer, but the gesture is lost; the slight man looks up when he says the word morning, then all the men do as though it is the signal that makes them notice the heat and the height of the sun, and they begin to move back towards the shade thrown by the garage. While they were talking of him, Rusty was here; now Joe sees he's gone, gone like he'd never been born, been a boy, grown up and married and had Gene and had him. Rusty Handy? Nobody here by that name. Mistaken.

Joe almost believes this. Then the men begin to move towards the shade and their stir and movement bring Joe back to himself: a boy who will not give up on his father.

He leaves the gas station. He doesn't know where he's going but he believes he will know, something will tell him, and this belief seems part of his belief in his father. Belief spreads in him, a sweet tidal roll.

Joe is near the marina now, the sky a dome of blue stitched to the blue basin of water, the water cracked with white. He heads down the pier where speedboats are moored and the half-day and full-day and night fishing boats that take parties out after blues. He looks out over the water towards the invisible line where the marina becomes the Atlantic; from where he is the ocean looks calm, nearly flat, the tide gently rucking the surface, the surface the color of cardboard, and he thinks for the first time about some other place: about where his father might be instead of where he is not.

You a fisherman son? a man calls. Joe aims for the place the voice came from, hits it and squints. The man's on the bow of a large fishing boat, the sun behind him. Parties of 50, a sign on the starboard side says. The boat's the scooped shape of a cradle. Take y'out, the man says, get ya back in time for supper. *With supper!*

Joe looks at the boat as though he's weighing the attributes of this large one over one that is smaller and faster, of day over night fishing, of blues, though he has no money and if he did, would not spend it on a boat that is always in sight of the shore. He looks out again, at the ocean. He says, I'd like to go farther.

Father? the man says. I ain't got no kids, that I know of! and he laughs, a spluttering sound that turns into coughing and scares off the gulls that hang like a mobile over the stern, drawn by the fish smell, by the bucket of chum.

Joe looks back at the man; his eyes move but no part of the rest of him. It's not a boy's stillness and the man laughs again, and when he speaks it is louder, as though Joe's maybe deaf as well as motionless.

Joke, the man says. Old bachelor joke, matter of fact. No kids, he says and holds his palms up showing they're empty. No lady ever liked me enough *to* get married!

Joe nods, as though this is what he's come to hear. Thanks, he says to the man though he does not mean for the confession or the offer of fishing. He knows what he will do now. If his father is gone, he'll go too. Go *after* his father, he thinks, hearing the double meaning in it: either he'll find Rusty or he'll be the next one to leave. Either one.

Joe goes home because, until he has money, there is no other place for him to go, but he knows his return is temporary so he doesn't mind it. He does not stand out on the sidewalk the way he did earlier or stop just inside the front door and hold his breath against the smells of his mother, and he does not slow or answer when she calls – Gene? Joe?

He goes up to his room, stands facing inwards. If she follows him he will continue on into the room, throw himself down on the bed. Waiting, he looks at the narrow metal locker which serves as his closet; at the sparse collection of toys, sports equipment, boxes of battleship models: somebody's idea of what a boy must like. He has never been one for toys. A desire for things – if it had ever been there in him – atrophied early, and it was not just covetousness followed by disappointment followed by a returning and stronger covetousness that got snapped off close to the root because it was useless to covet. He had simply not wanted the things most boys wanted. All his wanting, since as far back as he could remember, had gone into his father.

Now it is money he wants, and when he is sure his mother is not on her way up behind him, he walks his quiet, holding-back walk into his parents' bedroom and he slowly opens his father's drawers and kneads into the underwear that is old and soft, almost translucent from washing. He is not expecting to find money here, he just needs a place to begin, and he continues on to the bathroom and takes each thing out of the medicine chest and opens it to see if there are bills, folded and taped into the lids. He goes next to Gene's room where there is a narrow camp bed, like his own, and another gray locker and where there is also a desk, crowded into the minute space, that LuAnne and Rusty bought years ago in the midst of one of those rosy spells that followed Rusty's returns. Gene's never used it, too small and too frail, plywood with glued-on veneer that wept compacted sawdust. In the center is a hubcap where Gene dumps the change from his pockets and things – a keychain, a saint's medal, an earring made out of pink and mint-colored and frosted glass – forgotten or given to him by girls.

Joe carries the hubcap with the rim cutting into his chest and slides the change out on his bed. It has the dirty cold smell of tarnished metal, a tang he can feel in his teeth. He thins the pile down to one layer and picks out the silver and two bills he finds folded and buried – a ten and a five – then he puts back the pennies and refits the hubcap into the clean circle inside the surrounding circle of dust on the desk.

There is $22.90, counting the ten and the five. It does not feel wrong to Joe that he is taking this money, or the wrong has no intensity. The money is Gene's, but it only sits there, as unused as the medal and keychain and earring.

Then he waits. Gene's not home, still at work or out with a girl. His brother's life is distant and hazy to Joe, a thing he does not see and so does not think about the way he does not think about other lives which brush but do not intersect his: teachers, the kids in his class, the man on the fishing boat. It has never occurred to him to envy other lives, as though his parents had neglected to teach him this, too.

Joe walks all the way to the Last Gas Before Highway, though it is more than four miles. He is planning to hitch when he gets there, but he doesn't hitch now. It's the still-dark part of the early A.M.; cars won't see him at the side of the road until his still form jumps into their headlights, and by the time the drivers are sure what they're seeing – a boy in jeans and a light, zippered jacket, his straight dry hair falling into his eyes – they will have already swept past. It's maybe four or four-thirty, the time he felt it was safest to leave, after Gene got home and Joe heard the slide of cloth off his brother's body, the zippers and laces.

He waited until he was sure Gene was asleep, then waited longer. He went down the stairs, stopped at the bottom, his heart kicking hard so that he could feel his carotid artery beat. His mother was still in the living room, upright in her chair. He waited for her to move, to drink from the glass she was holding, balanced, on her leg, or to light a cigarette, but she'd done none of these things.

The road's dark as he walks, he can't even see his own feet moving below him. From a distance, the lights of the Last Gas smoke; the station has the look of a lit, empty room. In the dark and at this distance it seems as though the earth ends there.

Joe walks past the gas pumps to where the highway heads south. He doesn't know why he is sure that his father's gone further south except that he can't call up a picture of Rusty headed in any other direction – towards a city, towards a tropical climate, towards a crowded, distant state. He only walked off, like he was going someplace nearby for his dinner.

He waits for a ride a long time. He is patient and the patience is pleasurable to him. Traffic begins to pick up as it gets lighter, though there is no moment when Joe, watching, could have said the increase had begun. He stands with his hand out, his thumb cocked. He feels he has stepped outside of the whirling mass of debris that is his childhood and when a car stops and Joe sees himself in the opaque silvered glass of the closed window, he's surprised that the outside of him is still a boy.

The door opens and Joe bends to look in; sees first bare knees and then cut off shorts and a pink halter top, a girl with both hands on the wheel.

In or out, the girl says, not looking at him. This is not my idea of the world's greatest view.

Joe gets in. The girl pulls the car back onto the highway.

I can take you anyplace, the girl says, long as it's south. I'm goin' all the way to fucking Cape May, she says, meaning the southernmost point of this part of New Jersey. Hell, I'll maybe park in Cape May and keep going, cross on over to Europe. I'll disappear off the fuckin' map of the earth, she says, pardon my French.

I just had a fight with somebody, the girl says. Four hours and one hour minus ten minutes ago. I been driving around ever since. She sounds proud of the accumulation of time, as though it adds up to something.

So, she says. Where are you headed?

Joe looks at the girl. Her thigh spreads slightly upwards into her shorts. Her skin is as creamy as wet soap and pink; paler, though in the same spectrum of pink, as her halter. She's maybe sixteen. Joe knows she's not interested in where he's going. She's only looking for troubles to measure her own up against.

After my father, Joe tells her.

Where's he at?

Don't know for sure.

The girl, who is interested in endings, says, Think you'll find him?

Joe says, I do, and sureness kicks in him again and he looks at the speedometer, willing it to move faster.

The girl nods. She says, Well, you just tell me where you want to get out.

They drive. It's fully light now, almost seven. Joe reads the signs above and at the side of the highway.

See, it's this boy, the girl says as though she's returning to a subject she'd started before. My *boy*friend, she says, my *ex*-boyfriend, that's if he was my boyfriend to start with, I don't know.

I'm not a *chump*, she says. What does he think, I'm fuckin' *stupid?* Pardon my French.

Joe only listens.

He tells me he has to go over his mother's, there's this *squirrel* problem, there's squirrels upstairs in her house and at night they come down and they run across her in her bed. We're supposed to be goin' someplace, an engagement party, my best friend, well, one of, but he has to see to those squirrels, so I say okay, it's like an *emergency*, right? even if his mother is wacked. She pauses, pushes the cigarette lighter in on the dashboard, tumbles her hand in her bag, looking up, looking down, looking up.

So he says he'll be by for me later, after the squirrels. So I'm ready, you know? I'm dressed (Joe looks at her halter, pictures a dress the same pink) and I'm sittin' there waiting and it's six and it's seven – the party's six-thirty – and it's eight and it's nine and it's fuckin' ten-*thirty* and don't ask me why I am sitting there all by myself all that time, I guess I *am* stupid. But I'm worried too. I mean maybe something *happened*. Maybe the fuckin' squirrels *attacked* him, so I call up. Mrs. Esterhaus? the girl says, holding the hand with the cigarette up to her ear like a phone.

Mrs. Esterhaus? she says again. The old witch won't let me call her her first name which is Minnie, like who'd *want* to. Mrs. Esterhaus, I go, how's the squirrel problem? and you know what she says to me? Squirrels? she says to me. Where do I think I'm callin', the *zoo?* Fuckin' squirrels? I mean, where'd he get that from? Who makes that stuff up?

She is suddenly crying and Joe looks over at her. Her shoulders are hunched and she has both her hands on the wheel, and he touches her, one finger rests on the jut of her shoulder bone. The girl cries harder.

Joe shifts slightly nearer, in case he needs to lean over and steer. The girl cuts the wheel hard to the right and he does lean, his hands shoot up into the air, but she's pulling off the road. She sits for a minute, her head resting against the wheel, crying. Joe doesn't speak or touch her, just waits for her to stop.

I don't suppose you carry tissues? she asks him, and he takes off his jacket, hands her the sleeve and she wipes her eyes on it.

Thanks, she says. Whew. Believe it or not, I'm not a crier. The last time I was maybe twelve when my mother said I couldn't shave my legs till I was four-teen. I didn't even cry when my grandmother died. I am so fuckin' *mad!* She takes a deep breath, another. I'll shut up now. She looks down at Joe's jacket, spread like an apron over her lap. She runs her nail down the zipper.

You're a nice boy, she says and looks up at Joe; her eyes are red and white and blue and there's a pink band spanning her forehead from the wheel's impression. She raises her hand, brushes the hair out of Joe's eyes. His hands raise and hover just over his knees.

The girl leans in towards him, her eyes close as she comes; Joe sees her nos-trils flare once, delicately, and then her mouth is on his mouth, her tongue on his lips so that he knows to open them and his teeth, though he has not ever done this before, and he touches her tongue with his own. His hands are still raised but he doesn't use them, doesn't touch the girl except where their tongues are touch-ing; does not move his hands on her arms or her legs or her throat though she is all skin, and when she sits back he does not lean in after more. He is still a boy. He knows the kiss belongs to some upcoming part of his life.

The girl, facing front again, holds her hair up off the back of her neck, rolls it in a skein around her hand. Look, she says. You think you can pick up another ride here? I changed my mind. I'm goin' back.

Joe nods.

I'm sorry, she says.

Not on my account. Joe smiles. Watch out for squirrels, he tells her.

The girl says, I been goin' with him four years. Four *years!*

Joe gets out of the car. The girl calls him back and he bends to the open window thinking "kiss," and watches the way her mouth moves when she speaks.

There's not always a choice, she says. Sometimes you only get yes-or-no answers. Then she edges out onto the highway, illegally crosses, and heads back in the direction they came.

It's cool outside the car, and Joe puts on the jacket, feeling the residual dampness from the girl's tears on the sleeve. He stands a long time, hours, he can tell from the progress of the sun and from the heat. No cars stop.

He's hungry, he can't remember the last time he had food – the corn dog Rusty bought him? – and once he knows that he's hungry it's all he can think about, but he won't walk off the highway to get something, like his one ride might approach and drive off while he's gone. Gene's money is still in his pocket. He is conscious now in a way he was not earlier of the collective weight of the quarters and nickels and dimes.

Heat makes the passing cars waver, car after car, and in the heat on his shoulders and face and back and bouncing off cars and the highway, Joe begins to think about shade, then shade's all he can think of, the intensity of this want dimming his want for food, for a ride, for his father.

He is so focused on withstanding the force of his physical needs that for a minute he does not notice the car pulled onto the shoulder a few dozen yards short of where he is standing. He blinks at it, sun bouncing off chrome, a white blaze that scars his vision and blinds him to all but the shape of the car, then he walks towards it. When he gets to the car, the passenger door's open and Joe looks inside and it's Gene.

Joe stays where he is for a minute, bent, staring at Gene in the car, then he gets in.

She's at it again. Dead drunk, Gene says the first thing after Joe's in the car, as though this news is the thing Gene drove all this distance to tell him.

Joe nods. He says, I gotta have somethin' to eat.

Gene pulls into a place off the highway, a tipped concrete hut set at one end of a vacant lot, weeds pushing up through the blacktop. It has the look of an abandoned drive-in and Joe thinks, The food here must be old.

You pay, Gene says as they wait for the hamburgers and fries and the two large Cokes, extra ice, that Joe ordered. It's the only time Gene mentions the money. Joe takes the ten and the five and puts them on the tray when the food comes.

The hamburgers are gray, they sweat grease, and Joe thinks again of the age of the meat and sticks to the two Cokes, the ice clicking against the side of the tall waxed cup, the cup sweating and softening in his hand.

You almost made it, Gene says when he's done eating. He looks for a napkin, lifting the hamburgers Joe hasn't touched, finally using the wax-coated wrapper.

To? Joe says.

To him. The old man. That's where you're goin'. I'm right, am I right?

Gene pulls out, licking the salt from the corners of his mouth. The hamburger wrapper is still in his hand. He keeps his foot off the gas, lets the car roll down the grade of the empty off-road as he looks for the place to get back on the highway, but they drift past the north-bound entrance, turning at the on-ramp marked south.

Where? Joe says, his voice high and squeaking. He clears his throat, Where're you goin'?

I said you were close, Gene says. Might as well go the distance.

For the slice of one second, Joe thinks he and Gene want the same thing. A picture comes into his head of their father standing out on some street waiting for them. He sees himself tumbling out of the car before Gene's fully stopped – from behind him Gene's voice saying Whoa!, but he knows Gene's smiling from the way the word lifts at the end – and he runs, his legs churning and awkward as though they are suddenly longer than the last time he used them, and he hurls himself into his father.

He's shacked up with some babe with big tits, Gene says, and Joe's confused. There is no point of meeting between Gene's voice and what's going on in Joe's head. What? he says.

The old man. Where he goes, where he's gone all these years. Big tits and bucks, Gene says.

No way, Joe says. How the fuck would you know? His father is farther away and cleaner than that.

I know, Gene says. I been out here. I followed him too. More than one time.

Bullshit, Joe says. If he was dead right in front of you you'd take a step over. Bullshit.

Joe, Gene says. I *know!* I *been* there! Gene takes a breath. Years back, he says. I don't know, he didn't used to stay gone so long then. You probably don't remember. I felt like you then. I did, he says when Joe turns his head and looks out the window.

So this one time, he's gone and I get in the car. I'm thirteen, fourteen. Needless to say, no license. He smiles, waits, but Joe won't look at him.

I follow him. He was easy, standin' there right by the Last Gas which wasn't the Last Gas then. I just followed. He goes to this house and he goes in and I wait and that night he comes out with the babe. I sat there for two days. Probably you don't remember that either, those two days I was gone.

Joe closes his eyes, shakes his head, but he does. He does remember.

He stayed put in that house. When he came out, she was with him.

Joe suddenly can't breathe; the air rushing into the car's open windows feels solid to him and dense and clotted, and he says to Gene, Stop!

Stop? Gene says. I'm finished. You hadda know this, Joe. He ain't worth . . .

Stop! Joe says. Pull over! Stop the car!

We're close, Gene says. We're almost there, his voice the murmuring voice of a dentist or doctor.

Stop! Joe says again, and when Gene doesn't stop, when he doesn't slow or pull over, Joe pulls up the lock on his door and though there is wind pushing against the outside of the door like a gang of hands, he gets the door opened, moves to the edge of the seat, watches the asphalt coming up, coming up, coming up, and Gene's shouting, What the fuck's the matter with you, are you nuts? Are you crazy? his voice dimmed by the roar of the wind.

Gene leans across Joe, the hard roped muscles standing out in his neck and his arm, and he holds onto the open door's handle with one hand. When there's a big enough gap in the traffic he slows, he pulls off the highway.

Fuckin' maniac! he yells. He throws himself out of the car, he's coming around to Joe's side. What the fuck's *wrong* with you? You need a fuckin' psychiatrist?

I'm not yours, Joe says. You don't get to choose for me. He thinks of the girl saying "not everybody gets choices."

Joe, Gene says. He makes his voice quieter, it is a physical effort and he hates his father: hates him. I know you don't understand this, but I only did it for one reason. I can't stand it, watching you always *expect* something from the son-of-a-bitch! He's not worth it! I can't stand it, that's all! Gene walks away down the shoulder of the highway. He walks a distance, like he is not intending to stop, but Joe never thinks he might just keep going.

Look, Gene says, when he's back in the car. I didn't plan this. I just came after you, it was like me all over again, but I didn't think about doin' this till I saw you. I'd of let you go, if there was something to go to, but there's nothin', there's not. There's less than what you got to go back to and Christ knows, that's nothin' either.

Me, Gene says. I got a girl. I'm gettin' out, gettin' married. His voice is low and joyless; he speaks with his head turned away from Joe, towards the window. The back of his neck's a pink-brown to his collar from the time he spends out in the sun at the Last Gas.

I only wanted, Gene says, his head still turned, to save you from pain. He stops talking and in the cessation of sound in the car, the outside sounds seem fresh: the rush of the cars slapping past them, a plane overhead.

But that's the thing, Joe says, into the noise and the quiet. I don't want to be saved. That's the thing.

CHAPTER 4

G̲ene drives him back. Joe gets out of the car, stands on the mingy-sized squares of sidewalk looking up at the front of the house. The shade in one of the two ground-floor windows is pulled lower than the other. The house has the dazed and lopsided look of a stroke victim.

Inside, it is a sealed cave, murkier, smaller, fouler than Joe remembers, as though months or a year has gone by since he was last here, and when they have gone in – Joe first, Gene right behind him – Joe turns and looks out at the light through the front door. LuAnne is not home.

Gotta go, Gene says. I hadda get someone to cover for me at work, but he hovers near the door, hands dug and moving inside his pockets, waiting to see if Joe forgives him.

Joe's eyes are batting around the living room like panicked birds and Gene frowns and crosses the room, touches him.

I'm goin', Gene says. I gotta go, okay? and he does leave, but not until Joe looks at him, nods, in a way Gene takes as normal.

Joe paces from the dim living room into the kitchen and back over and over, until he hears LuAnne's car pull into the driveway. The living room wall shimmies then darkens again in the fan of her headlights. Before she has turned off the engine, he's out the back door.

Joe spends as little time as he can in the house where his mother is mostly drunk or passed out or frenzied. He is in the house only to sleep and there are nights when he can't sleep and he goes down the stairs and out and sits in the tiny patch of backyard in a metal chair curved like a rocker.

He can't be in the house when LuAnne's there, and he can't eat the food she cooks and leaves for him in pots; distaste spreads in his mouth when he thinks of her touching the food; of her stiff white-gold hair; of those parts of her – flaked skin, dandruff and spit – that he can't see, and he eats only foods sealed inside plastic that he steals or, when he has money, pays for.

LuAnne will not give him money. Joe tells this to Gene; sits up and waits until three, four in the morning, when Gene gets in, his eyes pink from the lights of the Last Gas or from drinking.

It's like jail, Joe says, his voice grieved. He looks at Gene's face while he talks and at his hands, striated pink and grease-colored, laid like two plates on the table.

She's afraid. She doesn't want you takin' off, Gene says and then he stops and in the leftover space Joe hears "too" and he stands and sits and stands again because hearing this is also like jail.

Gene gives Joe money, most often a five and a ten so Joe thinks of the five and the ten he took from the hubcap and he says to Gene, Can't you make it two tens? Money in his pocket settles him while it lasts, but it doesn't last, so when LuAnne is drunk or asleep Joe takes bills from her wallet. He buys food and cigarettes and, in a short while, booze, bourbon or sour mash of his own, and though it is not the way that he wants to be – furtive and stealing – he accepts that it is the way, for now, that he is.

He drinks for the first time the night of the day Gene returns him from hunting his father. The bottles of whiskey on a shelf above the TV set were the only things with a shine to them in the whole dim, tarnished inside of the house. They were gold or reddish, warm colors, though they did not taste warm at first, they tasted jagged and sharp. But that did not stop him and after a while the whiskey warmed him up and tired him out. He went on drinking so that he could go on living in this house while he had to and not choke here and not die.

In April, eleven months after Joe took off after Rusty, Gene does what he'd said he would do: he gets married. It seems to Joe as if it's not a thing Gene really wants. Gene is only eighteen and seems always tired and bled of pleasure.

Her name's Patty, Gene says one night. Joe does not know if Patty is the one Gene's been planning to marry all these months, or if she's just some girl who was handy.

Gene gets an apartment and moves out and says to Joe while he's moving, You come to me *any* time. You just call. I'll come on over and get you, so Joe goes, remembering the fierce way Gene said *any*. He goes without calling, when his mother is home and his need to be gone from her is instant; when he cannot wait for a ride, wait even for the time it would take him to dial Gene's number.

They live downtown, which was what the three or four facing blocks of stores with apartments above them were known as. They live in the last building on the street over Greschler's, a store that sells cheap plastic toys and brushes and combs and bathing suits covered with dust soft as talc, and when Joe gets there, Gene's never home. He's working at the Last Gas, unusual hours that he tells Joe but that Joe can never remember. It's always Patty who comes to the door, her hair wet, or walking with her weight rocked back on her heels because she'd been polishing her toenails, and Joe sees surprise or delight start in her face then spoil when she sees that it's him.

She tells him to sit in the living room where there are a couch and two chairs, stiff and blue-gray and massive, like the shadows of large zoo animals. She leaves him there and goes to the phone in the kitchen and talks with her hand cupped over the mouthpiece, her voice low, and Joe can hear not words but the stresses on words, the complaint, so he stops going by Gene's.

He has no place to go. In the two years and five months since his father's been gone, Joe is down to this: nothing. He says these words over and over again to himself, I have no place to go, so he walks, cruising the neighborhoods of the town. He walks through downtown, full of old stores, their deep fly-speckled windows decorated with criss-crossed flags and with photos of President Kennedy cut out of *Life* magazine and set in cheap frames, the light picking up wrinkles in the paper. Sometimes Joe stops to study the pictures. There is a pained look on President Kennedy's face, as though he knew what was coming.

Behind the blocks of downtown is a parking lot big as a lake with new stores ranged around it like prefab apartments. The train station borders the lot and makes a divider, too, between the black part of town and the white part and, walking, Joe sees how there are layers of white people and that the lower your layer, the closer you thought you were to the layer above you, the farther from the layer below.

One morning, Joe's following the train tracks north out of the station and he looks to his left – made to look, he'll think later – and sees an old shack set in a weedy lot down from and behind the train station.

Joe stops, breathes in the flint-smelling air, and he looks at the shack: ramshackle, tipped. Because of its nearness to the train tracks, to the black section of town, and because of its shabbiness – long shards of wood scab off under his nails – Joe thinks it once had something to do with freed slaves, but it had been built twenty years ago as an interim ticket shack between the demolition of the old stationhouse and the building of a new one.

He waits for days to make sure the shack is unused, though he can tell from the weeds in front of the door, equal in color and height to the weeds in back, that nobody's been here for years. Still, he waits; goes back each morning and hunches down in the weeds fifty yards from the back of the hut where he cannot see the door, but where he is invisible.

On the sixth waiting day he goes in. He brings with him a hand spade he found in LuAnne's garage that wept rust when he lifted it and stained his hand brown-red and made him think "Indian," and made him think of his father. He had not seen this spade before; the small square of backyard behind LuAnne's house was untended – bald mud and the one chair, nothing else – and even the chair had been left by some previous tenants.

Before he can get into the ticket shack Joe has to clear off the weeds. He does not need much space – at not quite fifteen he is still small and his bones are like water – just enough room to open the door.

He kneels and hammers the spade straight down so it bites into the layer of weeds. He hacks his way from the door out and back and around ending opposite to where he began. He can feel the beginning of burn on the back of his neck and through his T-shirt to his shoulders. He shifts his grip on the spade, holds it as though he is loosening cake from a pan, and punches the spade under and under to break up the roots of the weeds; feels them resist and then give with a sound like the ripping of cloth. When he's finished he has a kind of a mat like the ones at front doors that say Welcome.

It's hot inside the shack, the heat different from outside: baked and red and consistent, the same in the back as the front; the same at the height of his head and his ankles. The shack is faintly lit from the one barred window, the light through it the same parched dun as the weeds outside the door.

He knows that the shack is his for now, while his need of it lasts. He's calm, almost grave and ceremonial accepting the shack as something passed down to his keep, unconditional except for the one condition he sets for himself: he cannot spend the night here. It is the one way he has of distancing himself from his father.

Joe hears the scrabblings of mice but he does not care, does not even look towards the sound. Later he'll hear the soughing of the weeds and the dense and infinite sounds of crickets and insects and the crowding noise of the trains that begins as a delicate tremble up through the ground making the window chatter and that Joe takes, the first time he feels it, to be his own excitement.

Two days after he finds the ticket shack, Joe goes downtown. He wants a lock for the ticket shack door and he goes to the hardware store where he looks at the locks that he has no money to buy. The one he wants would be easy to palm, his fingers close right around it, but he wants his tenancy there to be clean, not tainted by stealing. Then he walks across the big parking lot, passing the movie theatre and the supermarket that also sells liquor. As he passes the drugstore, he sees a sign in the window that says Delivery Boy Wanted and he goes in.

The drugstore's laid out to lure bennies: sun products and makeup and tampax and aspirin up front and farther in, hangover cures and sunburn medications, sunglasses and styrofoam coolers and warm glass bottles of juice and beer can liners and floats and kickboards and tubes shaped like seals and like dragons and wire bins of beach balls and of rubber thong sandals. Joe goes to the counter at the back of the store where the serious medicines are, the ointments and creams, and then the pharmacist's alcove behind them, and he waits, his eyes snagged on yellow boxes and on condoms.

I'm here for the job, he says when the pharmacist comes from the back.

Good, the pharmacist says. When can you start?

When do you want me?

I wanted you two *days* ago, the pharmacist says. I wanted you *yesterday*. His voice is both joking and peevish, as though it was Joe who did not show up for work the last two days.

Joe nods; the pharmacist looks at him and smiles, then says, Can you start now? and, Every day after school, and Pay's a dollar an hour and tips, which you might get or might not, depending on goodness, and Joe does not know if this is good money or not, or if the goodness the pharmacist means is other people's or his own.

There's a bicycle for him to use, old, the color of rust but it has been tended, the rust curried to smoothness, and in the course of the first few days he works, Joe feels attached to it; greets it with a hand on its seat, on the nose of its fender. He spends most of his working time riding and so it is not really a job to him, or not really work.

After his third day Joe has enough to pay for the lock that he wants: small, unexpectedly heavy, black. He does not want a silver lock blinking and preening itself in the sun. When he has bought it he goes to the ticket shack and locks it to the door and he wears the key on a string under his shirt. During the day he fingers his shirt, pressing the outline of the key to his chest and when he rides, feels the light slaps the key makes on his skin.

Most of his deliveries are for sick children and sometimes for old people. Joe stands outside the doors of the houses, inside which are fever and rash and the smells of close air and sickness and the yellow and pale green smells of the medicines he brings. Sometimes the women who come to the doors take deep breaths of air and smile and tell him, I haven't been out in three days, and Joe stands inside the arc of his own good health and feels that this, too, is something he brings them.

He sees some women over and over – if they have a child with recurring sickness or more than one child. If their kids are asleep sometimes they ask Joe in, offer him cake or a Coke and one day one woman takes him through the darkened downstairs of her house and then upstairs to a bedroom where she strips a blue spread off the bed and opens a window. The first time, while he watched the blue spread peel down, the petalled white of the sheets emerging like the inside of some firm pale tropical fruit, Joe was not sure he would know what to do with the woman and thought of the girl on the highway, her lips and her tongue, but then he did know. He could feel the woman's need tumbling the air that touched and hovered around them and all he did was listen and answer the need.

After the first time there are other times, other women, so that there are days when Joe stays a long time in one house and leaves with the tops of his thighs slick and then sticky and with a smell on his hands that is the rutted, explosive longing of women. These afternoons become a part of his days though he does not need or ask for them; he goes to the houses only when he has reason to go and he talks to the women when they need talk and touches them with his hands and his tongue and his teeth and his cock when they have time or the need to be touched and if they do not, he is not disappointed and he does not ask. He knows this is one of the reasons they want him and knows, too, that there are other reasons: that he comes to them afternoons, which is the part of their day that is separate and bereft of men, and that it is also because what Joe sees is the deep down womanliness in the women. He does not see how they dress or if their faces are made-up or plain or how old they are. He does not see the things that the women see and worry and pinch at in themselves – pouched bellies and breasts and thighs fretted with wine-colored or silvery stretch marks. And he does not see that they are not simply women, that they are mothers and sometimes, late at night and inside the smells of cooked dinners and laundry and of soap and bleach, which are the cleanest smells of their day, and of the sweat on the feet and bodies of their husbands and of diapers and of the faint, heated-up rubber smells from the cords of electric appliances, that they are also wives. Joe sees them only as women and he hears, in a way other men do not hear, the high singing sound of their longing. It is his gift, meant to be used, as the job was meant for him, as the ticket shack was, and he gives it when it is wanted and if it is more than one time in one day, he stands at the sinks in the bathrooms of the second houses and washes his hands and his thighs and his balls and goes to the second woman the same way he went to the first. He never feels tired; sleep takes him by surprise, waits and then hits, so he has found himself some mornings fully clothed and shod, lying on top of his bed as though he had fallen face down and in the process of falling was asleep. And he has woken, some mornings, hunched in the chair in the back-yard and, once, with his head on his arms at the kitchen table but he has not ever spent the night in the ticket shack because he has sworn to himself he will not.

And then one morning he wakes and waits for the shadings of dark gray and light gray and black that are what he first sees to resolve into the colors and objects of his room. He waits a long time, but the colors and shapes he is seeing do not become the colors and shapes of his locker, his bed, the cracked linoleum floor, and he begins to know that he is not in his room, he is at the ticket shack. He thinks "afternoon" because he comes here afternoons and drinks and sleeps – but as he comes back to himself, feeling the soreness at the places where his bones press into the wool blanket underneath him and the sleeping bag and the floor under that – he knows it is not afternoon, and something in him topples; it gives way.

He does not move, though moving would ease the soreness and stiffness in his legs and his arms, and he tries to remember why he is here, some special instance that he could allow and forgive in himself, but there is no reason other than tiredness and drinking and the failure of his will.

He gets up, smooths the sleeping bag and the blanket and picks up the empty pint bottle he finished last night and goes outside where the sky and the sun and the acres of weeds in the lot are all white and do not turn into colors. He fires the bottle, holds it in the span of his hand and leans down and launches it high where it does a slow tumble, neck over end, filled also with white. He tells himself, I won't drink again, but the bottle has not even hit the ground yet when he knows that he will; that he'd be drinking now except that the bottle was empty.

He walks downtown, buys cigarettes and two Cokes and he takes them into the stationhouse where it is quiet and empty and cool. He drinks one Coke and sits with the second wedged between his thighs and feels the twin cold spots through his jeans and smells the wet brown paper bag. He smokes and waits until the time he knows LuAnne has left for the day.

Then he goes home. While he's walking he thinks of a shower and clean clothes – he can't stand not being clean – and he thinks these are the first and the second things he will do, then sees that he is not really seeing these things, or that he is seeing them second and third. The first thing he wants is to open the bottle of Coke and pour it into a glass and pour bourbon into that.

At home he does the three things he's thought of: drinks, and then, second and third, showers and puts on clean clothes, but he does not go to school. He sits on a chair in the kitchen pulled up to the open back door so he will not smell the layered smells of the house and so some neighbor will not say to his mother, Joe sick? I saw him sitting out back.

He tells himself he is waiting until it is time for him to go to his job and then it is three and three-thirty and four and he does not go and that day the pharmacist closes the drugstore and gets in his car – a small car that looks like a toy because the pharmacist's tall – and he makes Joe's deliveries and hears and sees, also, the disappointment in the voices and faces of women.

Joe doesn't go back. He meets the pharmacist one day on his way out of the market, hears the whispering sound of the cellophane on the cookies and chips in his bag and feels, when he shifts it, the liquid weight of the bottle. The pharmacist stops and looks down at him and says, You been sick? and Joe knows he could say yes and be believed and get his job back, but he says no; sees the pharmacist's face go from concern to scorn; hears, though he is no longer looking at the pharmacist, is looking just past his white-coated shoulder – I guess it's just summer, that it? Can't keep you boys off the beach? and Joe, who is pale, moon-colored, and paler under the dark of his hair, nods. He says, That's it.

He does not have a job. He does not see the women, or sees them, sometimes, on the street downtown, or in the supermarket or at night, waiting in line for the movie, white sweaters buttoned like capelets on their shoulders. They are with children or, sometimes, with men and the need Joe saw and answered in them is invisible. If they look when they pass him their eyes do not stay on his face, he is only a boy, straddling manhood, but they do not look. They are with children and sometimes with men and they do not know who he is.

It is the beginning of summer. Joe looks for another job. The places he goes are all fully staffed, set for the onslaught of bennies, though Joe knows this is not the reason he cannot find work: it is because he has lost or forfeited the need in himself. It's dried up, pea-small and pea-hard, and there are no jobs in the stores and the diners and coffeeshops and carwashes he goes to.

Still, he makes himself look. He starts in the morning on the nights he's slept at home – now he does not always sleep there – and wakes and washes and leaves early, when there are still crescents of white soap under his nails, and he goes to place after place, but there are no jobs. When he gives up for the day he goes to the liquor store part of the supermarket and he takes bottles of bourbon and pays for them with the money that's left from his job, or he does not pay – he is fifteen, they would not sell him liquor – he leaves money in the gap on the shelf that he takes the bottle from. And then the money is gone and he steals.

In the afternoons he goes to the ticket shack and he sits in the motionless heat and he drinks and when he opens the door to go out, he is sometimes sick.

It is a Wednesday late in July and still early enough so that the downtown is shaded and there's a breeze coming in off the water and below the short sleeves of his T-shirt, Joe's arms are cold and he rubs them. He's been into and out of three stores so far and he stands now in front of Jack's, a diner behind a motel. He goes in – it's cool inside too, the air conditioning matching the cool of outside, but airless. Joe stands at the cash register and waits for someone to come over.

I'm looking for work, he says to the waitress whose uniform looks like a black skirt and a white-bibbed black blouse and white apron until he sees it's one piece.

Al, the girl calls. She steps back and looks down the length of the counter and Joe takes a step closer, then a step back when he jostles a basket of mints.

Al! the girl calls again and a man dressed like a baby in a pale yellow shirt and pants lifts his head, then comes towards them.

Help you? he says.

Joe looks at his face, the skin shining as though it's been oiled, and he says, I'm looking for work, and before he's even got all the words out, Al's shaking his head.

Sorry son, he says. All hired out. Try again, maybe, say September? and Joe nods and says Thanks and he leaves. Outside he stands blinking in the parking lot while his eyes readjust to the sky and the colors of cars and the pink stucco diner that have an intensity he doesn't remember.

I hear you say you lookin' for work? a voice says behind Joe and he turns and it is an old man with white frail-looking hair and a shirt and pants a greasy green-black color gimping down the steps of the diner. Joe looks at the man, waits for him to approach: when he does, there is a faint smell of piss that Joe turns his head from. The man looks almost familiar, and Joe thinks of the faces of men that he's seen – teachers, store owners, Al, the husbands of women.

I got somethin'. Not glamorous, the man says. Not steady, either, maybe it might be one, two days a week. Hauling, mostly. Which I'm gettin' too old for myself.

Joe nods and the man says, Follow me, and starts walking and says, over his shoulder. Gas station. Not the Last Gas. You know where I mean? and Joe knows, then, the man is Claude Freemont and he stops walking.

Comin', not comin'? Freemont says.

Joe doesn't move. He is on the verge now of some difference in his life the way he was on the day after the first night he spent in the ticket shack, and he almost does not follow Freemont; does not move even when Freemont says, I do not have all day, and then he does move, he follows.

42

CHAPTER 5

....

Isabel wakes Joellen, who opens her eyes to the dark of her room, the trembling white of her sheets, her pillow case. Isabel's hand on the pillow smells of soap.

Joellen dresses in the clothes Isabel hands her. They are yesterday's clothes; she can taste their sourness. Isabel does not say where they are going, Joellen does not ask, but they have done this before: gotten up in the part of the morning that is still night and gone down to the beach and hunted beach glass in the arc of two flashlights. Isabel follows the tide charts in the paper, waiting for the first low tide after a high tide after a storm. This is the best time for beach glass and also for shells and seaweed and stones and broken-off crab legs and plastic cups and pink plastic tampon dispensers and hunks of cardboard, bled of color to grayness.

Let's go, Isabel says, and Joellen says, But it's dark! and Isabel says, But it isn't going to stay dark!

Joellen thinks of the first eclipse she saw, when she was seven or six, the sun snipped, halved, quartered, until it was just a corona battering the flat dark lid of the moon.

It's so dark! she says again, feeling her mother's limbs, the knob of wristbone, of elbow she keeps banging into as they walk. She remembers only the darkening of the eclipse, not the slow lightening back. She clicks her flashlight on and off.

Stop! Isabel says. You're wasting the light.

They take their shoes off on the boardwalk which is lit by tall streetlights, the glow from each lamp a separate white moon. The sand is cold, though it's July, and packed, like refrigerated sugar. They each have plastic sand pails; the first pieces they find hit and then jigger inside the pails, then there are more and more pieces, the pails heavy, the sound, as each new piece drops, a muffled click. It gets light, the dawn muted by fog into grays and lilacs, the pieces of glass the same colors.

They are home by the time the fog burns off, at the table in the small room at the back of the house, the kitchen a long dark cord, the room a bump at its far end. They sit in their usual places: Isabel with her back to the door, Joellen under the window. There is a red glass pitcher and glasses, too delicate for ordinary use, on the ledge of the window. The glasses are green and blue and pink and tint sections of Joellen's and Isabel's skins.

Isabel is sorting the glass into piles of lilac and lavender and root beer and a green that is like sugared mints and a blue the color of chlorine, the chips of color pale cousins to the colors of the glasses. From time to time she hands Joellen a piece and says, Look how smooth this one is, or, How flat, or, How shapely, which are categories too, but which do not cause their own piles. Joellen takes the pieces her mother hands her, rubs them or weights them, but she does not help to sort. She knows by the focused greediness on her mother's face that the sorting, for Isabel, is not a shared pleasure.

They are waiting for Leon to wake and come down: then they will have breakfast. Of course, Isabel and Joellen have already eaten, they ate on the beach, the fried clams Isabel loved and that they ate sometimes on nights when Leon didn't get home from teaching until late. Joellen does not like the taste of the clams, rancid and rubbery, but if she opens her mouth as she chews so the clams cool and cure in the salty air, she is able to swallow them.

When they hear Leon stand, hear his feet on the carpetless floor of the bedroom, crossing the carpetless hall; when Joellen hears or imagines the faint slaps of his slippers hitting the soles of his feet, Isabel begins cooking the pancakes and Joellen brings dishes and syrup and forks to the table and carries the plate of oranges in, quarter moons rocking.

Leon comes downstairs carrying the briefcase that he takes with him from room to room of the house or into the yard, and he stops at the seam in the linoleum that separates the kitchen from the room with the table in it.

Isabel's carrying a plate of pancakes. Passing Leon she bends slightly to him because she is taller and because she is expecting a kiss. Joellen watches the pancakes steaming in the space between her parents' two bodies.

I wish we didn't have to eat in the kitchen, Leon says, his voice breezy and tuneful as though this is a line from some breakfast song.

This isn't the kitchen, Isabel says, her face vague and surprised as she looks at the room where Joellen is sitting.

It's *near enough* to the kitchen, Leon says. It *might as well be* the kitchen. It isn't the *dining room*. He speaks as though he is conjugating.

Joellen looks at the archway that leads from the kitchen into the dining room. This room is vacant: uncurtained, unfurnished. It is bleak and cold in the winter. Leon sees this as Isabel's failing: he sees it as emblematic. Periodically, he brings it up.

You get the *smells* here, Leon says.

Isabel raises her head, sniffs at the air. It smells like food, she says.

Joellen nods. Oranges, coffee, the steamed smell of pancakes.

It's like living with some kind of *echo*, Leon says. How can I eat cake, for example, when I'm smelling garlic or fish. *Fish!* he says, and there is a leap in his voice as though he has located the single true source of his displeasure. I can smell *fish* at breakfast!

Joellen raises then lowers her head, breathes into cupped hands and takes a deep sniff. Maybe it is the clams Leon is smelling, or her own salted flesh.

We won't have fish then, Isabel says. She looks past Joellen, past the colored glasses, out the back window.

We hardly have fish, Joellen says. Her hair is lank from the fog and salt coated. It hangs in separate strips the width of flypaper.

That's not the point, Sal, Leon says; Sal is what he calls her, a name from a song, when he wants to show that she has no part in his anger. It is his way of abandoning her compromise name – Joe, for his father, Ellen for Eleanor, Isabel's mother. Jo*ellen*, Isabel says it, as though that is the real, the important, part of the name.

That isn't the point, he says to Isabel, and Joellen can dimly see that it isn't. It is not the phantom fish smell that he minds; it is that he smelled the salt off Isabel's skin, knew she'd been out while he slept. He would not have minded if she'd only been grocery shopping. He goes to the table and sits down. His place is at the foot, facing Isabel's place. The colored light from the glasses does not reach there.

If we used the dining room, this would be a nonissue, Leon says. He folds his hands over the briefcase.

Now, he says, his voice pleasant: this discussion is finished. I'd like some coffee please. Their fights were elemental, always about food.

I'll get it, Joellen says. She jumps up, knocking the table. Oranges fall off the dish.

Careful, Sal, Leon says, but she's already gone.

Isabel's pouring a fresh batch of pancakes. She kisses the top of Joellen's head. The weight of the kiss moves Joellen's chin nearer the coffee pot she is holding; she can feel the metallic gleam of its heat.

I should be married to *you*, puss, Isabel says in a low voice, and she smiles and Joellen is first proud and then, quickly, guilty and repelled.

Joellen brings Leon's coffee to him at the table, Isabel carries a fresh platter of pancakes.

Can I go? Joellen asks. She is looking at Isabel, then turns, for an equal span of time, to Leon.

To? Leon says.

Charlieo's, Joellen says, meaning Charlie O'Casey, her best friend. To the picnic. For the Fourth of July. I go every year.

In fact she has gone only once before this, last year when she and Charlieo were ten and eleven. Charlieo told her that his family has these parties every Fourth of July. It seemed like he meant going back generations.

It's the ninth of July, Leon says, smiling.

Raindate, Isabel says. On the fourth, it was raining. She is forking pancakes onto his plate. She is busy.

Are you going like that? Leon asks, lifting his chin at Joellen. His hands are still folded as though they are just ornamental.

Joellen looks down at herself. She is wearing the same clothes, shorts and a T-shirt, she wore yesterday, the clothes she put on this morning. Even if she had thought of changing before, now she will not. A stubbornness she cannot help sometimes keeps her from pleasing her father.

Oh, she's fine, Isabel says. It's just a picnic. It's not black tie.

Isabel's wearing the same clothes herself, the same clothes she wears day after day in the summer – shorts of a blue-and-black plaid, a white sleeveless blouse. The shorts stay pouched in the seat when she takes them off at night, the tubes of the legs retain the shape of her thighs. The blouse is puffed out in front with air breasts and the large rounds of her shoulders, a headless, limbless bust. Joellen imagines her mother washing these clothes when no one is home; crouched, naked, on the floor of her room waiting for the washer to finish.

There's no reason she should not have clean clothes. We *pay* Ida, Leon says. Ida is the woman who comes Wednesdays to put their clothes in the washer, to add soap and bleach, to hang them out on the line in the backyard.

Isabel closes her eyes. They stay closed a long time; Joellen thinks she's asleep. Or counting.

Joellen kisses Leon, then moves to her mother. Isabel lifts her hand, curves it to Joellen's cheek. Her mother's hand is weighty and large, larger than Leon's, it is almost too large for a hand. Sometimes, looking at it, Joellen imagines it is not a hand, it is some other thing, hand-colored, hand-shaped. It has a beachy smell, though Isabel's touched pancakes, coffee, oranges since the beach. Joellen turns her head into the cup of Isabel's hand and she puts out the tip of her tongue, tasting the deep-down salty taste of her mother.

She waits for Charlieo on the porch. He is picking her up. Joellen knows where he lives, has been there hundreds of times, but the O'Caseys believe a girl should be escorted to a party. It makes her self-conscious, although she is also glad she will not have to pass alone through the flank of O'Casey uncles and aunts in Charlieo's backyard.

She sees Charlieo every day, he comes by every morning in summer, stands with his face pressed into the screen door, his lips small fleshy pockets. They go to the beach or the man-made lake, which they call the fake lake, one block inland where there are turtles and ducks and high-strung geese whose down powders the air, or they go to the train station and lay coins on the tracks for the trains to elongate and flatten, or they check on Charlieo's experiments. He has cut fruit and vegetable and sometimes flower seeds in half and carefully taped them to some other, different half seed. He wants to grow car-beets and bean-matoes and pea-a-golds, he says. Foods that are twice as nutritious or useful. Then he will take them to countries where food's scarce and teach the people to grow them.

Joellen waits a long time, the brick of the front porch cool on the backs of her thighs. Charlieo is at Mass; when he comes he is dressed not in shorts and a T-shirt and bare legs and sneakers, as he is most days, but in long pants and a plaid shirt that's been ironed. Joellen comes down off the porch. The sun lights his shirt fabric: she sees the delicate rounds of his shoulders, his arms and the flat rosy smears of his nipples and she looks down at her sneakers, made shy by his sheathed bareness.

You went to Mass? Joellen asks. She is shy, too, in the face of religion, its catacombed richness. We are not worshipping people, Leon says. Your mother and I do not believe in organized religion. He is Jewish; born Episcopal, Isabel says of herself, and Joellen saw or imagined a wistfulness when she heard this, not for Episcopal, for born.

Charlieo nods but does not speak and Joellen feels that his silence is related, somehow, to Mass and she feels chastised by it and distanced. They walk facing forwards not, as they usually do, facing each other so sometimes they trip or have to take scissoring steps to keep up.

Anyone there yet? Joellen asks and Charlieo says, The Marines have landed, and Joellen smiles and knows who he is again. This is something they say when they are talking about Charlieo's family: his father, his two brothers, Douglas and Herman, ten and eight years older than Charlieo, and his three uncles, Bernard and Brendan, who are twins, and Francie. They all had been or were or were going to be Marines, as Charlieo would also be. An inherited trait, Charlieo said, like how those old kings and princes were bleeders.

They were always there at the O'Caseys' parties, Christmas, Easter, the Fourth of July. The clan gathering, Mrs. O'Casey called it and Joellen pictured men wearing bear pelts, dipping gourds into barrels of grog, though she had seen them before, the men and their wall of wives: Francie's Agnes who was short and wide and whose dresses hugged like tight pillow cases, and the twins' wives, Bridie and Margaret, or Margaret and Bridie, both brown-haired in shirt-waisted dresses and twin-like themselves; and Douglas's wife Daisy – Daisy O'Cazee, they called her, and his "new" wife though they'd been married three years.

Charlieo lives on a block of neat, precise houses and trimmed lawns and swept sidewalks. His house is aluminum-sided and white and starched-looking, like a nurse's cap. They can hear the sounds of the party from across the street and see the smoke from the barbecue rising over the top of the house. Smoke signals, Charlieo says, pointing.

A green plastic trash barrel's set on the concrete patio and the men stand around it, holding bottles of beer that drip on their clothes and the concrete. They

48

laugh, batting each other's backsides and shoulders, a little embarrassed by the deep twin pleasures of each other's company and of drinking so early in the day. The wives are inside, busy with food, drinking also, tall glasses topped off with soda and ice. Only Daisy is outside, bored and ornamental, her webbed garden chair partly crushing the roses.

The sun is bright in the yard, on the turned, parched-looking rose bed, and off the back of the house and the concrete and the blinding white front of the garage and Joellen stops, stranded by brightness and by the voices of men. They call to Charlieo – Hey, Charlie, and Chas! Charlieo is not what he's called here, it is his school name, Charlie O., because there is another Charlie.

Joellen! one voice calls and Joellen looks up – it is Charlieo's father. He is a small man, trim, his hair mowed like Charlieo's hair, though his is silver.

Welcome, he says and takes her hand and almost bends over it, as though he is asking her to dance. In the face of his courtliness Joellen feels insufficiently dressed.

Can I offer you something? A beer? Mr. O'Casey asks. He does not smile, he winks solemnly and walks, hand on her shoulder, to the barrel and fishes out a soda.

Charlieo frees himself from the circle of uncles and meets Joellen at the food table. Potato salad, he says, pointing. Macaroni. Ambrosia – his eyes close when he says this. He stands too close, his breath pesky against the side of Joellen's face so she keeps brushing her cheek. The smell from the barbecue drifts over – the turp-like smell of lighter fluid and smoke and grilled meats.

For dessert, Charlieo says, his hands folded in front of him: watermelon, then cake and ice cream. The cake all with sparklers.

Did you memorize this? Joellen asks.

Nope. Don't have to. We have the same exact thing every year. Charlieo rotates the bowls until all the serving spoons are facing the same way.

It is hot in the yard and the heat and the wavering smoke from the grill and the colors of the dresses the women have on – patterned and bright or flowery – and the different brightnesses of Daisy's clothes and gold hair and gold bracelets, and the fact that she has been awake since well before dawn give a dreaminess to the day Joellen can't shake over the course of the long, slow afternoon. When

Charlieo says, Let's go out back, meaning the back of the L-shaped double lot behind and to the west of the house where he does his agriculture experiments, Joellen moves after him in a dreamy torpid way.

There are trees back here though not many; there are bushes and vines in dense circles, like twined Maypole dancers, pools of shade at their centers. Joellen is drawn to the shade, and she stops near one circle of shrubs letting Charlieo go on ahead.

The grass looks lush and dense from a distance but it is scanty up close, bald patches of earth showing through. She lays her palms here, feeling the brown coolness up through her fingers, and when she lies back feels the earth's gravitational pull and its movement which is not a slow, imperceptible creep but a whirling and she is dizzy. She hears the sounds of the party: voices, the scraping of chairs and the chinging of Daisy's gold bracelets and then she hears, also, Daisy's voice: it says, Herman.

There? an answering voice says, and Daisy again, saying, Yes, and then, There, and then, Yes.

This is what Joellen hears and knows, also, that she could not be hearing – the voices are low, heavy rasps; she's too far from the party to hear sounds so distinctly – and she gets up, runs, to find Charlieo.

Who she does not see, and she calls CharlieoCharlieoCharlieoCharlieo in an urgent way because he seems to have vanished.

He steps out from shade into sun. Here, he calls, waving her towards him. Jo!

When she gets to him she's panting, her lips and the back of her neck sweaty, and she sucks on her lip and tastes salt.

Charlieo steps back into his rectangle of garden. The earth is an unnatural orange to Joellen, her eyes still tinted by shade. She sees the rows of experimental vegetables; straggling green stems, thin as thread, dragged onto the ground by the minuscule weight of their heads. They make Joellen sad, though Charlieo says, in the cause of science these are acceptable losses.

Charlieo bends to the marigolds; there are dozens, their foliage rusty, their gold and orange heads frilled. His hands pick through their bushiness like a mother's hands combing for lice through a child's head. UNDER, he says, grunting, pulling on something. Look! he calls. Look at this! This could be a car-beet!

He comes towards her, holding a thing that looks like a small hooked finger on the flat of his hand. There is a cloud of gnats over the garden, stationary and hovering; moving through them, Charlieo swats, in an unconscious way, at his face.

What do you think? he says looking up, and then he says, What? Jo, what? because Joellen seems paralyzed.

Her mouth opens for speech then she remembers the gnats and it closes. She points at Charlieo. His hand goes, fast, to his fly – a check, a pat. *What?* he says, his voice stricken.

He is all gold. Gold winks on his face and his arms and dazzles in patches over his fingers like rings or ornaments.

WHAT? Charlieo says again as Joellen comes towards him like a sleepwalker, hand out. He's been transformed, she thinks and something else: something that is like Daisy's voice saying "Herman," like Isabel's "I should be married to you," something she is just on the cusp of knowing, that this Charlieo, gold and shining, is supposed to tell her. She touches his cheek then looks at her finger. It is powdery, the whorl of her fingerprint visible under the gold, and then she thinks "pollen" and it is no longer miraculous, the miraculous folds in on itself and is subsumed by what is rational, ordinary, though for a moment, the two stood side by side, she was seeing them both, deciding which one to give up.

Joellen walks home. She is tired; her scalp and the back of her neck itch where the sweat's dried. On the blacktop of her street there is a pile of glass chips, pale green, the color of fish tanks, and she blinks and looks at them, remembering the start of this day: the black sand, the glass pieces.

She goes up the driveway, through the backyard that has only the naked clothesline, some bushes, the grass a few tufts over bareness. Inside there are roses on the table, the pale yellow of eggs stirred into milk. Seeing them, she remembers the roses from the day President Kennedy died. Ida brought them, though it had been a Friday, not her day to come. As she thinks "Ida," Ida appears in Joellen's head; her smooth, lickable skin the color of mocha frosting; the soft and faded black pedal pushers, the sleeveless pink blouse she keeps on a shelf in their laundry room and wears to do their laundry.

And then Joellen walks into the kitchen and Ida is there, or another version of Ida.

Hello baby, Ida says, her voice low and musical, though this is not how she talks to Joellen on Wednesdays; grunts, mostly, or sucks on her teeth or says nothing.

Joellen turns her head: The sink, the stove, some chopped fruits or vegetables whip by. This isn't Ida, she thinks. This woman's wearing a dress, a design of red ladybugs in black-and-white windows fanning over her hips. This woman's wearing stockings, the hairs on her legs mashed under the nylon, as fine as the legs of spiders.

Maybe it's Wednesday, Joellen thinks and walks to the back window, checks the clothesline, although she passed it on her way in, saw it empty.

You want to help me get the supper? Ida says, still in that low sugary voice, and Joellen is sure: this isn't Ida. Ida doesn't eat here, though Isabel tries to tempt her. Joellen's seen Ida say no, and no, and no thanks. All she ever takes is a sugar-water she makes for herself and does not share. She sits at the table, her hand circling the glass, her back not touching the back of the chair.

Ida takes down a carton of salt and shakes some onto the flat of her hand, then tosses it into a black iron skillet – it makes sounds, it pops – and then puts in meat which hisses; something is off about this too: Ida reaching for salt, not detergent, not bleach, not clothespins.

Ma, Joellen calls. She heads for the stairs.

Ida lets her call once, twice, the time it takes her to turn off the flame under the skillet, to bang it onto the next burner, to follow.

Ma, Joellen calls. She's looking up towards the top of the stairs. It seems a long way.

Joellen, Ida says. Come on in the kitchen – but her voice doesn't mean kitchen; her voice means sweet/sugar/honey/dear/darlin'. The small hairs on the back of Joellen's neck start to rise but are trapped under dried sweat and salt.

Joellen? Ida says again. Your mam's not upstairs, child.

She says, Jo?

She says, Baby? her voice warm and runny – she does not talk to Joellen on Wednesdays – and Joellen turns on a step and she says, She is too, then where is she?

Joellen's two steps up, her head level with Ida's; when she turns she looks into eyes that are dark, almost black, the whites tarnished as though some of the black has leaked off.

She's gone, baby, Ida says and Joellen thinks, gone: the beach, the market – but while she is thinking this she can see a different gone next to the plain one – and she closes her eyes because she can think of many meanings for gone and because she hates words. Ma, she calls, turning from Ida.

Ida's behind her, Joellen can feel Ida's breath on her neck. Stop *tracking* me, she says, then goes on calling Ma, because the hum the word makes is familiar and soothing.

The door to Isabel's workroom is open, the pieces of glass she and Joellen found this morning on her table in old peanut butter and mayonnaise jars.

Joellen steps into the room, Ida behind her. This room is *private*, Joellen says. Has Ida ever been upstairs before?

Baby? Joellen? (*Joellen*, Ida says it.) She's gone, Ida says. There is a rushing sound in Joellen's head, a sound like being knocked underwater by a wave, and she thinks she is pressing her palms to her ears but when she looks down, there are her hands, right beside her.

Joellen turns, she goes into Leon and Isabel's room, though she does not expect to find anyone there. Her parents' bedroom is an anonymous space. There are no objects or pictures, no perfumes or creams: Isabel does not like the smells of these things. There are no books. Leon reads, but not lying down. There are a bed and a dresser, the kinds of pieces you see in motels.

Ida takes Joellen's wrist, the white wrist cuffed by the brown one. They sit on the bed.

An accident, Ida says, and then she says Car, and then Hospital.

All's I know, Ida says. She holds her palms out on the white and the black and the red of her dress, stretching the fingers so that her hands are not only empty but convex: nothing could sit there. All's your daddy told me.

Leon! Joellen says, hearing his name. He would've called *me*, she says, almost smiling, her voice almost triumphant the way Leon's was this morning when he said Fish!

He called me, little girl. To be here for when you got home. He had to go with her.

Accident. Car. Hospital. Gone.

Come on downstairs, Ida says. Help me get dinner. Porkchops, she says. You like porkchops? but she doesn't move off the bed. She picks up Joellen's hand, smooths the palm like she's about to tell Joellen's fortune. Joellen bends to their two hands, looking also. She smells onions and meat fat and she throws Ida's hand off her own and gets up.

Ida follows her to the head of the stairs, starts down.

I'm chilly, Joellen's about to say, changes to cold: chilly is Isabel's word: it is gone.

She says, I'm getting a sweater.

Ida nods, says, Then you be down.

Joellen goes back into Isabel's workroom. There's an unfinished mosaic attached with long screws to an easel. It is all pinks and greens; standing back Joellen sees what Isabel wants you to see: it's a meadow. She sits at the table, a door laid over bricks. The top of the table is pocked. She dips her hands into the jar of glass pieces, touching the pieces no one's touched since Isabel touched them, and not looking, picks one. It is frosted and flat on one side, slightly arched on the other. She puts the piece in her mouth, her tongue fitting under the curve. It is smooth and thin, like a sucked-down candy, but it tastes, it tastes, it tastes like salt.

Joellen watches TV, stands twisting the dial, liking the static of different velocities in between stations, on the lookout for shows she is not permitted to watch. She turns and turns, hectic, ecstatic.

Ida is cooking. Foreign smells come from the kitchen – meat juices and floury gravy and onions. Joellen does not know if she likes porkchops, has she ever had porkchops? We are not porkchops people, she can hear Leon say.

From time to time Joellen goes into the kitchen, drawn by the smells and by a stark boredom: she is not used to watching TV. Nothing happens. The Road Runner falls and is deflated, he is hammered and bashed. Then he gets up and walks away.

Mashed potatoes, Ida says when Joellen comes into the kitchen, or she says, Apple pie, or, You say you like porkchops? Joellen looks at Ida's hands as she slices apples or onions. The knife makes a heavy clopping sound on the cutting board, the wood rebounds, echoing under the knife. The roses are still on the table, mostly furled, a petal or two peeling away from the buds. They are not like the President Kennedy roses, the last of the season which, warmed by the heat of the kitchen, had opened and bowed under their own heavy weights.

They had watched TV that day, all day, sad and monotonous. The day was dark gray and light gray and black, the colors of TV, and of trains and dark veils.

The roses seemed bleak, shedding color.

Joellen touched the screen, Mrs. Kennedy's head. Static crackled around her finger, drawing dust.

Leon comes in the front door, Joellen hears it, the knob turning, slipping under his fingers, they must be damp or slightly greasy. She hears it turn twice, hears the brass tongue recede from its pocket, hears the movement of the hinges, each sound separate as though dark heightens sound.

It is dark now: the yard and the windows, the porch and the upstairs, dark stacked on dark. The only light comes from the TV and the grimed yellow light in the kitchen.

Joellen waits for Leon to come in, stand behind her, tell her to turn off the TV but he goes into the kitchen. Joellen can hear the tumbled soft sound of his voice, of Ida's, low sounds like the sounds of food cooking in pots. She gets up, raises the volume of the TV.

Then he is there, his shadow long on the wall, his nose the length of a ladder.

I'm watching TV, Joellen says. Leon touches her head.

*Pop*eye, she says and waits, holding her breath so even if he speaks low she will hear him say, Turn it off now. His shadow moves, his head nods scraping the ceiling, the floor.

I'm watching POPEYE, she says. He's getting SMASHED pretty good!

Don't shout, Sal, Leon says. I can hear you.

Popeye, she says. Olive Oyl got choked. Her neck got all twisted. It was horrible, Joellen says. I loved it. It was the best part.

Sal, Leon says. He says, Joellen.

Joellen sits on the couch, her fingers hooked under the cushions, a grittiness under her nails – crumbs or sand. Popeye the Sailor Man, she sings. TOOT TOOT. She digs her nails deep into the cushion.

Joellen, Leon says.

I'm probably watching this show EVERY night. There's also other cartoons. They're all excellent.

Come eat, Leon says. Ida says dinner's ready.

TOOT TOOT, Joellen says, yells, goes on yelling until Leon comes around to the front of the couch and, finally, turns the TV off.

CHAPTER 6

···

After Leon calls, Ida hangs up the phone and walks from the sleeping porch, where the phone is, back to the kitchen. It is a small house; the rooms, small and thin-walled, are like stacked-up matchboxes, two bottom, two top.

Johnny, her husband, is out in the backyard. Through the flimsy walls he hears both the ring of the phone and the click when Ida hangs up. He comes around to the kitchen door when he hears it, would get to the table the same time as Ida only his hip ticks, paining him and giving him a slow side-to-side way of walking, the movement of his body like the shifting of sand in a bag.

What was that? Johnny says.

Him, Ida says, wiping her hand on a dish towel. While Leon was talking her hand wetted, her palm sliding back from his voice.

Him, she says again. It is how she refers to them, Leon, Isabel, Joellen's "the girl," and always there is a splinter of anger in her mouth when she says it, like they have invaded her home. The first day she went to work for them Leon was home, though in the white people's houses where she worked, men usually weren't. I'm Leon, he said. This is my wife Isabel? and Ida saw how "wife" was something he didn't feel fully sure of.

Says she was hit by a car, Ida tells Johnny. Says she's gone.

There is a pause and then Johnny is shaking his head, saying No! in his deep voice, the No sucking down into the heat of the kitchen. Poor little girl, Johnny says.

Hit-and-run, Ida says.

It's quiet in between Ida's talking and Johnny's and Ida notices the quiet. The houses are close together where they live, the yards joined. On weekends the whole neighborhood's usually out; there is the smell of barbecued meat, the rush of merged voices, but today there is no sound. The quiet sifts down around them like ash.

I got to go over, Ida says. She says, He asked me. He still at the hospital. Girl'll be coming home. (I'm sorry, Leon had said. I have nobody else. To call, and Ida had felt, again, that pinching of anger as though he had somehow arranged this to force her into playing some part in his family she didn't want to be playing.)

Johnny nods, his head moving slowly, the nod taking it up and down a long way. He stands then and goes back out to the yard and clips five or six of his roses. In the kitchen, he wraps their stems in wet newspaper.

Here, he tells Ida. Carry these. He holds out the roses. The soaked newspaper drips onto her skirt.

I got to stop, Ida says. Buy some food. Never nothing to eat in that place. Each sentence starts with a sigh. You got money for me? she asks, sighing.

Johnny puts his hand in his pocket. He has on overalls, the top flap undone, the straps dangling down to his knees, what he wears to work in the garden. He's bare-chested, his bigness a slow steady slope that begins at his armpits, his nipples dark purple and squinched like winked eyes. He looks huge to Ida, bigger because he is standing and she's sitting at the table, and looking up at him she has a sudden memory of Johnny calling on her at her grandmother's in the time after first her brother Solomon died then Ma'am followed. Ida was sixteen then, it was eighteen years ago. She sat at the table at Ma'am's touching the pads of her fingers to Ma'am's blue oilcloth cover and watching the steamed marks disappear.

Money's upstairs, Johnny says, and heads up to the bedroom. When he is upstairs, his weight makes the house tremble. Ida blinks at the place he was standing and looks around at her kitchen, unsure, for a moment, where she is. She has not thought of that blue oilskin cloth or Ma'am's kitchen for a long time, or Ma'am or Solomon either. She does not even dream them. It's as though in the eighteen years since Johnny brought her up north from Fontana, Miss., where they are both from, Ida has not thought about home. Now she sees them – herself, Solomon, Ma'am. It's like being asleep.

* * *

She is hanging wet clothes on the line stretched between two trees in front of the house, or it's what she's supposed to be doing instead of standing with her wrists dangling over the clothesline, her cheek laid on the smooth inner skin of her arm.

Won't dry anyhow, she says inside her head, her voice grumpy. She rubs her cheek back and forth, amazed that the soft silk under it's her own smooth self.

Clothes, Ida says, won't dry till Christmas. The day's hot, the air near liquid and green. Even her hands do not dry, damp from handling damp cloth, the air too wet to hold any more wetness.

*I*da, Ma'am calls, stressing the I so Ida knows it's not the first time she's said it. Where you at?

Ida stoops and picks up a wet shirt.

*I*da!

I'm right *here!*

You don't hear me callin' you? Where's that Solomon got to?

Ida frowns; then, in her head, she hears Ma'am's voice saying, Walk around lookin' like that, one day it'll stick, and she smooths her face out. People are always asking about Solomon who is thirteen, three years younger than she is. Neighbors pass and stop and say hey to her but as they stand talking, Ida sees their eyes peeling away from her to the yard or beyond, to the woods at the back of the house like their eyes can't help it. She does not know why Solomon called this kind of response from everyone. He wasn't so different from the boys he stayed with, except beautiful, a yellowy boy, skin and eyes too when the light hit a certain way, his elbows, his knees, the trough of his spine the color of toast. But boys don't mark beauty, not in each other, not even in girls till they get to a certain age and even then, their notice is just words: titties and legs and butt and girl.

Solomon came into the world with delight, Ma'am said, and I don't know why, but he ain't found no reason yet to change that.

How do I know where he's at? Ida calls. What do I look like, the FB of I?

Don't you be yellin' across no yard at me, girl, Ma'am calls back to her. You talk to me, you come on to where I'm at.

Ida rolls her eyes and sucks her teeth but she heads towards the back of the house, the yellow-green heat hard to move through, the air dense and oiled so dust clings to skin and hair and inside mouths and noses and attracts mosquitoes. Ma'am's sitting in her chair outside the kitchen door of the house, woods behind her, trees bent a bit at the top as though out of interest. She's blown up with the blood pressure that swells her arms and her legs and her hands and feet so, she says, she can hear her waters sloshing around and some days, the waters make her feel crowded inside her head. She's working a white collar, its ends curved and creamy like petals of a water lily flattened out. She sewed for white people, two dollars a dress, good money. Sometimes the ladies sent over cars and Ma'am came out of the house holding the dresses, wearing white gloves as though the darkness of her skin might rub off and soil them. She's not sewing now; the collar just lays on her lap.

Ida walks towards the chair where Ma'am sits in shade that's no cooler than anyplace else, though from a distance it looks purpled and dark. As she passes the kitchen wall of the house a snake glides over her foot. It's small, less than two feet, black with orange markings. It slides into the chinks of one of the cinderblocks that hold up the house.

Ida looks down at her foot even after the snake's passed and the hanging dust's settled. She almost yells, then she doesn't. Ma'am can read signs in any natural occurrence, and Ida is suddenly afraid of hearing that she will never marry, bear children, live a long life. She shudders, then waits to hear Ma'am say, What lies you told? because this is what shuddering means, in the heat.

Ma'am's sagged in her chair, her arms hanging, legs falling apart as though she is coaxing what scant breeze there is to her skin. She slits one eye, Ida can see the gelatinous band of white; she says, What you lookin' like that for? and Ida closes her mouth, feels the powdering of dust on her gums, the insides of her lips, and says nothing.

How 'bout lemonade? Ma'am says. You feel like goin' down for some lemons? See will Willard chip you a dime's worth of ice. I'm feelin' crowded inside my head today.

Ma'am takes some coins out of her pocket, they are wet and sticky with sweat, and Ida puts them in her own pocket. Her dress is the same as Ma'am's, a shift with two flat front pockets. Ma'am sewed all their dresses the same except for the fabrics and sizes: Ma'am has on a pink with gray rickrack, Ida's is blue.

Ida walks up the path to the road, the dust under her feet soft as talc, her soles and between her toes powdered a color like cooked squash. At the road she turns right, heading to Willard's, the small dark store the only one within walking distance, the only place that marks this town as anything but a small collection of houses. While she's walking, the foot the snake crawled over begins to heat up.

Was I bit? she thinks and kneels down in the road, but there is no mark, no puncture, no spot even where there's a sparking of pain when she runs her fingers over the fine fretted bones of her foot. She stands, keeps on towards Willard's, but the heat's worse as she goes so she stops; says, This fool foot's a sign. Somethin' will happen to me if I go on, so she doesn't go on, she turns back. She's not worried what to tell Ma'am; Ma'am will nod, say Ida was right to stand quiet and hear what the snake meant to tell her and to heed what she heard, though she will sigh, too, over that lemonade.

When she's back at the turn-off to Ma'am's, a cut in the trees wide enough only for one thin-sized person (when Ma'am walks through, the branches and vines pick at her sleeves and there is a whispering sound, though when Ida and Solomon pass they are utterly silent), Ida's foot still is not cured. She stands at the top of the path, her hands balled in the pockets of her dress, the knuckles bumping the cloth. Her weight's on her left, her cool foot, the other foot's lifted and as she is standing, a picture comes into her head of the wet-licked bodies of boys at the swimhole they go to, the sun like a zipper sliding up and down their wet arms, the slapped water, the constant, almost machinery sound of boys calling and laughing, and Ida smiles, knowing now what the snake meant to tell her.

She keeps on in the direction opposite to Willard's, heading for the swimhole, and with each step her foot's feeling cooler. About halfway – she is still too far off to hear the sounds she anticipates hearing – she hears only bugs chittering and the creaking of birds and she stops in the drilling sound and the heat and looks up at the sun, hand to her eyes, thinking, When do you plan to *quit?* And as though they hear and are answering that word, the whirring sound of the insects suddenly stops.

In the temporary cessation of sound from the insects she can hear another sound, moving water, and she remembers there is a small stream inside the woods, the tail end of mountain run-off. Ida heads for it, smiling (the insect sound going again) and she walks into the woods till she gets to the shallow stream, clear to the bottom, its surface broken by chippy patches of white where the sun breaks through the tangle of trees.

There is a large, flat rock on the far side of the stream, its surface creased from erosion. Ida crosses to it, steps over the stream – she could step twice as far – and she lies back on its surface. Coolness comes through the back of her dress and she edges down some so her feet can drop into the water. The stream passes over and around them, her feet causing jetties, and inside the coolness and the constant sound of the water, she sleeps.

Ma'am's dozing, has not moved from the chair where Ida left her, was asleep before Ida had gone up the path to the road, as soon as she'd handed Ida the coins to buy lemons. She gives herself up to the motionless heat and to the motionless feel of her body. Her head bends, near to touching her shoulder. Her breath hums, going out.

She stays as she is. Time passes, minutes maybe, or hours. Her head lolls, her arms hang. The pink of her skirt is poled by her knees and held taut. In the part of her mind that is not fully asleep she is waiting for Solomon and for Ida.

After some time (she still cannot tell, minutes, hours) there are other sounds, the distant shouting of men, far enough off so it is not intrusive, a crepey sound, like coughing. The sound moves closer, it penetrates her sleep and she rises one layer closer to consciousness where she waits for the sound to move off so she can sink down again.

Ma'am, she hears, Ma'am, and opens her eyes to the round face of Johnny Lee Iron, to the tiny dark pits of ingrown beard on his cheeks, to neck rash. He is no longer a boy though he is not married; he lives with his sister, which makes him seem boy-like. Ma'am feels a coarse rubbing at the top of her arm; not fully awake she thinks the rubbing and the look of rash and of beard are the same. She covers her arm with one hand, sees then that the scratching's a rope Johnny holds, looped, in his hand.

It's Solomon, he says, he is breathing hard into her face, she can smell meat on his breath, the salted pink smell of ham.

Them boys, down at the swimhole? Saw him go in but he . . . They ain't sure he came up.

Ma'am's on her feet with "up," before it: Johnny's unprepared for the speed and agility of her movement, she knocks him off balance. She is out of the chair, on her way up the path, branches switching at her, her brushing them back; there will be tiny scars later, like stitch marks on her arms and her face. Johnny, he has to run to catch up.

The hole where the boys swim is shaped like an inverted inkwell, the sides sloped and faceted by rock and by gold-colored mud that turns to slip when it rains. Small, hairy roots and large crooked ones sit exposed on the slope; stunted trees sometimes fall, washed down to the bottom in a hard rain; the boys use them as floats.

At the bottom, the water looks flat and is mostly shallow, milky with mud. Streaks of slip dry on the boys' necks and their arms and the insides of their thighs as they come out. It's a steep way down to the water, the path worn slide-smooth by the feet and behinds of boys, though there's another way in: a rope knotted to a tree at the top, knotted at the bottom for a foothold. It's a drop of twelve feet from the rope, a free fall into the center where the water is coldest and deepest.

When Ma'am gets there, the water is empty of boys. Two or three men move slowly in the water tipping to dive, the jeans they still wear waterlogged and white where the sun hits. Boys stand on the bank their lips purple although the heat is still fierce. Some of them jump up and down shouting – there, there – pointing to the spot where Solomon went in with a whoop, teeth wet and glinting. They will not believe in disaster, even when the men stand and shake their heads, throwing droplets of water.

Ida wakes up in the dark, looks straight up at the leaves, dark silhouettes against the less intense dark of the sky. She gets up, lifts her feet delicately from the stream, and walks through the dark woods. She is not fully awake and so she is not afraid until she gets to the road, the moon bright and high and white enough for her to see her own shadow, and then she looks back at the woods and it is the idea of the woods, all that dark, that finally scares her.

Well, you're out *now*, she tells herself, speaking out loud, expecting the sound of her voice to dispel the fear, but as she heads home the fear stays.

Ma'am's still in the chair outside the door to the kitchen, same as when Ida left her, like she's been waiting all this time for Ida to get back with the lemons.

Ma'am? she says.

There is a humming, like bugs.

Cool out now, Ida says. Nice out.

Mmmmm, she hears again, a humming sound on the verge of tuneful.

Ida puts her hands in her pockets, touches the loose coins Ma'am gave her. Sorry about your lemonade, she says. I never did make it to Willard's. I . . . , and she thinks of the snake, raises her snaked foot, slides it half up the back of the other leg, under her skirt.

Solomon's gone, Ma'am says. She has her eyes closed as though it is noon, the light blinding. After she's said words, she goes back to humming.

Gone? Ida says. He ain't gone. Where'd he go, he's thirteen? She takes several steps to the door of the bedroom – the house is two rooms, like two boxes, each with its own door. He wouldn't go someplace at night without telling her.

Gone, Ma'am says. Drownded. Gone. Went offa that rope.

Ida thinks she might laugh then, a feeling that is like the beginning of laughter comes up in her and she opens her mouth to let the laughter come out. She is seeing the rope, the one at the swimhole, seeing the snake, sees now how they are the same thing, how the snake that hotted her foot meant her to go down to the swimhole, to Solomon. She was meant to stop him, keep him off the rope, *cut* the rope maybe. She could not have otherwise saved him. She can't swim.

Ida stands, her mouth open, waiting to laugh, a lump of laughter stuck in her throat. From someplace there is screaming. One dog starts to bark, then another.

Ma'am puts her to bed, or Ida is in bed, the bed they have always shared, she and Solomon, the bed where Ma'am's Virginia had borne each of them. She is wearing a sleeveless white shift that glows in the lit dark of the room, a match for the moon's white. She reaches her foot from her side of the bed over to Solomon's. He slept polite, a straight pole at the far edge of the mattress. Ida waits for her foot to reach and then rest against Solomon's knee, but her foot touches nothing and she knows for the first time that her life is not going to be one unbroken line of herself and Solomon and Ma'am. She had not known, before, that this is what she expected: thought "man" and thought "married," though there was no face, no body to "man," no life that was not this one to "married," and she lies on her back in the bed, splayed, one leg pushing itself to find Solomon's leg at the opposite side of the mattress.

* * *

The men search for three days, going down to the swimhole, diving until it gets dark. They tread water, waiting for breath, arms churning. They turn butt up and dive. It's what the boys do, though in the men it looks serious, as though dives are a thing they must master. They dive for three days, for continuous hours. The women bring food and the men climb out, clothes heavy with wet, and sit on the sloped banks of the hole to eat, water collecting in the creases of their flesh. They are silent and grim. When they're done eating they dive again, but it is too deep in the center, too weedy and they do not find Solomon.

Like a forest down there, the men say to each other. You remember it like that?

Weeds got him, they say. Don't want to let go.

Ma'am sits at the top of the slope looking down on the men who, treading water, look up and see her and keep diving. Someone carried her chair here, set it in the insufficient shade of a scrub tree, but Ma'am moved it out in the sun, sits with a red bandana tied on her neck, wearing a straw hat that is crushed and split, the straw a burnt color from age and from sweat.

At the end of the third day, Johnny Lee Iron climbs up the slope. Drops of water sit like transparent eggs in his hair; he's bare-chested, his arms and chest quilled with goosebumps, cleaner looking and smaller than the bumps on his neck and his cheeks.

We can't locate him, Ma'am, Johnny says. Them weeds. Won't give him up.

Ma'am doesn't answer. Her silence makes Johnny feel they – he and the men – haven't tried hard enough. We been at it three days, he says.

Ma'am sits still, like she's thinking this over, then she nods, she puts out her arm and Johnny Lee helps her up.

I did want to bury my boy, she says, but she's not talking to Johnny, she's on her way back to the road.

Johnny goes back down the slope, his body tipped, his arms stretched out for balance. A small shower of dried mud and twigs precedes him. We can quit, he tells the men when he gets to the bottom. Don't need to come back here tomorrow, but while he says it, he's wading into the water.

That night, through sleep or the veiled and restless time she passes at night and calls sleep, Ida finds she is facing away from Solomon's side of the bed and turns over. She makes herself lie the whole night facing Solomon. She believes if she lies facing his side, he will come back. Turning, she sees the curtain that divides their half of the bedroom from Ma'am's billow out. She watches the curtain, hearing the small bumped sounds of Ma'am's movements and the unconscious humming Ma'am makes, and then she hears Ma'am leave the house and she gets up and leaves also, wearing nothing but her white shift.

It is a mooned night, the moon whole except for a slice, the light artificially bright. Ida keeps way behind so that Ma'am will not turn and see her, and she follows Ma'am to the top of the swimming hole. She stands still at the top, watches Ma'am make her slow way down the slope, one step, pause, another, a lumbering pace, and Ida looks down at herself, at the white shift that is so bright it is near phosphorescent, and she takes it off, balls it up small in her hand and holds it against the small of her back and then she goes slowly, quietly, down to the water behind Ma'am.

Ma'am is undressing too; folds her pink dress and bloomers the size of a bucket and lays them down. Ma'am is short and wide, her head small, no neck, the squared head on the massive body like a small buffalo. The flesh on her buttocks and arms and thighs is dimpled and curled, scoops of flesh on top of scoops. She stands without moving, though to Ida it seems she does move: the flesh active, swinging, dimpling, even in stillness.

Ma'am bends to the water, pats at the surface with her hands and then she walks in, paddles out to the center where she struggles to turn herself so she can dive the way the men did. She is grunting. In the quiet, Ida hears her. She watches Ma'am turn, turn again, trying to find the right angle, trying to dive. She does it over and over, but it makes no difference. There is too much of her, she is too buoyant, she floats.

Time passes, a week or ten days. Ma'am sits outside in the shade that does not provide coolness; since the day after the night she went diving for Solomon she has sat here, left the maintenance of the house, the sweeping and washing and preparation of meals, to Ida.

All day, Ma'am just sits, humming in the back of her throat, a sound so constant and other than human that when she comes within reach of it, Ida sometimes bats at the air near her face thinking mosquitoes, or bugs.

They don't talk, except when Ida opens the kitchen door and calls Ma'am? Bed! or announces a meal.

At night, when she does not know if she's awake or asleep, Ida sees Solomon. He's running. She can see glimpses of him in between trees; he is the color, the fleetness of deer. She believes he has taken off for some reason she does not know and she waits for a sign to make this part clear. She spends her time waiting, waiting is under the chores, the preparations for meals, the washing. She believes it will arrive in her next breath, the next time she sits down or lies down or stands up; she does not know when it will arrive. She is always ready to be startled.

Ma'am? Ida puts her head out the door and says it again, Ma'am, and thinks of the times she was the one had to be called more than once.

Ma'am?

Earth was not meant to be this hot, Ma'am says, fanning at herself. This heat makes me can't breathe.

Ida goes back into the house, wets down a rag and carries it outside to Ma'am. She wraps it around Ma'am's neck, watches the water collect and then stay, shallow rivers inside clefts of fat. Dinner, she says. Come and eat?

Mmmm, Ma'am says. Her eyes are squinted though they are shut. Just let me rest here a minute with this cool. My head's real crowded today, and then she takes up the hum again, in the back of her throat.

Ida goes inside and she sits at the table and turns the dishes she's set on the blue oilskin cover. There are slices of ham she's fanned out on one plate – six slices, she counts them – and cold peppered potatoes, which she counts also, lifting the top ones with a spoon, laying these on her plate till she's got the bottom ones counted. The potatoes leave a skin of wetness on the plate. There are peas also; she thinks, I'm not counting those, but then she is counting, putting the counted ones on her plate and on Ma'am's, and when she is finished she gets up, goes, again, to the door and calls, Ma'am!

Ma'am doesn't answer, and Ida thinks – sleeping – and frowns, as Ma'am would, thinking Ma'am should not sleep so much sitting out in the heat. Ma'am!

Ma'am doesn't stir. Ida comes outside, approaches Ma'am's chair. There is a quietness, an absence of some sound. Ida lifts her head hunting for it, one half of her thinking because she is always waiting for signs that this could be it, the other half – It's so hot, even them flies have quit. Ma'am, she's still calling, her voice lower the closer she gets.

The rag, half fallen off Ma'am's neck, trails down her front like a flag pointing down and Ida looks down at Ma'am's hands, holding each other in her lap.

Ma'am? Ida says and touches her. Ma'am rocks a little, the rag falls and covers her hands and Ida raises her head, knowing all of a sudden that the sound she was missing was that hum, was Ma'am.

Ida sits at the table. She does not sit in her usual place, back to the door; she has moved to another chair now, what was Ma'am's, so that she does not have to twist around all the time to see who's coming. It's the one thing she's decided, or the one thing she thought of then did in the days or weeks or however long she's been here by herself at the table. She keeps telling herself, sit down and think, and she sits but then she cannot think, as though she's forgotten the trick of it. She sits at the table, pressing the pads of her fingers to the blue oilcloth, watching the gray steamed spots disappear.

She is wearing Ma'am's dress, pink with gray rickrack, the hooks up the front rusted out. The dress is six or eight times too large for her, she's got it tied with a length of rope at her waist, the front pockets meet and flap over each other in back. Ma'am would not ever let them – Ida, Solomon – wear anyone's cast-off clothes, even hers, even each other's; bad luck, she said, but Ida feels clear of bad luck now. Paid up in bad luck.

People come, knocking, the sound of knuckles and then of the door, loose in its frame, knocking back. Ida smiles at them and nods, smiling, as they talk and blinks at the door when they leave, not remembering who they were, what they said.

The women all come, but only one man as though he is the other men's elected representative. Johnny Lee Iron, he calls out, knocking on the door frame. Ida looks up and smiles. He stands inside the door, big, taking up space in Ma'am's kitchen.

My sister, that's Dilly? she said me to carry you this, Johnny says, and he sets down a plate, more like a platter – porkchops and gravy and greens, the dish towel covering it hot and wet with fresh steam.

Porkchops, Johnny says, reminding her what the food is like he reminded her of his sister's name. He says, You eat them now. Keep up your strength.

Ida smiles. When he has gone she's still smiling. She can't remember a word that he said.

He keeps coming. He brings her other small gifts, announcing their names as Ida holds them – a gold plastic comb, a stone so flat and so thin looking through it is like seeing through fog, a bag of pastel candies, their white and green disks painted with flowers.

Ida smiles at these though she doesn't eat them; when Johnny is gone she thinks of the flowers painted on them and takes the candies outside and digs shallow holes and buries them in a half circle outside the door to the kitchen. She marks each covered hole with a pebble so she will remember where they are planted and step over.

Always, he knocks on the frame of the door and announces himself – It's Johnny Lee Iron – and when he comes in and says, How you feeling today? Ida is smiling.

She is smiling, also, the day Johnny comes and knocks and calls to her, It's Johnny Lee Iron, and asks, in a roundabout way, if Ida will marry him. She does not really hear what he says because after his knock and the sound of his voice naming himself, she sees how all the people she knows are named after things: Irons and Kettles and Hills and after Oak trees and Pines and after Peaches and colors – White, Black and Green. She is thinking of this as Johnny sits down in the chair back facing the door, though he does not usually sit.

Ida, he says. You maybe noticed how I've been coming by here every day.

Ida is smiling.

And why, he says. Why. He lays his large hands on the table.

And Brown, Ida thinks, Brown is also a name, and she smiles.

Well, I got reasons. Ida, I got these cousins, moved up to New Jersey, they found a house for me to move to, a house I could go to. It's near a ocean, a beach . . .

Beech! Ida remembers, and smiles.

And I'm fixed to go, to quit here – he waves his hand, stirring a fly that has lit on his wrist.

And I'm asking you, what I mean . . . He looks down, he looks out the back door; Ida thinks of the candies she's planted, pictures like seed packet covers.

I mean, what I'm askin' is will you come with me. To that house. Like I said.

Ida stays smiling, smiling as he says the marry-him things that slip out of her head like cold water as soon as he's said them, and Johnny takes her smiling for yes; maybe she meant yes, even years after, she can't remember.

She can't remember yes or the wedding they must have had, as she can't remember packing the things in Ma'am's house and shipping them up to New Jersey and following after with Johnny in a car that had busted three times on the trip and gone, finally, someplace in Virginia so they'd come the rest of the way on a train. It was like she had slept through those things, dreamed of something else, and when she woke up, they were done.

* * *

Ida walks from her house to the large supermarket downtown where the parking lot sucks in the heat of the sun and throws it back again, walking slowly because once she gets where she's going – Leon's house – things will be different. She walks with a bag of bought food, Johnny's roses laid on top, down shaded streets and she remembers the shade from back home: how it looked cool but wasn't and she stops, caught by remembering.

Families pass her on their way from the beach, half-naked white people, the bare-chested men pink and skinned-looking like mice or guinea pigs. They carry coolers; folded webbed chairs dangle at the ends of their arms. Their eyes slide sideways to look at her. It is always like this: the shifting of eyes and of bodies, the crossing of streets, the speeding or slowing of cars and of bicycles, the way conversations halt and skitter as though the white people couldn't keep their minds on what they were saying when she passed. She had not expected to be so noticed, up north.

On the blacktop two houses from Leon and Isabel's house there's a spray of green glass, the pieces small and thick and evenly cut. Ida scrapes them into a pile with the side of her shoe meaning to go inside and come back with a broom and sweep up the glass, but inside she looks for a bowl for Johnny's roses and then arranges them in it and then she unpacks the potatoes and onions and apples and flour and porkchops and then she is chopping and slicing and then Joellen comes home.

You want to help me get supper? Ida says.

The girl hikes up her shoulders, dips her ear as though Ida's voice is too loud, too high pitched, then she goes to look out the back window.

Ida throws a handful of salt in a skillet and she waits for the sound to draw the girl back.

Porkchops, Ida says. You like porkchops?

Ma, the girl calls, still looking out the back window, then turns, calling again – Ma, only Ida hears Ma'am, Ma'am and she stands blinking, she does not even see Joellen go out of the kitchen, then has to turn off the flame she's got going under the porkchops and run out to catch her.

The girl's standing on the steps, two up, her shorts caught in the crack of her behind. Ida comes up on the sweet dirtiness of child sweat and then the girl turns, still two steps up and Ida sees her face, streaked the yellow of saffron, and it's not Joellen she's seeing, it's Solomon. She has forgotten his yellowness until now and, inside remembering, she loses Joellen again.

Stop *tracking* me, Joellen says when Ida comes up the stairs after her, but Ida does not stop. She sits the girl down on a bed and holds onto her yellowy wrist and, her eyes on the yellow, she tells Joellen the things Leon's picked out for her to hear: Accident, car, hospital, gone.

Ida is chopping onions and apples, her wrists supple and schooled so that the knife never falters, moved by her hands and her wrists that move, also, when she is ironing, that twist up her hair every morning so it is smooth, running over her head, twisted into a smooth knot in the back. Her hands do what they do in her own house, in the houses of white women: hold needles steady and thread them and make stitches that are as small and precise as fly's wings, and make knots. They take silverware out of drawers, plates out of cupboards, they wash plates, making circular motions, they fold clothes, deft at pleats, making piles. She watches her hands as they chop, hearing the sound of the TV from the other room clear and then blurred when Joellen changes the channel; hears, also, the hissing sound of the rinds of fat cooking. She smells the different parts of the meal she is fixing, the smells layered: onions and under that pork fat and lower, the winey smell of cut apples, and she sees she is making the same meal Johnny carried to her from his sister and she stops with the knife in the air.

She feels suddenly heavy as though the heat of the stove and the day and the remembered heat from back home have laid down on her skin in ribbons. Solomon. Ma'am. The babies she carried and lost in the years she and Johnny have lived here; the first after two months, the others longer or shorter than that so sometimes she did not even know she was pregnant until she felt a giving way or a loosening of something inside herself and then she knew she had been. Other times she carried for months so not only her belly and breasts, but her hands and her feet and, she felt also, her lips and her eyelids began to swell, but she lost these babies too and she begins now to do what she has not ever done: she counts them.

She counts them, losing the count, revising it, starting again, the counting a repetitive grind in her head. To make it stop, she starts to count other things, potatoes and onions and porkchops and then she opens a cupboard and counts plates, opens a drawer and counts forks and spoons.

And when Leon comes in, looking too old and too young, his hair and his teeth when he smiles (he smiles; she is holding a plate. Is that supper? he asks) all licked and silvered in the light from the kitchen, she is the one who says, You'll be needin' me now, see to the house, to your suppers. She is fierce, the fierceness a surprise, and he smiles again. Ida looks down, away from his teeth; his knees under his shorts are ashy and pocked and she thinks of the glass on the street, of him kneeling, and she holds out the plate. Porkchops, she says. You like porkchops?

Leon takes the plate and Ida sees herself taking the plate of food Johnny brought her, the heat from the steamed cloth on the inside of her arm. She was wearing Ma'am's dress, pink with gray rickrack, though it was five or six times too big for her and though Ma'am had told her wearing someone's old clothes was bad luck, but she had not cared: what more bad luck could there be?

I'll take care of the girl, Ida says, and the man nods, smiling, bending close to the plate and then closer, until his head disappears in the steam.

CHAPTER 7

....

These are the things I remember.

The bones in my mother's wrist; round, dear, the size and the weight of ball bearings. The silvery cracks on her palms. Her hands: squared off, flat, you could use them for flipping things, pancakes, she said, flipping her hands.

Other bones, the clavicles, heavy and knob-ended and the tender V in between them as if the bone had forgotten to fuse. I lay my hand there, in the small space, (two fingers, not my whole hand) to see what the bones would have looked like, fused.

Her kneecaps, elongated, shifting under the skin like jar lids and the scars she showed pointing, this one and this one, like sites on a map. One in particular, just under the knee, invisible when she stood, she had to bend so you could see it. She was a girl, she had fallen on flagstone, there was a piece, a crumb of it still in her knee. Here, she said, bending the knee. We watched the seamed hill of the scar emerge, a tiny bleached island in the pink and chapped sea around it and under the scar, a dot of gray-blue, milky, the color of old eyes.

We bent to see it, she told the story, I see this over and over. Our heads almost touch. Our mouths close to kissing.

I see the twin juts of cheekbone and brow over/under her eyes, though not her eyes. They were green, but the color is gone; not the color of bottles, book covers, the ocean on overcast days; not the color of lawns, of limes, of sugared mints. Her eyes are missing. I remember bones.

And hair and nails, cousins to bone, the nails on her hands ridged like shells, the hair the colorless color of water and straight and fine and too sparse to balance the head. The features slightly larger than life-size, and the limbs, their marbled whiteness, her legs like twin monuments.

This is what I remember.

PART II

CHAPTER 8

....

Nothing stopped. I thought we would stay where that day had left us, as random as marbles: we'd head on into winter still in summer clothes. But things stayed nearly the same. Leon went to his colleges. Ida was there mornings now, handing me plates of fried ham and grits and tomatoes. Leon left money for Ida in envelopes on the table, the bills green and soft like an assortment of leaves. Maybe they talked on the phone. Maybe Leon called her at home or at our house during the day when I wasn't there. Maybe they never spoke – Leon left, Ida came, like some mechanism, oiled and silent, they did not expect me to notice.

Leon stopped driving after the car hit my mother, as though he understood, for the first time, the real and ferocious power of cars. He backed our car, a Rambler, into the garage and left it to ripen into an antique. When I go in for my bicycle, I try not to look at the car, the plastic headlights and flashers devil red in the light from outside, the hidden and ominous bulk of the car lurking behind them. I am afraid of the car. In the dark it seems almost living to me, secret and feral, like stray cats.

Leon took trains now, trains from our town deeper into New Jersey or out to Long Island or into New York where his colleges were. Sometimes there was no direct route and he had to go hours out of his way, then double back. He was gone from home more now; he left earlier and got back later, sometimes as late as eleven, the last passenger off the last train, unsteady with tiredness, loose pages from that day's newspaper swooping and diving at him like bats in the station.

I hardly saw him and never knew when I would. Sometimes he turned up at five, so the next night I'd wait to eat with him – Ida cooked suppers for us and left them on plates covered with sweating plastic. But the next night he'd come in at nine or at ten or eleven. I'd be numb with tiredness and would not eat the food that had dried out or congealed, the meat juices like a skim of thin ice on a pond. I sat at the table, my head propped on my arm, in need of company, but Leon hardly talked. Shouldn't you be in bed, Sal? It's late, he might say, but that was all and he made no move to shoo me.

On his late nights I missed him. On the nights he was home early, though, I couldn't bear him, the precise and clipped way that he spoke, his half-lowered shuddering eyes. I could not stand the faded, parchment-like shade of his hair, his teeth the same cast as though they'd been dyed to match. I could not stand watching him eat.

Ida crowded the food on our plates – meat and vegetables, potatoes and pieces of corn bread that crumbled, absorbing meat juices and vegetable liquid, until it was reduced to the grist it had come from. Sometimes she left dessert – plain cakes, pies that were scant-sugared – these things too, heaped on the same plates.

Leon ate everything, dipping his fork from food to food, lifting it to his mouth. At first I thought it was some vast and unstaunchable hunger, though he did not ever seem to want more. After weeks of watching him, I saw he did not care what he was eating. Where I kept the foods separate, herding them back, Leon's fork stabbed from food to food, the way the beach cleaners did, long poles bayonetting as much as possible. I saw him spear greens, then his fork moved to cake, wet green strings still trailing down from the tines.

Is it cold? I sometimes asked or, Does it taste good? He looked up, blinking, confused.

He didn't care, he must never have cared, and I thought, watching him chew, watching him close his eyes when he swallowed – how could he live with it, finding out now that my mother hadn't deprived him of things that he liked, that there were no such things, that he could not tell the difference between smooth and chunky or viscous or sweet or food that balked on the way down? His mouth knew only that it was full, that the molars were grinding, that the tongue lifted and turned lozenges of whatever it was and I thought: How can he bear eating? This constant reminder of how he had cared about food with my mother?

Leon does not talk and Ida talks only sometimes, and then about things that she chooses. She asks if I have on clean socks; if it's cold she tells me to wear a sweater. If I hum in the morning she tells me – Sing before breakfast, you'll cry before supper.

Ida was full of sayings, things she knew that doomed you to bad luck or sorrow. You could not open umbrellas in the house or leave a hat on a bed or put your feet on a table or rock an empty rocking chair, not that we had one. If I forget something, a book or a paper I need for school after I've gone out the door in the morning, I can't come back in to get it. Ida gets it for me while I stand outside on the porch.

Some days Ida does not speak at all; some days she's talking as soon as I come in the door, seems to be talking before I am even inside. It is often unclear to me what's going on in her stories, as though I've missed their beginnings.

Woman? Ida says. Fifteen hunnert and fifty-three pounds. That's half a ton, she says. Over.

Fifteen *hundred?* I say. I hear the way hundred comes out, stress meant for amazement, but it sounds as though I'm correcting the wrong way Ida said it. I sit down, waiting to see if she's offended. She is testy, suspicious, and I feel always close to guilty of something.

Ida does not speak, stands ironing, it is the last task she does every day before she goes home at 4:20. I hear the slap and glide of the iron.

Couldn't fit her in this place, she says at last. Her voice is grudging, she would rather not tell me, only there's no one else here to tell.

Have to take all the doors off of the hinges, she says.

Where'd you see her? I ask.

I just seen her, that's all, Ida says. She is full of such stories – the Monkey Man, the child with two heads – beings she seems to know well, though she will never say how she knows them. I imagine that they may be distant relations who come for visits. I know nothing about her. I know she works here. She is married to Johnny.

You hungry? Ida asks. The iron slaps and glides. The air in the kitchen is full of the crisped smell of ironing. Isabel never ironed. The washed and dried clothes Ida left folded on top of the washing machine Isabel stuffed into drawers. The clothes took up space; wrinkled, full of air, they lofted on top of each other. Tags and triangular pieces of collars stuck out of the drawers. When Ida took over, things were flat and smooth. I thought, at first, that I had fewer clothes. Things disappeared. Isabel's drawers and closet had been emptied, as though she had never had clothes.

Ida holds the shirt she is ironing, white and sleeveless, up to the light.

What's that? I ask.

I said, Was you hungry?

No. That. I point to the white shirt. It is familiar to me though it is breast-less and shoulderless now; it is flat.

Ida says, What? She frowns, not liking to break the rhythm of work. When she speaks, ironing, her words slap and glide. She spreads the blouse on the iron-ing board so the end of the board curves through the armhole then sprinkles the cloth, dipping her hand into a glass of water. Inside it, her fingers bloat to the size of small carp.

That shirt, I say.

Blouse, Ida says, correcting me, only she says it blooze, as though it's some French word.

Blooze makes me sad, like the other words Ida missays: mahonica, she says, and pin meaning pen.

I get up, go to the ironing board set up in the middle of the kitchen. This, I say, fingering the fabric.

What I said, Ida says, pushing my hand off, and I close my eyes again, wait-ing for blooze. I feel the radiant heat of the iron approach and retreat from my hand.

No, I say. I mean whose?

Her eyes narrow. Not *mine*, she says. I got my own iron. Or you maybe think I'm doing my own work on your daddy's time. You think colored people are thieverous?

No, I say, no, though when she says this I wonder: Do I? I think of my mother's missing clothes, the things of my own that I missed. At night, some shirt I had not worn or thought of in a while sometimes came into my head and I got up, went scrubbing through my drawers in the dark, the shirts flat and folded and ironed, each the decompressed height of an envelope. I always found it, down at the bottom, my fingernails scraping wood.

No, I say again. I mean I think it's my . . . and I miss Isabel with a force that is so sudden, so unexpected, I can't speak. Isabel was clear, and solid. It was not hard saying what you meant to Isabel. I grab the end of the ironing board and lean over.

What? Ida says. Joellen? You sick? Her hand moves, touches my collar, not skin.

The shirt, I say. I'll take it.

What for? Ida says.

And this is something else. You cannot say any words to Ida that are simple, that do not have to lead anyplace, that she meets simply with yes. I feel the weight of her wordiness, of having to explain everything. I have to sit down.

It's my mother's, I say. I say, I could wear it.

Don't you got clothes of your own? Ida says, turning to face me, her neck as slow-moving as the sound of the words. Don't you got enough in those closets?

Closets? I want to say. I have only one closet.

She stands facing me, hands on her hips, the pink blouse gaping away from her arm so I can see the secret white strap of her bra, the tight screws of hair like whorled knots in her armpit.

Don't you know it's bad luck to be wearing somebody's old things?

Bad luck? I say. Why? Who says? I am near crying. Ida's rules are like the meanings of words: arbitrary, iron-clad.

My Ma'am, Ida says. That's who.

Your mother? I hear my own voice – too loud, too full of amazement. Ida never said anything more about family to me than "Johnny." Maybe it was bad luck to mention the names of your family to white children.

I say the two words again, quietly, so they will not sound out of the ordinary to Ida, so she will go on. Your mother?

My grandmother, she says, grudging, and looks at me. What you think *Jo*ellen, God just set me down here, fully grown, in New Jersey?

I shake my head. I picture a grandmother – tidy, frail, a gray-haired version of Ida as Johnny is a pants-wearing one.

She live with you? I ask.

You writin' a book, Miss *Jo*ellen? she says and thumps the hot iron down on the stove and folds up the ironing board, which shrieks.

Leon and I are eating breakfast. It's a Sunday, Ida's not here, Leon's not talking so I am, talking and talking, because without it the house is empty of sound.

You want to go someplace? I ask.

I want to *not* go someplace, Leon says. I don't want to go *anyplace*. I *go* places all week.

No, I say. I mean just the beach. For a walk on the boardwalk.

It's November, Sal. I don't want to go to the beach in November – though there is no time he does want to go to the beach. He is not a beach person.

I know it's November, I say. I like the beach best now. Off Peak. It is my mother's word, my mother's favorite time on the beach. Leon looks up, he looks at me. My mother is suddenly there, a shimmering glare behind my shoulder. He looks down again and she's gone.

You could put me up for adoption, I say.

What? Leon says.

Nothing, I say. I look down at the table. There is a reamed orange rind on my plate. I look at that.

What made you say that, Sal?

Nothing, I say again. I shrug, drawing my shoulder close to my chin. When he is not looking, I kiss it.

Children who don't have *parents* get adopted, he says. You have me.

I nod. I know, I say. You're not ever here. I don't know where you are.

I have to work, he says after a pause that leaves a gap in the air like a missing fence post. I have to make us a living, small though it may be. I come home. You have Ida.

Ida, I say. Ida's a . . . and I stop. I don't know what Ida is, only what she is not.

A what? Leon says, his voice frozen into politeness. Finish please.

I look away, wishing to erase the last things that we've said. I know that Leon is ready to pounce: a *servant*, he expects me to say; a *housekeeper*, a Negro, for each of which he has a speech ready. He is as prickly as Ida, always on the look-out for slights, a kind of sheriff of prejudice, his senses honed for it as though there's a particular smell lurking under the skins of the people who have it, a slightly metallic tang the people themselves do not notice. We, I know, are not a prejudiced family.

She has her own . . . I start to say, then can't finish. Is it a family – Johnny, a grandmother, the fifteen-hundred-pound woman, the Monkey Man, the child with two heads?

Ida loves you, Leon says.

I look at him. How did he know this? Did Ida tell him? I can't conjure the sound of her voice speaking those words, not just about me, about anyone. "Love" was on the list of things Ida would not say out of superstition or delicacy, like certain parts of the body, like "panties."

Ida's a part of this family, Leon says and I do not speak then either. In what way? She didn't eat the meals that she cooked in our house. She drank only once in a while, when she was tired: cloudy glasses of sugarwater. She didn't sleep here. She arrived dressed – dresses and skirts that made her look different from the way she looked in the black pedal pushers and pink blouse she wore in our house. She shook out her clothing before she put it on again to go home. If I walked in on her when she was changing down in the laundry room, she pressed her hands flat on the top of her chest hiding not her skin, but the lace of her slip. She left only the pedal pushers and shirt on a shelf in the laundry room and the scent of the hand cream she used, a smell that was pink, like the shirt was.

Come here, Leon says, his voice gentle. He takes my arm, pulls me towards him as though he is not sure I will otherwise come. He draws me between his two knees.

I don't know why I didn't do this before, he says. I must think you're still a small child when you're not. He smiles, he winks. We'll *pretend* you are not a small child, he means.

I'm eleven, I say. I'll be twelve. I do not smile. Twelve sounds like a serious age to me, nearly grown.

He opens his briefcase. A smell yawns out of it, a parched and cracked smell like dried leaves, and he takes out a chart. It's his schedule, the hours and phone numbers and places he teaches, the times he is there, the time of the trains he takes home. The days of the week are in capital letters and underlined, the lines so straight and precise I know he used a ruler to make them.

Ida has one of these, he says. I thought that was enough.

Ida, I think. When did he see Ida? There was nothing, I knew, in the envelopes he left for her but money.

Leon is waiting for me to look down, his finger patient at the first line of the chart. Now you'll always know where to find me, he says. He takes me through the days of the week. I feel his knees pressing against me, pointy and thin through the cloth of his pants. I lay my hand over one knee and then, though I look down at the chart and follow the sound of his voice, I think of his knee. It jumps every now and again, slides up on its own. I feel his knee and think of it and of his fingernails gliding across the chart. They are opaque and fretted like the papery outer skin of garlic. I try to follow his words, but it is useless. I am so little touched.

Leon taped the chart up on a wall in the kitchen along with a train schedule and a map, the train routes darkened in red so they looked like sections of arteries swollen with blood. Little red vertical lines marked the stations.

It was better, in some ways, knowing his schedule; in some ways it was worse. Before it always seemed possible that he'd walk in the door any minute; with the chart I knew exactly when he'd be home. He factored in things like how long it took him to walk down the platform. He'd counted the number of steps from the station to home.

On Mondays he got in at five and Mondays were fine, only half an hour between the time Ida left and Leon arrived. On Wednesdays and Fridays he got home at eight and I could stand this, too, though it stretched me thinner. I sat at the table doing my homework. The house was soundless and airless. Sometimes I couldn't stay there. I went and sat in the station and watched passengers get off the trains and waited for one of them to be Leon.

Tuesdays and Thursdays Leon didn't get home until eleven and Tuesdays and Thursdays were endless. I tried to get Ida to stay or to take me home with her. I said I was sick. I said, My stomach, my throat. She'd have on her home clothes and stay where she was in the laundry room near the back door (maybe it was bad luck to walk through a house wearing a coat) and tell me to get the thermometer: mer-thometer, she called it.

You're not sick, you're fine, she'd say, looking at the thermometer, as though the two things, sick and fine, were so close nothing could fit in between them. Go eat, she'd tell me and she'd leave. I went through the kitchen to the front door, opened it, watched her go. I stood with my face pressed against the rust-smelling screen willing her to turn and see me, but she never turned, she never waved, she never looked back.

It's December. In one month it will be the start of the first year Isabel is not in. I make myself think this, a fact, though there are times, too, I run from where I'm standing when the thought comes. I can smell the oncoming dark on my way home from school. I no longer go early to visit the horses, not since the day of Crisis and Missiles. The horses seemed, that day, to know of disaster, and they stood, placid and inert, keeping it to themselves.

Mostly I take the bus in the mornings, but I like walking home. This day, though, I feel odd. My feet slap the sidewalk as though I am misjudging its distance; the cool squares of cement seem about to come at me as though they're loose boards I have stepped on.

It takes me a long time to get home, though I don't know this until I get there and see Ida not ironing – *past* ironing, she says when I ask, her voice cranky. What was I, *po*lice?

She has on her home clothes, a jacket the color of calamine lotion. She's in the vestibule near the laundry room ready to go.

Why you so late? she asks me. I still got shopping to do, my own dinner to think of.

I feel funny.

Yeah, you always feel funny, what's so funny about you?

I feel – I have to say funny again.

Ida huffs out through her nose, shakes her head. Tuesdays and Thursdays, she says. Those your funny feelin' days.

I'm goin', she says. She opens the door, holds it with her foot.

You're okay, Ida says. Your daddy be home before you know it.

I nod.

You know where I am, Ida says. You got my telephone, 'case you need me.

I nod again.

You lock this door, she says. I turn back to the inside of the house. Only the kitchen light is on, Ida turns off all the others before she leaves, maybe Leon scared her into doing it – we were not a light-burning family. Most afternoons I ran through the house as soon as Ida was gone turning on every light. I gave myself only a minute to do this, like I was a winner of one of those shopping sprees they gave as prizes on radio stations. I liked the combination of fear and giddiness.

But today, I can't do it. The top landing's dark and looming and far; the light from the kitchen is sallow. I am suddenly afraid of the house, afraid of the stairs, the light, afraid of the living room furniture. I can't go upstairs, I can't even go back to the kitchen. I go out the front door. I follow Ida.

She's easy to find. She walks slow, her hips hula-hooping under the spread of her skirt. I stay behind her – there might be some taboo against speaking to a person you'd just said goodbye to.

She stops at the market, one of a horseshoe of stores around a big parking lot – a drugstore, the Busy Bee Launderette, the Goodwill where people bought and wore other people's unlucky old clothes, and Hauptmann's Bakery where bennies lined up on summer Sundays, barefoot and shirtless and rude, to buy donuts and drink orange juice out of quart cartons they took from the cooler and finished and then put back empty.

I wait for Ida outside, by the market's dumpster. She takes a long time. She must have seen me, snuck out a back way. I am near the train station, I can cross the tracks, go wait for Leon, but it can't be any later than five, I'd have to wait for six hours. Then Ida comes out of the market.

I let her get a ways up ahead, then follow behind. We cross the train tracks, walk on until we get to where houses begin to crowd up on top of each other, close as weeds. No two are the same size, the same color, the same distance apart. Where there is a gap from a house torn down, the remaining houses seem to lean in towards each other as though too much distance between makes them lonely. This is where the Negroes live in our town. The streets have no names. The walls and the roofs of the houses are patched over with shingles in various colors and with hubcaps and flattened tin cans that glint and seem to be winking.

It's not fully dark yet, I can see the front yards, the washed-out color and texture of worn-away carpet. There are flowers planted in wooden boxes and in jumbo-size cans that say Tomatoes, Sauerkraut, Beets. The flowers are mostly dead or stiffened by cold but still recognizable: the red and hot pink of geraniums, the dusky purples and golds and mauves of fall mums, as though all the people who live here are saying, this is what "colored" means.

Ida goes down the narrow dirt strip that separates her house from the house next door. The windows aren't flush with the walls of the house: light sluices through cracks. I stand with my back almost touching the next-door house, they are that close. Inside, Ida puts her groceries on the table. A man comes up behind and slides her jacket off by the shoulders. He is large and old, his skin dark and creased like raisins. It's not till later that I think Johnny. He doesn't look anything like Ida.

It's cold out, then dark, and I'm just standing, the cool coming up through my shoes, watching Ida and the man pass in and out of my view. I imagine Ida cooking their supper now and the man maybe helping, though I can't see this. I can only see what goes on between their chins and their waists.

I stand a long time. This is what I am thinking will happen: Ida will spot me, she will be happy to see me, she'll bring me in. After a while Ida comes to the window and I think: it's happening now! I take a step forward, but she doesn't see me. She pulls down the shade. The light from inside shines like light through the skin of an onion.

As the shade lowers, the cold lowers too. I shiver, my legs vibrate all on their own and I slide my hands down to my knees, cup them, try to warm them, but I feel the cold, then, in other parts of my body and the shaking won't stop and it is so noisy – a dense galloping sound that doesn't move off until I yawn and inside the yawn the sound stops and I know I am hearing my teeth chattering from the inside.

I don't go up on Ida's porch, knock on her door, I know I can't, as though we'd made some kind of bargain about this: that we'd be seeing each other afternoons until 4:20, no more, no less.

I go back out to the street. I have no idea, now, where I am, how to get home; before, I'd just followed Ida. Neither end of the street looks familiar. It's dark, there are no streetlights, the only lights come from people's houses, illuminating, sometimes, the chrome of a parked car, a hubcap, a tin can flower pot. I walk, turning down blocks; I might be walking the same blocks over and over. Then I come into a patch of air that smells like salt and I follow the smell. You can't really get lost in our town. You just have to get down to the beach.

It takes a long time to get there. Everything's dark except for the lamps that lay circles of light on the boardwalk. My cheeks are frozen now; when I touch them I feel their smooth outer surface but they don't feel back and I can't feel my toes either. The sand was hot the last time I was here with my mother. Let's take our shoes off, she said, so I do and then I walk out of the circles of light towards the water.

Each step is cold, though I am expecting the next step and then the one after that to be warmer. There is no moon. I walk. The water is dark up ahead, its surface oiled and eel-like.

Where's she going? a voice says in my head, but it doesn't seem to be talking to me so I don't answer.

Find any? I say to Isabel. I don't think this is such a great time.

Hey! the voice says, the same voice or another one, Hey!

I take one more step, then another, then stop, something stops me – the wind, maybe, stiff and identical to my own force. I am pushing forward.

Hey, hey, hey, the voice says, a man's voice, this is surprising, though maybe it's my own voice, deeper than I remember, or Isabel's. Why is she shouting? I'm right *here!* I can *hear* you!

My mouth opens, fills with taste and with texture, something dense and dog-smelling scabbers over my lips and my tongue and my teeth. Wind? Water? I can't breathe or move, something holds onto my arms – seaweed or ropes – and I'm twisting and kicking, my neck stretching for air and then there's a light in my face, full and blinding – a buoy! – I grab for it but it bobbles away.

Hey! the voice says. I know her! and in the light of the buoy (not a buoy, a lantern) I see a face, eyes, skin, a mouth.

I know her, the mouth says. She's a friend of my brother's. Charlie's.

That right? another voice says, but I do not see who says this and then the first voice speaks again.

Jo, right? the voice says. You're Jo aren't you? and I say, I am *not* Jo, I'm Jo*ellen*, the fierce way Isabel taught me to say it, reminding me over and over, the way she also had given me dime after dime to keep in my shoe for emergency phone calls. Jo*ellen* I say and try to move sideways to where Isabel is.

Hey! the voice says again. I pitch forward, heading for my mother and there's some deep sound that's not the first voice or the second, that is me: cold and sick and sheared off by loneliness.

Arms come around me, Isabel's? then she hands me to the voice – it is Herman, Charlieo's second brother.

Night fishing, he says, packing me into his car, tossing his keys, ordering his friend to get the blanket he keeps in the trunk then wrapping me in it. It smells of wet wool and car oil; it smells delicious. He has his arm over my shoulders, he drives only left-handed, I sit close as a girlfriend pressing up against him, attentive to the shifting of skin and of bone.

He takes me to his house, carries me up the steps and in the front door.

Mom, Herman calls. The word hums in his chest and his throat, full of M's, an M word.

I've been afraid of something like this, Mrs. O'Casey says, her eyes owlish and concerned behind her round lenses.

The house is warm, the heat dry in my mouth and my nose, but it stays outside me.

Hot, Mrs. O'Casey says. She's burning up. Get the thermometer, Charlie, she says. *Ther*mometer, it is such a relief. But it is not Ida's fault, I want to tell someone. The way she says words.

Warm, Mrs. O'Casey says, touching my forehead and then she says Soup, and I turn to look at her, saying these things that I want.

Honey? Mrs. O'Casey says. I'm calling your dad. She moves near me and I look at her lips which are chapped, several strata of skin, some with traces of lipstick.

Honey? she says again. What time's your dad home?

He's not home, I say. He's working. At this college. The words sound far off, like somebody else talking.

Oh, Mrs. O'Casey nods. There are two small Joellens in her glasses, one in each lens.

Home at eleven, I tell her, nodding my head, the heads of my small twinned selves nodding back. Tonight's an eleven o'clock night.

I lie on the sunporch, on the couch Mrs. O'Casey's made up as a bed. She smooths the hair off my face, her hand's movements smooth and repetitive. After a while she gets up and turns off the light, though there's light, still, from the kitchen. The phone in the kitchen lifts, I hear the forward then backwards sweep of the dial, then it's replaced. She does it again and again at intervals, maybe three minutes apart, as regular and methodical as the backward brush of her hand on my hair. She is calling Leon, wants to get him the minute he walks in the door, before he has a chance to see that I am not in my bed, though I don't know if this is something he does: checks on me.

I hear her voice finally – Leon is home, he has answered. Her voice comes to me and drifts away, a murmuring tone. Here, she says, and then Sick and then Keep, I'll keep Joellen and I let go then. Inside Keep.

....

CHAPTER 9

It was the summer of miniature golf. I was thirteen, Charlieo fourteen, though we were in the same class at school. I'd skipped, shuttled out of second grade into third one day in the middle of the year.

By this time I was spending every Tuesday and Thursday night at the O'Caseys', had been for a year and a half, another silent arrangement of Leon's as the one with Ida was, as my mother's burial had been.

Cremated, Leon told me after. It sounded like something to do with milk; something like "pasteurized." He had spared me without asking.

Leon called Mrs. O'Casey my Emergency Person, which I heard in capital letters and with its underlying intent: as distinct from father. She signed my school trip forms, my notes home from the teacher. Guardian, she wrote under her name: a good word. Less dire than Emergency Person, I thought it called up a kinship, something like godmother, aunt, though I never said this to Leon.

Charlieo named our summers: I would not have thought of it. This was the summer of miniature golf, last summer was the summer of coins, the summer of seeds was the one before that. We were never quite free of the summers we'd already been through. We made pilgrimages to our old places the way other people visited battlefields: to feel tied to a history.

I had no further interest in coins, but for Charlieo there was no such thing as pure pleasure. We had to go back to the train station to lay nickels and cents on the tracks the way we had done last year, then wait for trains to run over them. We had to race, the same way we'd done it the summer before, to be the first to feel the distant train vibrations up through our legs; to yell TRAIN! TRAIN! at each other down the platform.

When a train pulled in, we stood on the platform, grit pinging our faces, until it pulled out again; then we went down for the coins. The long hooked chin of Lincoln was longer, Jefferson reduced to a few sketchy lines. I still liked their immediate heat, the smell of scorched metal, but I couldn't remember the covetousness I had felt a year ago: now they were only flatted metal oblongs, scalding, then cool.

The miniature golf course is down on the boardwalk and opens at eight. We're always there early: Charlieo likes being first. First in line, first scorecards, choice of clubs, first to pick out a pencil. The pencils were fresh-sharpened, the fragrance of shaved wood overpowering, for an instant, the stiff salted wind off the water.

We went early to avoid the crowds of children whose high whining voices were like assault weapons, and especially to avoid the bennies, boys mostly, in cutoffs with the round cardboard beach tokens that conferred summer resident status in our town pinned to their shorts. We hated the bennies because they were rude and disregardful, and because hating bennies is what made us a town, at least summers. On Sunday mornings the white-haired, patrician Republicans who went to the Episcopal church and the shopkeepers and their families, mostly Catholics, and the Baptist Negroes, acknowledged each other as they came out of their various churches, ranged around the fake lake like stores in a mall. Standing in line at Hauptmann's Bakery they found each other's eyes and nodded over the heads and behind the backs of the bennies.

The bennies travelled in packs, always half drunk, sour smelling, licks of salt like peeled skin making ragged crescents on the insides of their thighs. They liked to walk around shirtless. A few were weight lifters, their bodies carefully tanned, huge arms held away from their sides, ropey thighs chafing at the tops when they walked. Mostly they were just soft, fat boys, their bellies a pink jiggle, the dark shadows of the navels obscene. Visual Pollution, Charlieo and I called it. After golf we roughed out letters to our elected officials demanding a Shirts Only ordinance.

Dear Sir, I began.

Dear Honorable Sir, Charlieo said. You have to address them as Honorable.

How do you know?

He shrugged. I just know, he said. Don't you just know some things?

I nodded but I could not think of anything I just knew.

We sat under the boardwalk. The ocean was just a wrinkled sheet in the distance, a hard glittering white. It was like one continuous tarp of aluminum foil, as the summer was one continuous sheet of days, of family dinners at Charlieo's house.

* * *

Food, for the O'Caseys, was a secondary mealtime characteristic. It was there, they ate it, something out of the weekly double shopping carts of plenty Mrs. O'Casey provided, but what made them sit down was nostalgia, a lowing tenderness for their own golden days gone by.

They told stories that began: Remember when Herman . . . ? Or, Tell the time when Douglas was four. They laughed at these stories, the same ones over and over. Their eyes teared, they touched each other's shoulders, backs.

Tell the raft story, Mrs. O'Casey says one evening.

Listen to this! Charlieo says, punching me in the arm. Herman and Douglas roll their eyes.

One day, Mrs. O'Casey says, prompting. Charlieo took a raft . . .

Herman snores.

Mrs. O'Casey says, Charlieo took a raft . . .

They did not tell Charlieo stories often – he had missed the heroic era of Herman and Douglas's childhoods. The Charlieo stories they did tell made him seem slightly ridiculous, heedless and potty.

A hot May, Mrs. O'Casey says.

Hotter than hell, Herman says.

Herman!

No lifeguards, Herman says, leaning over, speaking in a confidential tone.

He launched himself at low tide, carrying the raft over a sandbar.

I remember the squabbling of birds, Mrs. O'Casey says. Not used to that heat.

Then the tide *changed*, Charlieo says, a boy who couldn't wait to get to the good part.

The tide changed, Mrs. O'Casey continues. We thought he was gone.

Europe, Mr. O'Casey says. Ten days or so and he would've hit England.

You thought I should go, right Pop? (Charlieo).

Mr. O'Casey nods. He looks serious. Said so. Said, if the boy's that set on going . . .

I stood on the shore, Mrs. O'Casey says. He just sat there, his little hands gripping the side of the boat. (Charlieo frowns slightly. "Little.")

It was blue, she says. Same as the ocean. It looked like he was sitting there, right on top of the water.

Charlieo's pleased as punch, a drunk bunny, his face pink and ashine, his eyes buggy. He looks from parent to parent, brother to brother as each tells their part of the story.

I wanted to call in the *Coast* Guard, Mrs. O'Casey says.

Right? she says. Douglas?

Hmmm? Douglas says.

The Coast Guard. I wanted to call them in. Charlieo is still smiling, but the rhythm of the telling has faltered.

Charlieo says, To *England*. Right, Pop?

No need for the Coast Guard, Douglas says. The O'Casey boys to the rescue! We hopped a fishing boat, he tells me.

The Dangerous Duo, Herman says and grins at Douglas who grins back. That's what we were known as, Herman's explaining to me.

"Known as!" Mr. O'Casey hoots. He is addressing me also, or addressing himself in my direction. His grin matches his sons': cartoonish.

It's what they called themselves! Mr. O'Casey finishes and hoots again, walloping back to those years.

Charlieo's bobbing his head. You never knew those old boats could do time like . . .

How would you rather die, Herman says.

I look around the table. I must have missed something, what did he say? Herman stretches his arms over the backs of the chairs to his right and his left. Sits grinning.

The choices are, he says: Jumping off the world's tallest building . . .

I thought it was "jumping off the Empire State Building," Mr. O'Casey says.

Yeah, well, is it? Still? I don't keep up with these things. I'm just trying for accuracy, Herman says.

As far as I know, Mr. O'Casey says. Charlie? You're more or less the expert in these things.

Charlieo's picking at something invisible on the speckled formica table top. It has his undivided attention.

More dessert? Mrs. O'Casey says, fluttering behind the seated men. I see her put a hand on Mr. O'Casey's shoulder, shake her head when he glances up at her.

Charlie? Mr. O'Casey says. I'd like the courtesy of a response, as would your brothers. Have you heard of them building anything bigger, taller than the Empire State? His voice is steady but with an edge.

No sir, Charlieo says. I have not.

May I go on? Herman says. His father nods at him.

Jumping off the *Empire State Building*. Being eaten alive by sharks. OR, sliding down a chute made of razor blades.

Douglas, who has not spoken, adds: Or, you forgot, the Electric Chair. Hanging. Having your limbs torn off one at a time.

Asunder, Mr. O'Casey says.

Asunder, says Douglas.

They don't stop, don't hear, I guess, the sound that I make, someplace between a hiss and a groan, or their mother say Boys! or the scraping of Charlieo's chair as he gets up fast so that I look to see if the chair's left skid marks. He walks stiff-legged away from the table.

You know how he hates that game, Mrs. O'Casey says.

Oh come on! Herman says. He's, what is he thirteen? It's a *game*, he knows that!

*Four*teen, I say. How could they not know this? They look at me, puzzled. They look away.

What does he think, we're planning an execution for the evening's entertainment? Herman says.

It's a fiendish word: it alters the feel of the house. Then Mrs. O'Casey's large back, her flowered print dress, crosses my sight and the house reverts to safeness.

He's sensitive to it, she says. It bothers him, that's all. Maybe there's things used to bother you.

I nod. I think of our car, the green cat-eyed Rambler backed into the garage.

Maybe, Herman says, but I doubt it. He's grinning.

Mr. O'Casey shrugs, looks at his wife. Far's I remember, that's right, he says. A hell raiser. Scared of nothing.

Herman clips Douglas on the side of the head.

Yeah? Douglas says. I'll save you the trouble of choosing. You die by the fist! and they are scuffling, hooting, forgetful of the size of their grown bodies. They take up too much space; a coffee cup gets knocked over, a pile of bread gets swept to the floor. Their knees hammer the underside of the table.

Joellen go on. Get away before these wild hooligans get you, Mrs. O'Casey says.

I go out back. I'm sort of looking for Charlieo, not sure he wants to be found, though it's not squeamishness he'd mind me having witnessed, it's outsideness. He is the one who knows if the Empire State's still the world's tallest building.

I head towards the seed farm, kicking through the ankle-high unmowed grass that whips and itches my bare legs. The grass is full of varied shadows – black, a smoky pine-blue and the flat inflectionless color that is plain crayon green. It's like a miniature physical map, various rugged terrains seen from above. I nearly step on Charlieo, sprawled on his back under a bush. His bent knees are pale moony humps in the landscape.

He tips his head upside down to see who it is. Hey, he says.

Hey.

I could feel you coming a mile. Right up through my back. He tilts his head, sideways this time. Echo, he says. Magnification. Pull up a piece of dirt.

I do. Lie back so the cool comes up through my shirt. It smells of mud and something pungent, garlic or onion. I try to remember what we just had for dinner.

What is that? I say, sniffing.

Onion grass, Charlieo says. Here. Chew. A stalk with a white bulb, slightly swollen, appears over my head. I twirl it in front of me but don't put it in my mouth.

How do you know all this stuff? I ask.

Like what?

Magnification of sound, I say. Onion grass. Dear Honorable Sir.

I don't know, it's stuff. Read. It's no big deal.

It is. I don't know, like, *any* of the stuff that you know.

So, you know other stuff. You have a good vocabulary.

I do?

Joellen, you know so.

We are quiet for a while; in the wake of the fluster Herman and Douglas always make, it stands out.

Then: If you could wish to know one thing, Charlieo says, what would it be?

I say: I would wish to know and be able to use every *useful* word in the English language, not counting the ones nobody's ever heard of, and to be able to remember them, but not to have them all cluttered up in my head so I could never think of anything else. I am very specific, as Charlieo will be, also, when I ask him the same question. We always covered all eventualities. Said the whole wish in one sentence or it might seem like two wishes and you'd only get half, like saying – sail to a beautiful island, and forgetting to say "and back."

You? I turn on my side, feel the faint downward shift of the tiny breasts I am just beginning to have. I think of Isabel's white shirt. It's nearly dark, down where we are. The shadows of the bush and the lawn are darker than the sky.

Charlieo's still on his back, his knees up, his arms under his head. I wait for him to wish something geological – to see what the earth was like when the dinosaurs lived and then to come back – but he says: Or getting separated from your spacecraft. Lost in space.

What?

My brothers. How Would You Rather Die? They never remember Lost in Outer Space, that's the best one. You'd just orbit until your body burned up, but you'd get to see some really great stuff first. That's how I'd go. No question. He plucks a blade of onion grass. I hear the almost unhearable slide that it makes coming out of the earth.

See the world, he says. Then, pffft. You're gone.

We are in the train station, the waiting room. It's dark, which makes it seem cool, though it isn't. The station has its own smell, furniture polish and under that, the smell of musty concrete: a cave smell, except for the lemon of the polish.

We'll be back in school soon, Charlieo says. Two more weeks.

We are starting at the high school, an old-fashioned building made of stucco and brick; you can picture women in long skirts and sensible black shoes and men who slap canes in their palms teaching there. It sits on the top of a hill that has steps cut into its slope, in but apart from town: the location of insane asylums and orphanages.

Summer's almost gone, Charlieo says. He takes a deep breath.

I can't wait for fall, I say, stretching. It's not true, it's how I separate myself sometimes from Charlieo's rampant nostalgia.

Really? he says. I know he's looking at me, I know how.

I take my comb out of my pocket, strum its plastic teeth. The station is quiet except for this sound. Come on. Let's make a coin, I say to appease him. We have not played golf today. Today we are touring old haunts.

We walk down the length of the platform, heading for the steps at the end that lead down to the tracks. I keep my eyes down, away from the glare: the sun rings off the tracks.

I pat my pocket for the comb I've taken to carrying as though it is something that goes with my new breasts. I'd spent time in Greschler's one day picking it out. Now that I had it, I hardly used it. My hair's straight and fine. It knots in wind, the salt and spray off the beach solders the knots. I wash it at night and comb the knots out with my fingers.

My comb! I say, I am already running back towards the stationhouse. I'll meet you.

Coming back down the platform, I see Charlieo coming towards me. My eyes aren't adjusted, he looks monochromatic, a shadow. I'm surprised that he's not down on the track laying coins.

Too hot? I call.

He doesn't answer. Mad, maybe. Has he said anything since I said that thing about fall?

My eyes are down on my feet. When I hear from the sounds of his feet that he is close I look up, but it's not Charlieo – I can see him now, down on the tracks, squatting and standing and squatting again. I stand watching this other boy come towards me – not exactly a boy; whatever's between boy and man – watching his face, his hair, that is stiff and dark and falls into his eyes; his eyes are dark too.

He keeps coming, watching me, I know his name now, Joe, I've seen him at school, he's older than we are.

Joellen, Charlieo calls. Jo, he calls, El, Len.

Joe is still coming. The hairs on the back of my neck rise. I think of them, they have my attention. I do not move my arms. My two arms hang down at my sides.

He is half smiling.

His breath is a column that reaches my cheek.

I think: he is going to kiss me. A kind of creeping feeling spreads from the back of my neck into my stomach and under my arms: I am a girl who got kissed.

He opens his mouth. The smell of whiskey comes off his lips and his teeth and his tongue. It makes the day seem hotter.

He dips his head towards me – permission: I'm going to kiss you. May I?

Joellen, I hear again, from far off. Charlieo, calling.

Joe does not move in to kiss me. I think: first he is going to speak, but then he does not speak either, turns his head and throws up, pink spewing out of his mouth onto the tracks, arcing like the spray from a fountain.

I think of looking elsewhere, of turning, a kind of polite and invisible curtain, but I don't. I keep watching. Veins stand out in his neck. He keeps his arms down at his sides, his hands cupped inward, oddly graceful.

When he's finished he straightens, wipes his mouth on the sleeve of his jacket – Jo! Joellen! – and he winks and then smiles and moves off down the platform. I half turn to watch him. There is a slight trembling below my knees as though the ground is less solid. I watch the loose legs of his jeans, the small hitch where his leg meets his hip. Down the steps, beyond the far end of the platform Charlieo's yelling, Train! Train!

CHAPTER 10

....

Joe walks down the length of the platform like a commuter off the train that he can taste and hear and smell behind him. As soon as he turns from Joellen he ceases to see or to think about or to remember her. She is not even a blinked image in back of his eyes.

He is on his way to his mother's; he does not think "home" when he goes there. He thinks "her house" as he thinks of his mother as LuAnne or she or her. Every morning after LuAnne has left for work, Joe goes to wash and to change and to walk through the house touching and looking at things, the house a museum of disgust. Her clothes are all over, the kitchen chairs, the couch: long bras like armor with stiff satin cups, stockings black at the feet. When he runs them through the eye of his hand, smells loft: stale cigarettes and perfume and the almost hysterical smell of female dirt.

Sometimes there are notes for him tilting over a page in LuAnne's blowsy writing.

I got a call from your school! the notes often begin. Or, Don't think I'm stupid, don't think I don't know, KEEP YOUR HANDS OFF MY BOOZE! Joe always went for a drink when he read that, though most days he didn't drink in the morning.

He never sleeps at his mother's house; has not since the morning more than two years ago when he'd spent the whole night in the ticket shack by accident. His body is used to the constant press of heat in the summer, a physical burden, the way weight lifters become used to the burden of weight. It is always hot inside the shack, the heat from the new day a layer added to the accumulated heat from the days before. Coming outside in the early, cool part of the morning, Joe sometimes can't recall what season it is.

In the winter, when it is too cold to sleep in the ticket shack, Joe sleeps on the floor of the office at Freemont's, his face pressed to the oily concrete, or he sleeps in his car, a dark blue VW with a freckling of yellow paint across the hood like drifted pollen. Claude Freemont rebuilt the VW for him, Joe holding the caged worklight, handing up the tools that made a breakable sound when he put them down on the concrete floor again.

Joe did not expect to like working on cars – he didn't like new cars, pampered, spoiled and mewling – but he likes the old ones, the junked or abandoned ones, their insides scoured like the carapace of insects; he likes bringing them back to life. He likes scrounging for parts in junkyards and in the hills of old carburetors and fuel line sections and single brake shoes and door handles, clean as licked chicken bones, Freemont tossed behind the station, and in the year and a half since he began working at Freemont's he has become able at rebuilding old cars.

And Joe also likes Claude Freemont, who he thought he would hate because he harbored the useless men. But Freemont is not of them. He allows them the use of the yard, the shade – live and let live is my motto, he has said more than one time to Joe. The men are just there, junked bodies amid the junked, rusted bodies of cars. Freemont doesn't speak to them, except sometimes to say 'Scuse me there boys – gently sliding the men out of his way. He keeps himself clean of the men as Joe keeps himself clean of his mother.

Despite the notes that are sent to LuAnne, Joe does go to school: he goes sometimes. He wanders in that direction and looks up at the high school looming down from the top of the hill, its darkness and severity the same as the darkness and severity of "education." He is never carrying books or papers, though he does the work when he's there, borrowing pencils and paper and books. He keeps his school books in the ticket shack and in the afternoons reads them and retains what he's read. He is not expelled because he is sometimes there; because he takes the make-up exams they arrange for him, he and a teacher sitting alone in a quiet classroom; because he does well on these tests; because when he is asked by his teachers, the principal, where he's been, he lies to them: talks about illness, about hardship, about family deaths. He is steady when he tells them, lets them look in his eyes which are steady, and he knows from the way that they look off and falter over their words that they believe him. That in exchange for the care they do not take, for the help they do not offer, they let him come and go as he pleases.

When he is not at the ticket shack or at his mother's or at school, Joe is at Freemont's; walks past the useless men whose names and faces he refuses to know. Some of them called to him the first few times he came here – Hey, you, Rusty's boy! – but he would not answer, resistance stiffening his neck and his hips and his shoulders, and now they do not call.

At night, when he is finished at Freemont's, he unbuttons his shirt and takes his arms from the sleeves and lets the shirt trail down from his waistband. He stands at the deep sink in the back of the garage, where there are tufts of grease cleaner, white and solid like shortening, and scabbed patches of oil and droplets of water trembling on top of the oil, round and intact. He washes his hands and his arms and sometimes his body where the oil has soaked through the cloth of his shirt. Then he goes to the ticket shack. He reads and he drinks and he waits for the next part of his life to begin.

CHAPTER 11

....

The three years I spent Tuesdays and Thursdays at the O'Caseys' were Douglas's Daisy O'Cazee years. He was not living at home then, but more often than not there were six places set at the table and when Charlieo and I came in for dinner, we heard Douglas's voice in the kitchen over the sounds of flatware tumbling in the drawers.

She's *shopping*, he said.

She's out with her girlfriends.

Come on, Ma, I'm starving, you want me to starve?

Herman and Douglas horsed around at the table while Mrs. O'Casey shook her head and said "grown boys" under her breath as she moved back and forth, serving: Douglas was twenty-six, Herman twenty-three. Mr. O'Casey beamed or laughed out loud. They're just *boys*, he'd say. "Boys" didn't seem to mean the same thing to Mr. and Mrs. O'Casey.

There was something odd about Douglas and Herman: a married feel. If you saw one, you always looked behind him for the other.

On the rare Tuesday or Thursday Douglas did not turn up, Herman was off his feed, mournful and edgy.

What is the *matter* with you, Mrs. O'Casey said. You're like a moony cat.

On those nights, Herman hung around Charlieo and me after dinner while we sorted our coins by size and quality or watched TV, or he followed us out back to the garden.

Charlieo loved it, the attention. I think he believed "three" was the problem, that two was the right number of O'Casey brothers: if Douglas wasn't around it could be Herman and him. He didn't notice the way Herman chucked the coins back any old way when he was done looking at them or that if he followed us out to the garden he stepped backwards, trampling things under his heels.

Douglas did not "sleep home" as he put it, the demarcation between married and not. When he left for the night, Herman went out too – Walk you home, he always said, though Douglas drove. I pictured him standing outside Douglas and Daisy's apartment waiting for their lights to go out.

My bed was a couch on the sunporch downstairs, everyone else slept above. I pictured them all asleep on their backs, breathing in, breathing out, a regular cadence.

Sometimes, as part of sleep, I heard the sounds Herman made coming back into the house. The refrigerator door. Water running in the sink. A chair. These sounds were part of the night to me. I never fully woke up.

And then.

Yelling, yelling, heels coming down hard, running. A harsh sound: nose breath. The asthma squeal of someone who can't breathe.

Dreaming. I open my eyes in the dark and in the dark I close them.

And then. I can't breathe. Somebody has me. Water. Breathing in wet, breathing in wet. My eyes closed, that must be the problem, my eyes open: dark still, and wet.

I think, night. I think, the beach. I think, Herman is taking a long time to stop me.

A light, remember the lantern? The wet dark streaked with red, with yellow, the colors bleeding to black, smeared and phosphorescent. Mrs. O'Casey appears, hands on Charlieo's shoulders, Mr. O'Casey two steps aside, Douglas, Herman, who saved me. I need to be grateful.

They all drip water, droplets dangle from their ears like stud earrings. Water darkens the light-colored wood of the floor. Wet, wet, wet, wet.

I am a girl. Somebody else's. They are over there.

And then water drips into my eyes, it drips on my shoulders. The yellow of my nightgown is gone, changed for a gray translucence, my skin, pinkish-brown through the skin of the nightgown. I pull a wet blanket around me. The mattress of the pullout couch is wet.

Charlieo, hands pressed between thighs, shivering, teeth chattering. I hear the discrete clicks, sound's return a reminder of sound's absence.

Douglas and Herman and Mr. O'Casey are spluttering, laughter sliding off wet tongues and wet lips.

Charlieo: chatter chatter chatter.

Herman, Mr. O'Casey says. Go get your brother a bathrobe.

104

Herman touches Charlieo as he passes.

Everyone into the kitchen, I'm making tea, Mrs. O'Casey says, a whole block of outrage and complaint hovering just behind the skin of her face, as her eyes sit just behind her glasses. Her face makes rebellious little tics and bolts on its own that no one seems to notice.

Those boys.

When the rest of them are in the kitchen, I get my second nightgown, flannel, thick and consuming, and put it on, its flounced hem tumbling to the floor, though it is summer.

Marines, someone says in the kitchen and Anniversary and *Have* to, little boy whines in men's voices. I hear: Remember the time we . . . ? and a pause and then laughter and Remember when Uncle Brendan . . . ? and laughter.

They're all at the table when I come in.

Sit, Mrs. O'Casey says and holds onto the back of a chair until I sit in it. The kettle's steaming up the window behind her.

Fish the girl out of the ocean, bring her back here so you can drown her. Makes sense, Mrs. O'Casey says. She smacks cups down on the table.

How about coffee? Herman says.

You'll have tea.

They're quiet as she stands looking down at them, a reminder of goodness, purely external: they merely pause in her presence.

You could *apologize*, she says finally and Herman jumps out of his chair, makes a sweeping bow. A droplet of water leaps off his arm, lands.

Please accept our apologies, mademoiselle. He says: madam-oiz-el. It's a tradition. Marine Day. We always do something to celebrate.

Commando raids, usually, Douglas says.

Mr. O'Casey laughs.

You've a wife at home, or am I mistaken? Mrs. O'Casey says. The three of them, Douglas and Herman and Mr. O'Casey look at her. The smiles on their faces don't change.

Mrs. O'Casey rubs her hands up and down Charlieo's arms, a sparking friction. Charlieo, in his bathrobe, looks skinned, like an animal with its fur damped down. His hair's tufted, his thin lips blue. They make me think of paintings, of the colors painters see in.

Why don't you get up to bed now son, she says. You're all of a shiver.

Pretty soon now, Mr. O'Casey says, you'll be a Marine your own self. His voice is loud and hearty.

He's a pre-Marine, Douglas says, in a matched loud voice. He reaches across to clip Charlieo on the chin.

A baby Marine, Herman says.

Bed, says Mrs. O'Casey, gently shaking Charlieo's shoulders.

Charlieo leans toward and smiles at his brothers. Droplets of water spot the table in front of him, knocked off his hair by his shivering.

That was a good one, he says, looking up at the ceiling.

That . . . , he says through chattering teeth.

Was . . . , he says through blue lips.

The best one ever.

CHAPTER 12

....

Joe is at the market where he can now buy his liquor, though he is not quite seventeen and looks younger, because the woman who works the checkout thinks she knows him.

How's your Ma doin'? she asks. Joe's told her his mother's been sick with one thing and another.

Better, Joe sometimes says or Not so good: he varies what he tells her, lowers his eyes, shrugs, meaning – what can I do but buy groceries, liquor? The woman likes hearing the tales of his goodness. She gave him a muffler for Christmas and a bottle of scent for LuAnne. These things, still in their boxes, are in the bottom of a fruit crate at the ticket shack.

Hey Joe, the woman says, bagging his two fifths of bourbon. It is July, but the store's over-cooled, she has on a sweater, light blue with a brown stain over her breast.

How's Ginny today? she asks, looking down at the stain, her chin doubling, looking up.

Joe's blank for a second – Ginny? he thinks. Then he remembers it's the name he said was his mother's. He thought the woman might be acquainted with LuAnne. Her hair is beauty parlor hair, the kind LuAnne's beauty shop turned out.

Not so good, Joe says, troubling his eyes. The heat ruffles her. I'm saving up to get her an air conditioner. Right now, he can't remember whether he's told the woman he has a job.

The woman nods, says, You are a good son, Joe. Believe me. Her head shifts from nodding to shaking, on account of his goodness. She only charges him for one fifth.

Joe comes out of the store, into the sun and the expanse of the parking lot, the asphalt white-crusted as though the ocean has lapped here. He blinks at the ground, at the parked cars, and heads for the Goodwill, one of a string of identical stores, like white concrete boxes, to the right of the market: the Goodwill, the Busy Bee Launderette, a sub shop, a limousine service, a real estate. They have all been here for years, though they have the look of businesses that will fail soon.

Joe walks into the Goodwill, away from the smell of detergent and bleach that comes from the Busy Bee's open doorway, the monotonous thrumming of the washing machines audible through the wall. His eyes grow used to the dark and he heads towards the table of boy and man things, trying not to breathe the musty smell of the store. It is the smell of age, the smell of the teeth of the old women who tend this place, sitting on folding chairs like wallflowers at some dingy church dance.

Joe sifts through the things on the table: he buys clothes here to work in at Freemont's; buys them, wears them, throws them away. He folds what he might want. There is a corduroy jacket, well kept, a deep green pine color, in among the pitted T-shirts and ripped pants. He carries it to the mirror to try on.

No! a girl's voice says. Don't!

In the mirror he sees it is the girl who he does not remember from the first time, at the train station, but who he has seen over and over this last year, a burr in the side of his vision. Once he stepped out of the ticket shack, locked the door, turned, and there she was, crouched in the grass at his feet. She looked up at him, small and atwitch, like a rabbit.

Joe looks at her in the mirror. She is small, her legs long in shorts. The sun's behind her, she's not wearing a bra. Through the pale blue gauze of her shirt Joe can see the tipped, darkened crowns of her nipples. She's been following him for a year, but now's the first time she's spoken.

What d'you want? Joe says. Why're you following me? He waves at his head like there's a fly buzzing around, but it isn't a fly, it's the girl.

Don't put that on, she says. She is intent, she will not change the subject. It's bad luck, she says. Wearing other people's old clothes.

Joe laughs. He says, You some kind of a witch?

She sees the white of his teeth, a white band. He has not turned, she is still watching him in the mirror.

Who says it's bad luck? Joe asks.

She can't think of an answer. Ida's who says, but she can't say "Ida," then have to explain who Ida is. She stands watching his teeth.

Who are you, anyway, Moses? Joe says, the only Bible name he can think of and not who he means. He means: a prophet, a Messiah.

The girl shrugs, looks away from him then. She knows less than he does. She is not even sure about Moses.

He lets the jacket slide off his arm back onto the table. You could've saved yourself all this alarm, he says. I'm not buyin' it. I don't like corduroy. Coo-droy, he says it. Though the truth is, she's spooked him.

He nods at the girl, then heads out of the store. The shirts he folded to take are still on the table, a small island of neatness.

The girl comes out behind him. Her feet, bare inside sneakers, make squelching sounds. Out in the sun she stops, she can't see him, she holds her hands screwed like binoculars up to her eyes.

Joe sidesteps, clearing the door. He watches the girl: there is something about her singleness, the thin crooked arms, the locked knees, that spikes at his ribs, makes him keep looking. See ya, he says, but he doesn't move off.

Look, the girl says. I'm sorry. About that jacket? She tries to remember the way he pronounced corduroy. I just . . . it's bad luck, she says. To be wearing . . . Like I said.

Who says? I mean, it's not like some law, that I know of.

Well, the girl says, then she's quiet. Well, it just is. It's like word spellings. Sometimes it doesn't make sense. (Coo-droy, she remembers. She says it over a few times to herself.)

She looks at him. She cannot think of one other thing to say. She is thinking of his teeth, the white glints that are visible beneath his lip. She thinks, Joellen, Jo, Joe and Jo.

He spares her the need for conversation. He steps into the space between them, though she has not seen him move. Later, she will think about this single moment and she will not remember him moving.

He kisses her, is kissing, his lips are warm and resilient and have the heated taste of whiskey, and his teeth and his tongue.

It is thrilling.

His hand spans her arm; he touches her where he wanted to touch, his hand merged to her arm, of one thickness.

He kisses as though he is thirsty.

Joellen's not breathing, inside the kiss. It is deep and thirsty. It goes on and on. It will never stop.

Joe pulls back, she looks at him, the hair on his forehead is wet, the hair tapers to points, the girl thinks water, and thirsty, and wet. He is still holding her arm. His fingers meet, nearly.

He asks, Come with me? though he does not need to ask. For a year, from the day she first saw him throw up on the tracks (she will ask him about this, he will not remember) she has been heading for this: for yes. She has been tracking him, he was easy to find which thrilled the girl who attributed this to her detective powers, not to the limited and predictable course of Joe's day. Her attention has been elsewhere.

Concentrate! Charlieo said when they were golfing, his eyes where hers were supposed to be – on the clown's lips, the mouse-sized door to the windmill, the crooked bridge over a moat in which other balls swam on the surface, their curves like crocodiles' eyes. Concentrate! – but she kept looking over her shoulder, as though Joe might have started to follow her too. Which he had not.

Joe and Joellen walk the length of the station, the tracks a ticked white. She and Charlieo spent a lot of time here this summer. Let's do coins! she said, and Charlieo nodded, his surprise fast, his enthusiasm just a half beat behind hers. A needle of guilt, a temperate grief for Charlieo taps at her, passes.

Things change, she had said. When we're eighty do you think we'll still be here, playing miniature golf? Charlieo looked at her, his face stricken, and she could see, it is what he'd thought, or not *not* thought, the same thing.

She follows now, lets Joe lead her, "Joe" she says to herself and looking, "Joe's hand." She has imagined them like this. As they cross the parking lot, the train tracks, she thinks: I walked with him here. It is strange. The things she remembers have never happened.

Here, he says, when they get to the ticket shack door. This is it. But I forget, you know that. He smiles, the left side of his mouth lifts; the left eye.

She touches the front of his shirt. There is a crackle, a small static shock.

He says, Better watch out for me. Electric.

They stand outside the door. He uses the key that he still wears under his shirt. Inside, the heat is a physical thing, solid and block-like, pressing her shoulders, her head. She looks around; if she is not braced by something – a wall, she thinks. There is no furniture. A wall, she thinks again – she will topple. She is sweaty and slick. When he touches her arm again, his hand slides. He moves to kiss her. She tips her head back, palms flat on his chest, another shock. She is wet, she thinks – Will I die?

On the floor in a corner is a sleeping bag, a wool blanket. The wool itches her wet back. He takes off his shirt, using one hand – it is dark blue and damp – he tucks it under her. She feels the buttons pressing into her spine like vertebrae more widely spaced than her own. She breathes in the breaths he breathes out.

His hands slide and slide.

CHAPTER 13

....

How did I know how to do it, the things we did three, four, five times all those long afternoons?

Take his fingers into my mouth, divine up and down their steep slopes. He left the whorls of his fingerprints under my tongue.

How did I know to start at his collarbone, tapering from the thick to the thin of the bone, my kisses as wet as the territorial markings of wolves?

I followed a straight, natural line, bordered by ribs. I made my way down. I might detour, licking my way over the cleaved ribs, the flat cork-colored nipples, the riven parts to the east and the west of his sex, but I never stopped.

How did I know it was an option, me on top? I looked down at the place where we fused. The skin on my stomach creased, my nipples sore, kissed to the color of cherries, my lips, his lips the same color.

I lay with my leg over his, my sex tender and ticking. I waited for him to rouse, rise, begin again.

How did I know these things? What did I have to prepare me?

I did not even know my own anatomy. Mrs. O'Casey had bought me pads and a belt when I got my first period, at thirteen. She called it my month-lies and said I'd have cramps and gave me a booklet from the church titled "The Duties of Womanhood" that spoke in dark, wormy euphemisms about "relations" and the need for resistance.

Ida found the box of pads on the floor of my closet; not the same box by then but the same paper bag, the brown paper worn soft as cloth, some superstition I made up but cannot remember. She called me upstairs, pointed to the box she had set on my bed, and she slapped me. In the stunned pause right after the slap, I thought she was angry. Offended that it wasn't her I had gone to.

But she said, My Ma'am done the same thing to me. You do the same thing if you have a girl. It's to remember how being a woman follows the footsteps of sorrow.

No one said ovaries or fallopian tubes or eggs. No one said uterus. Mrs.

O'Casey used the warmer and cozier womb. For years I thought the two things were different, like I thought whore and prostitute were.

It was Joe who told me things; knew them, I thought, because he had worked for a drugstore.

He used rubbers which I disliked. Joe, once removed.

No, I said one time, watching the delicate way he handled himself. I said, Skin on skin, and then was embarrassed at calling attention to his over-niceness and by the word, said twice.

He went on unfurling the condom. We don't want a baby, he said, and I snagged on the we and thought maybe we did.

He told me about fertilization, the passage and growth of the egg. His voice was like his hands were when they touched me: present, nonjudgmental; there was no part of my body that did not give him pleasure. In the wake of his words I felt the internal functioning of my organs, like planets around the significant sun of my womb.

Joe had bursts of talking but mostly did not talk except for small words: Here and Oh. He said Jo and I did. We screwed and we rested from screwing before screwing again. His ardor was patient and needful and quick to replenish and, mostly, enough. Mostly, I did not think about talking.

Sometimes, though, the absence of talk galloped inside my head: was sex enough, and for how long would it be? Then, I thought I meant for him. It made me restless for speech; not just words, conversation. I talked. I told him things so he would know me. Leon, I said. Isabel. Gone.

Gone where to? Joe asked.

Well, I said. This green car . . . and I paused, shrugged, leaving the impression that she had gotten into a green car and driven away, that she was gone in the way I wished her to be.

Where? Joe said again and the word made it seem possible that she was some place, actual and specific.

Joe nodded. Yeah, he said. My father's gone too. He looked towards the ticket shack window, stared for such a long time and in such a way that I thought somebody was out there and I covered my breasts. And then I had this idea: Isabel had gone off with him, with Joe's father.

Shacked up with some dame, Joe said and I pictured them living in a place like the place we were in, because of "shacked."

Some dame with big tits, he said, and I was surprised, almost offended – my mother!

What's his name? I asked after a while. I could see them, some tropical place like where Gauguin went. Palm fronds for thatch, no mail service.

Who? Joe said.

Your father, I said and he told me – Rusty – and then I was sorry I asked because I could picture Isabel with someone named Hector or Ivan or Rupert or Charles. Not someone named Rusty.

CHAPTER 14

....

I came and went all that summer and into the fall, my
days divided as my self was, between Joe and Charlieo; between afternoons and
mornings and the differing heats of the ticket shack and the O'Caseys' kitchen
and sunporch and yard.

To Charlieo, this was the summer of movies. To me, it was the summer
of Joe.

I had not told him about Joe by September – yet, still. I kept meaning to.
Charlieo and I went to movies almost daily in our town or the towns to the north
and south that were strung like large beads on a necklace. Each town had one
theatre, one noontime show. We saw the same ones over and over, I didn't care, it
used up the time until I could see Joe.

We took the bus that, Charlieo said, came only once every twelve hours and
ran only in parallel lines as though it had begun life as a trolley and never learned
to do turns.

We sat side by side, shoulders rubbing, our thighs stuck to the dark green bus
seats, our voices murmurs inside the kick and hover of the bus engine, the rush
of sound from the open windows.

I am going to tell him. Charlieo, I am going to say. You know how I always
have something to do afternoons?

Daisy left Douglas, he says.

What?

Left him. Ran off, or some such.

With who? I say. Herman's voice and Daisy's that Fourth of July. The ching
of Daisy's gold bangle bracelets.

Who? he says. I don't know. Is there supposed to be a who?

I don't know, I say. How should I know?

Well, all's I know, Douglas waits for her for dinner but she's late so he
goes into the kitchen to fix himself something, and there's no plates or forks or

whatnot. He thinks: I've been robbed, they robbed me. Charlieo sits nodding, like this is the same thing he'd have thought too, had it been his kitchen.

Then he sees Daisy's closets are empty, he says. Totally. No one even knows where she is.

We are stopped at a light on the outskirts of the town next to ours. Everything, the abandoned storefronts, the sidewalks, the bricks of the buildings, the clock hung on the outer wall of a bank, the air, is all various tints of brown. The dinginess seems part of the story. I cannot say "Joe" inside this. I'll wait to pass something beautiful.

Labor Day came and it got cool and, as if this is what we'd been waiting for, we went back to school. The halls smelled of floorwax and new clothes; sitting behind kids in class I saw the tiny snipped threads, the sized stiffness of their new shirts, the pristine white of the labels flapped out of new sweaters.

At the end of October it got suddenly hot again, strange, unbearable. You could smell fall and see it, the trees on our street tipped yellow and orange like frosted Halloween cupcakes, but the air was balmy and moist. School felt like a mistake. I sat in the stifling classrooms feeling divided from Joe and reminded of the division by the heat.

Charlieo and I had left off movie-going when school started, but one Tuesday, when we had the day off because of teacher conferences, we decided to go. Movies were our Pavlov's dog's reaction to heat.

There's a bench at the bus stop: the William Hollis Stone Memorial Bench. We sat on that.

Who the heck is William Hollis Stone anyhow, Charlieo says. He has asked this before, when he is hot, riled, testy.

Don't know. A signer of the Declaration of Independence?

Why a bench? Charlieo says. What kind of memorial is that, a bench?

Maybe he didn't like having to stand here waiting for buses.

You mean the man's got money to buy a bench but not a car? Charlieo says. Unlikely.

Maybe he didn't like his *mother* having to stand here and wait for the bus. Maybe he couldn't drive a car. Besides, how much could a bench cost? Benches are cheap.

Maintenance.

Maybe in his will he left money for a building: The William Hollis Stone Memorial Center? After they paid all his debts there was only enough left for this. I tap the bench slats, a hollow toot sound.

Charlieo will not be jollied. A bench, he says, shaking his head, looking down at the brown-painted slats in the V between his legs.

He raises his head then squints down the street where, I know, there's not much to look at. The high school is a block behind us; ahead is a line of houses, aluminum-sided in pale, Easter colors; the marina's a white spark in the distance. I'm looking at the back of Charlieo's neck, the cleft bones, the gold burr of his hair. Then his head drops so I suddenly see the sidewalk beyond him. And there's Joe. He is just present. I did not see him approach.

Joe's effect on me is a physically altering thing. The Joellen I am with Charlieo is not the Joellen I am with Joe. I look at his hands, one hand is holding the other, cupped underneath like the hand is a fish, and I think of the way those hands have touched me, the remembrance of one touched part blooming into another. We don't speak. He walks on. I watch the stir of muscle and bone under his shirt, the way his shirt creases then flattens again between his shoulders. I tell myself: he didn't see me.

Who's that? Charlieo says, watching.

Don't know. Somebody from school?

He looks at me, he looks astonished. He drops his head again, shakes it.

I say, Joe, I think his name is. It is painful to say it. To give it away.

Actually, Charlieo says. I know what his name is.

I think: Tell him now, but I do not.

So. You know him how? Charlieo says. Old drinking buddy?

Excuse me? Who says I drink? And who says I know him?

How do *I* know what you do, Joellen? I know you don't drink in the morning, that's all I can testify to. What do I know?

He waits for me to tell him.

I could say, He's sort of my boyfriend, though I'm not sure this is so.

I could say, I haven't introduced you because I didn't think you'd like each other. Joe, you can't see him in groups.

I could say, I don't like your tone. Your implication. I could sound like Leon.

Down on the ground the shadows of four legs, four hands, Charlieo's shaking head are all clear in the sun. I don't say anything at all.

Joe walks on. His hands bunch and then flatten in the pockets of his jeans. She is not even beautiful, he thinks.

She is not even beautiful. She is small, brown-eyed, slippery-haired; when he tries running his hands through her hair his fingers get lassooed by knots.

She is small. She is a child.

He has thought these things before, lying on his back in the ticket shack when she is not there. Sometimes, not always, he can work up a distaste or dislike. He smokes, the clamshell she brought him to use as an ashtray anchored to his chest, the smells of the sleeping bag – spilled booze and the almost beachy smell of sex – under that. She is a child; she is not even beautiful – but the dislike and distaste are illusory, they are fraudulent. What he feels in her absence is longing.

Joe walks straight until he gets to the marina and can't go straight on anymore. Freemont's sent him to the junkyard – if that's where he's going, he needs to turn right, down a nameless street known as the Basin, but he does not turn, he keeps walking parallel to the marina. It doesn't matter if he gets the part now or tomorrow or if he does not get it at all. Freemont and he pretend an urgency about the cars they rebuild but there is no urgency.

Joe heads down the two-way, four-lane spur of the highway, on the opposite side of the marina. He just walks, eyes tipped away from the jumpy whiteness of the water visible in between cars, trees. A horn honks and he's startled and hops onto the sloped shoulder where he walks a few steps on bent ankles. The car honks again and again. Joe squints across at it.

Hey, hey, Joe! a voice yells, alternately clear and drowned out under the horn. An arm waves out the side window. It's Gene in a new gold Buick. Joe starts across the highway.

Hey! Gene calls when Joe's halfway, waiting for a break in the flow of oncoming cars. What're you doin' here?

Joe doesn't answer because he is watching the traffic and because he is not in any unusual place.

Hey, Joe says when he gets to the car, puts his hands on the top of the door. The heated up metal burns his palms, but he doesn't move them away.

Hey, Gene says again, swats at Joe's arm, grinning, happy to see him. Long time no see.

Joe nods, looks away over the hood of the car at the water. They haven't seen each other since Gene tracked him down at the station and they'd talked and then fought on the platform.

Ma asked me to find you, Gene said then. She's upset.

Joe pictured the notes his mother left him. KEEP YOUR HANDS OFF MY BOOZE OR ELSE!! He laughed.

Says you're cutting school, Gene said. Are you? His voice was reasonable; it was – I won't take her word till I hear what you have to say.

Who are you, my fuckin' father? Joe yelled: it was the reasonableness that got him. What's it to you anyway? You get a job with the fuckin' school board?

You should stay in school, Joe. You won't get shit for a job if you quit out.

Yeah, Joe said. An education can get me a fine job. Like you got. A great future. He thought of the lights at the Last Gas, misty and sulfurous in the dark.

How ya been? Gene says now, and Joe blinks a few times, clearing his head. There's no trace of the argument he's been replaying in Gene's face or his voice.

You should come by some time, Gene says. Don't want my kid knowing only his old lady's side of the family.

Joe nods. Gene has a son, Adam. Joe can't remember how old.

Here, Gene says, squinting up at Joe. Come on and get in for a minute. I got the AC goin'. He's cranking the window shut while he speaks.

Joe walks around the back of the car and gets in. Gene tosses a box of disposable diapers off the front seat. Man I love this, he says, spreading his fingers towards the air conditioner vents. I could *live* in this fuckin' car.

You workin'? Joe says.

Off. Shopping. Gene turns his head towards the back seat, the diapers. Patty's pregnant again.

Joe just nods. He does not know if this is good or bad news. He looks at the radio dials, the cigarette lighter. There's a rectangular hole in the dashboard, wires dangling below it.

They stole my tape deck, motherfuckers, Gene says. Can you fuckin' believe it? He leans forward, bunches the wires. The sun catches on a gold cross around his neck. Lapped Catholics, LuAnne once called them. Joe hears his mother's voice. He hears the sound of ice in her highball.

I gotta go, Joe says, suddenly jumpy. The car feels stuffy to him, airless, though the air conditioning's going.

Yeah, Gene says. Where you headed, I'll drive you. He kicks at the dangling wires with his foot. He says, Fuckin' bennies.

Joe's got the door open.

No, hey, wait, Gene says. I got something I wanted to tell you. I was gonna wait till it was for sure, but seein' you. He shrugs, smiles.

Joe sits with the door open, a leg and an arm out in the sun. Maybe you should wait then, he says.

Shit you are a *hard* man to talk to! Gene says. You still workin' by Freemont's?

Joe nods.

Well, I'm thinkin' of *buyin'* the fuckin' place. That's my news. Gene sits, grinning.

Buy it? Joe says. How you gonna buy what's not even for sale?

Everything's for sale, baby brother. Trust me. Ever-y-thing. Gene drums his fingers on the steering wheel, pumped. They are not from people who buy things – houses or businesses. The word "buy" excites him.

You talked to him then? Joe says, or you just makin' blueprints?

Once, feelin' him out, so to speak, Gene says, and laughs.

Joe looks at his arm out in the sun.

He's old, Gene says. Thinkin' about his retirement, got to be. Somebody makes him an offer, believe me, he'll take it. He'll jump at it.

Yeah? Joe says. Well he never said nothin' to me. About selling. He thinks: where's Gene going to get that kind of money? The most money he can picture is the stack of bills Rusty used to come home with, scattered over the floor in the bedroom.

Hey, Gene says, Look, I got the AC goin' here. Do me a favor, keep the fuckin' door closed? All right? All right Joe?

Fine, Joe says and he gets out of the car and then he closes the door.

* * *

The bus takes us two and then three towns away. The town we are going to is much larger than ours, wider and longer: there is a convention center and a casino at the beach that was built in the twenties. The downtown is farther inland here than in our town, you can't smell the beach on the air; instead there's a rusted, flint smell. On the sidewalk, in line for the movie, I feel panicked: I don't like the air, I feel too far from home.

Inside – what is the movie again? – I watch the alterations of light off the screen as though I have contracted a shadowy blindness. The theatre walls are not walls, are heavy pleats of crimson velvet, black in the velvety dark.

We've seen this movie before. Charlieo watches, sometimes nodding his head when a part comes up that is the way he remembers. I look up at the screen, but the screen reminds me of where I am and of Joe and of how much longer I have to wait before I can leave. I push back in the broken, bouncy seat willing the movie to end: when it does, I don't remember a thing.

We wait for the bus back, leaning against the dusty double window of an empty storefront. The sign's been removed from the front, its individual letters unscrewed, but the name of the store – JULIO'S – is still clean and readable, outlined by the filthiness around it. What time is it? I ask.

What time is it always when the movie lets out? It's two, Charlieo says. It's past time for a pizza.

I shake my head. I wish I were walking back. It would take me forever, but I want to be moving, making something happen.

Do you? Charlieo says.

What?

Pizza!

Not hungry, I say.

You might be, by the time we get home.

I can't stand his peskiness, the way he pursues everything. I won't be, I say. I've got stuff to do anyway.

Like what?

I say, Things.

He looks away from me, down the street, against traffic.

* * *

Joe's not at the ticket shack when I get there, a long hour and fifteen minutes later, sticky and soaked. The bus lumbered. It feels late, though it is earlier than I get here most days.

I pace in front of the ticket shack door, then go around back. Joe does not want anyone to see us coming or going and get suspicious and make a report: There's kids using that shack. Us, Joe says, but he means me, because if someone were spotted, it would not be him. Out back, the weeds are nearly waist tall. I come around to the front again while Joe's unlocking the door.

He looks up, looks back at the lock. He swings the door open and goes in. He doesn't speak, but he leaves the door open. The sound of sweeping starts up inside.

I stand in the doorway; inside it's too dark to see him.

Hey, he says and I don't know if this is a greeting or if he is saying, Get out of the way. He comes close – it is like the first time he came close, the day on the train station platform: he is going to kiss me I thought then and think now. But he doesn't; he guides me away from the door with the broom.

I wait for him to finish. The sweeping takes a long time, though the place is small and nothing – cooking, the unwrapping of packages – goes on here.

What? I say finally. You not talking to me? But I am not sure if his silence is hostile. He never talks. How do you know the difference between one type of silence and another?

So, I say. Maybe you saw me with this boy at the bus bench? Charlieo, I say. Know him?

His whole family's Marines, I say, a family trait. Like how royal families used to be bleeders?

He's like my brother, I say. We sort of grew up together. It's a long story.

The movies, I say, on and on and on and on. In the middle of each sentence I tell myself stop before you get to the next, but then I am speaking the next. It is a burst of dust from Joe's sweeping that stops me.

He leans the broom in a corner and comes towards then goes around me, closing the door. As hot as it is out, it is cool compared to the heat he shuts in. He takes my arm, his fingers press into my flesh – hard. I try to remember if this is the same force with which he always touches me – and leads me to the sleeping bag. He lifts the hair off the back of my neck. Strands stick. One by one, he lifts them.

Now, he says, holding my hair up, his breath, his voice in my ear. Now.

Charlieo's on my porch when I get home from Joe. Where you been? he calls. I been looking all over. As though he hasn't seen me for days.

I told you. I had to do something. For Leon. I can't remember if this is what I told him: for Leon.

Yeah, so, what takes so long? He's sitting on the top step of the porch. Under the rose and gold of his skin, his knees are two bony chalk shields. He seems girl-colored compared to Joe who is dark, nearly brown, though he is lighter under his clothing, like two colors of coffee. I sit one step down from Charlieo, my back to him. Behind me is the heat from his knees.

Charles, I say. Let's go to the beach. I picture waves buoyant and large and cool, me the only swimmer pocketed by the ocean's creases, almost invisible inside its vast grayness.

Joellen, he says. It's six o'clock. It's 6:10. We can't go to the beach. Dinner. It is a Tuesday, an O'Casey night.

Charlieo pokes my back, my shoulder blades flex. Come on, he says. We'll be late. My dad's barbecuing. And of course there'll be your lemon meringue pie for dessert.

I turn to him, smile, I have to though it makes me feel crowded and pressed, my lemon meringue pie. It is true, it is my pie, I am responsible for it. I once told Mrs. O'Casey how good it was, though I don't like pie, sweets, too used to Ida's scant-sugared desserts. Mrs. O'Casey beamed, her round clock face pink and shined up with pleasure. Now every Tuesday and Thursday, she made one.

Never tell my mother you like something, Charlieo told me when it was already too late. Herman? Got bologna every day, four years straight in high school.

Wonderful, I always said when she served it. Good as always! I spoke around the sugary sweetness that made the pulp of my teeth ache.

I couldn't face it, saw a room full of sun-colored pies hitching towards me. I couldn't face the two nightgowns, always clean, always washed after only one wearing, waiting for me in the drawer of the sunporch. They were not the same nightgowns; Mrs. O'Casey gave me two new ones each Christmas in appropriate sizes, one flannel, one the same sheer yellow the pies were. She hovered, watching me open the box.

I hope you like them, she always said.

Wonderful, wonderful, good as always.

Pleeease, I say to Charlieo. Just a dip. I tip my head back, look at his face upside down. I can see into his nostrils. He holds his head still though his eyes move, slightly, away.

We go to his house. The barbecue smoke hangs in a wedge above the back-yard. Smoke tamps the heat down and holds it. We eat outside, the smoke shifting into our faces. We slide up and down on the benches at the table, out of its path. It is just Charlieo, Mr. and Mrs. O'Casey and me. I picture Douglas and Herman out hunting for Daisy. When Mrs. O'Casey carries the pie out, I put up my hand, smile. I say, No thank you. Not tonight. I say, Too hot for pie.

Heads bow. They eat with their heads bowed to their pie plates as though they are saying a long, difficult grace.

My head is up. My hands are spread on the table. Leon does not approve of grace-saying, or would not if he knew grace came before every dinner I had here, the way pie came after. If he knew, Leon would tell me to excuse myself. We are not Christians, Leon would say, as though what we were was *un*christian, unchar-itable, mean.

After dinner, I shower. The heat, I say again. I smell like smoke. I sniff at the fabric of my shirt, make a face. I put on the nightgown and lay down on my bed on the sunporch. It is too early. Mrs. O'Casey's still doing the dishes. She comes to stand in the doorway. Joellen? she says, then stops, as if this is the whole of her question.

You hardly touched dinner, she says finally. Could you be sick? She comes in, lays her hand on my forehead. It's still damp from water and dishwashing liquid. I force myself to lie still under its weight.

It's the heat, I say and fan at my face. I know I am saying this over and over.

She turns off the light in the kitchen. Through the common living room wall behind me I hear her voice, then Mr. O'Casey's, then hers. I hear Charlieo. I imagine him reporting to them: At six o'clock she wanted to go to the beach! At 6:10! Then there are no voices as though, separately, they are pondering what this could mean.

I hear the murmuring of the TV; after some time it's turned off. I hear their procession up the stairs, then their footsteps fanning out in different directions. The toilet flushes three times.

I look down at my breasts, the way they hold the gauzy material of the nightgown out and away from my chest; the way my stomach and ribs rise and fall but my breasts do not move. I can see the divot of my navel, the gravelled patch of dark hair below that. I can't sleep. Late, two or three in the morning, I get up and put on my smoke-and-sweat-smelling clothes and go out.

I come to the station and walk down to the end of the platform, down the three steps to the tracks. My feet blush in the fire-colored light from the signal. The ticket shack is set back a ways, a thicker box-shaped darkening in the dark. I push on the door, expect it to yield, but it is locked or something is shoved up against it. For the second time in one day I think Joe's changed his mind about me.

Well the hell with you then, I say: no sound, but I am moving my lips.

Even this does not make the door open. I am embarrassed and angry and at the same time, I am knocking.

I'll give him two knocks, I say, already knocking a third time, a fourth, a fifth, knocking until the door opens and Joe has my arm and is pulling me in.

I am sitting in the one chair in our dark living room waiting for Leon. The kitchen light is the only one on. The dining room window is open. There is no breeze, but there is a difference in the density of the air outside and in. It's Wednesday, an eight o'clock night.

When Leon comes in I stand. You look tired, I say, though I cannot tell how much is the true pallor of his skin, how much is the kitchen light. I think the word beat, he looks beat, as in beaten, but I don't say this. I choose my words. I choose tired.

Hello, Sal. This is a pleasant surprise. Seeing you. His voice is tuneless and spent.

Wait, I say. I hold up one finger, watch his eyes focus on it, then leave him to go to the kitchen. When I come back, he is still standing.

What is it? he asks, taking the glass of sugarwater I've made him. He's pleased, tries hiding the pleasure. Leon likes it when women bring him things to eat or to drink. He holds up the glass, examines the stirred cloudiness in what light there is from the kitchen. He sips it. I watch him pull back from the sweetness.

Sugarwater, I say. For revival. I hear Ida's voice. *Re*vival, she says it, as though "vival" is also a word.

Leon puts the glass down, says, I'm too tired even to drink. Drink has an innocent sound when he says it: coffee or water or weak tea. Not the same drink Joe's is.

Leon, I say. He sits as though he is trained to do this at the sound of his name. Leon, I'm fifteen. I don't want to sleep away from home anymore. I want to sleep in my own bed. I say this, though it isn't true. I want those hours, late and dangerous, with Joe.

I watch Leon's face change as I talk, paler than it was, if this is possible, or shinier maybe: it takes on an opalescent gleam that is like the inside of a shell; later I realize he was sweating.

Go on, he says. His lips are a thin line.

I'm finished.

What if something goes wrong, Sal. If you get sick.

I won't get sick. I'm fifteen, I say again. It's not the same.

He looks down, runs his hands down the section of his leg available to him, thigh to knee. He says, It's happened before.

Once, I think. Once. The room, the house seem crowded with things that have happened already. I suddenly know he will not marry again.

I won't get sick, I say. If I get sick, I'll call the O'Caseys. She's still my Emergency Person. I smile. See? I am saying. Things are the same.

Leon nods slowly. All right, I guess, he says, his voice conditional, "I guess" is like quilt batting, insulating him from the absolute.

You call Mrs. O'Casey? I say: a question. It seems right to me, neat and correct, that he silently un-arrange what almost three years ago he silently arranged.

Perhaps you should, Leon says.

I thought you, I say. So it's official.

"Official," Leon says. I can hear his lips peeling away from his teeth, know he is smiling. I don't think "official's" precisely the word you're after, Sal.

What then? Sanctioned? Permitted? (Official is right, is what I mean.)

What about "agreed to"? Leon says, although that's of course two words. What about discussed, considered, allowed?

Later, I have to go out on the porch, swing my arms, take deep breaths. The containment of talking to Leon.

CHAPTER 15

···

The heat quits, suddenly, fast, shuts down as though it has never been. Cold leaks from windows, wind gullies off streets and is so fierce off the beach, walking parallel to it you don't make any headway. Sidewalks, buildings, things made out of concrete and metal and wood that held the heat all that long summer were frigid to the touch; mailing a letter you thought about your fingers freezing and sticking to the mailbox. The weather mocked memory. Even the sand was ice cold.

Joellen thinks she could not have conjured a cold this fierce. It feels personal to her, as though it has set out to thwart them, her and Joe. The ticket shack is unheated which makes it seem as though it is also against them. When Joellen is not angry, she is on the verge of panic. They have no warm place to go. She comes up with alternatives that usually Joe, but sometimes she, herself, vetoes. "My house" was the first place she mentioned though as soon as she thought and then said the two words she knew her house was not possible. She and Joe would leave traces; Ida, who could detect if ice cubes were missing from the freezer or if a piece of fruit was bruised in a way different from when she had bought it, would discover them, tell Leon in whatever still-mysterious way information passed between them.

"My house," Joellen says and then thinks the things about Ida and after that, sees the steps Leon would take to restrict her. So *that's* why you didn't want to sleep at the O'Caseys'! he'd say, his voice triumphant as though he'd been searching for an answer to this all along, the months and months since it happened. There was not much Leon could actually do – he would still be home some nights at eight, some nights not till eleven; Ida would leave at 4:20 – but he could police Joellen, ask her questions: when did you get home and where did you go and with whom and what were you doing, and then he would say, We are a truth-telling family. We are not liars.

What about your house, Joellen asks instead.

This is it, Joe says.

Your mother's house. She has not asked this before, some internal caution warning her off. Now, with her fingers icy, toes numb, she tells herself she'd been mistaken. There is no reason not to ask. Your mother's house.

What about it?

Is it heated?

It's heated. We're not goin' there, Joe says. He gets a cigarette, strikes a match off his thumbnail.

Why?

He does not answer, turns his head from her, from the picture of LuAnne she's called up: the smells, the closeness of the house, the spoiled food left on the dishes in the sink which LuAnne did not wash and which he could smell even from the front door. He is afraid if he brings Joellen to that house she will become, somehow, part of it. He is afraid LuAnne's smells and the lint from her clothing and hair and flaked bits of the skin chewed off her lips will seep and sift onto Joellen so that when he touches her, she will be composed partly of his mother.

What about my car? he says. It has heat.

Joellen's eyes brighten on "heat" and they go out to look at the car like it's an apartment they're thinking of taking.

Joe's VW, is parked in an alley not far away. Looking at it, Joellen thinks of the nights Joe sleeps in it, imagines finding him in the morning frozen, immoveable, hands fused to the insides of his pockets. They'd have to jimmy him out, move him (his body L-shaped) to some warm place until steam began to rise off him and his body began to drip.

It's so small, she says as though it really is an apartment. All they would do here is fuck and then leave.

Joe nods, fingering the curved roof of the car. Desire chuffs in him like wind under a coat. This happens: some small thing – a curve, an angle – makes him want sex. Now it is the humped roof of his car. He wants with a fierceness he is slightly afraid of. He thinks something in him might break if the want is put off and it is not in his prick and his balls that he feels this (though it is there, too) but in his lungs, in the boxed back of his throat, in his knees. Some-times he wishes he could hate Joellen for calling this from him and sometimes he longs for the part of his life before he knew her though when he says that it is just words; they do not cut near to the bone.

On the way back to the ticket shack they stop for take-out coffees at the bakery, which is as different in winter as the heat from this cold. No bennies; at this hour – near four – not any customers. It smells of yeast and heated ovens though, in the few minutes they stand waiting for a fresh pot of coffee to brew, Joellen begins noticing drafts, slips of cold in the warmth.

They walk what's only three blocks back, but by then Joellen's freezing. She shivers, waiting for Joe to unlock the ticket shack door, her teeth chattering hard, her body trembling so Joe has to turn to block her from his sightline. He's holding the bag with the coffees in his teeth.

Hurry, Joellen is thinking, and that it has to be warmer inside, *somewhat* warmer, though she knows it is not. Still, she can't call up a cold colder than the one she is standing in and "shelter," even when it is only a shack, implies protection, some warmth.

Joe opens the door and draws her inside and holds her against him with one arm. In the other he's holding the coffees, scalding through the cardboard cups and the bag. He looks behind Joellen, at the interior of the shack. He does not want to go other places – her house, his mother's, his car. He wants to be here, though there are no curtains or beds or dishes or pans; no cupboards, no table or tablecloth, towels, sheets; no running water, no electricity, no forks or spoons or cups, except for these cardboard ones; no heat.

Joellen starts crying, standing inside a sheltered and still ominous cold. Joe sets the cups down, his hands hot then quickly cooling, and touches her face with hands that smell like coffee and says, Shhh, and, What is it?

It's so *cold*, Joellen says. The cold comes at them, pulled by the residual warmth of their bodies, suckling off them. Their exhaled and visible breaths mingle, seem to become something leering and animal. Joellen's skin, the walls and the floor of the shack, are cold as iron.

Joe picks up the coffees again, carries them to the sleeping bag which he has smoothed and neatened after yesterday's use. He pours bourbon into the cups, but by now the coffee has cooled so he drinks from the bottle, swallows twice then calls to Joellen.

You'll feel better, he says, swinging the bottle.

Joellen gets under the blanket – they are still wearing jackets, shoes and (Joellen) wool gloves – and Joe feeds her the bourbon, one hand on the back of her head, the other holding the bottle, tipping it gently – she does not like what she calls the flavor – and she drinks. It is not warmth exactly, but the illusion of warmth, or a feeling of travelling away from the cold, a gold river.

There is no place to go. The gas station is in the process of closing. Gene's bought it, like he told Joe he was going to. (How? Joe thought. All that money?) He was tearing the old place down, building a new place, a Gaseteria he called it. Freemont's office with its warm, oily floor was already gone, the yard in front partly dug up. When the demolition began, the useless men scattered like perturbed birds that ruffle and squawk and fly up in the air, then light still in a group, someplace near. They stood now around the LAS BATTERIES sign, a long pole stuck in a wobbling cake of concrete, huffing into their hands, scowling and cursing at the torn-up yard, the sparkling chipped glass that had been the window of the office. The Gas Man, they call Gene. The Tycoon.

Joe feels pressed – by the cold, by the loss of the gas station so that, at night, his choices are now to sleep at LuAnne's, where he will not sleep, or in his car. He holds Joellen under the blanket, his forehead and eyes are uncovered, a triangle of blanket like a bandana flapped over his mouth and his nose so he inhales the oily sheep smell of wool. Joellen's entirely buried; Joe rests his chin on her swaddled head.

What? Say again? he says when she speaks, pulling the blanket away from her face.

A motel, Joellen says, though her voice is flat. A motel. Beds slept in by bennies.

Joe says no, shakes his head, says, No money. Not since my brother shut the gas station down on me. Joe could pay, maybe, for one day or a week of days, being off-season, but they'd just end up back where they started and it would push him quicker to the time when he will be stealing again.

What's wrong with here? he says, his breath whiskied and warm on her cheek. What's so bad about here?

Joe sets down the bag he is carrying – coffee, a cruller glazed with brittle sugar – so he can unlock the ticket shack door. Inside, the light of the shack is smoky and blue, a patch of sun on the floor under the window like a neat, trapezoid rug.

The coffee has leaked, dampening the cruller and his hand which he rolls in the hem of the sweatshirt he's wearing. He sits on the sleeping bag, drinks, replacing the cup's plastic cover after each sip to keep the heat in, though when he is here alone he does not notice the cold, the bareness, the absence of comforts.

Joe half lies on the sleeping bag, propped by the wall, and stretches the kinks out of his back and his hips and his knees (Joellen's vision of him frozen, L-shaped and immoveable inside his car is not so far off) and he thinks about her, chaste, in school. In his head he sees empty classrooms, Joellen, a teacher, a blackboard, the windows. No noise, no other students. He stays with the picture a long time, as though he is walking her down the halls, the brown floors winking with the smeared, reflected colors of clothing.

Joe thinks of the rusty cold smell of Joellen when she gets here in the afternoon. Thinks of his palms, flat, running over the front of her sweater, the wool smooth and then dimpled under his hands, his palms rubbing over her nipples. He sees her open to him, sees himself starting inside her, and he's dizzy, runs his hand over his face where he smells, on his hand, the ways he had touched her yesterday; the juices, wet then, now dried. His lip brushes texture; he sees an opaque, brittle circlet on the inside of his wrist. It is glaze from the cruller. He puts his tongue out, waiting for it to melt, expecting an infusion of sweetness. But it is not glaze, not sweet, it is come or juice from Joellen, a day old, picked off the hand that smells also of booze and the scorched undersmell of spilled coffee and he moves his hands, holds them out and away from himself, noise clicking in the back of his throat, because the hands he'd been touching her with in his head were not clean.

He does not know where to go to get clean. Gene's, where Patty will answer the door, her mouth pinched with dislike and with the effort of being civil to him. He can see her complaining to Gene – he always *wants* something. Never even brings anything for his nephews.

He's my fucking *brother*, I don't give a shit what he wants, what does he want? Give it to him.

She would suffer him taking a shower, hovering outside the door to the bathroom and when he came out, squeezing herself past him to mop the floor, the tub; to gather and remove the one towel he'd used and hung neatly.

He thinks of how he used to wash at the sink in the gas station office, his shirt unbuttoned, pulled off his arms but still tucked – fuckin' Gene, he says, because the gas station is gone: the sink, the office, Freemont. And thinking Freemont's name, Joe decides he will go to Freemont's: in the second it takes him to make this decision he's seeing ahead, a future of days when he will go by Freemont's house every morning with fresh crullers, the paper. They'll have breakfast together, he'll shower. He will not go to Gene's or his mother's.

Joe has not been inside Freemont's before; *to* it, when Freemont asked him to drop something off (leave her outside, he had said) but not inside. It's a small, mean house the brown of oiled logs near, though not of, the streets of the black people's houses, a house maybe four or five times the size of the ticket shack but no more.

Freemont's glad to see him – This retirement shit, is the first thing he says, turning sideways to let Joe step into the kitchen. Joe's shoes stick to the tacky surface of the linoleum. There is a burnt-coffee smell.

Coffee? Freemont says, hoisting a dull aluminum percolator, and Joe nods and feels, still, that he is inside the picture he'd imagined.

Freemont brings coffee that pours like it is oil. The table is covered with oilcloth, the walls with newspapers, comics, old calendars sent over the years by suppliers to the garage.

Fix you somethin'? Freemont offers. Got fish froze in here. This retirement shit, he says again. Fish and TV, but Joe sees the grease thick and amber-colored like cooked gasoline on the stove, on the walls and spattered all the way up to the ceiling and he says No, no thanks, already ate, and covers his stomach with his arm. The kitchen is tiny, cramped, his chair butts up against the refrigerator door; through a half-opened doorway he sees a bed, greasy blankets slid half to the floor, the door banged up against the foot of the bed. The two rooms are the whole house.

Freemont sees where Joe's looking. Bed I used to have? he says. It was smaller. Joe says, You been here a long time?

Freemont nods. He says, Built her. He says, Fella who owned this particular piece didn't want it no more when the coloreds started building them shanties. He cocks his head sideways, the direction of the black people's houses, better built, cleaner than his is. For a second Joe thinks how old Freemont must be, Civil War old or at least Reconstruction, which is when he imagines most of the Negro houses got built, by freed or by runaway slaves.

Got it cheap, the land I'm talkin' about, when I was nineteen, could've been twenty, Freemont is saying. Nobody bothers me. Them, he says, his neck, his head pulling again towards the houses. They know to leave me alone. He leans across the table to Joe, his breath strong and whiskied. Got protection, he says. Flash it around ever now and again. Live and let live I always say, Freemont says, and he grins.

Place got a bathroom? Joe asks and Freemont snorts, amused, as though he's built it in some clever, disguised way, as a challenge for visitors.

The bathroom's too small to turn a full 360 degrees in: you stand facing the sink or the john, the only way to get into the shower is sideways. The stall shower's rusted, the bottom two-thirds of the plastic curtain mildew-black. Even the gas station bathroom was cleaner.

Joe had not planned to actually shower this first time; thought he would strip, wash himself as he stood at the sink the way he had at the gas station, but the sink is black also, the towels putrid and black, there is not even toilet paper he could use to pat himself dry. He turns the hot water tap on with his elbow, then turns it back off and goes out to the kitchen and tells Freemont, Thanks for the coffee.

Yeah. Come see me again. Call up my secretary though, make sure I'm free, Freemont says and laughs. Busy man, he says, sputtering laughter.

Joe waits for Freemont to stop because it seems hard, leaving a man standing there laughing all by himself. He looks past Freemont's house (shack, he thinks, shanty) dwarfed by the two-story houses the black men built here. Freemont's house leans slightly, as though it is yearning towards these other houses, their straight backs, their shuttered eyes, and Joe closes his eyes against Gene's house and LuAnne's and now Freemont's: the choices it looks like he has.

He goes directly from Freemont's to LuAnne's. He is dirtier now, Freemont's grease and filth and stale breath layered on top of the dried juice, the dried come, the booze, the spilled coffee, the dirt that's his own. LuAnne's house seems clean after Freemont's. Joe showers, puts on clean socks and jeans and carries a clean folded shirt with him downstairs, already used to the warmth of the house so he is not thinking: shirtless.

Walking into the kitchen, his eye catches on color: a streak of yellow on top of the table. A spilled yolk, is the first thing he thinks and disdain changes his face and he looks up at the ceiling so he will not have to see it, but it's a pad of yellow legal-sized paper. LuAnne's left an envelope for him on top of the pad. When he had not been by for several days after the letter came she drew a clutch of waxy red arrows on the sheet, their V's pointing in towards the envelope. Crayon, Joe thinks, but they're lipstick; his clean arm and wrist, from where he leans on the pad, are scored with what look like fresh whip marks.

It's his draft notice. Selective Service, it says in the corner of the envelope which strikes Joe as he holds it: how it means they are choosy. He does not open the envelope yet, puts it in his back pocket to open later, now he tears the top arrowed page off the pad and rips it up small and buries the scraps in the trash can under the sink. He takes the legal pad to the living room, looks for a place to stash it, a place LuAnne will not look until days or weeks have passed and the sight of the pad will trigger no memory, and finally he stuffs it under a strew of newspapers and clothes. It is the way he blots the droplets of water off the faucets, the walls, the floor of the shower. So she will not know he's been here.

CHAPTER 16

....

They are in the ticket shack, Joe and Joellen, tangled
and wet, their clothes twisted down to ankles and knees and waists though still
attached to them, like leashed dogs. They lie tilted towards each other, crowded
to one side of the sleeping bag, avoiding spongy wetness. Joe's holding the capped
fifth of bourbon in the crook of one arm, the glass of the bottle between them.
Joellen lies with her face pressed to the opening of Joe's shirt smelling their two
mingled smells and the smells also of must, wool, mothballs. She thinks of
Goodwill, that he is wearing this bad luck piece of clothing, and she shivers and
Joe chafes her arm with his free hand in an unconscious way, the way you touch
a dog or a pencil, because he is used to her shivering, and Joellen feels that, behind
his touch, he is absent and she rolls on top of him so there is no space between
them and still, she feels distance and bears down.

Hunh, Joe says, her weight pressing the air from his lungs, thinking, still, that
she is cold.

She lies flat, her shoulders and ribs fused to his and it is still too far, too much
skin and bone in between them. She wants to be inside him, his features cupped
over hers, her eyes looking out through his red lit skin. Sometimes, when his body
shifts, when he moves an arm from one position to another she does likewise, but
it is the strain in her own shoulder she feels, not in his.

Joellen lies quiet except for a fidgety rolling she can't control caused by the
rolled tops of Joe's thighs.

Settle down, he says and steadies her, touching her ribs with the tips of his
fingers and right then there is a knock on the door. Joe stiffens, Joellen feels all his
muscles tense, her attention's on not falling off.

Joe's breath squeals through his nose; he opens his mouth to breathe quieter.
He's not sure what he heard. Could be wind, he tells himself. Could be some animal, maybe a rabbit. The thought is calming, it is logical: he has seen rabbits
before in the high grass that spreads like a lake behind and around the ticket shack

as though the shack is becalmed in dun-colored water, though he has not seen any rabbits lately; it is late February, the grass has died back.

A stray rabbit, he says; his voice is soft but he says this out loud.

What? Joellen says, her head popping up: she could never have known he'd be thinking of rabbits. What?

Joe does not answer; waits for the knock or the butt or the rattle (he is no longer sure of the sound) to repeat.

A knock. Someone knocking. Joe stands in one movement, Joellen rolls off him, the bottle rolls out of his hand, rocks and then stills on the sleeping bag. He's got his jeans up and buttoned as fast as if he has practiced. The bourbon, capped, does not spill.

Joe is motionless watching the ticket shack door. Something to do with the station, he thinks; he thinks – Not me, I'm careful – and then, Somebody followed Joellen, and he is suddenly angry at her and though she is huddled behind him hissing – What is it? What? – he keeps his back to her, won't speak.

He takes a step towards the door.

Don't *answer* it! Joellen says. She's rolled off the sleeping bag and is squatting beside it, her underwear, her tights still pulled down, tethering her ankles. But Joe goes to the door. They'll only come back. He does not want to wait to find out what's coming.

It's Gene. Joe blinks into the light – no sun, a whiteness. Yeah, he says.

So this is it, huh? Home sweet home?

Joe doesn't answer. He stands straddling the thin ticket shack door, the door bisecting him. Gene's wearing a parka, dark blue lined with orange, the colors of road crews. What? Joe says. What do you want? His voice is uninflected and steady.

If you'd just *call* me sometimes, say where you're at, I wouldn't be having to find you, Gene says, his voice pleasant, steady also.

Call you, Joe says, closing one eye, half smiling. You're not fucking there, I get Patty, I get your wife. We have great talks.

Gene puts a hand on the outside wall of the shack; weight on the hand, he leans in. Yeah, he says. She's got a bug up her ass about you, I don't know what it is. Forget her. As he talks Gene catches movement behind his weight-bearing arm, sees the face of the girl, pale and small in the dark. He looks at her, at Joe, his eyes flick back and forth between them. He winks, says, loud, so the girl will hear him, Sor-ry. Didn't know you had company, then he moves in towards Joe, his lips, his bad teeth looming; says in a quieter voice, Let me come back in a while. When you're finished.

Joe's waited a long time for this wink; knew it would come and that he would hate it and now he does not even pause. His head comes down, his shoulder hikes, he dives at Gene. Gene teeters then hops back once, twice before he goes down flat on his back, raising a few puffs of dust off the ground. He lies with one hand pressed to his chest, the other raised to show he is harmless, and Joe looks at him a minute, then sits on the ground next to his brother. As fast as it came up, his anger is finished.

Gene sits up: the rustling nylon of his jacket, the creak of his work boots, the scrabbling sound of movement on dirt. Christ, he says. I came to fucking *talk* to you, Joe. He sits rubbing the weight-bearing arm.

Not here, Joe says. I don't want you here. His arms circle his knees. He looks past the ticket shack, out to the grass, now mostly stubble. If he squints, he can't make out where the grass ends. He could be some other place.

Fine, Gene says. I get the picture. Can we fuckin' go someplace? Can we fuckin' do that?

Joe shrugs, he stands up. When he hears the sounds of Gene standing, he starts walking.

Hey! Gene says, bent over, dusting the knees of his jeans. Joe doesn't stop, Gene has to chug to catch up. Wait up, you fuck! he says, coming even with Joe. He means to take Joe for coffee, for lunch maybe (Christ is he thin, Gene's thinking; before, when Joe's jacket was hiked, he could see the protuberant bones of his pelvis, the flatness of his jeans strung between).

You ever eat? he says, thinks: get your "girlfriend" to make you a meal, but he does not say this. He realizes it is the way he talks most of the time to most people, wise-ass and joking. He can't talk this way to Joe.

I eat, Joe says.

What? What'd you have last night for supper for instance? When he says supper, Gene sees the pink-orange flame from the broiler in his kitchen, remembers the smell of its cooked heat.

Joe stops, turns, looks up at his brother. Why? You writin' a cookbook?

You're so fuckin' skinny. No . . . (. . . no girl goes for a guy who's so skinny, is what he's about to say, but he thinks of the girl in the shack and can't say it.) You got to eat Joe. Come eat by me, let Patty cook for you. Or not Patty, go home for supper. He tries to think of the meals LuAnne cooked but can't remember anything other than ice. Now he says, Did she ever cook? Ma? When we were kids, I'm talkin' about.

She cooked, Joe says. When he was around. Some of the time. She cooked.

If it was somebody else, not Joe, Gene would laugh, say, Could be why he left, not thinking of LuAnne or Rusty while he said it. He'd say it to be funny, the kind of thing people expected from him, the kind of man he'd turned into.

They're at the gas station. They both stop at the yellow line and look down like boys at a lake, toeing the water. They are parallel with the LAS BATTERIES sign, the useless men. Joe takes a step back, zigzagging the line.

Fuckin' cold, Gene says, shoving his hands in his pockets, squinting up at the sky. It won't quit, it's fuckin' me up. Can't get my new tanks in till the ground thaws. No tankees no laundry, he says cocking his chin back, the way he does to receive laughter, but Joe's quiet, looking at the torn-up yard. The old tanks, half dug up, are humped burrowed behemoths. Their size makes him breathless.

Wait'll you see the new motherfuckers, Gene says. Six. Each one the size of a football field.

When're they goin' in? Joe asks, because he does not want to be here then, to see them.

When it thaws, knock wood. Gene bangs his knuckles against his own skull, then he looks up again at the sky. Fuckin' me up. It's like I'm payin' for it, you know? Fuckin' cold.

Joe thinks, as he has before, about the money. What did it cost to buy six new football field–sized gas tanks? He thinks of the money Rusty used to come home with, green covering the floor, the bed, like a quilt stitched out of bills.

Where'd it come from? he says now. Dad? All that money.

Where? Gene says. You don't know? She gave it to him. The bimbo. So he'd come back.

Joe waits to feel something – surprise, injury – but all he feels is cold, the sharpness of the cold air in his lungs.

Gene's looking at the new office, mostly finished, three sides are cinderblock, the front a single sheet of glass. Daylight catches the glass at an angle, making it look tipped. Wanna see it? he says, already walking.

Inside, the office is empty except for a filing cabinet and one chair. It smells like fresh glue. Their voices echo like voices in an indoor tiled pool. The useless men are watching them. Joe thinks they could break this new window, they are that close to lawless. How long you had this up? Joe says.

Couple, three weeks. Gene's opening and closing file cabinet drawers. Joe hears the sounds of tissue paper.

Think fast, Gene says and Joe puts his hands up, a dark blue thing coming at him. It's a folded shirt. The fabric is new and sharp, like fiberglass.

Open it, Gene says, still grinning.

The shirt says Gene's Gaseteria on the back. Over the front pocket it says Joe, stitched in red.

You like it? I thought about red, I thought about gold, Gene says, flipping his hand back and forth. What do you think? The truth.

Joe thinks the shirt's meant as a joke, the way airline pilots give wing pins to little boys. He wonders if Gene's second child's been born yet. Yeah, so? he says.

So? So, when this show's on the road I want you working for me. Around school naturally. Part time, flexible schedule.

Fulltime, Joe says. He balls the shirt, tosses it onto the chair.

Hey! Gene says. This is brand fuckin' new! He picks up the shirt, refolds it along its pressed lines. Fulltime? he says. You got school, it's your last year of school, right? Am I right Joe? Help me out here.

Joe shrugs. It is irritating, the way Gene says his name in each sentence. In a way, it's the irritation that makes him say – What's the difference. I quit school anyway. He hasn't been there in weeks. Still, Joe's surprised at the tiny wisped feeling of loss at what he's just shut himself out from.

That's good Joe, wonderful, they're gonna come for you anyway, you don't have to send out goddamn fuckin' invitations!

Yeah? Joe says. And who's that?

Uncle Sam, Gene says. Uncle Sam?

Joe looks at him. She tell you? he says. He means LuAnne.

Gene almost nods, turns his head sideways instead. She told me you got a letter. Said you hadn't been by in some time, she was worried, some such. His voice trails off. He sounds too much like his mother.

She tell you all my business? Joe asks.

Gene says, Like what? What else is there?

Joe looks out the window. The useless men are still there, like ex–house cats that are no longer civilized. Rusty's been gone seven years.

I'm right, am I right Joe? Gene says. Your notice? He can't keep the prideful note out of his voice, for guessing.

Joe shrugs. He rubs his back pocket where he carried the envelope around for days before he opened it, but it's not there anymore. He's already gone for his physical.

He says, They want me, they got me. If I'm goin', a high school diploma won't be all that useful. If not . . . , he shrugs.

Shit, Gene says. He sits in the chair, shaking his head, bouncing the navy blue shirt that says Joe in his hands. Shit, Joe!

We got a deal? Joe says. Fulltime. Take it or leave it.

Gene tosses the blue shirt in his hands a few more times, then he hands it to Joe. Who steps out of the glue-smelling office, out into the air that is so cold, it hurts just to breathe.

CHAPTER 17

I stay on the floor a long time, packed small, my skirt stitched down by my arms. I keep looking down to make sure my bareness is covered like a woman expecting guests who keeps checking that all her knickknacks are turned the right way. The white oblong crotch of my underwear, taut between the two poles of my ankles, shines in the dim ticket shack light. It was like those air raid drills in school, the triangular strips of white and flower-sprigged underwear curved over the secret places of the girls who sat against the wall facing me, knees up, hands on their heads.

Skirts down! I want to yell at them. Skirts down!

I am afraid to stand up. I am afraid that the moment I do, the door, still partway open, will open further; that the man Joe went out with will come in. I know he saw me, though it is dim. I saw his eyes sweep and then rest, stopping full on my face.

I wait a long time for the man to come back, for something to happen. Fear begins to mingle with boredom – this was like the air raid drills too: you can only stay on that cusp for so long before it loses your attention. I look around the ticket shack the way I had looked at the girls' underwear.

Sometimes, lying with Joe, I think about how the shack would look if we fixed it up. I think of curtains – pale blue with white dots; a blue rug, maybe a bed. I always think these things in the same order: curtains, a rug, a bed, like a chant. I said it to Joe once – his eyes closed, "no" in his face. I went on thinking it though.

I said, What about a hot plate? We could cook up baked beans, canned spaghetti.

No outlets, Joe said, on his back, eyes on the ceiling.

Well, *butane* then, I said.

He said no to that too, brought it out of himself slow – No, no, I don't think so, a slow and luxurious drawl.

Curtains, I thought, a rug, a bed. Baked beans. Canned spaghetti.

Squatting here, I realize: heat. A hot plate would have thrown off some warmth. Not much, I can hear Joe say to this. Not enough to make a difference.

Maybe it would make a difference, I tell him in my head. Maybe it would make a difference to me.

You got blankets, Joe says, his voice and inflection so clear I almost turn to see if he is behind me.

We got this – holding a fifth by the bottle neck, chiming the booze back and forth. You got me.

Thinking of these things, solutions to cold, brings me back again to the cold of the shack, my exposed skin, so I stand. My knees tremble a little, the muscles hop, and this, too, is like the air raids. I didn't care if the man walked in then, maybe I didn't remember the man under "cold," and, the fact that Joe left me here. He'd never done this before. Even when we went for Cokes, we both went, he locked and unlocked the door like he didn't trust me.

I pull my tights up twisted so they spiral like Ace bandages around my calves, thighs, waist.

This place is a dump, I say, loud, into the dump and saying it I see that it is, see it small and curtainless, rugless, bedless, what it will always be.

Joe comes back to the ticket shack, stops a foot or two shy of the door near the scrabbled marks Gene made when he went down. He can make out Gene's boot print, see Gene as though he's still here, doing pushups on the one weight-bearing arm, and he can see LuAnne too, her hair streel-like, her voice the sound of ice cubes, and he looks past the door, out over the stubbled grass, past that, as though his eyes need a fresh place that hasn't been tainted by family.

The door is unlocked and he goes in, expecting Joellen; he is surprised not to see her squatting the way that he left her, frozen like a rabbit in headlights. He does not know where she is, what to picture. He's never been to her house. Except for the time he saw her sitting on the bench at the bus stop, he has never come upon her doing what she does when she is not with him. It is like when he reads: historical action, the life of a character occurs only in the back-and-forth sweep of his eyes.

Joe steps into the ticket shack, takes a step back to close the door. Something is different, some change in air or smell or presence. He has felt no presence here other than his own and Joellen's and the ghosts of those black men, their shoulders sweat-damp. Now he feels Gene and behind Gene he feels his mother, and a truth starts in him and grows: this place is no longer mine. The feeling – a seed that becomes a belief – starts in his head, spreads through him like water or covering paint, and even while he is watching it spread he's thinking: would it be true if I hadn't just thought it, like when he told Gene he was finished with school?

It's not what he expected.

Expected he would be the one to leave, to outgrow his need for the shack, that it would let him go fondly, stroking his back, like one kind of parent.

He sits on the sleeping bag; opens and takes several hits from the bottle of bourbon. He begins to make plans. Work for Gene, he thinks, lifting the bottle, swallowing, the bourbon sliding up and down the glass, a sound that's like jewelry. He can work towards a trailer; maybe in six months, working fulltime, he'll have a down payment. He'll buy a shell, won't be money for furniture, which is fine. All he's after is shelter.

I go home, though it is not where I want to be, the house empty except for the smells of Ida's handcream, old cooking, the scorched smell of ironing. I don't see Ida much; she has receded for me the way people's aged grandmothers do. She is like Mrs. O'Casey or like Isabel: a presence once larger than now.

I go up on the porch, peer in, making sure Leon's not home. The house is dark except for the kitchen light Ida always leaves on, but Leon might be sitting there in the living room in the dark saving on electricity. I don't see Leon much either. He makes me edgy. It's the way he speaks, his nitpicking precision – I've always hated lima beans, I might say over dinner, and he'll look up and say, *Always?* this hunting-cat smile on his face.

I don't recall feeding you lima beans for the first several years of your life. You didn't taste lima beans, I think it's safe to say, until Ida began making them for us when you were what? Ten? – and he goes on like that, the talk shifting to the meaning of always, to my lack of precision, lima beans only a springboard.

I can't bear hearing him speak, watching the things he does – the intent way he looks through the mail, carefully reading each envelope, sometimes holding one up to the light. Why? Bills, circulars, ads, there was never anything different.

There's nothing there, I always wanted to shout at him.

But he'd say, Nothing? and fan the stack in his hand. Pretty weighty for nothing.

I could see why Isabel left him – I sometimes think this, "left" rather than died, hit by a green car, cremated, gone.

He misses the point. His pleasure in talking is in tripping you up, but he is so high on precision he misses the big things. He'd smelled booze on me once, leaned in close and inhaled.

Is that *alcohol* I smell? he asked me. Have you been *drinking?*

No, I said. Cough syrup. It was what Joe told me to say. I cleared my throat. Cough syrup.

Are you sick? his voice rich with parental concern: he liked this too, uncovering sickness or need.

No, I said again. A tickle.

He nodded. He wasn't a drinker, liquor was not kept in the house. Sometimes, if Isabel wanted a brandy, he brought it home for her, one or two tiny bottles, a medicinal dose.

Good, he said. You know we are not drinkers.

We who? I wanted to ask him. We, you me and Isabel? We, you? Some larger cultural entity or tribe? But I would not ask, make the point, again, words, when that wasn't the point. I hardly drank, I drank to get warm, I hated the taste, I don't even like coffee, I wanted to tell him. (I know, Sal, he'd say. I've *tasted* your coffee.)

I like sex though, I could say, being conversational. I go to a falling down shack and I fuck with my boyfriend. I probably reeked of it when I got home, the smell off my skin was sometimes so strong it made me dizzy. Strips of my clothing – my underwear, sometimes the cuff or collar or tail of my shirt soaked in it, dried and stiffened. Dogs knew. Dogs pulled their owners to me across parking lots, streets, frantic to push their noses into my crotch. I'm so sorry, the owners said to me, jerking choke chains. Dogs knew. Not Leon.

I come down off the porch. There's a moon I can't see lighting the street, shining the slant roofs of houses. I think I'm just walking around but I end up in front of the O'Caseys'.

It's cold. The doors are all closed, the storms up. Leon has not changed our windows or doors out of screens for years, not since Isabel, and I see for the first time: Isabel did it, a singular fact that changed nothing. I stand on the O'Caseys' front steps, my eyes tracing the cut-out aluminum flamingo on their storm door.

The inner door opens, Mrs. O'Casey opens it. She is not wearing her glasses and looks squint-eyed and piggy. The two empty milk bottles she's holding clink in her hands.

Yes? she says, her voice muffled, the storm door still shut between us.

It's me, I say, hand on the door. The metal is cold.

Oh, she says. It is you. Did you want something, Joellen?

I take the empty milk bottles from her, put them in the milk box outside the door. The lid is cold, the box the same dingy silver as tooth fillings.

When I straighten Mrs. O'Casey is wearing her glasses, her eyes magnified three or four times behind them. Her fierceness and distress are magnified too. I see Charlieo at school, but I have not been here since the hot and odd night in October when I did not want any yellow pie, when I took off the yellow night-gown and left. I know that the nightgown has been washed, that it sits in the drawer with its fellow. They are somehow naked without me.

If you're out of milk I could go get you a carton.

She seems to be thinking this over. Her lipstick is chipped, like nail polish. He's out, she says finally. You missed him. With some friends, she says, tapping her cheek with her finger.

I feel what I'm sure she intends me to feel: Friends. Who?

He does have other friends, Joellen, Mrs. O'Casey says, though I haven't spoken. Other than you, she does not say.

Oh, I say, and then, I know, and then, *Good*. Each thing is the wrong thing, false or condescending.

Well, if you'd let him know I came by? I take a step backwards, too far, I lose my footing, I half-jump, half-fall and land kneeling.

Joellen! Mrs. O'Casey says and hustles outside. The warmth she has kept sealed in behind her, guarded by the flamingo, charges out. I smell piped heat and steam, from the kitchen.

She kneels beside me: my knee is scraped and superficially bloody. Our heads both bend, like mine and Isabel's used to, our eyes on the tiny blue island of flagstone in her knee. We watched for a long time, as though it was inhabited.

Mrs. O'Casey helps me up, guides me inside. This, she says, should be seen to.

The kitchen looks and smells pink as though it is heated by a rotisserie coil. I sit on the table holding a wet cloth to my knee; Mrs. O'Casey hovers with antiseptics, bandages. It is what we are doing when Charlieo comes in.

Hey, we tell each other, both shy, but there is my knee for us to look at.

Fall?

Sort of.

Graceful. Same as always.

You've been fast, Mrs. O'Casey says, taking the container of milk he's still holding. Her voice is disapproving. She hurries the bandaging, angry at me again.

Wanta do something? Charlieo says. The movie? He's still peering down at my knee, as though it is interesting. He taps down an edge of adhesive.

Sure, I say and am proud of the swiftness of my answer; how it proves I am not even thinking about Joe.

Hungry? Charlieo asks. Mrs. O'Casey's back stiffens. He forgives me, she will not, or him for his easiness.

I'm not prepared for company, she says, her back still to us. I'm sorry but I've not got food for . . .

Oh, I say. No. Really. I don't want a thing. It must cost her, to turn me away, to say this.

Maybe a movie, I say to Charlieo, already on his way to the door.

Mrs. O'Casey has turned, she leans now against the lip of the sink, her head turned from me. I'm sorry, she says. I just have enough for my family. Which you were once, I hear. Which you are no longer.

It's me should be sorry, I say. I resolve to do better, to spend more time with Charlieo, her. On my way to the front door I am sure I will do this. And then I am outside and I know I will not. The cold is white and smoky and makes me miss Joe in a way that cracks inside my bones.

I push on the flamingo to shut the storm door. It's very dark, the steps shadowed. I go down them slowly, slamming my heel into the back of each step. It's not until I am all the way down, out on the sidewalk where Charlieo's waiting in a cloud of his own exhaled breath, that Mrs. O'Casey turns on the porch light behind us.

Joellen, a voice says, calling from a distance, Joellen. I rise one layer out of a sleep that is nourishing, dreamless. I try to sink back, but that level's gone, peeled back like the protective skin of an onion.

Joellen, Joellen, the voice goes on, unvaried in tone or inflection like the back and forth squeal of a glider. I am awake though I pretend not to be, furious, as cold as the voice. I do not want to be wakened this way. Isabel touched. She did not use her voice.

Joellen, Joellen.

What! I scream finally, wild, my eyes open. Leon flinches, teeters away from the door. What? That's how you wake someone?

Someone is downstairs to see you, Leon says. A boy.

Joe, I think first and the long night of thinking about him, not sleeping, comes back to me. After the movie Charlieo walked me home. We stood outside. He talked, I was too tired to hear him.

Who? I say.

How many boys do you know?

What time is it? I turn onto my back.

Nine, Leon hisses. Eight after. It is *Sunday*, he says. My day off. My one day.

I didn't know someone would come, I say. Go back to sleep. It is not true that Sunday is his one day off, he is off Saturdays too, but he will not sleep in on Saturdays: the day he sleeps late is Sunday.

Back to sleep, he says, his voice derisive and whiny. You know I can't sleep once I'm up. I'm up! He throws his arms out, his robe looks like a box suspended from a broomstick. I get up, not looking at him. Head for the stairs.

At least put on a *robe*, Leon says. The whole world doesn't have to see . . .

I don't have a robe, I put on a sweater. It barely covers my hip; you can see a white quarter moon of my underwear. I walk tipped slightly forward, to cover it.

The downstairs is freezing, the front door partway open, I can feel what scant heat Leon gives us snaking out of the house. I kept turning the thermostat up, Leon kept turning it down, a silent war like the one he and Isabel had over the plugs of electrical appliances. Leon's hush puppies sit side by side on the bottom step. I put them on, try not to think of his prissy nervous sweat oozing under the soles of my feet.

It is Charlieo. Charlieo! I say. Leon didn't say it was you! He is standing outside. He never came in: used to stand with his hands and lips pressed to the screen when he came to call for me summer mornings. I remember the tiny pillows of flesh, raspberry and cream.

Why don't you come in? Why didn't Leon make you? You look like Rudolph, I say. You look Rudolph-ized. His ears, the tips of his nose are unnaturally red, as though lipsticked.

Where were you, Joellen? Can you tell me that? You know how long I waited? Where were you? A mournfulness I can see and name comes off him, but it does not touch me.

I wrap the sweater tight around me. It's freezing, I say. Will you please come in?

He looks away off the porch like there's something he's keeping an eye on.

I waited for hours, he says. I didn't go. I made them go without me.

And I remember – fishing. It seems like something I dreamt, some plan from years ago. Last night, standing in front of my house, him talking and talking. Fishing, he'd said. A boat, a friend of his father's. I remember this now, the same picture I'd seen in my head then comes back: a blue day, the sun, white and chippy off the blue water. I could hear the water slap-slapping the hull of the boat. I had thought: Joe will not know where I am.

Today? I say. It was today?

You know it was today, this morning, I probably told you only six thousand times: 5:30 A.M. The marina.

I can see him standing out on the bow of the boat, scanning for me, refusing hot drinks, his whole face red as it is now in parts, the red clashing with the orange of his life vest.

I'm sorry, I say. I mean it. I guess my alarm didn't go off. I was so *tired*.

He's still looking away, down the street.

I'm sorry, I say again. Really. Why didn't you just go without me?

He looks scornful. His hurt is as weighty as a paper bag filled with plums.

LOOK, I say. I'M SORRY! I'm using the last patience I have, carried like the dimes Isabel gave me for emergency phone calls. What else can I say?

You can explain, he says. You can give me a reason. Where were you?

I was here, I was sleeping, but I've already said that. He doesn't believe me, or does not want to hear it. So I say, I was with my boyfriend. Joe? You remember him? Fucking, I say. I go on, I give details, made up ones since I was no place but here. But I can't stop. I say things that are like rips in fabric, that make his neck, the rest of his face flush, though he does not move.

I look at the front of his pants – my interest is clinical. It is flat there, the zipper flat and smooth under its tongue of khaki. I picture his balls and curled penis cupped in his briefs. I close my eyes.

He is down off the porch – I hear it, then open my eyes. Which was the one unforgivable thing that I said? He is striding down the street, hurt streaming off him like vapor.

Go *after* him, a voice says in my head, and I do, in a way: unlock the screen door, step outside. I hug myself inside the sweater. Leon's shoes stick then drop off the soles of my feet.

Charlieo, I call, but my voice is dim-sounding. Charlieo, I call louder, but I am not loud or insistent enough. Not like all those times at the station when we laid our coins on the tracks, waiting to be the first one to feel the vibrations, to straighten, to yell at the other one, Train!

CHAPTER 18

....

The cold eases some, not so Joellen and Joe really notice, but the ground thaws and Gene's able to get the new tanks in. He throws a Grand Opening party in February; hundreds of plastic triangular pennants like flaps cut from beach balls snap in the air that is as chill and as clear as the plate glass front of the office. The party is catered: spiked red punch spews from a fountain. The useless men stand across the road, their final retreat after the LAS BATTERIES sign was hauled off, the new gas tanks sealed in. They seem alert, better dressed, as though they are guests who never quite make it to the party. Gene tells Joe to come wearing his navy blue Gene's Gaseteria shirt. Joe nods, knowing he will not wear the shirt, he does not even go to the party, though he starts working for Gene the day after.

Joe walks carefully holding his weight back as he crosses the new concrete of the yard. The cement has something shiny in it, like pieces of milk glass; when the sun hits the yard has the opaque blueness of ice. Joe thinks of the six buried gas tanks, enormous steel bladders sloshing with gasoline under the yard. In his mind they are animate the way, when he'd first seen it, Gene's living room furniture also was.

The work is different than what he'd done with Freemont, some of this, some of that, not the rebuilding of cars he'd done before. No pumping though. The new pumps, sleek as soda machines, are automatic; customers go to the little raised glass box Gene added on to the side of the office and asked for three bucks or five or a fill-up. Customers pumped it themselves. Joe or Anthony or the two other boys Gene hired locked and unlocked the pumps without coming outside the glass box.

Cafeteria, Gaseteria, Gene said. Get it?

Sometimes this is Joe's job, to sit in the glass box where he feels himself to be a spectacle, and make change and say over and over – Which pump? Sometimes Gene tells him to stand outside with a squeegee and wash off all the women's windshields. Forget the men, Gene said. Let them do it themselves. You stand there, a lady drives in, you smile, etcetera, etcetera. You know what I'm sayin'? Leeean right across, Joe, Gene said, leaning across the desk in the office. Go the whole nine yards. Summer? Open your shirt. Bennie chicks love that shit.

Joe hates it. He hates the glass box. Hates wearing the shirt that says "Joe" so people whose names he doesn't know come up to him and say, Joe. Give me a ten's worth, Joe. One night, in the light of the kerosene lantern he keeps in the ticket shack he bit at the red thread, pulled the "Joe" out of the shirt, but it was still there, a darker blue permanent stain under the stitching. He feels owned, and it is not just the jobs Gene gives him to do or the particular way he wants these jobs done but, Where're you goin'? Come on over and eat, come on out for a beer, a clap on the shoulder, a wink, Tell me what the fuck you got to do that's so god-damn important?

Gene knows how he takes his coffee, that he sometimes spikes it, that he craves sugar for breakfast. Shit, Gene said watching Joe eat two crullers one morning. You are a sugar *junkie*. You never used to eat sugar like that.

You weren't that way before, Gene's always saying, as though in his tastes, the way that he speaks, the growth of his body, each thing that is not the way Gene remembers, Joe has betrayed him.

It's not like you're the same either, Joe said once, thinking – Patty, Gene's one or two kids; thinking about the pink-and-green frosted bead earring in the hub-cap in Gene's old room.

I'm not? Gene said, surprised. He thought it over. Then he said, Sure I am. He'd brought sandwiches that day, wrapped in waxed paper, from home. Meat-loaf, he said, tossing Joe one. Patty made 'em.

No thanks, Joe said, tossing it back, the two ears of the waxed paper package unfolding.

It's meatloaf, Gene said. Don't tell me you don't like meatloaf! You used to love it.

Did I? Joe said. He can't remember foods that he had liked or disliked as a boy. He remembers himself always hungry. So maybe I changed, he said. People do that. What about you?

What about me? Gene said and smiled like it was the question he wanted to be asked. A bit of the soft white bread from his sandwich was plastered to his front teeth. He took a pen from his pocket – the pens also said Gene's Gaseteria on them.

A newspaper was spread open across the desk and he leaned over and signed his name, huge, covering the whole of the paper on the diagonal. There, he said. See?

Joe looked at the signature upside down. He didn't know what it meant. That Gene's signature hadn't changed, or that because he was here, writing it, Gene hadn't?

Still, Joe does not quit. He stays for the money he gets every Friday, walks to the ticket shack feeling the folded bills smack inside his pocket. In the shack, under the sleeping bag, he takes up a piece of the floorboard and digs up the Wonder Bread wrapper he's buried there, his roll of bills rubber-banded inside it, and he adds the new bills to the old ones and counts them, then rewinds and reburies the bag which has a musty old smell, like muskets and cannons and maggoty cloth and freed slaves. He counts the money and thinks about how much it will be the next Friday and in his head he skips over the rest of the days of the week.

He stays. Spring comes, it warms up and then it is almost summer and he stays until the letter comes telling him to report for basic training in North Carolina, then he quits.

Quitting? Gene says, like the word doesn't mean anything to him. What for?

Places to go, Joe says. Think I was in here for life?

What places? Gene says. Go when? And then he says Oh. Shit, Joe. When?

Soon, Joe says. I don't remember.

Well, stay at least till you go. You can probably use the money. He clips Joe's shoulder, then digs his hands down in his pockets like all Joe has to do is say "money" and Gene'll give him some.

Joe ducks away from his brother's reach. He doesn't want to be touched. He nods but he knows he will not stay. That day, he unbuttons the blue shirt that says "Joe" in a shadowy, dark blue and walks back to the ticket shack that way, half stripped.

CHAPTER 19

I t is the morning after the day Martin Luther King was shot and died at 7:05 in Memphis, 8:05 here, at five minutes after each hour, someplace. I pictured his fluttering soul, winged, a sound like calm heartbeats, saying goodbye to each time zone. The soul looked like the moist underbellies of fish.

Don't expect Ida in tomorrow, Leon said last night. It was a Thursday, an eleven o'clock night. I watched TV, until he came home, by myself. Heard over and over: A high-powered rifle, his necktie blown off by the blast.

The shooter was said to be driving a late model white Mustang, wearing a black suit, a black tie.

Our TV's hard to watch. Never serviced, to show Leon's disdain of TV. The picture rolls; hands and shoulders, then shoes. The antenna is wrapped in tinfoil.

As if he was being respectful: a black suit, a black tie.

Leon came in and sat down on the couch. Did not take off the overcoat he's still wearing though it is April and warm. The coat's missing one front pocket.

Don't expect Ida tomorrow, he said, sitting hunched towards the TV, his knees spread, his hands dangling between them. Ordinarily he sat in an effete way, one thin leg crossed over the other, his delicate ankles kiss-kissing. This news called for something more manly.

How do you know? I thought though didn't ask. Leon likes to be asked. Had she called him at his college? Long distance? Did they speak often during the week? How long did their conversations go on?

My eyes felt gritty, full of the same sandy static as the TV.

It sounded like a firecracker, one witness said.

It was a tremendous blast, like a bomb, said another.

How could he be dead in Memphis at 7:05 and still be alive here?

How do you know? I asked him. About Ida.

TV light strobed over Leon's face. He smiled, almost invisible, almost a shift of the light.

* * *

Leon is right, Ida's not here. On my way down the stairs I notice the absence of cooked smells, of sounds: the iron slap of stove burners and pans. I am very quiet in case the creak of the steps, the sounds of my bare feet are covering Ida's morning noises, which they would not. Ida takes no pains to be quiet, liking to wake me.

I turn on the TV to see if, overnight, the outcome has changed. They could have been wrong. The wound could have been superficial, the bullet deflected by his black tie. He could be not dead. Waiting for the sound to come on I see time retreating, from 8:05 Eastern to 7:05 Central. I think about California, where he had not died yet.

Sometimes, watching the films they still show of President Kennedy's motorcade that day in Dallas, watching the sun slide from front to back off the patent-leather black cars, the crowds and waving and teeth, the motorcade in slow motion, I think: maybe this time it is not going to happen.

I go looking for Ida. I am not going to school, I don't want to be around white people. I think of my empty school desk, my name called out in class after class: Joellen Stein? Joellen? The answering silence. I have been absent so often, my name called, my seat empty. Still, today it will sound different.

I want to take something to Ida the way she brought us the President Kennedy roses, but nothing grows in our slap-muddy backyard and the fruit, the food, in our refrigerator are things she has bought or made. There are oranges, there are bananas. The particular brown spots on their skins Ida will recognize.

I walk through downtown. There do not seem to be any Negroes around. This seems strange to me, though I cannot remember if it is always this way.

I look at cars: a late model white Mustang. It could be anywhere.

I have not thought how I will find Ida's house. I was there only once, the sick day I followed her home.

I cross the tracks. Bottles have been broken here; green and brown glass glints between pieces of gravel, like lichen and moss. The air has a gunpowder smell, or is this the usual smell of the tracks? There have been riots, I know, in close cities. In this town, white boys live in houses hung with Confederate flags and NRA decals.

And then I am where Ida lives and it is like I have stepped into a different time or day: Easter. Everyone who lives here is out on the streets, the streets are packed and vivid with the colors of clothes and with brown and black and yellowy faces. Mothers are out, and babies in carriages and small clusters of men in white shirts and no jackets, their hands in their pockets pulling the pants fabric taut at their butts. Small children scuff their shoes into the seams of the curb and bigger ones kick at the smaller ones' shoes to get them to quit, but there is no squawking or scolding, no noise, and I think maybe I have gone deaf, except then a plane flies overhead: I hear that.

The people wander around, eyes down, as though they have lost and are looking for things – wheelbarrows, doll carriage wheels, buttons, rusted skate keys. Their milling is purposeful, they are all part of some united action, some custom of grief or loss I have not witnessed before. I stay where I am: separate, white, invisible.

CHAPTER 20

....

Ithe last day, Joe's last day here – Until I come back,
he says, or Joellen makes him say that. He does not think "return" or its possible
inverse. "Going" is all that he thinks.

You don't have to, Joellen says. I'll hide you, and she lies crosswise over his
body. He doesn't move, his arms pinned, though he could get free without effort,
breathe and his breath would lift her. He doesn't speak.

They talked about it only once before, a few weeks back when Joe told her
he was going.

What? Joellen said. What do you mean?

What I said. United States Army.

No, she said.

He was silent.

She said, You can't. You don't have to.

I have to. I'm drafted.

The word distanced her: Drafted. Something she was not; something that
belonged only to Joe, the way Mass had belonged to Charlieo. She shivered,
though it was the end of May. Joe ran his hands down her bare arms: habit.

We could leave, go up to Canada, Joellen said. She pictured blocks of
three- and four-family houses, boxy porches protruding from their upper floors.
The houses were dark brick or dull painted colors, a dirty gray, a dark green. She
could not picture sun there, in Canada.

People do it. We could get jobs, she said. She saw them eating cereal for
breakfast before leaving for work. Not enough heat, they'd be wearing their jackets. They'd get to know the names of their neighbors. She pictured these things
though, even while she was seeing them, thinking "we," "us," Joe was not really
there, in the picture.

Joe had pushed himself up on one arm, shook a cigarette out of the pack he
kept on the fruit crate along with a box of Strike Anywhere matches. He scraped
his thumbnail over the flint.

I'm not goin' to Canada, Joe said when he'd got the cigarette lit, inhaled, frowned down at the lit tip. He held the smoke in his lungs a long time.

Joellen nodded, watching the cigarette also. She said, How come?

Well, for one thing, I'm not Canadian. And I just told you. I'm drafted.

So what is that, some kind of Biblical commandment? Thou shalt not go to Canada? She was vaguely pleased by the sound of that, its air of learnedness. For a second, distracted, she was not sure what Joe was talking about when he answered.

Look. This isn't something you get to weigh the pros and cons of. You don't get to choose. You . . .

People do. People decide to go to Canada. It's a decision.

Not me. I don't see it like that. You get called, you go. It's like being born, he said, and . . . He inhaled. Families, that's another one. He thought of his own family: Gene, LuAnne, Rusty. If he could choose he'd want no family. He'd pick no one.

You want to go, don't you? Joellen asks now. You don't mind it, do you?

Joe thinks about this though he knows the answer. He does want to go, though it is not Vietnam or anyplace in particular he wants to go to.

I don't mind seeing things, he says, but this is not right exactly: never having been anywhere there's no specific thing he's got a craving to see. What he wants isn't leaving *to* something, but leaving, plain. He wants it to be time to go and then to be gone. He can't even picture where it is he's going. When he thinks basic training, the screen behind his eyes is silvered and blank.

There is a rolling panic inside Joellen made up, in small parts, of concern for Joe's safety and of loneliness but mostly of knowing that this life will change. It will not be the same. He will see things she will not. When she pictures him during the day he will not be looking at the splintering ticket shack walls or at the tipped tiers of donuts at the bakery or at the goose down that hangs like a static blizzard in the air around the fake lake where Joe had taken her, once, twice, trying to teach her to drive.

Theirs is a life of continual notice. How will they survive the absence of that?

If it was me, Joellen says, I wouldn't want to go. You can bet on that.

Joe looks up at the ticket shack beams, at the wall behind him. When I get back we won't have to be here anymore, he says. I been savin' up. Buy us a trailer.

Us, he says. Joellen wants him to say it again. She closes her eyes. Joe's eyes are near black; his skin dark, the color of the shells of walnuts; his hair dark and dry and stiff, like horse hair. Still, she can't call up a composite picture though he is beside her, and panic rolls in her again and she opens her eyes, touches his arm with one finger. She thinks of Isabel's hands and the words she has always used to describe them: square and flat and squared off. She thinks of the size and heft of her mother's legs; the scar on Isabel's knee, a pale pigmentless hassock, the setting for one blue-gray flagstone chip, but these memories are no longer tactile; whatever she does, she keeps losing parts.

I'm afraid you'll forget what I look like, Joellen said the day Joe told her he was going.

Joe touched the back of her head, the hair bunched and knotted. He buried his fingers in the knots. You'll give me a picture, he said.

You too, she said and nodded so Joe's hand came with her.

The photos are in her jeans pocket now, sheathed in a double thickness of tinfoil. There are four, from the booth in the back at Greschler's where they sold droopy parakeets and turtles whose shells were the same wet sliminess as jars of green olives. The photo machine was backed up against a window, the window unwashed; a brownish, grimed light came through the glass the same tint as the photographs.

Joellen almost did not take these photos. The booth did not seem private enough, the curtain did not come all the way down to the floor or close completely either: the metal hooks stuck at one end of the runner.

I'll ask someone to take a real photo, she said to herself, but it seemed a physical, almost a sexual request. And who could she ask? Did Leon even have a camera? There were no photos of the usual kind in their house: Joellen at various heights in hang-hemmed dresses standing in front of the house, on the boardwalk, in the backyard. There was no wedding photo of her parents, though there were some childhood pictures each of them had brought, separately, to the marriage: small black-and-whites with crimped edges; the aqueous-tinged color snapshots of the fifties.

It's not pornography, Joellen! she told herself, and this was the thing that pro-
pelled her into the booth.

Inside, there was a rank smell like old hair dressings and musk that made her
think "pornography" again. There were circles of gum and rusty scratches in the
walls. Joellen fed in her quarter and smiled or looked with what felt like longing
into the light. For the last shot she lifted her shirt – maybe it was "pornography"
that made her think of it – then sat back on the seat.

Her skin looked shiny in every picture as though it was wet, and streaky, some
fault of the chemicals. The final shot, where she had lifted her shirt, showed just
the tops of her breasts, her T-shirt a striped bandage riding above as though, at the
last minute, she'd changed her mind.

Hey, I almost forgot, I have something for you, Joellen says now, hoping her
casualness at least sounds authentic. She hands Joe the foil-wrapped package. She
has cut the four-photo strip in half, two and two, to make loss less likely.

Hey! Joe says. Look at that! The pictures seem odd to him, of someone not
familiar. Their color is odd. He rubs his thumb over the pictures as though he is
rubbing off excess layers of color.

Don't lose them, Joellen says.

He says No, though these photos do not make him think of Joellen.

Where's mine? she says.

Joe says, which one do you want? and holds the strips out to her.

No, she says. Mine. The one you're supposed to give me.

He doesn't answer. They're sitting knee to knee on the sleeping bag.

See? Joellen says, her voice high-pitched. She knew he would not bring her a
photo. When he'd said that he would she was surprised, it seemed outside the
scope of his ability. But she had counted on yes.

She is about to cry. She holds still so she will not shake the tears loose.

What? Joe says, looking at her, moving forward to look closer. You're not
cold? he says, because she has not ever cried for any other reason. He chafes her
bare arms. The skin is soft, hairless and frictionless, and for the first time he thinks,
I may not ever touch this again, and a bubble of pure loss rises up through his
chest so he looks at the crate near the sleeping bag which is where his bottles of
booze always are, but he's out. He has not thought of losing Joellen, not in the

160

way he is thinking it now: a true loss, like blindness or the loss of the sense of touch. Me. Gone away, is what he's thought, but until now, he never saw Joellen as absent. He opens the fingers still wrapped around her arm and pushes away from her.

He imagined their last day different. He imagined sex and release, over and over – Are we going for some kind of record? he thought Joellen might ask and he was ready to laugh but not answer, thinking there were maybe just so many fucks allotted to them and he'd use up the ones they had left. Now he's afraid to touch her. His hand hovers, not touching, so that she has to thrust herself up, groaning, arching her shoulders, her nipples bunching like steel shavings drawn to a magnet.

He does not want, even, to come; wants to enter and lay still inside her, just lay there, and say to himself: This is what it feels like.

He thinks of telling her this; he turns to speak into her ear. It is a clean pink, a delicate curve he hasn't noticed before because he has not looked or looked closely enough or he has looked and has not remembered. He wants to memorize her and he knows he will fail, is already failing and that one day, months from now, a part of her he's forgotten will float through his head, suddenly clear, and that it will make him buoyant with longing. He rolls away from her, sits up, begins putting his shirt on. Let's go for a walk. Let's get out of here, he says.

Joellen lies still, watching Joe's skin disappear inside his shirt: his collarbone, the shallow divot where his ribs meet and fuse. Today is not what she thought it would be either.

Joe waits while Joellen sits on the sleeping bag tying the laces of her sneakers. He is already packed, a pile of things that he washed in the laundermat and folded and packed into a suitcase he got from Goodwill.

The Wonder Bread bag with the money he saved he put in a shoebox and wrapped tight in brown paper and tape and wrote on the top in black pencil: FOR JO, and her address, and brought it to the gas station.

You shouldn't of, Gene said, winking.

Yeah, well, I didn't. Lock this up? Anything goes wrong, see that it gets where it's meant to. He said this fast so Gene wouldn't stop him at "wrong." Joe looked down at the box. FOR JO, he saw and thought: Who? He did not call her Jo. He picked up a pen from Gene's desk and next to the black pencilled JO he wrote a blue ELLEN.

It is almost summer, the light through the ticket shack window clear and yellow, and waiting for Joellen Joe closes his eyes, feeling the loss of the moments he's still living through. When he opens them again, Joellen is straightening the blanket, bent over, the fabric of her pants pulling across her butt.

Stop! he says. It has already started, his grief at the discrete parts of her body. Stop! What're you doing?

Straightening the . . .

I'll do it, he says. Come on. I'll do it later.

It is warm out, hot in the sun. They walk to the marina. The water is fractious, small waves like scallops of curled hair white against the blue. There's a low tide smell. They walk close, they sometimes bump into each other, Joellen wants to touch him, but Joe's not one for public displays of affection.

One of the fishing boat owners is hawking gutted fish at the foot of the pier – baby sand sharks, Joe can tell by the white, almost pearlescent meat, though the heads are gone with the tiny, incisor-like teeth.

Sea trout, the man calls, barking to passing bennies in white pants and gaudy T-shirts, their faces vivid with the season's first sunburn. Joellen slows, caught by the white of the fish, the viscous red and pink buckets of chum. Joe keeps walking.

Sea trout? she says, catching up. I never even heard of sea trout – but one level down she thinks of Joe's hand.

Joe stops suddenly, where the marina ends, turns into a park: a strip of haggard grass, public tennis courts, swings rusted out by salt air. Strung across the highway, like an awning hung the wrong way for shade, there's a banner: Fireman's Fair. Joellen sees where Joe's looking. She says, Let's go there.

They walk down the Midway, past booths where balloons pop, where coins get tossed into boxes, past feathers and fishbowls and the odd, coughed language of barkers. The air smells like cooked sugar.

Joe stops near a booth where pyramids of Indian clubs are set up. No one is pitching at them, but the tuneful creaking sound the clubs make collapsing is clear in his memory. Joe does not know if this is the same booth Rusty stopped at all those years ago; if the barker, sullen and silent, his hands folded under the flap of his dirty canvas apron, is the same. Things have happened. Rusty's been gone seven years.

Joe steps forward, puts a dollar down on the counter. For three, he says.

Two bucks, the barker says.

No. Three for a dollar, Joe says.

Two bucks! the man says. Can you read? The sign's only the size of a cow!

Joe looks up; there is a sign, black on yellow: 1 throw $1, 3 for $2.

Expensive, he says, but he takes a second dollar out of his pocket.

The man puts down three balls, the same balls Joe remembers. They are wrapped in white tape, the tape dingy with blurred fingerprints. Joe picks one up, strokes his thumb over the tape, then he begins to rotate the ball slowly in his hand.

Will we have a winner, a winner, ladies and gentlemen, the barker calls, clapping his hands, startling Joellen. Take a Chance, Find Romance, he calls, his voice loud and slow. Then he leans in towards Joe. Let's go, he says under his breath. This ain't the fuckin' Olympics.

Joe doesn't pay any attention. He rotates the ball slowly, taking his time until the ball is where he wants it, held, delicately, by three fingers. He sets. He feels the weight of the ball – weighted, he knows, with lead slivers. Then he pitches, the ball leaves his fingers, he feels the same pop that was in his father's shoulder, the involuntary "hunh" from his chest, the follow-through: elbow, wrist, fingers tapering out.

The musical sound, the clubs falling.

Joellen hoots, the pitch of her voice matched to the note of the tumbling clubs.

A winner, a winner, the man calls, looking past Joe and Joellen at nothing. One down, two to go, the man calls. Two to go, Don't be Slow.

Joe picks up the second ball, rotates it in his hand, his thumb tapping gently, almost a caress. Joellen is watching his fingers; can feel the soft scrape of his thumb as though the curved edge of the ball is her hip, her breast. She keeps watching his thumb.

The man beats his knuckles on the counter, a drum roll.

Again, Joellen says, her voice soft: she is wishing.

Joe does it again. He knows before the ball's gone from his fingers that it will hit, it does hit, he hears, again, the broken crockery sound of the clubs falling.

A winner, a winner, the man calls again. He pounds on the counter, the last ball jumps, Joe has to lean in to block it from rolling.

Joellen is smiling, leapt when Joe brought the second pile of pins down. She looks behind her, wants other people to be watching. If there were other people they'd be thinking: that boy who just hit all those clubs? Hers.

A few people do stop, look at the back of Joe's head, keeping a distance as though there is something noteworthy or contagious about him.

Win me something, Joellen says, low, close. She points up.

Joe looks at the big-winner prizes clipped to the struts of the booth: green alligators with white plush teeth and goggling eyes, yellow monkeys, pink panthers. Their fur is long, matted, like shag carpets. The booth smells of packed sawdust and Joe thinks of LuAnne's house and that his father used to live there and while he is thinking this he knows, in a solid immutable way, that he will never see Rusty again.

Let's go, he says. Let's get out of here. He can't look at Joellen. If he looks now, she will disappear too.

You can do it, Joellen says, her voice coaxing; she thinks he has lost his nerve. One More, You're in the Door, she says, smiling.

Let's go, Joe says, but then it is he who doesn't move. He picks up the third ball, holds it on his palm, turns it, scraping his thumbnail over the tape. He picks at the tape until it works loose, then he begins to unwind. The inside of the tape is clean, an almost dazzling white, the clean white of the flesh of the sea trout. He unwinds and unwinds. The tape makes an unzipping sound. As he does this, it seems less significant to him, to know that the balls were secretly weighted. It had seemed like something, that day Rusty was pitching. Now it seems less, something maybe everybody knows.

Hey! the barker says. What the fuck do you think you're doin'?

Joe steps back, still unwinding. A sliver of metal, fine as the lead tip of a mechanical pencil, is stuck to the inside of the tape. Joe loosens it and lets it drop out on the counter.

He unwinds again until he comes to another small piece, then another, and he pushes them off the tape and into his hand like they are fruit seeds.

Hey! the barker says. Give it!

Joe holds the lead pieces out on his hand. Lead, he says to the three or four other people he has drawn to the booth. It's under the tape in all them balls. You're not meant to win this, he says, and as though this is a demonstration he picks up the ball and hurls it towards the back of the booth. It caroms around, streaming tape like a kite tail. It hits the pink panther which spins, showing its left shoulder, showing its right.

Lead, he says. Remember that.

Get the fuck offa here, the barker says, crawling across the counter after Joe. What the hell're you doin', you're effacing private property! I'll call the fuckin' cops, so help me, see if I won't! He yells this, kneeling on the counter.

Joe's walking away, his head down, eyes on the soft Midway dust powdering his shoes, moving in the same direction Rusty's shoes had that day he never meant to come back.

Joe's leaving tomorrow: a train into New York then another one to North Carolina. He's never been to New York, most of the people who live in their town have not, though it's less than three hours due north. When they left the cluster of shore towns, strung in a line parallel to the ocean, people tended to go further south. Joellen, who knows which train Joe's taking, is meeting him at 6:10, at the station. Gene knows too, resets his alarm for 5:30 so he can get to the station himself; when it goes off, Patty will draw her knee up and kick him and say, Thanks. Just what I needed. Less sleep.

But Joe doesn't wait. (Five fuckin' thirty, Gene will recite in his head, jiggling the change in his pockets. I haul my ass out of bed at five fuckin' thirty, he's ditched. Son-of-a-bitch is already gone.) In his head he's talking to Patty though he knows, even while he hears her voice answering his, that he won't tell her.

Joe can't wait. His need to be done with the limbo of waiting is too strong, he takes the last train out that night.

I'll write to Joellen, maybe call her, he tells himself on the train. It's so dark, it's hard to tell if the train's really moving. The windows are blank and opaque. All he can see is himself, looking out.

CHAPTER 21

....

When I was five we moved here from Queens, in New York City, where Leon had lived all his life until then. I do not remember it so well. It was a small apartment house, the rooms had a fustiness as though smells – cooked cabbage and vaseline and the inverted airlessness of steam heat – had been stuck down under layers of pinkish-brown paint. I did not love that house, a place where you had to keep lights on even in daylight. It didn't get sun. You could look out the window and see sun and blue sky framed by the sharp sides of other brick buildings, like a painting.

Still, I didn't like the idea of moving. I hadn't seen our new house, the house Isabel had picked out, before we moved into it: I think I was not sure there was such a house. If we packed everything and moved out and there was no house, where would we go? Maybe Isabel and Leon had given their money away and been tricked. I did not believe in their practical sides.

The day we moved I walked through the apartment, full of brown cardboard wardrobes and barrels and boxes, their dingy brown clashing with the calamine lotion color of the walls, and I marked off the end of my relationship with the place.

This is the last time I'll brush my teeth in this bathroom, I thought, tapping the wet bristles of my toothbrush.

This is the last time I'll put a glass in this sink.

This is the last time I'll pee here, hear the sound of this toilet flushing. It seemed mysterious to me, that this apartment would continue to have a life; that other people would do in it the things I'd done, without me as witness.

I said my goodbyes that last day; walked through the rooms and touched things so that my fingerprints would remain and made marks, also, inside a hall closet, on the underside of a door, first with a pencil then ink. I thought of some other child finding those marks and thinking about me, me specifically, though I had made marks only. I did not write my name.

I remember these things. And that I knew to pay attention.

As I meant to pay attention to Joe, our last morning, hour, minute. I wanted to keep the last thing he said to me the way other girls kept gifts – a gold necklace, a dried rose – given to them by other boys. Words were what I wanted, but then Joe left early and cheated me out of my portion.

I tried to remember what he said without my knowing it would be the last thing. I wanted, Be good, I'll be thinking of you, Don't go anyplace, Wait.

Not so much. I did not expect Love, Marriage, Forever, but something that linked us: Take care of yourself (for me); be good (as I will also be); don't go anywhere (without me); wait.

But I did not know, I could not remember. Let's go, he'd said, we were still in the ticket shack then, the last time: I had not known this either. I thought we would meet there the next morning. We would not fuck, but we would touch. I would taste the inside of his mouth, his skin.

Three for a dollar, he said, but this did not count, he hadn't said it to me.

Let's go, he said. Let's get out of here and then later, I gotta go.

Go was the last thing I heard, I think it was go, but maybe not. I hadn't started to flag the last things: the last time in the ticket shack, on the platform, the last sound of a train while Joe was still here, the last kiss, as I had not with Isabel. I hadn't known to pay attention, to carve marks, to make them say my name.

CHAPTER 22

....

"Please do not stand until the train has come to a full and complete halt in the station," the conductor's voice says over the loudspeaker, but Joe looks up and he's the only one sitting so he gets up too and stands in the aisle. The car reeks of cigarette smoke and of the lavatory at one end and of used, air conditioned air.

The dense noise of the air brakes disperses; when the doors open there is the dense noise of passengers moving and the gritty feel and smell of the track. Joe makes his way to the huge domed center of the station. The noise here is overpowering, a clatter, like thousands of horses across cobblestones, like thousands of dishes being slammed on top of each other in a tiled room. It is one immense burr of sound, a motorized din that does not rise or dip or alter. Joe stops at the gate to the track and just listens, trying to accustom himself to the noise, but he's picked a bad place to stand; people bang into his shoulder, his shoulder and arm swing out and then back like a saloon door, so he moves on, follows the signs to Track 48 where his train to North Carolina will leave from.

Track 48's down a short flight of stairs in a corner of the station. The ceiling is lower, the noise less rampant, but there's less air, Joe thinks. The air is visibly green and has the sweaty odor of canned soup. At Track 48 the gate's closed, but there's a line of men and boys standing, squatting, sitting on suitcases, that snakes out from the gate, curls in and around on itself and Joe stops, looking at its pattern.

Whoa, a guy says, walking into Joe's back. Dangerous place to hold up!

I guess, Joe says. Whole place seems like a dangerous place. He looks up at the ceiling. He thinks of the weight of the people on the level above them.

On or off, the guy behind Joe says.

'Scuse me?

The line. You're holdin' things up.

Joe moves, closing the gap between himself and the rest of the line. Must be one big train, Joe says to the guy.

Gonna be one *crowded* train, the guy says. He's tall and blond; his hair, when his head moves, picks up the pinkish tones of the overhead lights.

Time's it leave? Joe asks him.

Coupla three and a half hours. But I don't think they're too worried about leaving on time. Where all are we gonna go, know what I mean?

Look, Joe says. I'm hungry. I never got any breakfast. What about if you hold my place here, I'll go off for a while, then I'll do the same for you.

The guy grins, like he knew he'd run into friendly people even though back home, before he left, they all told him bad tales of New York. Good, he says, still grinning, chugging his suitcase forward with his foot. When Joe turns to hunt for him – tall blond guy, Joe tells himself – the gap's closed. The whole line seems to be tall and blond.

Joe makes his way back in the direction he came, his eyes picking out those men and boys likely to be heading for Track 48. He's adjusted to the noise and the rush or thinks he is until he gets upstairs again, where the combination of sound and movement is so strong it takes his breath.

Joe makes his way over to a row of phone booths, waits for one to empty and when he gets one, is surprised at how much insulation the closed booth gives against the sound and the rush beyond it.

He thinks about calling Joellen; hoists himself up to dig change out of his pocket, then sits turning the coins on his palm. He waits but does not make the call. Someone stands outside his booth so Joe picks up the receiver and drops a coin in the slot but he still doesn't dial any number.

There are names and words scratched into the walls of the booth: For a good time call . . .

It's what I need, Joe thinks, a good time, though he doesn't mean the good time of the telephone number, more like a stretch of time that is good, even and peaceful, alone in good weather with all his needs taken care of. And while he is thinking "even" in the sense of flowing and smooth, he begins to see the crowd outside the booth as flowing. He sits and watches. There is something seductive about it, a single overall rhythm.

You could get lost in a crowd like that, Joe thinks and then he stands and moves out into it.

You could pick your feet up or stop dead and it wouldn't make any difference. They'd carry you. You'd be carried, he thinks, which in one great rush that makes a compass of the station, circling the information booth, hurtling up a ramp and outside onto the sidewalk, he is.

PART III

CHAPTER 23

....

Vietnam is so green. I can tell this even on black-and-white television, a drenched vivid green saturating the landscape. I watch the six o'clock news every night. Sometimes Leon watches with me. He has things to say about the war or some demonstration against it, but that's not why I watch. I don't look at the newsmen's faces, at the people being interviewed. I look behind them, at the trees, their leaves like long strips scissored from paper, flat in the blow from a helicopter. I look at the vegetation, the huts the people live in. I want to see the things Joe's seeing.

He sent me a picture, one of those instant Polaroids that was already fading to its own queer green by the time it got to me, but I could still tell the true greenness – the trees in the background dense and opaque. There was sun and no shadow. Joe was standing alone. He was wearing green fatigues and a webbed belt and a canteen, green and green. Pfc. Joseph Handy, he'd written on the back, the letters wavering as though he had written them on some unsteady surface: green water.

When I went out, I hunted greens the way I used to hunt words, my eyes hopping and settling on car paint, on lawns, on sweaters, on our shaggy polite-looking trees, their leaves regular, heart or hand shaped. I wanted my eyes full of green, to wake to a watery green light, to breathe the green, almost underwater air Joe was breathing, a satiety of green, but my greens were not his. They smelled like grass clippings, like turf, like the water from hoses, domestic and tame.

CHAPTER 24

....

Joe had drawn me a map to his house: his mother's. He didn't want to since he did not mean me ever to go there, but distances are hard for me to imagine.

I don't want to go there, I said. I want to know where it is.

I had never heard of his street though this is not a large town, bounded by the marina, the ocean, the Last Gas, the next town in a string of similar shore towns. Some of the towns are richer, some shabbier, some have only white people as residents, some fill up with white people in summer so the rest of the time the black people spread out on both sides of Main Street. Some towns are like small, segregated African countries.

My town has layers, like an ecosphere or a terrarium. There is the sea life: fish and mussels, clams, starfish.

There is the animal-vegetable stratum: Jersey corn, Jersey peaches and tomatoes. There are the horse farms, some that bred Eohippus-like trotters and pacers, some the fleet, fully evolved thoroughbreds I had loved.

And there are layers of people, starting with the slovenly white boys and their underage wives who live on the shabbiest blocks in from the beach. They are jobless, as though the Great Depression touched down where they live and then never lifted, or the Civil War either: there are Confederate flags tacked to their front doors, hung over peeling porches, pinched under top story windows like pissed-on sheets. Where did they come from, these lazy and vicious and drunk boys who draped themselves over their porches, pants riding down below the cracks of their asses? Who bred them? There did not seem to be older versions of them, though once in a while you went to high school with a girl who took up with or married one. They are the mutant and rumbling underbelly of the town.

There are the men, one layer up, who stand across from Gene's gas station, silent and shifting. Perhaps they are the fathers of the mutant boys, though the boys seemed evil, the men, boozy and benign.

There is the Negro part of town – strips of blocks that are shorter and more densely built up than the blocks anyplace else. The houses look stuck together from a distance, made of found objects: glass, pieces of wood, hubcaps. They look abandoned, but are not. The life there is hidden. Shadows twitch behind shades; voices and laughter spill from the cracks in the walls. Behind curtains, up driveways, through back doors, inside garages, there are businesses. You can smell the sulfurous smells of a beauty shop passing by; you can find men who do All Appliance repairs, dressmakers whose stitches are small and straight and thin as the legs of an insect. No signs. You just have to know where they are.

This part of town is bordered by the train tracks and, on the far side, by a huge vacant lot. The earth is reddish and poor, a few scanty shells scattered across it as though once, in a previous geological era, it had been ocean. There are a few shacks, like border patrol huts, scattered across this lot. Lone white men live there, mean as wild dogs, stubblefaced, drunk, shunning and shunned by the whites and the blacks they lived in between.

Starting down at the shore are the rich people's houses. These houses are huge and old or they are new, with lookouts and large plate glass windows that glaze orange and pink in the sunset. There is more sun on these blocks and high, old trees that act like umbrellas so there is less rain.

Two blocks in from the shore is the fake lake. The houses here are also expensive but polyglot: red Colonials, pink adobes, yellow stuccoes with shutters. You expected to see women in long gray-stuff dresses and men in serapes and yellow-haired children in red clogs greeting each other like extras in various ongoing movies.

The blocks spoking back from the beach, stopping at downtown, picking up again, running into the highway, this is where most people live: the white people who worked, ate dinner, had their hair done. I live on one of these blocks, Charlieo lives on another, but not Joe. When he said the name of his street I said, What? and then I made him draw the map. I watched his hands move as he drew, fluid and swift, his street was a circle around a circle.

Is that a park? I said, pointing.

Joe kept drawing. Meant to be one of those man-made lakes they like around here. Changed their minds, though. Figured nobody with money was gonna live this far from the beach. They left it, it just overgrew – and his hands worked, feathering up and out from the paper, drawing trees.

I came across Joe's map a few weeks after he'd gone: picked up my notebook one morning and the map slid out. I had not seen Joe's handwriting since the single photo he sent me, my address all that was written, and PFC Joseph Handy at the top of the envelope that I licked, in case he had also kissed or licked it, and I had not seen his hands in longer than that. I saw them then, long-fingered and agile, holding a pencil, stroking then moving the shift knob of his car, and there was suddenly not enough air in the room. I had to sit down.

Ida looked at the clock. What *now*, she said, as though she had private things to do that she wanted me gone for. You better be gettin' yourself to school!

I went out to the porch. It had rained and was still damp: wet stains on the sidewalk, on halves of tree trunks, halves of buildings. It was grim, like pictures of Eastern bloc countries in textbooks, and it left a loneliness as heavy as a damp coat.

I missed Joe – I do not even like to say that: I miss him. The word is too ordinary and paltry; a sock could be missing or a hairband. Missing is absence and this Joe feeling was not absence, it was something added, like the pain of a toothache. He was a click or a smell in the air, just ahead of me, just behind. I saw his car everywhere, not parked behind Gene's Gaseteria, where I knew he had left it – I saw it driving. I saw his leg, the way his jeans flapped when he walked, the heel of his shoe passing through some doorway. I once heard him ordering coffee and crullers, his voice so distinct I followed it into the bakery. The rope of bells on the door rang. The bakery women in dresses white as flour looked up.

I got up off the porch, headed for school, but I did not go. There was no click or smell in that air; no residue from time spent because Joe had not spent time there. He was not at school as he was not at my house, inside the hard thumping sounds of Ida ironing, under Leon's comments about the news.

I went to the ticket shack. Around back, so no one would see me. I could not go in: no key. I pressed against the splintering wood. My breasts and my hipbones, the tops of my thighs, my left cheek, my right cheek pressed in. Morning gave way to afternoon, my body numbed from its farthest points inward: hands, feet disappeared like the horizon in fog and I stood on until I finally said to myself: this is a wall Joellen. This is a wall.

I did not go to school the next day either, though it was sunny. I went to the station, the point where Joe's map began, and headed on from there. I followed the map. It took me a long time to find Joe's house: I am not good at maps. I am not good at a certain kind of pretense or imagination: the transposition of small to large, flat to fleshed-out. I do not get mileage keys: one inch = 100 miles, or the cartographed outlines of states. Inside a car, I cannot picture the car fitting into a parking space. I cannot look at flat blueprints and see rooms. But I knew, from Joe's drawing, that I was there when I got there. There was the circle of dirt, maybe two-thirds of a mile around, a little smaller than the fake lake, the ground humped like the plastic islands sold for turtle tanks, the trees thin and almost bare; the few leaves they had seemed grudging. A road ringed the treed place, then a horseshoe of houses: spare, drafty, miniature, as though they were built only for show, not to be lived in.

Joe had not written his house number, I looked that up in the phone book: Handy, G., it said and underneath that, Handy, R., the letters of his father's name as clear and upright as any other citizen's.

Joe's house was the same as the others except that the single front concrete step was cracked. I wondered how long the crack had been there, if it had happened when Joe was a boy. He had been a boy in this house! Walked around with a fake guitar, wearing a Davy Crockett cap, sat on the stoop that had or had not been cracked then. I could see him plain as in a home movie, the colors bleached, the sprockets at the sides of the film. This was where Joe had been a child.

I wanted to leave, but I did not: I stood on the island of trees watching the sun blind the front windows of Joe's house, staring too long so that when I looked away, I was also blinded and thought of the day of the eclipse I'd watched with Isabel.

I had never seen Joe's mother. My picture of her was tough, her skin chicken-stringy, her hair a lacquered helmet, her nails long, polished, dirty, the image that matched the distaste on Joe's face when he said "LuAnne," or "my mother." But I had never seen her, there was no proof, she could as easily not look that way. I softened the picture. Her hair lengthened down to her shoulders, a soft brown, not metallic. Her nails became clean. I could introduce myself, she could ask me in, we could drink coffee. I wanted that, though Joe would not want me to want it.

Hey! a voice yelled: some mother after a child. There were children here, an astonishing number in a place where the houses were so small. Kids spilled out onto the street as though the houses spit them. Sometimes there were mothers chasing after.

Hey! the mother yelled. It had begun to get dark. I did not look, kept my eyes away from the voice, a two-note shrill, not clearly human.

Hey you! You!

A woman was stalking across the crescent-shaped street waving her hands.

You, I'm talking to. What are you the friggin' FBI? What are you, spying?

LuAnne, of course it was LuAnne, her face red and bunched, her teeth bad, lint in her hairdo.

Hey! she screeched.

I looked once, quick, behind me, then started backing away. She followed.

Don't you let me catch you hanging around here again, you hear me? I'll fuckin' shoot you, I'll do it. What do you want?

I could have stopped her with one word. Joe, I could have said, my mouth wet with it, Joe, but I couldn't say his name to her. I looked behind me. I ran.

I wrote to Charlieo.

I wrote because I wanted to write to Joe and could not. Joe might write back. His letters, I knew, would be unsatisfactory: C's or D's. They would be short; they would not say "with love," they might not even start Dear, Dear Joellen – one word I could count on and invest with tenderness. Any ardor there was (I did not think there would be any) would have faded by the time the letter reached me, as the ink on the back of the photo he sent me had faded, as the photo itself had. Something was not better than nothing. When the mail came I held my breath, hoping there would be no letter from Joe.

I was going through some of our coins, is how I began my letter to Charlieo. It was not true but I knew it would make him nostalgic, make him go up to his room and open his top bureau drawer where he kept his coins and old golf pencils, like yellow and red and green miniature logs, and old shoelaces he'd been fond of. I could hear the delicate tink of the pencils rolling against one another in the drawer.

Days later – time for my letter to reach him, for him to think about it, to answer – I got a letter back from Charlieo. It was lying in the hall, on the sideboard that had been Isabel's mother's. The phone was there and it was where Ida put the mail.

Charlieo's letter was blue, an envelope, a matching blue sheet, like a coat and a dress. It stood out from the uniform white of flyers and bills.

We had not seen each other, except in school, in passing, for six months, since the day he stormed off my porch. Our letters were third parties, mediating between us. My letter proposed, his acceded to, a meeting.

We are to meet at the beach, two blocks from the miniature golf course. I get there first. The wind is stiff, my hair whips my cheek: small stings. Someone comes towards me – Charlieo, I think, but it's not: it's a tall and solid blond man.

It is Charlieo. In my head he is fourteen, thirteen, a boy.

You can close your mouth now. What, did I forget to get dressed?

But it was his growth, a physical testament to the passage of time. The next time I saw Joe, what would he look like?

Are there any pictures of us? I say.

Pictures?

Photographs. Photos.

There are, or at least there were. I remember the two of us side-by-side in his backyard, the waistband of my shorts twisted. We stood squinting into the sun.

I say, Remember? Fourth of July? The Marines had landed.

His mouth twists, a half smile. Don't know, he says. We could go take . . . I could look, he says.

I nod. I hear: I am not welcome in his house.

We sit far back on the boardwalk, leaning against a boarded-up store, our backs and butts against wood. We have had a wet spell, all the wood is damp, cold. I didn't know wood was such a good conductor, I say.

He says, Ever heard of lightning?

Lightning? I say. It is cold. Cold conductors is what I was thinking.

That's why houses shouldn't be wood, Charlieo says.

But they are, I say. I think of the ticket shack: all that time Joe and I had not been safe.

Charlieo shrugs. He means, my house is not wood; your house is not. He says, The wood ones are the ones that get hit.

I see you still know everything, I say.

That's right, he says. I still do.

We both nod, as if there is music going in the background, but there is the roar of the ocean, distant and miniature.

Been a long time, I say.

He looks at his watch, a chronograph: I have never seen it before. Someone had bought it and wrapped it and given it to him as a gift. Joe was seeing things too that I was not seeing.

Six months, five days and . . .

A long time, I say. Did they ever find Dazee O'Cazee?

Nope, Charlieo says, they never did. Although there may be a few small, underdeveloped countries they still haven't checked.

We try to pick subjects that are neutral, but in fact, there are no such subjects. Association, history, event bloom out of everything we mention. We had been children together.

Did you walk here or drive? I ask him.

Drive. New car. Well . . . my father's, he says.

Really?

Yeah . . . It's . . . it's nice. It's . . . He speaks in a hesitating, stuttering way, as though some words are too personal to be said between us. I lose the thread of his sentences, wondering what the lapsed word could have been.

What? I say.

He raps his knuckles against the boardwalk, a tattoo.

Look, I say. I'm sorry. That's why I wanted you to meet me.

He says, I guess I knew that, but . . .

His mother. I say, I know. I say, It's been a really long time.

Well, Charlieo says. It wasn't all bad. We haven't had lemon meringue pie once!

I laugh. You know, you've known me longer than anyone else, except Leon and Ida, I say and, the words hardly spoken, the pleasure of them recedes: present, absent, like the ocean. He has known me longer than anyone, longer than Joe. Joe and I had not known each other as children. Our history was the smallest of legs on a map: an offshoot, a side road, a shoulder.

Joe, I say. Remember Joe? He's gone. The Army.

Charlieo flushes, the red and the gold of his hair mutually intensifying: the red is redder, the gold more gold. That so? he says.

I say, I feel like I've known him my whole life.

I say, It's so hard. You know? but Charlieo won't look at me.

I really miss him, I say, and then I am angry: that lightweight girly word, diminishing Joe, diminishing me. A public word, a word for the censorious and even miss may be too strong: a spoonful of whiskey in the tea. So, she's running to you to fill up the void? I can hear Mrs. O'Casey say. I should not have written to Charlieo, he should not have answered. It was my fault, I had not completed the sentence: "I want to see Charlieo," I had said. But I had left out: "And have him turn into Joe."

Look, I say. I should go.

Charlieo sits still, hands tucked under his thighs. The ocean comes and goes in the distance. Too bad the miniature golf course isn't open, he says.

I stop. Too bad, I say.

He says, Has your hand-eye coordination improved?

I should think so. I've been working on it.

He nods. He turns his head into the light. There is pebbled stubble above his lip and I think "man" again and my longing for Joe is terrible, physical, like waves. I should not have come.

Come on, Charlieo says. I'll drive you home in the new 'mobile.

He puts his hand out to help me up. I look up at him, tall, his hair shining like metal where it is struck by the sun. Friends? I say.

A beat. Another. Friends preceded by "just," the booby prize offered to those not called for that other lush thing.

Friends, he says. Absolutely.

CHAPTER 25

....

Charlieo's teaching me how to drive. He's a good teacher, patient, though a little conservative. He won't let me go over 30. I am allowed to drive only in straight lines on side streets where there's very little traffic. Charlieo says I have to earn my way up to the big streets, then turns, like they are Boy Scout badges. He borrows his father's car for these lessons, a huge Oldsmobile with a wraparound windshield. The car is a sky blue, the color of painted eggs.

Charlieo believes driving lessons should simulate reality. Well, he says when he pulls up in front of my house. I need to pick up a few things at the drugstore. He often needs things at the drugstore or feels like going for pizza, places that are straight lines away from my house.

Driving's a good thing between us, a thing with no history.

Poor, Charlieo says. That was poor. We're parked across from the drugstore. He gives me critiques. The best I've done so far is semi-bad.

I have this theory, I say. It may be genetic.

What?

Driving. Being a driver.

It's not genetic, he says. On the ceiling of the car there are tiny dark pinpoints that vibrate when you stare at them. There is no gene for driving.

How do you know? Have you read up on brain chemistry and the driver?

Okay, fine. What about before they had cars? What did the driving gene do all those years?

They had horses, I said. Or maybe it was latent. It was – what's that word? Like tonsils.

Vestigial. Tonsils are organs. Driving's not tonsils.

But it was, look at Leon. He'd taken me out once in the Rambler nobody had driven in years, since the day of my mother's accident. I'd asked him at breakfast one Sunday. I didn't expect him to say yes, but the next Sunday there it was, purring in the driveway. He said he'd had somebody over to tune it, jump the battery.

Who? I said. I thought maybe Gene. I thought maybe Joe's brother was standing here, in the driveway, saying things like jump start to Leon.

Who? Leon said.

Came to tune it.

A mechanic, he said. Who do you think?

He had washed the car too, or hosed it down. Water sparkled and dripped off the hood. The car is a dark resinous green, an antique wallpaper color. You don't see cars that color now.

Leon drove us to the parking lot at the supermarket. Empty on Sundays, it had the stillness of an unused pool. He did maybe 25 all the way there. Cars rode up on his back, then went whizzing around him even though there's a solid double yellow line. There was a lot of honking. Leon's knuckles were white. He was breathing small shallow breaths out of his mouth. I rolled down my window. When he looked over to see what I was doing, the car swerved.

ENTRANCE and EXIT are painted side by side on the blacktop at the parking lot in flaking yellow letters. Leon drove in where it said EXIT. He braked hard. We both rocked forward then back.

Rule Number One, he said. Obey all signs. He moved the stick on the wheel to reverse. He threw his arm over the seat and looked out the back window.

Leon, I said. What are you doing?

A thing's not done if it's not done correctly, Leon said.

There's nobody here, Leon. It's Sunday. Nobody cares if you enter at the exit.

I care, he said and put his foot down on the gas. He must have missed reverse, the car shot forward, it went quite a distance, Leon still looking out the back window as though we were going that way. We went right into a dumpster. Old lettuce leaves and tomatoes sprayed over the hood of the car, their colors delicate against the dark background green.

I hadn't told Charlieo this or about the driving lessons I'd had with Joe. They were a long time ago. They were tied more to sex than to motion.

Joe took me to the fake lake. There was hardly any traffic there and a speed limit of 15 – a good training road, Joe called it, though at the westernmost curve of the lake, white down from the snarling geese hung in the air, distracting.

Joe had no patience. His car was a stick shift. I kept forgetting the clutch, popping the gears.

What are you doing? he said once, after I'd done it again. He smacked his hand on the dashboard then stroked the place he had smacked. The car seemed suddenly female to me. I took both my hands off the wheel.

What's wrong with you? Joe yelled, though the car barely drifted.

This isn't a toy. A car's a machine, he said. Potentially dangerous.

I thought of the Rambler, confined in our garage, of the car that had hit my mother. Maybe I don't want to drive. Maybe cars are too dangerous.

We were stopped at the entrance to the fake lake, opposite the beach. There's a flag pole there, the flag as big as the tarps that cover ball fields. There's a monument in the shape of a tombstone, matched to the flag in proportion. The stone is a liverish pink and reflective in the waxy way of new cars. The names of local boys who died in wars are carved into it: World War I, World War II, Korea. The stone is large, there is plenty of empty space. The space seems expectant and hopeful.

Do you want to do this Joellen? Is this something you want to do?

I didn't answer. I kept staring out at the stone. Joe clicked the glove compartment open and shut.

Yes, I said. All right? Quit asking me. When I looked away from the monument, the windshield, the intense overcast sky were tinged a transparent mauve.

Well then, Joe said, clicking the glove compartment. Pay attention.

I put my feet back on the pedals. My feet were bare; it was a surprise each time I touched the brake or the clutch or the gas that they did not feel the way that they looked, like blackboard erasers.

Ready? he said. His hand, three fingers, were on the shift knob. The fingers curved and spread. A blue vein ran up the underside of his arm.

I'm going to show you, he was saying. This is the last time.

I watched his fingers fan over the shift; his thumb stroking up to the swelled tip of the bulb.

Slide over, he told me. You go under me.

He lifted himself over the shift, weight on his arms and thighs. I slid under. The muscles in his ass bunched and released. My front touched him, the backs of his thighs, my hands on his back for balance.

He shifted. His hands stroked. He drove using only one finger.

* * *

It's hot, Charlieo and I are on the beach. We don't go much in summer, no one who lives around here does after the age of ten or eleven. The bennies come back, we scuttle around in dark corners so we don't have to see them. Every Labor Day, we forgot about them again, the way you forget fever or cold, so when Charlieo says, That time again, I say, For?

You know. The Jack Bennies.

I have my shoes off, my feet burrowed into the cool sand. We're sitting way back, in the wedge of shade thrown by the boardwalk.

So, Charlieo says. Decide what you're going to be when they ever let you out of the hallowed halls of high school?

They were making me do another half year, I had missed so much school my Joe year. You sound like Leon, I say. "Have you given any thought to your major?" Leon was pleased with the punishment the school had come up with – summer school, then school until December: academic prison. Leon thought it was exactly right.

Have you? Charlieo says.

The ocean's a silvered metallic color with light bouncing off it. When I shrug, a horizontal band of white raises then lowers across the water. I'm sick of school, I say. Maybe I'll take some time off, go someplace.

Great, Charlieo says. You can come visit me. Southeast Asia's a great vacation spot.

He's going into the Marines, some ROTC-type deal where he went in eight weeks after graduation. His brothers had both done it, but neither of them had been sent to a war.

When do you go?

Four weeks, three days, Charlieo says. Want to know how many hours?

He's burying one of his fists under sand. I want to touch him, but we are not touchers. Even in first grade, when we had to form buddy lines, we'd scramble to be each other's buddy. When the teacher told everyone to hold hands, we stood close but not touching.

Remember buddy lines? I say.

He nods. Of course. What doesn't he remember?

He says, So? You didn't answer my question.

Which was?

What do you want to be?

I say, A ballerina, a princess, a sheriff, a mommy.

He rolls his eyes.

It's a generic response.

I'm serious, he says. He's pulling paper, two pencils out of his pocket, always prepared. We'll make lists, he says. We'll keep them. In ten years we'll come back to this spot and see how they turned out.

These are golf pencils, I say, loud, to cover the sound of that: ten years. The same place.

Now, Charlieo says. Write down all the things you might want to be. His pencil is poised in the air, he looks like a proctor for the SAT's: Ready. Begin.

I DON'T KNOW, DON'T MAKE ME DO THIS, I write at the top of my page. The paper is almost unnaturally white, like milk in the shade.

NOT HERE, I write. NOT IN HS.

A DRIVER!

Married, I write. To Joe, I keep myself from writing.

A lamp salesman, I put down.

Gimme, Charlieo says.

This is stupid. I wrote stupid stuff.

He reads through my list with the exaggerated and serious attention adults pay to the political opinions of children.

Married, he says, he looks up at me, he looks down. We both put that. His face is pink.

You, me and the rest of the world, I say. I don't know, maybe I won't get married.

He is still looking down. The pink fades.

Okay, I say, sliding my foot over the sand, in his direction. Let's see what you wrote.

He holds his paper by a corner, it snaps in the wind. A marine biologist, it says. For a minute, I think that means a biologist in the Marines.

Agricultural research.

Horticulture (but there was a question mark next to that).

A husband, a father.

Crime.

Crime? I say. Who writes down crime as a possible career?

He shrugs. I'm being thorough. I don't feel my true nature's necessarily set. It's speculative, he says. Covering my bases.

You're kidding me, I say. You won't even pick up change off the street in case the person who dropped it comes back.

It's speculative, he says again. Anyway, that's what we'll do. Come back in ten years and reread them. Okay?

He stands up, turns in a slow tight circle, his feet piling up a small bunker of sand. I know he is memorizing where we are, this spot, chosen at random, significant now.

CHAPTER 26

....

Ⅰt is hot. I come out of sleep slowly. The stickiness of the air is a weight: I can't come all the way up.

I am lying inverted on my bed, head where my feet go, what I do on those nights in late summer when the breeze off the water just stops. Lying this way gives me the illusion of air – if anything stirs I will feel it – but last night there was no breeze and it is not August, only June.

Joellen, Joellen. Leon's voice, droning on and on, the same monotonous pitch. Joellen, Joellen. It is what wakes me. I open my eyes, disoriented. The light through the curtains is the same translucent yellow as my nightgown.

Bobby Kennedy's dead, Leon says.

John Kennedy, I say. When it was John and a classmate at school told me President Kennedy's shot I said, No. That was Lincoln.

No, he says. Now Bobby. His voice is both sharp and weary, as though he's been sitting up all night with an invalid.

A breeze stirs the hair on my forehead and I look at the window, but the curtains are motionless; the breeze is only Leon's swift movement past the door of my room.

I am tired of loss. I am tired of new death, the way each one looms by itself, the red-pink of hooked meat carcasses, and I am tired of the reprise of old deaths the new ones call up so it is not one death or two or three or however many there are now, but these same deaths counted over and over. I am tired of filmy veils and slow trains and the serried bursts of words from TV newsmen – cortege, caliber – used, like company dishes, only on these so special occasions.

Leon is gone, Ida is downstairs. She looks up then down at the stove again. I think she is checking to see how I am taking the news of this Kennedy's death, though what she says is: You're wearing *what* to school, Joellen?

I look down at myself: cutoffs, a T-shirt, no shoes. It's too hot for clothes, too hot to even be thinking about it.

I sit at my place at the table, the sun hotter here, streaking through the hot colors of the windowsill glasses. There are no roses on the table the way there were when President Kennedy died, though that was November and roses were harder to come by. Maybe Ida does not know, and I am back at the moment of hearing: the fresh news, the sinking down. But the radio's going, men's voices mumbling out from the kitchen. Maybe Ida has not brought roses because I did not bring any when Dr. King died.

Sit, Ida says and puts a plate of food down on the table. Steam billows up from the plate. Underneath, the oilskin tablecloth sweats.

There is a knock on the front door and I get up. Standing, even in the hot kitchen, it is less hot than it was near the plate.

You *eatin'*, Ida calls after me.

It's Charlieo, a surprise. We do not do this anymore, come to each other's houses. I taste the rusted metallic smell off the screen door.

Yeah? I say. We don't want any.

He smiles, but without showing teeth. He is so big, his size a constant surprise. I can't correct the memory of him, of us both, as smaller.

You see it? he says.

I nod. I say, On the radio.

They had it on TV, he says. The whole thing. It was earlier. California.

I feel, again, the stagnant weight of these public deaths. The motorcade in Dallas. The motel in Memphis. California is a distant time zone. Maybe this will end different.

I'll take you to school, Charlieo says, as though this segue makes sense. I . . . We thought you shouldn't be alone.

I don't get it, why, is it dangerous? I'm not alone, I say.

Charlieo stands at attention, looking over my head, into the kitchen, at Ida. Come inside, I say. You can eat my breakfast for me.

He shakes his head. Can't. I'm not going today.

Me either, I say and grin – we can ditch school together, play miniature golf. I am not allowed any cuts but it's an old habit, not going, and hard to just break.

He shakes his head again. I'm going to Mass, he says, still looking over my head. I came to drop you.

I'll come with you, I almost say, but I don't, and he doesn't invite me.

Ready? he says.

Yeah, well I'm not. I have to have breakfast. I have to change. It's okay, I can walk.

Sure? he says.

Sure. You can drop me off next time they shoot some rabbi.

I shut the screen. I latch it. I say, This is in the public domain.

Look, he says. I just came by to see you to school.

I say, Yeah, well, it's not any farther than it was yesterday.

Go, I say. Go. SCAT!

It's hotter outside than in, it is only 8:30, the heat – sudden, unexpected – is surreal. Something tickles the bare flat place between my breasts and I touch there, my fingers wet under my shirt. Charlieo has made me jittery. I think "blood" before "sweat."

It is quiet outside the school, another vague consequence of the heat, as all day everything will be, but it is also quiet in the halls, the classrooms. Desks are empty. It is like one of those holidays: the Ascension, the Assumption, the Feast of the Virgin.

The teacher calls the roll and after the names of the kids who are Irish Catholic there is a silence, a pause, the heat from the open windows bearing down. It is exclusionary, their absence. Collective, spontaneous, or perhaps they called one another up, a round robin.

When the teacher comes to my name, I don't answer.

Joellen Stein? she says and there is the same dense heat, the same quiet. I could be anything.

Joellen, she says. I know she is looking right at me, though it is something I feel rather than see, as I am looking out the window. Still, in that silence, the loss? it's mine too.

CHAPTER 27

....

The O'Caseys are throwing a party. It's Charlieo's last day at home before he is shipped what he calls "overseas." There's something World War II–like to me about this word; something Italian or French. It does not call up the dense and saturated green of where Joe is.

Charlieo has already been gone the whole summer: basic training. I was in summer school. Classes were held in the high school, but it didn't feel real, learning things in the heat. We could wear what we wanted: shorts, tank tops. Girls in waitress uniforms buzzed in and out on mopeds, their apron strings flying behind them. All the uniforms were either dark formal colors or the pastels of party mints. I sat in the back of the room and memorized them: black-and-white, Perkins Pancakes; pink, Pat's Diner. On a quiz, I'd have gotten 100.

Because of summer school and the other half year they were making me do after that, I didn't get to graduate with my class. The O'Caseys had thrown a party for graduation, too.

Come rested, Charlieo tells me. It'll be an all-nighter. The night before being shipped out? No sleep.

It's an indoor-outdoor party. Black-and-gold crepe paper streamers are twisted and taped in loops around moldings and the rough bannister down to the basement. Japanese lanterns hang from lengths of clothesline in the backyard. The light from the lanterns is an electric yellow. Moths bat around them, their wings creamy and translucent.

Whenever I spot him, Charlieo is jammed in the center of a group of men: uncles, neighbors, people the O'Caseys play cards with. The talk and laughter of men crackle and echo across the concrete patio covering the music from the phonograph cranked loud in the basement.

The men cluster near the trash barrels, bottles of beer in their hands, or they sit on the rented tables covered with paper cloths. None of them eat, as though there is something delicate or unmanly about eating. The women don't eat either, waiting for the men. The food stays the way it was set out, the same symmetrical heaps and mounds. The paper cloths pleat and tear under the thighs of the men.

Joellen! somebody calls: Mr. O'Casey. His clipped hair casts a silvery light of its own in the soft dark. He pulls me into the ring around one of the barrels loaded with ice and beer. I am the only female, a violation of tribal custom.

You know Charlie here's from a long line of Marines, don't you?

I am confused, of course I know this, he knows that I do, then I see he is not really speaking to me. I am his straight man. He is playing to an audience: all men. They stand around Charlieo making physical contact.

Yes sir, I say. I knew that. I don't know why I called him sir, I never had.

I can tell you, I'm proud of this boy, Mr. O'Casey says, punching the air. No telling how far this boy's going!

He is charged up, they all are, the uncles, Douglas and Herman. Even the men who had not been Marines, who stayed, humbly, on the outskirts of the circles, had adopted the strut, the chest-forward stance of the O'Casey men.

This boy, he says, is a legacy. An offering to his country from his family.

The men don't break contact with Charlieo – a hand on his shoulder, a finger ticking against his elbow – but Mr. O'Casey has their attention.

Something cold presses against the top of my arm: Herman offering a beer.

Why are they so happy? I say to him. Why is this a good time for a party?

Herman looks at me, the smile from the beer offer still on his face. Why? he says.

Now, I say. This party.

He's being shipped out tomorrow, Herman says.

To a war. He could get killed. People get killed.

Yeah, well, some. Acceptable loss, Herman says. In every war. But don't you worry about Chas. He's an O'Casey. We're lucky charmed. He leans close, I smell the beer and cigar smoke on his breath.

We, Herman says. Don't. Die.

Around midnight Charlieo comes up behind me. What do you say we get out of here? His voice is soft but it stands out from the single whir of many men talking and laughing, and from the clink of beer bottles and ice and the distant and dreamy sound of some slow song coming up from the basement.

I thought you had to stay up all night. Some moral duty.

He looks down, then up again. Light slides off his hair. It is crewcut like his father's, both their heads the color and gleam of precious metals: Mr. O'Casey silver, Charlieo gold.

Yeah, he says. But I'll never make it if I don't get out of here, get some fresh air.

I say, It's your party.

He grins. Be right back. Don't move.

He goes back to the beer. The men's voices get louder and faster, they close in around him. Charlieo's movements become small and curtailed, like a moth in a bottle.

We meet up in the driveway. He has a six-pack, the cardboard waterlogged, dripping cold spots. There's a small knot of men on the front stoop. The yellow porch light is on and the light from the living room behind them, a white light that dilutes the yellow.

Have a good ti-ime, someone calls, waving, as we stand at the doors to Mr. O'Casey's car.

Don't do anything I wouldn't do.

Be go-od!

If you can't be good, be careful!

What am I, the sacrificial virgin? I say.

Charlieo says, I'm not gonna touch that!

We get in the car. We just drive around, splitting the beers.

I say, Is there an object to this motion, or are we just cruising till we run out of gas?

Charlieo says, Or beer.

What about a game of golf? Or a round or a chukker, or whatever.

Charlieo grins and nods, up and down, up and down. The motion of his head makes me vaguely seasick.

We never played at night, too crowded, too many bennies: too many now. It takes us a long time to find parking.

Bennie alert, I say, getting out of the car. Three boys with premature beer bellies, fleshy and shirtless.

Fuck 'em, Charlieo says. Live and let live, I always say.

You never say that.

Well, now I do.

We lean on the low fence that separates the golf course from the boardwalk like paddock from pasture. The fence is wood posts and a green plastic mesh that gives when we lean in against it, our stomachs and knees pouching through. There are tall pole lights at the golf course's four corners: in the light, the bennies look pink and hairless. They move from hole to hole carrying six-packs like purses. One of them has on a pith helmet with two slots for beer cans and two clear plastic straws running down, like oxygen tubes.

I figured by the time we played the first hole, the bennies would be finished and gone. I'm slow, it can take me twenty strokes to get the ball through. What's par for this hole? I ask. It's a windmill.

Charlieo's watching the bennies clustered around the shack where you pay like the three little pigs. I thought they were leaving, but when we get to the third hole, they're coming around to the first, starting over. They catch up to us on the fourth, a clown's head. You have to hit into its mouth.

Comin' through, comin' through, one of the bennies says.

Hot stuff, watch your back, says another. The three of them crowd up behind us.

Whoa, Charlieo says. You see her trying to putt here?

Who are you, Arnold Palmer? the one with the pith helmet says.

You the resident golf pro? says another one. He is so close, I can see the hairs around his navel, stuck down, as though he'd dropped jelly on his stomach.

Excuse me? Charlieo says. He takes a step towards them. He's taller and harder than they are, the sharp planes of his body stand out next to their pink doughiness. Together, the three bennies look like a wad of chewed gum.

What's the problem here chief? the third bennie says, the smart one, the one who built his house out of bricks. Go ahead, play your game. He steps to the side, the other two follow.

Charlieo turns back to the clown head. Its goggling eyes and lewd moving tongue are goofy looking in daylight but in the flat, shadowless light from the lamps they are tinged with menace. He sets up his ball. I hadn't finished my putt but I let that pass. Later, back in the car, I'd say tonight's win didn't count. Buzzzzzzz, I'd say. Forfeit on a technicality.

Come on Arnie, what do you say, let's step it up, the pith helmeted bennie says.

Hey, the second one says. You in a rush? I'm not in a rush. Classes don't start for another three days. He yawns and drapes himself over the one in the helmet. When he lifts his arm I smell deodorant and sweat and the piggy oiliness of suntan lotion.

Charlieo turns to them. I'm so glad you have no place to go, he says, his voice pleasant and eerie. I myself have a pressing engagement. I'd like to enjoy my last game of golf for a while.

A *pressing* engagement? the brick house bennie says. You mean, like, *ironing?* He grins (maybe not the smart one); the other two snort and guffaw.

Charlieo flushes, his face going almost as red as the clown's lips and tongue. Which part of that, he says, did you find funny? He glares down at them, tall, lunatic, ready to take them all on. Clenching and unclenching his fists.

The bennies look elsewhere, shift and knock into each other.

I step right in front of Charlieo. Are you kidding me? I say.

I say, Is this a *fight?*

Nobody looks at me. I am as invisible as the women at the O'Caseys' party.

Oh, I say. I get it. You go ahead and keep the golf course safe for democracy. Don't let me get in the way. I'll see you, I say. Give me a call when you get back. Send me a postcard.

I don't even go out at the exit, I go over the fence. My feet, on the wooden slats of the boardwalk, make a hollow almost tuneful sound, like wind chimes. Where are you going, Joellen? a voice says in my head. Not home, the house silent except for Leon's breathing; not back to the O'Caseys' party. Where is there to go?

I stop, and when I do Joe's there, sudden and whole. I see the length of his leg, his hair, thick and dry, falling over his forehead. I can see his thumbnail scraping the flint of a Strike Anywhere match. The intensity of my longing keeps me still. I close my eyes. Wait for him to touch me.

Jo? a voice says and I open my eyes expecting Joe, Joe's chin, the hot inner crease of Joe's neck, but there is gold where I am expecting dark hair and pink where Joe's dark skin ought to be.

I'm sorry, Charlieo says, and I think he means: Sorry, it's not Joe. It's me.

I don't know what came over me, you know me, that wasn't me out there. He points over his shoulder, at the golf course. The lights spoke out of the dark like masts.

It felt good though, I'm not gonna lie to you! Ridding the world of Jack Bennies!

I feel, again, vaguely seasick. The lights weave. The slats of the boardwalk goggle and bob like the eyes and lips and tongue of the clown.

We're in the front seat of Charlieo's father's car looking out at the various darks: the frilled trees like paper silhouettes laid against the paler background of the sky. Charlieo opened the car door when we stopped – to spill out the last of a warm beer? to spit? – and the door hadn't clicked to when he closed it. Every so often the light goes on, a tiny intermission in the dark.

It's at least three A.M., it may be later, Charlieo says the dashboard clock is unreliable even though the car's brand new. We've just been driving around again, finishing the six-pack we took from the party, stopping at an all-night package store for another. We're parked in front of my house. I feel strange, my head dense, my body weightless, from beer and Joe and this different Charlieo and from tiredness.

The car light goes on. In the instant of light, I see Charlieo's neck stretched by the weight of his head. His head is large, too big for his body. The light goes out again.

Look, he says. I'm really sorry. I don't know where that all came from.

I can't see him, but the words go with the humbled cant of his head.

You don't want to go, I say.

Tell me about it. They'll all still be up when I get back, sitting around. It's like a friggin' wake.

I picture his family – his father, his brothers and uncles in the living room, the aunts falling asleep in the kitchen chairs, the sweat from their highball glasses forming star shapes on the table. When Charlieo comes in the men will all hoot, the aunts will jump, startled awake in the kitchen.

No, I say. I mean tomorrow, today, whenever it is. Away, I say, I choose away. I don't say Vietnam, Southeast Asia, overseas.

He shakes his head, a tight shudder, the way horses ripple their skins to throw off flies. Of course I don't, what do you think, I'm friggin' stupid?

I hear Herman's voice: lucky charmed.

So why are you going? I'm so tired. I have said it to Joe, I have heard it from Leon.

He keeps shaking his head. Irrelevant, he says. It's who the fuck I am.

You could've waited, I say. Gone to college. Gotten deferred.

You don't get it, he says. They're all sittin' there, waiting for my mother to make breakfast. You know what's for breakfast? Eggs and pancakes and mixed grill and cakes and my mother's soda bread. The same thing she made for my brothers.

I remember that Fourth of July Charlieo telling me what was inside each bowl, on each platter. We have the same thing every year, he'd said, proud of the sameness.

You know how many years I've been waiting for this?

So you mean you'll go and get yourself shot at because you don't want to miss breakfast?

Yeah, he says after a while. In a way.

That's it? That's your whole reason?

Forget it, he says. Forget it, okay?

I don't get it, I say. Your *mother* . . .

Please, he says. Okay? The car light blinks on and then off.

I look out the window. So, I say after a while. Think you could've taken all three of them?

He smiles; I can see this even in the dark: his teeth are like his father's, that white. Yeah, he says. I could have. He takes a deep breath, holds it and looks around like he doesn't know where to exhale. Well, he says. Write me?

Of course, I say. I put force behind it: of *course*. I'll write every day. I'll knit socks. What else can I give him?

I turn on the seat so I'm facing him. The light blinks on, he's shifted also, and I move in to hug him: our first deliberate touch.

I don't want you to go either, I say into the beachy smell of his shirt, and longing for him blurs into longing for Joe. I don't want him to go. I don't want to be the only one left.

He groans, as though my arms on his back are too tight. I've waited so long, he says.

And then I am aware of *him*, not just a shape I am holding: his large hands, each one the span of my back, and the marble-sized muscles above his elbows and then his hands move, slide under my shirt, stroking the skin on my back. I'm not wearing a bra, I feel his hands stroke down and down looking for it, then they trail around to my front. They are large, not Joe's hands, and sticky, and I know: he has never done this before. I see his uncles, his brothers, waiting for him at the house.

I pluck at his hands, take hold of the wrists and pull but he doesn't let go, and I think of the lists we had written: a criminal, his list said. I pluck harder, breath and squeaking sounds come from my chest.

His hands move then, press in and then peel from my back, my skin sticking to his damp palms so that the separation is slow: bone and then flesh, the skin last. I say No, or Stop, some short, one-syllable word, gone as soon as it's spoken.

CHAPTER 28

School is a circling plane, school is limbo.

I had expected to feel singled out; called on expressly; made to do extra work: to live up to my potential. I'd pictured faculty meetings where I was the subject, and taken pride in the picture, but I am treated like a visitor, an auditor, like someone who does not speak English.

In June I'd felt suddenly younger than the seniors I was supposed to be graduating with; I feel infinitely older than this class. I have no interest in the girls, their faces clean and reflective, their plaid kilts and shetland sweaters and knee socks and jangling gold jewelry. They stood in small impenetrable clusters outside in the morning, their books shielding their chests, and talked about parties and boys and TV shows.

And the boys: maybe they'd heard about me and Joe. Maybe there'd been rumors about me and Charlieo. The boys came sniffing around like those random dogs had, pulling their owners across parking lots, streets. These boys were scrubbed and pink and had new shoes and new haircuts. These boys were puppies.

I have only three classes, I'm out by noon and home. Ida's taken to making lunch for me, sandwiches and glasses of milk, her way of saying: still a child. Still in school. My teeth clench when I see Ida's lunches, the sandwich neatly cut, a napkin folded beside the plate, the milk with floats of purple or red from the colored glasses on the windowsill. I want to yell when I see them. I don't yell.

You don't have to make lunch for me, is all I do say.

Ida raises her eyebrows. Have to? she says. Who you tellin' about have to?

No. I mean, it isn't necessary.

It's necessary. You tellin' me food all of a sudden's not necessary? You just sit on down and eat, let me worry about necessary. She turns back around to the sink. She wears the same pedal pushers as always, the fabric worn down to silkiness and slit in places, due to age.

I could not eat, inside the circle of Leon and school and Ida's lunches. Not hungry, I said the first few times, then I said nothing. The sandwiches sat on the table all afternoon, the bread beginning to stiffen and curl. They were always gone by the time Ida was, but the next day there'd be another one.

I woke every morning with a dim fury that I took to school and walked around with inside the smell of the shiny pages of textbooks and leather shoes and chalk and gummed reinforcements, and I took it home with me in the afternoon where it smelled like warm milk and sandwich.

We'd gone on a grammar school trip to an aquarium once. Two dolphins swam in a tank of grayed water. The tank seemed large to us, small children, but the dolphins swam back and forth from a small door at one end of the tank to a small door at the other.

They know where their food comes from, a cheerful guide told us, pointing to an envelope-sized window in the door. It had taken till now for me to know they were trying to find their way out.

It's the Thursday before Halloween, the air clean and cold and fragrant with the smell of damp and decaying leaves. In the halls between classes, you hear the zipping sounds of corduroy. I always get to school early. I like standing outside by myself the way, when I was small, I used to go early to visit the horses. There are no horses near the high school.

Groups don't usually form until a few minutes before the bell, one person first, their friends sliding to them like magnetized filings. Today, a group is already here, though not huddled. They stand side by side like swimmers toeing the edge of a pool. They do not speak to each other but straight out into the air. Maybe they're blind, I think and walk over.

There are three of them, two girls and a boy. They are all wearing jeans, faded and patched, they all have long hair. Not anyone I recognize, not from this high school. They are reading, their heads bent to what look like white sheets, folded in squares. The sheets snap in the breeze; their hair jigs out behind them.

Cherry, Stephen. Chester, James, they all say. Chester, Johnson. Chester, Walker. Chestnut, Arthur. Chin, Lee. Chin, Roger. Their voices are cadenced, like clocks.

They are reading the war dead. There is no sign or announcement of this, but it is what they are doing. They are wearing black arm bands. The patches on one girl's jeans are velvet. They must have been here a long time, to already be up to the C's.

Cruz, they say. Dahl, Daimler, Daugherty, Day, Day, Day, Day.

Were these brothers, the four Days?

The sheets snap: computer printouts with perforated edges. One of the girls loses a corner of the page she is holding. Her voice is missing from the next name, like a dropped stitch in knitting. The boy – he is standing between them – reaches over and catches the page for her. His hand waits until her hand is secure, waits one beat more, lets go. I had not noticed the boy before this, not as distinct from the two girls. Now I see how his cuffs are turned back, and how the veins standing out on the backs of his hands are a man's veins. I think of his hands touching things. I think of the possible smell of his hands.

What's going on? somebody says behind me. Who the fuck are these?

Got me, somebody else says. Not from the fuck around here.

What are they *talking* about? in a whine.

Acceptable losses, I want to say.

A crowd has built behind and to both sides of me. Heads are all I can see, the colors of hair, a chip of paleness or ruddiness under bangs. Sound rumbles forward and back like the sound of the ocean. I am Isabel's daughter, I cannot stand crowds. How will I move? How will I get free? There is no one in front of me except for the boy and the girl and the girl, heads bent, reading, but I will not step into the field created by their voices, mined with the names of the dead.

And then they say H. Haas, they say, Jeremy. Haase, they say. Craig. Their pronunciation is careful.

Haback, Habacker, Haber – Alan, David, John Anthony, John Leonard. They advance. Their voices move forward. They will get to Hand, to Handy, and I cannot be here to hear Joe's name read, even if they do not say Joseph Handy, even if the Joseph Handy they do say is not Joe. I can't be here to hear it, bad luck: no black cats, no old clothes, no mentioning the names of the living alongside the names of the dead.

I turn, facing the crowd, walk from one end to the other and back like a football game booster. I look at shoulders and jackets and chins, trying to find a way out.

Haberman, they read. Habib. Hack. Hack.

The wall is solid. I look for cracks but it is an impenetrable bank, a wall of dark jackets, arm pressed against arm, seamless and soldered and I start to shove, Move, move, the crowd pushing against me. It is not just that I cannot hear Handy; I can't be around when it is said. Their jaws could not go slack to say H, they could not smile into Eee, their voices could not part the air, the air could not tumble and break.

Hadrian, Haft, Hagan, Haggerty, Haggerty.

People move. People's shoulders swing back and I am through, running down the slope of the hill, my legs going faster than my torso: two people running. I run across the parking lot, my shoes slap-slapping, the asphalt stinging the soles of my feet and I don't stop until I get down to the beach, to the water, until the water and the stiff chafing wind and my own breathing are the only sounds left.

It is Halloween morning. People have put carved pumpkins out on their porches, the pulpy insides already beginning to brown from exposure to air. Leon and I sit at the table. He's cooked himself breakfast; nothing, I said when he asked what I wanted. Just coffee. I waited to hear him say, Coffee's not nothing, Joellen.

Are you on some kind of diet, Joellen? You're so thin, is what he says. Passing me, he picked up my wrist, showing how his hand could cuff it a time and a half. I didn't realize I was losing weight. It was Ida's sandwiches. I'd half given up eating.

Sure? Leon says. Pancakes!

I saw Isabel, that last breakfast, the steam rising off the plate. I shook my head.

Suit yourself, Leon says, cheerful, but you don't know what you're missing! Leon is always cheerful now when he is talking to me, a dense chipperness that doesn't suit him. Serious to morose is more Leon's spectrum.

So, he says, from behind his pancakes. Steam fogs the bottom half of the window behind us, opaquing the colored glasses. It gives the illusion of heat.

I hear you missed school, Leon says.

I look at him. I picture a telegraph tower beaming little Morse code bleeps to Leon.

Did they teach you Morse code in the Army? I say, but he doesn't look up.

Leon's cheerfulness when he is with me is for my benefit, but it is not personal. Often, he does not hear me.

There was this demonstration, I say. Against the war. I couldn't go in.

Leon nods. We are not a picket-line-crossing family.

Two days? he says.

Pardon?

The demonstration. Was it two days? You missed two days of school. Thursday, Friday.

I don't answer. The steam on the bottom half of the window is too dense to see through.

We've discussed this, Leon says. You are not to miss school. I thought that was clear. No?

I twist my coffee cup back and forth on the table. It is part of the punishment: not one missed day.

Don't do that please, Sal, Leon says. He looks up, he looks down. He is buttering his pancakes, each one right to the edge. Help me, he says, still holding the butter knife. I think he means with the pancakes.

I don't know what to do, he goes on, how to impress upon you the *importance* of school. What you're doing now – he waves the butter knife – has the utmost importance for your future. You won't get into college, he says. His voice is singsong, each word has its own note. Is that what you're after?

I know this is his bottom line question. I know all I have to do is sound contrite and he will bless and forgive.

A demonstration, I say. Against the war. You don't approve of my missing school for that?

He flushes, his face red, the thin line of his lips speckled the purple of plums. I say, What? What is it? Something is happening to him, a heart attack, something. I look from his face to the phone.

Don't you tell me the importance of anti-war demonstrations! And don't you try to pawn off your truancy as a political act. To my knowledge you've never gone to a demonstration!

This was true, I did not go to demonstrations, there weren't any in this town, there were parties when boys went into the service, parties when they came back. On Memorial Day there were parades.

You of all people should be actively opposed to this war, Leon says. Your so-called boyfriend's over there. Or am I mistaken?

The morning Joe was supposed to leave, I ran into Leon at the station. Leon had been in the Army. That day it seemed consoling.

Leon is still holding the butter knife, the tips of his fingers shiny with butter. Even while we sat in the train station over the watery coffees he bought us, even while I was telling him, I wanted to stop.

So-called. I walk around with Joe a small weight inside me; he was a deflated balloon, folded flat, that I carried. Now he is full-sized and solid. He takes up the whole room. He is not so-called.

This will not be repeated, Leon says.

You will not miss one more day of school. He looks up again, tipping his head. I'm working hard here, Jo. You've got to pitch in. Your cooperation is needed. Work hard this semester, we'll get you into college yet!

He winks, he looks at me, I know what he's seeing: me capped and gowned at some graduation, him in a seat on the aisle.

And I say, I'm not going to college. After I say it I tap the outside of my ears. My voice is a distant fogged sound.

Oh yes, Leon says. You are going to college!

I had not planned to say this; wasn't sure even after it was out of my mouth if it was true, or if I was saying the worst thing I could think of to Leon. It didn't matter. I liked being the visible reason for his discomfort. I had to go on. I wanted out from under Leon's expectations and Ida's lunches and the sniffing-dog boys and so-called.

I'm leaving school, I say.

Leon freezes. I'm afraid that's not open to discussion, he says. You will finish high school. It's three months more. What's three months?

Take it back, a voice says in my head. They are just words, you can take them back. But this was not true. There was no such thing as "just" words. I was Isabel's daughter, but I was also Leon's.

Education, Leon says, is *the* most important thing in this household.

We are an educated family.

We are not dropouts.

We are not flag wavers.

We clear our plates from the table.

We do not worship.

We are not Christians.

I am sick of we. We are not making this decision, I say. I am.

Oh, Leon says, that's where you're mistaken! You live in *my* house. *I* put food in your mouth, *I* put clothes on your back. *I* make the rules. You will finish high school! You will go to college! He looks at me; a streak of light off the butter knife hits his eye, bisecting the iris. His eye has the shattered look of the inside of a marble.

I'm not going back, I say. Maybe later. It is an out, but it has no power to save us.

People don't go *back* to high school, Joellen!

Correspondence, I say. By mail. I see myself thumbing through the day's ads and bills, the envelopes a blurred white in the polish of the sideboard.

Leon slams his hand down on the table. The knife on the side of his plate rings.

I'm going out for a walk, I say.

The violent red his face had become is fading. He holds his mouth open, as though this hole is causing the fade. Good, he says, after a while. Go for a walk, I approve, clear your head. I won't have this discussion when you're in this state. He nods, egging himself on: he thinks he has found the right tack.

When you can talk reasonably, we'll continue.

He does not move as I get up, does not look at me. His head is bent over his plate, his hands flat on the table, a posture of grace. The steam has begun to condense on the window.

Trick-or-treating, I saved the rich people's houses for last: the old shingled ones with creepy wraparound porches and the new ones, built around the fake lake. These houses seemed to be wearing costumes themselves. They were fronted by large lawns floodlit to the color of frost at night, and by hedges clipped into helixes and ducks.

Everyone went to these houses because rich people gave good candy, but I went for the moment the front doors opened and the splendor and light spilled out onto the steps. I went for the moment, always possible to me, that I might be asked in, fallen in love with, adopted.

It is a day of remarkable light like some layer of gauze or gas has been blown out of the sky: seeing is different. Colors – leaves and pumpkins and the colors of houses – are distinct and, in their distinctness, almost painful. The huge flag that was raised every morning above the fake lake rolled out in waves, its colors stirring and stark against the blue.

I am just half a block from the beach, can see the boardwalk from where I am standing, but I do not want to look at the sky and the solid gray band of the ocean and the cuff of dun sand. This light is too stark for the beach. I circle the lake and go down streets of old trees and houses bigger but shoddier than Leon's and mine: houses of four- and five- and six-children families. The shade blues everything.

Motion is soothing, so when I get to the highway, I keep walking. Cars pass, leaving gritty tunnels of wind. I walk by car and pool dealerships and contractors' offices and a furniture showroom and the thirty-foot papier mâché replica cow on the Beef-O-Rama building and a mini-mall of doctors' and dentists' offices. The buildings are concrete and low, tan or yellow or off-white. I know these places. Still, in the light, things look changed. The businesses I pass begin to look less familiar, even their names. I can't remember if I've ever heard them before, and I keep saying to myself: that must be new.

Buildings approach, draw even with me, fall back, but I have no sensation of forward movement, as though it is the highway that's moving, not me. When I stop under the roof overhang of some building, suddenly thirsty, the highway, the weeds, the buildings appear to keep moving. I have to hold onto the side of the building, the feeling of continuous motion is so strong.

Oh there you are, a woman's voice says from the doorway of the building, behind me. No car?

I shake my head.

Well come on in. I thought you weren't coming.

I follow her through the doorway into a room so cavernous and so dark I keep my eyes on her blonde head for illumination. The room is lit only by a few shaded bulbs that hang from the ceiling, fake and inadequate after the light from outside, like doll house fixtures. There are three or four old metal desks in the room and some chairs; at the front three plastic orange seats, the kind they have in laundermats, are bolted into the floor.

Bennies, the woman says. They steal everything.

She shrugs. Alice King, she tells me. Royal Real Estate.

She sits down behind one of the desks so I sit also. It does not seem strange to me, to be sitting here.

So, she says. How did you get here?

I . . . My lips stick to my front teeth. Do you have something to drink?

She stands and goes into the back, but with a sigh: she is not fond of waiting on people. The office is the size of an airplane hangar. Her desk has a cube of photographs on it and a pink silk rose in a vase made out of mirror and a white ceramic cup that says Somebody Loves You with a lipstick mark on the rim and they seem, suddenly, to be all the things that I want.

Rule Number One, she says. There's a fridge in the back? Help yourself to whatever, but the Tabs are all mine. Okay? She puts a can of Coke down next to me.

I nod. The sweetness of the Coke hurts my teeth.

Okay, Alice King says. So like I told you on the phone, there's some paperwork, there's some showing houses and apartments to clients, though you won't do too much of that, only when I and my other agent are too busy. We are VERY QUIET in the off-season. December through June, it's a zoo. She pulls a strand of her own hair out of her mouth: proof of how wild it got. Her hair is the creamy yellow of white corn.

Mostly, she says, what I need is a body to man the fort. My other agent takes off the off-season. I need a body here. Otherwise, I get stuck, I can't get out. Off-seasons, I like to go out for long lunches. She strokes the side of her coffee cup. Somebody Loved Her.

It might only be temporary, she says. Or, like I said, it might turn into permanent, but I can't promise anything. It all depends on the season we're having. If you feel you need more security, I understand.

But I like the sound of it. Temporary: a pause, a hiatus, a breath.

One thing, I say. I've never sold real estate.

Well we don't *sell* exactly, or hardly ever, and anyway you couldn't sell if we did, without a license. We rent. It's a bennies business, it takes care of itself. All's we have to do is drive them to . . .

Or drive, I say. Charlieo pops into my head.

Oh. Well, so they drive. All the reasons she has for not hiring me, she dismisses. She wants a body, so she can go out for long lunches. She takes a contract out of her desk. What's your last name?

Joellen, I say.

Ruth Joellen?

No, I say. My first name's Joellen.

Are you sure? I could've sworn you said Ruth. On the phone.

I shake my head. I'm sure, I say. Joellen. Ruth hadn't shown up. I sat in the huge office and said thank you to Ruth.

Dear Charlieo, I think. I'm writing to you from my new office. He was gone, I hadn't heard from him since the night of his party. Still, there wasn't anyone else I could think of to tell.

One thing, she says, still filling in the contract. Her handwriting is solid and big: I could see a stack of papers on a teacher's desk, hers on top yelling – Me, me.

You have to buy a gold jacket. This is my office, but it's a Gold Crest franchise. I'll give you the address. There's a place not too far where they sell them. Okay, she says. You can sign this. Any questions?

Yeah. Can you find me an apartment? One I can afford on my salary?

Absolutely, she says, standing before she needs to be; she has to bend down to her desk drawer to find keys. Let's go. I can show you the territory. I'm dying to get the hell out of here.

Dear Charlieo. I'm writing this from my new apartment . . .

CHAPTER 29

....

I stood on the porches and steps and long wooden exterior stairways of apartments while Alice King unlocked doors. These places were as unlike the huge fake lake houses where I'd gone trick-or-treating as it is possible for places to be and still be called dwellings. Light did not fall from these thresholds like gold coins and there was no one inside, but there was something the same in waiting for the doors to be opened.

Most of the places were horrible: dark, with streaky paint and heel- or fist-holes punched in the sheetrock. Gummed grease stuck to the stoves and cabinets. The refrigerators or the bathrooms smelled.

People *rent* these places? I said in one living room where newspapers had been torn into strips and crumpled into balls: the room was like a giant nest.

Not people, Alice King said. Bennies.

Still, I found something to like in most places: a piece of furniture, a porch, the placement of a window.

You know, you have good instincts, Alice King said. That's what you do, you talk up the features. When all else fails I always say, Great hot water.

She looked up at the ceiling of the room we were in, the giant nest. There was a brown water stain near the light fixture in the ceiling, like a birthmark on an upper cheek, stopping just short of the nose.

Except, like I said, bennies don't call for finesse, Alice said. Girls are a little bit choosy, the boys take the first places they see. Proximity to bars is the only qualification. It was a surprise, that Alice knew what proximity meant; that she had used it in a sentence.

I had to see every place. If I settled too soon, the next place or the place after that might be the perfect one. Trick-or-treating, I stood outside afraid I would be chosen at the first or second house I went to. How would I know if that was the best I could do?

Alice King didn't mind – she liked being out of the office – but she was noncommittal: she did not look at any of these apartments as potential homes. Once or twice I asked her, What do you think? and she roused herself and looked around: she had no memory of where she was. I pictured her own house, full of glass and lacquered surfaces and walls made out of mirror.

I took an apartment above a garage. These were common in our town, we were zoned for them, Alice showed me quite a few though this one was nicer than others. Some rickety wood steps led to the door. There was a platform at the top of the stairs where you could put pots with geraniums in them. I pictured myself coming home, walking down the driveway, my eyes focused on pinpoints of red. The place was a block from the highway, and about equidistant from Leon's and the beach, maybe a mile and a half.

The apartment had been recently painted, the paint smelled vaguely anti-septic. Even though crumbs of dirt had been painted into the sills it was cleaner than the other places I had seen. There was a white hot water heater in the kitchen standing like a sentry behind the door. I walked through the three rooms: the kitchen, the living room, one bedroom. Behind me, the hot water heater hummed.

I bought a gold jacket. On the way back to the office to sign the rental papers Alice King said, We can stop on the way for your jacket, and we did, though it was in the other direction, two towns away.

The gold jacket store was a tuxedo rental that also sold uniforms: hospital and kitchen whites, waitress outfits. Pat's Diner! I thought looking through them. Perkins Pancakes!

There were two types of gold jackets, one wool and more expensive, one of what the label called man-made fibers. It looked dirty; even though it was new, a gray seemed to ooze up through the gold. The buttons were gold tone, non-reflective, like on school band uniforms. The jacket was stiff with sizing: tissue paper, I thought first, squeezing one arm, but it was hollow. I took that one. Cheaper. Alice King had said temporary. The wool one wears better, the salesman said, not giving up. The wool one could last forever.

The apartment was furnished and had dishes and glasses and forks and a blue shower curtain. I spent time thinking of things that I needed: soap and a mop, a broom, sponges, scouring powder. Two towels. Alice King advanced me the money. Don't buy sheets, she said and gave me some of her own that she didn't use and that turned out to be king-sized, awash on my double-sized mattress.

I bought two plastic flower pots, mock terra-cotta, and some geranium plants and set them outside the door. Their musky, almost mildewed scent and the near-faded smell of new paint became the smells of my house.

I bought a glass bowl and three rubber fish and put them on the window-sill in the kitchen. The perfect pets, I explained in my head to the guests I did not have. Every morning and when I got home from work and stood rinsing a cup at the sink, I turned the fish over. They only wanted to float belly up.

I bought white paper and white envelopes and a small book of stamps. Dear Leon, I wrote. Here is my new address. I don't have a phone yet. I have a job. This is my work number. This is best.

I didn't mail the letter to Leon for a while. I liked seeing, in ink, the things I had done.

I went back to Leon's one afternoon when no one was there to get the blanket from my bed. The kitchen smelled of cooked food and ironing and the pink smell of Ida's hand cream.

I took the spread down to get the blanket but there was no blanket, no sheets, as though I had been only a foster child.

You gone, then be gone, I could hear Ida say, grabbing the sheets off the mattress so hard her fingernails bent.

I bought a basket to keep in the bathroom and I put shells from the beach into it. Their smell made me think of my mother.

I bought two coffee cups that said "Joe" on the outside. At night I sat at the table in my kitchen and drank from my cup, my thumb covering the E, lifting and putting the cup down on the red-and-white-checked plastic cloth that came with the apartment. I left the other cup out on the table and thought about Joe sitting across from me, drinking. I bought a fifth of bourbon.

Uh-huh, I said and nodded like Joe was telling me something. I had the hum of the white water heater for company.

CHAPTER 30

....

Joe's dreaming. The colors in the dream – the ocean's clear gray, the spectrum of sand from white to brown – are the colors of the temperate zone.

He wakes to a heat that is already building, already unbearable on his neck and his back. He's soaked under the poncho he sleeps in. The heat in his dream is dry, a color like dry straw, the ticket shack heat.

He fights the rise up to consciousness, to this landscape, wet heat, the tropical lizard greens, then he stops fighting. Turns away from the dream as he turns from the words for girls' bodies. He sits up. He begins the day as he does every day: he gets stoned.

After a while he stands inside the darkened, green-tinted light of the tent. Under the smell of damp canvas there is mildewing cloth and rotting leather, mixed with the smells of mud and stagnant water and plant rot from outside. Joe looks out at the jungle that seems to advance overnight, and he squeezes the pocket where his dope is.

He doesn't eat breakfast. He stands outside the mess tent flattening and re-forming hillocks of mud with his heel, smoking first dope then a cigarette, held inside his cupped hands for dryness. He waits for his restlessness to subside, as it usually does, but it has not by the time his sergeant comes out and tells Joe he can take off anytime and says, Don't forget to pick up a few things! Twinkies and a coupla six-packs – calling after Joe, the reach of his voice flattened by the green rubber poncho he also wears.

Joe is supposed to go scouting for snipers, a useless job: the snipers set up at night and are gone by morning and have never returned to the same place. Still, there is hardly anything else to do.

He keeps to the edge of the jungle – a rule: open spaces are more vulnerable. He's alone, though another rule's supposed to be "go out in pairs." By himself, Joe settles some.

He thinks of the freed slaves bursting out of the ticket shack and of the day, all those months ago, when he walked or floated or was carried out of Grand Central Station by the crowd, and he feels the same near-happiness he felt then. He could go anywhere and nobody but the tall blond boy who was holding his place in the train line cared where he was.

Joe begins to hear the rushing sound in his ears he heard that day, the combined sounds of air brakes and trains and the collective noise and rush of people, and he bears out and away from the fetid green air and the semi-protection of the walls of the jungle. He heads to the center. And the noise – a pop, another pop – comes as a total surprise.

CHAPTER 31

....

So where's this famous rush I've been hearing about? I say.

It's mid-December. On the day she hired me Alice King said it got wild, December to June, so on the first day of December I expected to find the place jammed with underdressed bennies: sockless, shirtless, wearing thongs and no jackets. I expected the constant ringing of phones; talk and some shouting.

Alice King shrugs. It's unpredictable, she says. It's been cold. People don't know how to think summer when it's cold.

The cold in the office was astonishing, and I did not think I could ever again be astonished by cold. There were two radiators, the color of the reverse sides of aluminum foil, but you had to sit on them to feel any heat, and there was a space heater under each of our desks, but their warmth stayed on the floor like a spilled, red liquid. I kept my jacket on all day; Alice King wore a fur coat, sleek and reflective. Some mornings she picked me up and drove me to work. She drove a black Camaro with beige leather seats and good heat. We sat in the parking lot and drank take-out coffees.

Well. Time to face the music, Alice always said at five minutes past nine.

In the office, Alice and I hardly spoke as if that was a violation of office etiquette. The phone hardly rang; when it did, it was mostly personal calls for Alice – Steve, the Somebody Who Loved Her. He sometimes sent roses. They turned blue at the edges like cold lips.

Calls came also from girlfriends it surprised me Alice had, though there were photos of her in the cube on her desk in three different bridesmaid's dresses, and from her father, Reilly, in Florida.

How's tricks there, little lady, he always said when I answered, the same words every time the way Alice always said, Time to face the music. I pictured the two of them talking in snappy sayings to each other.

Until this day in mid-December, the phone had never been for me.

Yes, I say, into the phone. This is Joellen. Alice mouths "Reilly?" and I shake my head, raise one finger.

Joellen? the voice says. Are you there?

I'm here. Mrs. O'Casey? How great to hear from you! How are you?

She must have gotten this number from Leon or it might have been Leon who called her. Maybe she'll listen to you, I can hear Leon say.

Can't complain, can't complain, Mrs. O'Casey says. Mr. O'Casey was down with a cold, but I've managed so far not to catch it. There is a pause then the sound of tapping. She is knocking on wood.

And yourself?

Well I'm working, I say. Did you know that? A real estate office.

Yes, she says, sounding impressed. Real estate! I'm told there's a future in that.

By who? I want to ask her.

Joellen?

I'm here.

Joellen? she says again. I, we. Charles, she says.

Charles? She does not call him Charles. Charles is his name for baptisms and confirmations, a formal name, worn with a suit. Charles? And I think dead, and then gone, Charlieo's gone.

There is laughter, someone is laughing, Alice, I guess, there is no one else here, and I turn to frown at her, but her desk is empty. Cans knock against each other in the back. The refrigerator hiccups and rocks as it closes. And then I feel the huffs of my own breath on the hand that is holding the phone. I am the one who is laughing. I cover the mouthpiece with my other, my serious hand, though by now Mrs. O'Casey must have heard me.

Oh, I say. What? My breath is coming in odd heaves. I try to breathe slowly and deeply, to calm it. I think: does this sound to her like distress?

Wounded, she says. She says "only." Thank God.

Thank God. I mean, not that he's wounded. All . . .

All right, I am about to say, but this is wrong, impolite: you do not say all right immediately following wounded. All right makes its own elision, into alive.

There is a pause, a stiffness. I have violated the etiquette that covers the sick and the injured, a set of rules I do not know as I do not know office etiquette.

Please, I say, my voice weak and tired. Which must be what softens her.

He's in Mercy, she says.

Mercy is the hospital two towns south, the only hospital near here. This has never occurred to me before. Under the brisk, nursely turn of her talk I think: what if something happens here?

He's just arrived, Mrs. O'Casey is saying. They transferred him. First he was in Taiwan, a hospital there. He was there quite a time. Many months, she says. Her speech is like the precise, rounded English that some Asians speak, forming their mouths, carefully, around the foreign vowels.

Here is his number, she says. Do you have a pencil?

I write down the string of numbers she gives me. I do not think "phone" until she says, This gets you direct to his room.

There is a scrabbling paper sound, as though Mrs. O'Casey is going through notes. Has she made this same informational call, call after call, flipping the same papers, reading out the same numbers to other people? I picture Charlieo's room filled with visitors. I do not know what's wrong with him, or has she already told me?

So, how's he doing? I say. Is he doing okay? Will he . . .

They say he'll be fine, she says. Not counting the leg he's got gone.

She stops. I think she is crossing herself. I do it too in a hidden way: scratch my forehead, rub my breastbone, one shoulder, the other. Even Leon would not be able to tell.

I was ready to go see him as soon as I got off the phone with Mrs. O'Casey. Emergency, I saw myself saying to Alice, my lips pressed together, but I knew she would offer to drive me: any excuse to get out of the office. I wanted to take the bus. I pictured myself waiting for it, and then the movement of the bus, the soot and dried dirt streaking the windows, the green seats, some stained on the backs by hair tonics which also smeared some of the windows. I'd go this evening, after work.

The Hospital, is what everyone from around here calls it.

A looming dirty-limestone facade. Patients calling out from the windows.

The Hospital that my mother had been in.

Let him get settled, I said the first week, though I had no idea how long he'd already been there.

He's loaded with visitors, I said.

I didn't go. I called the hospital every few days to find out how he was. Every time they told me stable, his condition good, so I pictured his leg grow-ing back, a slow start then a bursting, like marigold flowers. It seemed possible that this time it would come out all right. That this time the end would be different.

And then one day, after weeks and weeks, they say he's been discharged.

Discharged? I say. It sounded gangrenous, a turn for the worse: not stable, not good. Discharged?

Gone? the nurse says. Sent home? a bubble of laughter under her words.

So that means he's okay, I say.

Well, I guess he must be, she says. She has a sugary voice. I wait to hear her call me honey. He's gone on home. We don't send people home around here until they're better!

Better! What a relief! I say to the nurse, as though we have clocked back-wards: he had not been wounded, he had not been sent overseas. I did not have to go to the hospital.

There is a smoky coolness to the day, as though someone's been burning leaves. It is a Saturday, there are no leaves, there have not been leaves for months, and there is no fire. Just a residual smokiness in the air that is distracting.

This is what I think will happen: I'll ring the O'Caseys' bell. Somebody (Douglas, Herman, a crisp, hired nurse?) will answer the door. Follow me please. This way, they'll say and head back to the sunporch. (A nurse. Someone who wouldn't know I had ever slept there.) Charlieo, sweet and clean-looking and flat in a white-sheeted, white hospital bed. I will not look at the flat place where his leg will not be. I will not flinch when he pats the expanse of flat white sheet and asks me to sit down.

I ring, stepping into the picture I've just imagined. No answer: they're probably all back on the sunporch, with Charlieo.

I ring again; the door opens immediately this time, he opens the door, *he* does, leaning on crutches. He is massive, huge, as though the loss of a leg has inflated the rest of him. He is changed. Even his hair is changed: not long, but longer, and brown, as though the gold that it used to be has tarnished.

He opens the storm door, props it with a crutch: there is the chewed looking end of what is left of his leg. I look fast so that I do not begin by not looking, wait-ing for a better time to look. So that I do not go on, not looking. He is not wearing the chaste, striped pajamas I'd pictured, the empty leg neatly folded and safety-pinned back. He is wearing cutoffs.

So I say, Aren't you cold? and lift my chin in the vague direction of the leg.

One leg is, he says. A little. One leg isn't. A pause. He looks demonic, though maybe it's the distortion of the glass of the door.

So, Charlieo says. *Jo*ellen. His voice – sarcastic – is a surprise, somehow making fun of my mother. Jo*ellen* is how she told me to tell people to say it.

Fuller Brush? he says. Magazines? Yes? You must be new at this. You should work on your sales pitch. If it was me, I'd start out: "Hello. I was in the neighborhood. Stopped by because I have something you can't live without!"

Hey, I say. Who's writing your material these days? Some retired vaudeville comic?

Good material, he says. Don't wanna waste it. He hops a little, readjusting the crutches.

Don't you want to sit down?

Nah, he says. I sit down all the time. Down is my operative word.

I nod. So, I say. How you doing? With it – I raise my chin at the crutches.

Oh, he says. Superb. I'm becoming quite fluent. Crutch, he says. It's like Esperanto.

Well, then, you'll have to teach me.

He shifts again, hops, adjusts. Someone had taped a folded white cloth to the top of each crutch to ease what must be the pain of the whole of his weight settled under his arms, the two lines like stitched cuts. Somebody – Mr. O'Casey, Douglas or Herman – had padded and taped the crutch handles one night while Charlieo slept (downstairs, I was right, on the sunporch, though there is no hospital bed). They would have crept in. Picked up the crutches, one in each hand, so they would not clatter: a beach chair sound. In the morning, hoisting himself up, Charlieo would have noticed the padding; how he was now slightly higher than he'd been the night before; how the crutches with padding were incrementally more comfortable than the crutches without, but that the tape scratched.

White hospital adhesive, he'd think. He would not ask for it, though everyone in the house, on the block, everyone in town who knew him and half the people who did not would happily go to a drugstore. They would hold up their hands, the one not holding the dainty white bag, refusing repayment.

Want to know how *long* I was in the hospital? Charlieo says, and I can hear him that day on the beach: I leave in four weeks, three days, want to know how many minutes?

The hospital *here*, he is saying. Not counting the hospitals there.

I'm sorry, I say, if that's meant for me. I was planning to come. I . . . What can I do now?

Well – and there is that grin again, that devil-grin.

Well, he says. Just don't let them take me to court.

Court, I say. (A pad? A pencil? Should I be writing this down?)

Court?

Court, court, you know. Scales of justice?

I don't get it, I say. Don't let who take you?

No one, he says. That's not the point. His face reddens, he spits when he talks. Court? he says. You know what a court is?

I'm sorry. I don't follow.

COURT! I can't go to COURT! he yells. Don't you get it? I'll lose – and he lifts up one crutch. It bats the aluminum stripping on the side of the door.

I can't go to court! he yells. No leg to stand on!

CHAPTER 32

··

Mrs. O'Casey does not want to go to Joellen about Charlieo. For one thing, she does not know Joellen's address. This seems an insurmountable problem and it increases her anger: there is no dignified option. She can't just arrive at Joellen's (as Joellen has done often enough at this house, she says to herself). Well that's as it may be. *I* can't!

When Mrs. O'Casey talks to herself, the voice in her head is always thickened by a brogue. She is Irish from the other side, though Mr. O'Casey says: only on a technicality. She'd come out, with her parents, at nine months. Speaking, her accent is American but in her head, the voice has the thickness and cadence of her mother's.

These are her choices: call up Joellen herself; ask Charlieo for Joellen's address; ask someone at Joellen's job; ask the woman whose name she can't remember, who did for Joellen and her father.

In the end this last seems the least onerous choice, although how can she call up a woman having no name to call her? She does not know if the woman is a Miss or a Mrs. or which, to this particular Negro woman, or to Negroes in general, would be the more insulting if wrong. She tries to think which would offend her more but, truth be told, she can't remember what it feels like not being married.

Finally she asks Charlieo, although he is hard to talk to these days, insolent and sarcastic. She is nervous in his presence, nervous in a way she has not been since the boys were little and she took them down to the beach. She hunted out tide pools for them to play in where the water was placid and warm and safe, but the boys had no interest in tide pools. They went crashing into the surf while she stood on the shore scanning in every direction for their skinned, wet heads.

Charlieo's watching TV, the room darkened, depressing. Sometimes she is half afraid of him and thinks (then hates herself for thinking): but I can outrun him.

He's in the big chair with the cracked green leather hassock in front of it; coming at him from behind she expects his two legs to be up on the hassock. In the space of time that it takes her to get to the foot of the chair, see that there's no foot on the footstool, she fills up with grief for her boy.

Who will not look up. Who makes her stand in the flickering, depressing light. Who, when she begins to speak says – Shhhh!

Now, he says, at some clearly arbitrary time: it is not a commercial. Yes?

He has a routine: he watches TV for hours; at two or three in the afternoon he works out. The floor of the sunporch is mined with dumbbells and barbells that Mrs. O'Casey cannot even roll with a foot, and with the black plates that are like discuses: five pounds and ten and fifteen. She hears the ring and clank of the weights, Charlieo grunting, when she passes the sunporch in the afternoons.

Yes? Charlieo says and his mother says – I wanted to know, what was the name of the woman who came in and did for Joellen (on "Joellen" he looks back at the TV) and her father?

Charlieo does not answer. She waits, miffed and put off. It is sometimes like being alone with a large untrained dog in the house. When the boys were small, she would never say yes to a dog. How could you know what a dog might be thinking?

Charlie? she says finally. I asked you a que . . .

Ida, he says and she is so relieved. It has gone well! He has told her! Then she has to go on.

No, she says, pleasantly, gently. I mean her last name.

Ida, he says, splutters, in the frosted TV light she sees him spray spit. All I know is Ida. I don't know if she *has* a last name!

Ida? she would have to say. This is Eileen? Eileen O'Casey?

As it turns out though, she does not speak to Ida, Ida does not answer the phone, or perhaps she no longer works at the Stein house. For days Mrs. O'Casey dials Joellen's old number, her apprehensiveness rising with each ring, her palm sweating against the receiver. When there is no answer she is relieved, until she notices the relief and the apprehension returns, stronger or sharper, as though apprehension was cumulative.

And then at four one afternoon, someone picks up the phone.

Stein residence, a man's voice says. There is something dear and sad about it – this man, living alone, and Stein residence and Mrs. O'Casey has a fleeting and odd thought: what if I'd been married to him? So odd, so far from anything she's thought before that she cannot, immediately, answer.

Hello, please? Who is it?

Mr. Stein! she says finally. It's Mrs. O'Casey! Her voice is full of emphases that mean: hasn't it been a long while!

Oh! he says. Hello! his voice pleasant and hearty, then suddenly scared as he slides back into remembering Joellen's sick night, the night they (thankfully; he is still grateful) found her on the beach, took her home, or who knows what would have happened. It is still what he leaps to, hearing Mrs. O'Casey's voice on the phone.

I understand Joellen's got her own apartment? Mrs. O'Casey says. Her voice is even and reassuring.

Yes! he says. Yes! Can you believe that? An apartment above a garage, he says and says the address and describes it though he has not seen the inside; had gone, only, one Sunday and stood on the sidewalk checking out where Joellen lives.

I'm not altogether happy, he says and then, embarrassed, he says he'd better ring off, and Mrs. O'Casey remembers one more feeling from girlhood: when by some accident, she was given the largest, best piece of whatever it was. When it had come to her without asking.

They are having tea, tea in the strict sense: tea only. They are drinking it out of dark mugs, the tea murky and invisible except for its steam. There is a cracked saucer on the table, for the teabags, and two spoons, but no milk or sugar or napkins and no biscuits or toast. They sit lifting and sipping from and replacing their mugs on the sour-smelling checked plastic cloth; the tea seems to Mrs. O'Casey to smell also. She takes mock sips.

They have not spoken much to each other, though Mrs. O'Casey has said many things to herself, in her head:

Nothing! Not even a cracker! Not even milk for the tea!

You did stop in, Eileen. The girl didn't know you were coming. (She paused here, on this true thing.) Still. I would never have nothing! Milk! She sipped at the foul-smelling tea, frowning into the steam.

You don't have to drink it, Joellen said.

Oh no. It's fine.

Then you should've brought something. Soda bread, Mrs. O'Casey says to herself. Which Joellen does – or does not – like?

Do you like soda bread? she asks.

Joellen raises her eyebrows. They have not said very much; this seems an odd question to start with.

Sure, Joellen says, and then amends it. I guess. (All those lemon pies.)

So far, the only pleasurable part of this visit to Mrs. O'Casey was Joellen's surprise, her clear discomfort on opening the door and finding Mrs. O'Casey on the other side of it – a kind of payout, Mrs. O'Casey felt, for the pain Joellen has caused Charlieo. But this pleasure leaves her deflated and somewhat horrified at herself. Lately, her life seems sprinkled with venial sins and she smells then, as if it is coming from the tea mug, the musty and perfumed claustrophobia of the confessional.

Well, Mrs. O'Casey says now and sets down her mug. I came, Joellen, to ask for your help.

Joellen puts her tea down also.

Yes, Mrs. O'Casey says, as though Joellen has said to her – help?

Yes, with Charlie. He's not himself, Mrs. O'Casey says.

Joellen thinks, No. He's less than, he's only part of himself. She does not say it. She can hear Charlieo saying it, though.

Where is he? Joellen asks.

Mrs. O'Casey waves at the air in the kitchen meaning, Not here. Since he got back, she says, I . . . I don't know what to do for him. How to help him. He is so . . . hurt, she says.

She stops, shakes her head. Hurt isn't right, with its implication of physical pain, though she is sure there is that too. She looks at the purse she holds on her lap, snaps the clasp open and closed. She has probably had it for thirty-five years. The clasp shuts with a bit of resistance, a muted click she has always liked.

More like damaged, Mrs. O'Casey finally says. She sometimes believes that the boy they got back, the boy who lifts weights, watches daytime TV in the dark, is not really her son. That there is some network of substitutions – orphaned or amnesiac boys sent home as replacements for real sons; sent to where they were most needed. She feels sorry then for the boy lifting weights on her sunporch and for herself, the most fragile of mothers.

Damaged, Joellen says, nodding, appraising the word.

Mrs. O'Casey briefly closes her eyes, hearing this private word said back to her.

Damaged, Joellen goes on thinking. The word is large and powerful to her; she sees things: crushed cereal boxes, wheelless cars, houses with broken windows. Damage can be repaired, she thinks. Mrs. O'Casey must know how to do it. All she has to do is listen.

Out back, Mrs. O'Casey tells me, cocking a spatula over her shoulder. She's cooking hamburgers – meatballs, she calls them – and the smell of fried meat and breadcrumbs that I have smelled so many times follows me out the back door, across the concrete patio, into the yard. I head back to where Charlieo's garden used to be and for one long moment, I can't remember how old I am; where in history we are now.

I hear the sound of a spade on hard earth before I get to it, a ringing and scraping that travels clearly on the cold air. The yard has a verdancy that does not go with the weather. There are evergreens here and the grass, for some reason, stays a kind of tough, greasy green all year. I have to say to myself: it's winter.

I come around to the garden. Charlieo is sitting on the hard ground. The earth is the color of unbaked cookies. He is banging the blade of a hand trowel against the ground – smash, smash, smash, like a baby in a sandbox.

What are you doing?

He looks up, startled first, then malevolent. He goes on smiling, banging the trowel.

Quit it, I say. Will you quit it? I can feel the metallic ringing of the spade in my teeth.

Fancy seeing you here, he says. Won't you join me?

To do what? What are you doing?

Why garden work, he says. So therapeutic. Do sit down.

No thanks. I'll stand.

Something circles my ankle, soft first, a dried weed blown up against me, then it stiffens, a cup or a brace and then I am down, I come down on my back with my standing foot twisted under me. It hurts, a shooting fiery pain.

Son of a bitch, I fuckin' hate you! – and I'm crying.

Charlieo's face goes pale and chalky. Oh, God, he says. Let me help you. Are you hurt? He moves so close, I can smell the sour cold on his skin. I can smell cinnamon mouthwash.

Get away from me! I say and rock back. Pain shoots through my leg under the tipped weight of my body. My breath hisses.

He is quiet, tapping the heel of the trowel quietly against the cold ground. I always thought land, growing things was a kind of salvation, he says. You know what we did over there? Whole face of the land was blown away. You know what we did? Bombed the shit out of it to be sure, I guess, in the three or four days between bombings, nothing might grow. We did it, he says. The good guys.

The trowel goes pat, pat, pat.

So that's some kind of explanation for what you're doing back here?

I'm not doing anything. It's just someplace to be besides in the house. Trowel was out here. And he tosses it away from himself, as though he is putting it back where he found it.

Look, I'm sorry, he says. I didn't mean to hurt you. I really didn't.

I don't get it, I say. You never used to be . . .

I never used to be a lot of things, he says.

Yeah, I say. Like an asshole.

He holds his head still: I could say anything.

See if you can stand, he says. If it's . . . twisted or something. He lifts his chin at my hurt leg, still bent underneath me, the one he can't see.

Here, he says and slides a crutch along the ground. Use this.

But I won't. I stand on my own. I can put a little weight on my ankle, not much.

Look, he says. Stay here. I'll get somebody to give you a lift. Maybe he grins when he says this. He hoists himself up; the crutches rise like the splayed legs of a long-legged bird: a flamingo.

I wait what seems a long time. The ground is mottled with various trowel marks shaped like fish and like smiles. I count slowly to a hundred, angrier after each increment of ten. He is back at the house, watching TV. He hasn't told anyone.

Where's Joellen, Mrs. O'Casey will have asked him.

Oh. Gone home.

I start towards the house, very slowly. I can't put much weight on my foot.

The back door slams and Charlieo calls, Hey, Joellen. Hold up! Somebody's with him, Herman it turns out. He rushes across the lawn, reaches me, scoops me up. His speed is courtly. Charlieo stands still on the patio, leaning on his crutches.

Herman carries me across the yard, the bushes and trees moving quickly past. I let my head go against him, against the bones in his chest. At some clearly marked but invisible place I can smell the cooking smells from the house again: the fried meat and breadcrumbs.

The air in the yard is heavy with cooking and with its own smell, moist and familiar. A bird, a sparrow, chitters and the smell has feathers in it. Beneath these smells there are other ones: the ground heated by sun in the summer, pollen, ocean salt. The fried meat smelled heavier, then, than the air.

It is darkening in the backyard, the greens almost black underfoot though looking up, the sky is still light. Colors buzz in front of my eyes, on and off, like flickering neon. Look what's gone, they are saying. What won't be coming back.

I remember the bones in Herman's chest. I remember this bumpy ride. The tick of glass pieces in the bottom of a bucket.

There is no way to know which things you'll forget, which of the things you are smelling and hearing and touching and saying will come back at you, like the smells in this backyard, leaving you sick and weak and full of longing.

....

CHAPTER 33

The cold leaves to set itself down someplace else. Cold's not like rain or heat, temporary liquids and gases. There's a solidity to cold. I couldn't picture it resorbed into the atmosphere. Cold doesn't cease to exist. It folds its tent and moves on.

We have a stretch of near 60. The ground, frozen and taut, relaxes and gives off that rich loam smell that's like spring. The sand nearest the water turns slappy. Crocus and snowdrop shoots come up. I had the urge to hammer them back into the ground with my shoe. It was only the beginning of January. They'd get blitzed. When the real spring arrived, the flowers wouldn't.

Alice King was right though: the warm weather brought people in, and the phones never stopped ringing. People called wanting the same places they'd rented last year and got testy when I asked for more information. Let me speak to Alice, they said, hissing. *Alice* knows who I am! *Alice* remembers!

The other agent came back, an older woman named Vivian. She was tiny, she wore immaculate skirts and white blouses, her gold jacket so small it seemed to have been tacked together from mouse-sized fragments of cloth. Her gray hair was short, tightly curled. She was very efficient, although she sighed all the time, as though Alice had interrupted her usual six months of sleep.

The customers were rude and dismissive, shouting over each other's voices pushing ahead of the person in front. The married ones, lawyers and lawyers' wives, had money, according to Alice, but did not like parting with it. They were agitated and pinched and demanded attention. They brought whiny children. Are you in charge here? they said, battling the children out of their jackets.

I'm . . . I began, and they could tell, in one word, that I was not. They looked off behind me, pinched frowns. Your face'll stay like that one of these days, Ida used to tell me.

The girl bennies came in alone or in pairs to rent what they called group houses, which made them sound like halfway homes for mental patients. The girls were organized, sometimes they had checklists. The boys came in boisterous gangs. They wore puffy jackets. They laughed and elbowed each other. Their fingers closed and unclosed around phantom beer cans.

It was exhausting and loud. The office filled up with noise. At night, when we were leaving, there were empty soda cans and cigarette butts on the floor and a permanent blue haze under the ceiling.

Alice and Vivian had done it before. Vivian spoke quietly to people, leaning over her desk, her butt lifted out of her chair as she pointed something out on a contract. Her transactions were tidy: she was a gold-and-blue buoy of calm.

Alice King strode in and out, customers trailing behind her.

I mostly stayed in the office, answering the phones, handing out Cokes to already sugared-up bennies. I was uneasy, being there by myself, the only non-bennie.

Joellen! Alice King calls across the clamorous, open space of the office. There is too little furniture to absorb sound and hers is a voice that carries. She is holding a phone receiver, jigging it back and forth in her hand like a cocktail shaker.

Yes? I say into the phone. When Alice answers the phone she says – Alice King – loud and forthright. I creep up on my calls. I am never sure I want to know who it is.

Jo-El-Len, Jo-El-Len, I hear the voice chanting before I even get the receiver to my ear. Charlieo. He has been different since the night he tackled me. A strain, the doctor who came to the O'Caseys' house said it was. He sounded disgusted, as though strain was not what he'd gone to medical school for. He wrote the word on his pad with the T underlined – STRAIN – so we wouldn't confuse it with something more serious.

You seem to be having a fine time all by yourself there, I say to Charlieo.

Who is this?

Please.

Want to go for a drive?

Now? I say. I can't go now. I'm working.

Not now. Saturday. A *drive*, he says, hammering the word, then silence: he is waiting for me to say – Drive? *Can* you? To picture his absent leg, the empty column of air over the gas pedal. I am supposed to say, We can use my leg for the gas.

Through the receiver I hear him humming.

I say, Quit setting me up!

I am not set . . .

You are!

Just a simple invitation, Joellen.

But nothing is simple. He is different from how he was the night before he tripped me, but he is always different, he is never the same.

They refit the car, he says. Okay?

I think of his crutches, padded, taped.

Hand gizmos, he says. You'll be perfectly safe. His voice deflates: an empty balloon.

Yes, I say. I'll go for a drive with you Saturday. See how simple that was?

Yeah, well, I'm not sure I want to, he says. After all that.

But on Saturday he is outside the car, leaning against the front bumper across the street from where I live. I can see him pulling up to the curb, picking his stance. He grins that maniacal grin when he sees me, then grabs the roof of the car and swings himself in on his strong arms.

He is breathing hard, which I do not hear but see, his chest lifting quickly. There is sweat on his upper lip, almost invisible, like the camouflaged ova of insects. There are about five knobbed shifts spoking up from the floor, like a bunch of dead pond weeds. They give the car a rehabilitational air. In this car, you would not use the words "pleasure" and "driving" together in a sentence.

I say, Let's go to the beach. He doesn't move, he's considering.

What? A simple invitation. To quote you.

He says, Steps.

A series of long flights run down from the boardwalk, the wood a striated gray-brown. Charlieo was right. It is like learning to speak another language.

I say, Sorry. We could go under.

No problem, Charlieo says. He is busy with the gizmos, his large arm muscles swimming under his skin.

The beach is windy. Sand flings itself against the nylon of our jackets, stinging my face and hands. I keep turning around, thinking there are kids behind us, throwing it.

We sit almost under the boardwalk. Fuckin' *windy*, Charlieo says and sits down hard. It was a mistake, making him come here. It took him a long time to go the short distance, over sand, that we've come.

Hungry? I say. I could get us some . . . I stand up to scan the storefronts on the boardwalk. It's winter, nothing's open. I turn to look out at the ocean which, because of the curve of the sand, I cannot see. My self, standing, is like a curtain between us. He can recover in private.

And when he speaks again – Hey, he says. Come on down – he sounds calmer.

You know what? I say, We should have brought our lists.

Of? he says. Camp clothes for summer?

The when-I-grow-up ones.

We said ten years. I don't think it's been ten months. You're not even out of high school.

What are you? I say. A spokesman for Leon? I have forgotten about school, something unfinished.

Charlieo lies on his side, scooping up sand, letting it run through his fingers. His left, invisible leg could just be buried.

When I was little, I say, I used to try to count the grains of sand. I'd start with a small patch. I pick up a handful and show him the small amount in my hand.

It seemed urgent to me that somebody do it, I say. I don't know why.

If you carried one grain of sand at a time from here to, oh, make it easy, the parking lot, he says. When the whole beach was empty you'd still only be at the beginning of eternity.

What's that?

A definition. Of how long eternity is.

By who?

He doesn't answer, lies the way he was lying, sifting sand through his fingers. Then he says, You can throw my list out. If you still have it. I consider it irrelevant.

I will not throw it out! We said ten years. We made a bargain. I am suddenly panicked, the feeling I used to get realizing the impossibility of counting all that sand.

I won't be any of those things, he says.

You don't know that. You had good stuff on your list. Landscape, botany.

He nods. But I can't see him doing those plant-type things either.

There's only one thing on that list I still might get to be, he says. Maybe. Depending on circumstance. It could go either way. He lets sand pour through the funnel of his hand. It runs close to my hand. I feel its smoky coolness, close but not touching.

Which thing, I say, watching the sand.

He waits. When his hand's empty he says: Guess.

CHAPTER 34

Mrs. O'Casey calls regularly, either just after I've seen Charlieo or when it's been a while since I've seen him last. I can picture her at her kitchen table worrying the dry skin in the crotch of her thumbnail: Joellen's not seen him in, how long has it been?

How are you? Mrs. O'Casey always asks, but she means: how's he?

We haven't seen you in a while, she says, but she means: You haven't seen him.

Royal Real Estate.

Joellen?

I pause, the secret, still private second before I have to give myself away. Sometimes I think about saying, Who's calling? I'll see if she's free.

Hello?

Yes, I say. Mrs. O'Casey. How are you?

You must have the ESP or something, she says. Always knowin' it's me. Her voice is pleasured, a brief intermission in our business.

She asks me to dinner. Mrs. O'Casey has changed towards me. Where she used to be hurt when I said I was busy or that I would try to come over, then did not, now she is persistent. She will not take no for an answer.

You the official gatekeeper? I ask, as Charlieo opens then hops away from the door.

Not yet, he says. There's an apprenticeship period before they make you official.

Seeing him I never know what to expect. There is no carry-over from the preceding time, when things seem to be moving towards normal between us. The next time, we always have to start over.

The sound of men laughing comes from the kitchen.

Gang's all here, Charlieo says.

Herman and Douglas are at the table, Douglas with a beer, Herman drinking a glass of milk. They sit slapping the backs of each other's heads like two of the Three Stooges. I suddenly know that Douglas and Herman won't ever marry. Douglas's marriage to Daisy seems a long time ago, like a rumor.

I'm coaching a Little League, Douglas says.

Oh great! Mrs. O'Casey says. Isn't that great?

Same team as last year? Mr. O'Casey asks.

Douglas nods, eating.

Carl's Diarrhea! Herman says. He laughs, spraying food.

Lovely! Mrs. O'Casey says.

None of that! from Mr. O'Casey. This is a dinner table. People are eating their dinner.

What? Herman says. It's the name of the team. Carl's D . . .

Herman! Mrs. O'Casey clatters a butter knife.

What! Herman says. Carl's DAIRY, I was going to say. It's the . . .

Name of the team I *played* on, Douglas says. Like at the turn of the fuckin' last . . .

Douglas! – Mr. O'Casey.

Sorry, Ma. Century, Douglas continues. I don't even think Carl's (Mr. and Mrs. O'Casey look up) DAIRY, Douglas says, sponsors a team anymore. I don't even know if there IS a Carl's DAIRY.

Carl's Dairy was a dusty wood-floored delicatessen two blocks from the high school. There was a rusted metal sign outside that said Homemade Ice Cream, but there never was any. They were always out of chips and snack cakes.

Charlieo takes a hit off his beer. It is his fifth or his sixth beer. He's got the empties hoarded next to him like collectibles.

Gone for years, I say. What did they put in there again? Char? We all look at him; he doesn't answer. Picks up his beer and drinks.

I forget, a superette? I say.

A Kwik-Shop, Mrs. O'Casey says. We look at each other. She looks at Charlieo, shooing me back.

Charlieo, I say. What was the name of the Little League team you played on?

The other talk stops. Herman is gap-mouthed, food showing.

What? I say, looking around. He played Little League. Right? Right? I turn to Charlieo who is also looking at me. Almost smiling.

Right, he says. Yes indeedy. Vinnie's Pizza. I'd remind you what we called that, but it's not great dinner table chat either. On the other hand, Joellen, you should know better. We don't mention my Little League days in this house. You need TWO LEGS to play Little League, don't forget. We don't mention things that include Legs, even though a Leg, PART of a leg's an acceptable loss. Not a life. Still, we don't say Football, because then we'd have to say foot. We don't say – Pass me a leg, when my mother makes chicken. Dark meat, we say. We say dark meat.

He laughs, a raucous sound: he is the only one laughing. Mr. O'Casey reddens an un-human color, like jello or kool-aid.

Your mother, he says, made us this fine dinner. I suggest we honor her by eating the rest of it in peace.

I look down at my plate; what is it we're eating? Lamb, mint jelly, potatoes roasted in fat so that they taste, also, like lamb though they are sharp-cornered and leathery. I put my fork down.

Hey, Herman says. I came up with a new one. His voice intrudes into the quiet room like a car without a muffler.

Off a cliff in your *car!* Herman says.

Nah, Douglas says. It's too much like "jumping off the Empire State Building."

What is this now? Mrs. O'Casey asks. She sounds stricken. This is a game she never remembers.

In your *car*, Herman says. We don't have a car one.

"How would you rather die," Mr. O'Casey says, explaining to his wife. You know. That silly game.

Douglas is shaking his head. I challenge, he says.

Mrs. O'Casey gets up to clear the table.

Lost in space, I say, looking at Charlieo. I nudge his elbow. Remember?

I have one, Charlieo says. Listen to this. Captain goes out behind the hooches of this camp.

"How would you rather . . . " Herman says, peevish.

A little light R-and-R, Charlieo is saying. A little "alone time"?

Everyone's watching him. Douglas, Herman, their father are silent and uncomfortable. This makes them seem girlish.

There's a little copse, Charlieo says.

A . . . ? Herman says.

Trees? Charlieo says.

So there's sniper fire, Charlieo says, his hand up and cocked. Mr. O'Casey frowns and flushes again. That must be another rule: No guns at the table.

So they find him, Charlieo says. He's got his dick in his hand. He's . . .

Where? Mrs. O'Casey says. Where did this happen?

So what's the question, Herman says, impatient. "How would you rather die, before or after jerking . . . ?"

Nam, Ma, Charlieo says, and Mr. O'Casey stands up, his chair knocking backwards. Two potatoes roll off his plate leaving tipsy grease trails.

Maybe Nam is like leg: not something you say.

Wait, Charlieo says. I have others.

Your mother worked hard on this meal! Mr. O'Casey says. A vein has cropped out in his temple, purple, dangerous looking.

Look! Mrs. O'Casey says. Dessert!

She's gone to the counter, comes back with a pie held out on her hands. The meringue sweats and shines in the light.

I am carrying dishes from the table to the sink, where Mrs. O'Casey is doing the washing up.

That's it, I say. The table is empty of dishes, and men. I better get going, I say.

She nods. You're most likely tired, she says.

I am, I say. Long days at work.

What we talk about is never what we're saying. He's wearing us down, she is telling me. You too? But I will not answer: my gift to Charlieo.

I'll get one of the boys to take you, Mrs. O'Casey says. She wipes her hands on her apron and takes a step towards the living room, where the light from the TV hip-hops.

I'll take her, Charlieo says. He is standing in the arched doorway that leads from the kitchen to the sunporch. We did not hear him come in. Under the sounds of the dishes being cleared and the faucet running there was the ching-ching of his lifted weights.

Oh! Mrs. O'Casey says and retreats. We both stand with our backs against the lip of the sink.

Douglas or Herman could go either, she says. If you're tired.

Or I could walk. It's . . .

. . . dark and 38 fuckin' (he looks at his mother, touches his fingertips to his head) . . . degrees, he says. The thaw has ended. It is fully winter again.

They walk us to the front door, all of them, a phalanx closes behind us as we go out onto the brick steps.

Watch out for any ice, Mr. O'Casey says from between the shoulders of his two sons.

Safe home, Mrs. O'Casey says.

The rounds and protuberances of their faces are like cake frosting in the whiteness of the porch light. I am afraid, suddenly, of going out into the dark. The last of the light ends a third of the way down the walk. I touch Charlieo's jacket for balance.

I am settled in the car, he settles me. I do not look out the window at his parents, his brothers, still clustered on the front porch. I am not yours, I am telling them.

He opens the back door, lays the crutches across the back seat, arranges them as though they are sleeping children, then lowers himself into the front seat, smiling or grimacing up at the overhead light. When the door shuts, I can still see the throbbing white line of his teeth.

We drive to the end of the street, then stop. Where to? he says. His hands in his lap are green and pink from the dashboard lights.

What do you mean? I say. Home. My apartment. Where else?

We could play miniature golf.

Oh, I say. This is Charlieo. I know who this is.

In the winter? I'll take a snowcheck, I tell him.

Yeah, well, I suppose my championship golf days are behind me now anyway.

Please, I say. Does this come with a violin accompaniment?

You're right, he says. I should take up some other sport. Place kickers only use one leg.

Why can't you say "foot"ball anyway? I ask. It's not like it's FEETball.

This is Charlieo, I think again.

The car is warm and steamy. I hear the engine, the muffled clicking of the crutches behind me. We drive and drive.

You taking some *long* cut I don't know about? I say.

Is this the scenic route?

The car turns, the turn continues, pushing me into the doorknob. The fake lake, I think.

It's *closed*, I say again, meaning the golf course, which is not far.

I crack the window, sniff at the space for salt air. Which I do not smell. There is something else, something almost like burnt hair.

He drives around whatever this circle is, drives around it again. My shoulder stays wedged into the sharp little bone of the doorknob.

I'm a little dizzy, he says, laughing.

I say, How many beers did you have, are you drunk?

I'm a little lost, he says.

Lost? How can you be lost? It's not that big of a town.

I'm a little lost, he says again, as if I have not spoken. I'm pulling over. To get my ball bearings.

Don't pull over, I say. You're not pulling over.

He does though. Parks on a ring of houses that form the outside edge of a circle – the *fake lake*, I think again. The voice in my head is insistent.

It is not the fake lake though; even without the sound and heavy smell of the ocean it can't be. There are no floodlights whitening the house facades. There are no careful front lawns.

And then things start to happen, unrelated things happening in a seamless way that makes them seem dreamed.

I recognize this place. LuAnne, Joe's mother, lives here.

I say, Oh! I know where we are now. I can tell you how to get . . .

Alone at last, Charlieo says and I smile but then I hear him. He has turned towards me on the front seat. One side of his face is pale green.

He reaches his arm across the back of the seat, his fingertips touching my neck.

Quit it, I say and bat at his hand.

It moves away, then it comes back.

Turn this way, he says.

What for? No!

Turn this way, he says, as though this is the first time he has said it. I think: he is mad.

He turns me. I move in one piece, until I am facing him on the seat but, still, he doesn't stop pushing. My legs come out from under me, I'm stretched out.

Hey! I say. What are you doing? Cut it out! Quit it!

My head hits the arm rest in the dark.

A hand, not my own hand, rubs the back of my head.

My head doesn't hurt, then it is hurting.

He is kissing me – What? – his lips are spit wet, I almost laugh, turning and turning my head.

Charlieo! I say. The sound of his name is a comfort. This is Charlieo. He will save me.

He has not shaved. His face abrades my skin.

I push at him, my legs pinned. I try flexing my toes but can't feel them. I think: an accident. I think: dreaming.

He is straddling me, his thighs looming and white – when did he take his pants off? I lie across the seat like his crutches.

Get off me, I yell. Get off me, and Stop! and I'll call the police! I flash in and out of hearing myself. There are the things I am saying, the things that are happening, the things going on in my head.

He is straddling me, his two thighs strong and intact. He throws his head back. His neck, caught by a light from outside, is long, muscular, silver, like the neck of a wolf or a dog. He is riding me, still covered by jockey shorts as white as tooth-whitening toothpaste.

I move, going for him with my nails and hooked fingers, but he is fast and has all that available upper body strength. He pins my arms, using both his hands at first, then only one. My arms are as thin as stripped sticks. His thighs grip tight. I feel the warmth of one leg down my side, the coolness from the absence of the other.

Ever been fucked by a one-legged Irishman? he says. A one-legged Irish Marine? A line of saliva hangs from his mouth, drips onto my cheek.

I hate you, I say. I say it again and again. Then I stop fighting. I just stop.

He fumbles inside his briefs. I think of the man he told us about, the captain, shot with his dick in his hands.

His hand, his poling fist, punches into me. Move, it is telling me. Fight, move.

I do not move.

I make my brain patchy and dark.

And then he stops. Nothing has happened. He has done nothing. Maybe they can't get it up: one-legged Irish Marines.

Get out, he tells me, but he doesn't move, sits on me, his head turned towards the windshield, hand still in his shorts like he has forgotten it's there.

I am still pinned.

Go! he says. Go! Get the fuck out of my car, he says, almost howls: a wolf or a dog.

He shoves open the car door on my side, hoists himself up on his arms, one on the seatback, one on the dashboard, he is shoving at me with his knee. His breath drags inward, like sobs. He keeps shoving. I have no leverage, no place to hold on. I go out head and hands first, like a tumbler.

He takes off, the car door is dangling open, then it shuts. He leaves rubber, the substance and smell, on the street. For a long time – months, a year – those marks will remain visible.

It's dawn when I get home, the air cold and wet, the light silver. I've been walking around a long time. I didn't want to go home, take a hot shower and sleep only to wake up at three or four or five in the morning to my door shuddering under Charlieo's fist, the chattering glass, his crutches against the porch wall. I know he will drive around for a while, cool off, come to find me.

I stood for a time where he'd left me, on the dark, curved street, the porch lights dim as matches, breathing in the rotting, restorative odor of wet leaves. I thought about going to Leon's but we hadn't spoken since I moved out: what would I tell him? Charlieo tried to rape me?

I don't quite understand, Leon would say. He'd sniff at the air near me and be sure he smelled sex though he had never smelled it after I'd been with Joe three or four times in one day. Don't be judgmental, Leon will tell himself, but the look on his face will be curdled; he'll choose a more distant chair.

I thought about going to Ida's, going right up on the porch, knocking till somebody came to the door: Ida, her nightgown dipping down off her shoulder. I'd watch the shift and flutter of her flesh, creamy and boned.

I'm sorry. Were you sleeping?

She'd hitch up the gown, cover the formerly bare place with her hand. Her voice, when she said, What you want here, Joellen? or, You know the time? angrier than it would have been had I not stared.

I walked, skirting the neighborhoods of the people I was thinking about, skittish about slow-moving cars, too pumped up to stop moving. I walked all night. I walked until I was too tired to take one more step, then I took another step and was too tired to take the one after that. Exhaustion began at my feet and travelled upwards through my calves and thighs and hips. My muscles felt bruised, banged together. I didn't go home until it got light.

And there he was, sitting on the long flight of steps to my door. At each step I took, his head nodded.

Joellen, he says. Not Charlieo, Mr. O'Casey. I knew halfway up the driveway: the silver of his hair and no crutches.

He stands to meet me. I'm surprised by his size; I have always thought of him as tall and upright and broad, like his sons, but he is not. He is compact, well-proportioned, though years of keeping himself lean have turned him stringy.

It is cold and wet and quiet.

Not home? I ask and gesture for him to sit as though this is my living room. I sit too, the wood steps cold on the backs of my thighs. It's not until later that I think I should have asked him to come in.

Not home, he says. It feels like we're at the end of a conversation; the preliminaries have already occurred.

Thought he, the two of you, might've come here, he says. Ordinarily, I wouldn't've bothered you . . .

And I am suddenly angry at what they all assume I am: some girl, here to service his son. The night of Charlieo's send-off party, the wall of them seeing us off after dinner tonight.

I am not a sacrifice I want to tell him, but he is just sitting there, nodding his head like an old man.

Well, he says. Slaps both knees and stands.

Now what? I say, looking up at him.

Send out a search party, he tells me.

There is an absence of surprise in his voice. He's been expecting this, or something like it, though maybe I'm wrong and all I'm hearing is tiredness.

How long have you been here? I ask.

He stretches, arching his back against his spread fingers, something I've seen Charlieo do. Bones click in his back. Don't know, he says, his voice strained because he is stretching. I guess most of the night.

Maybe he's home, I say. By now. I haven't seen him for a long time, I say. Most of the night. Maybe he's gone home.

He nods. Maybe. He does not believe this. Someone would have come for him.

Do they know you're here? I ask him.

Unless they guess it, he says. He looks up at the long flight of steps to my door. It's lighter out now, the white-painted steps clean and shining.

He's not here, I say.

He nods. He says, Any guesses?

One. You won't want to hear it.

He holds still, looking at me.

It's "gone," I tell him. I think he took off.

He nods again. That would be my guess too. If he wasn't here.

And I see it is not sex that he believed would have brought Charlieo to me; it is sanctuary.

Do you want some coffee, I almost ask, but then I think of us sitting across from each other at a coffeeshop table – I don't have any coffee upstairs – waiting for our order, not talking. What would we talk about? Everything has already been said.

Alice King will not let me pick up the phone. All that day and the next I leap for it, but no matter how quick I am, she is quicker. For me? I mouth or make a gesture, my two hands flat on my chest, eyebrows raised. She goes on talking, turns her back to me or, in her own time, gives a little dismissive shake of her head.

Hey, I say pretending cheerfulness. The phones are *my* job. Read my job description!

She nods, doesn't look up, cleaning her nails with the dart-shaped cap of her pen.

I'm expecting this call, I say. Really important.

Look, she says. This is a business. I can't worry about who answers the phones. She was twisting the Somebody Loves You cup on her desk.

I kept my hand, as if casually, on top of my phone while I worked. Still, she got to it before me. She didn't rush: the phone just sprang into her hand like some trick she'd practiced with a gun and a holster.

When the door opens about eight on the second night after Charlieo took off, and first cold air, then a man come through it, I look up. I say, Hi. Can I help you? though usually it is Alice who does this.

Am I too late? this guy says.

I say, Nope. We're still open.

Alice speaks at the same time. You are if you came by to ask me to marry you, she says. I'm taken.

The man looks from me to Alice. He blushes.

She's kidding, I say, my voice low.

Pardon? the man says. He leans his left ear down towards me which gives him the quizzical look of a puppy.

Kidding, I say, poking my thumb behind me towards Alice. His naked ear is still pink from the blush.

So what do you have in mind? Alice says. Papers scratch on her desk. Have a seat. Joellen here can show you some photos. If there's something that interests you, we'll set up a time, take you out to see it. How does that sound?

Patronizing, I want to say. It sounds patronizing.

She hands me a clipboard; I take it without turning around. On it are the specifications of each house we have listed, xeroxed photos attached. The pictures are grainy and dark. It's hard to tell where a lawn or a garage leaves off and the houses begin. In some, you can't even tell you are looking at a photo of a house.

Have a seat, Alice King says again. She stands behind the chair to the right of my desk.

The guy nods. When Alice steps away he picks up the chair and sets it down on the left side of my desk.

Mind? he says. I don't hear so great in my right ear.

Tony Packer, he tells me. He takes off his jacket. He's wearing brown pants and a shirt the color of milk-lightened coffee, the kind of clothes mothers pick out for small boys. I don't realize it is a uniform until he gets up and I see the Highway Patrol patch on his right sleeve.

Well, I say. To start, why don't you tell me where you live now? I flip through the pages on the clipboard. I've never actually done this before.

He shrugs. He says, A trailer? Not a double wide, not on a foundation or anything. It's the kind you can hitch to your car if you want to. I always liked the idea of just takin' off.

A trailer, I say. I don't think we have any . . .

No, he says, smiling. He's clean-shaven but when he smiles, I can see the shape and color his moustache would be.

Look, he says. I'm not really here about a house, although I do sometimes think about moving. Trailer's small, he says, smiling again. He touches the top of his head, smoothing the hair down as if he is saying: no headroom.

Really, he says. I'm here to see you.

Me? I say. I doubt it. Why? Did I win something?

Joellen, right? he says. Who they told me to look for. Joellen . . . He takes a pad from his pocket to read me my last name.

I don't have a car, I tell him. I don't even *drive*. This is a fact that usually shames me; now it seems like good fortune.

He looks up. Really? he says. Then how do you . . . ? He shakes his head. I'm investigating, he says. This is an investigation. Charles O'Casey?

I don't get it at first. You heard from him? I say. Why would Charlieo call him?

Tony Packer shakes his head. From his father, he says. Reported him missing. A missing person, he says.

This is right. "Damaged," his mother had said but all those months he'd been home, Charlieo had been missing.

If you'd come with me, Tony Packer says. I want you to show me the place you last saw him, answer some questions. Okay?

I think of the circle where Joe's mother lives, where Joe used to, where Charlieo left me –

Dark, I say.

He says, Flashlight.

– where everyone's missing.

Alice and I turn out the office lights and go out together. There are no stars and no moon; the only immediate light comes from a coach lamp hung over the door, bleaching it yellow. At night I can't remember what color the door is.

Going home? Alice says.

No, I say.

Tony Packer had told me to wait for him here. He said: Two minutes.

Plans, I say.

Alice drives off; the absence of her headlights leaves everything darker. The parking lot seems vast, the light from the coach lamp paltry and faded. When I look away from it, towards the highway, yellow balls dance there like Christmas tree lights.

I wait a long time. Tony Packer doesn't come. A joke, I think. Somebody's setting me up: Charlieo! Although I didn't even know that he knew Tony Packer. I wait for one or the other of them to turn up.

Nobody comes. This could be dangerous, I say out loud. The sound of my voice makes me angry.

Son of a bitch, I say. Now I have to walk all the way home in the fucking freezing dark! Anger gets me up to the highway, a ribbon of black tar lit only by a blurred white snowball of light off the roof of some business up ahead.

As soon as I start walking the cruiser comes up, high beams smoking behind me. I don't stop; he pulls even, keeping pace. I picture another car, doing 70, coming up behind him, splattering me over the highway.

Look, I yell. Quit it. You'll cause an accident.

What? he yells. He rolls down the passenger window. The staticky voice of his police radio, a sound that is like cellophane crumpling, rolls out.

Come on, he says. Get in. You've gotta be freezing.

I was freezing standing in front of the office! I say. I was freezing in the fucking dark parking lot! For twenty-five fucking minutes, I say, a time I make up. Then I get into the cruiser.

I'm sorry, he says, lowering the radio. It is still on, but quieter. There is less static.

I went to get this. And he hands me a cup so hot the cardboard registers cold to my fingers. It is not coffee, coffee would be wrong. It is soup.

I tell him the place. That circle? I say. Not the lake, the one . . .

He's already nodding. Know it. All's you have to do is give me one clue, I'll know the place, how to get there.

I think: Big deal. I put the lid back on the soup.

Don't like it? he says.

It is annoying, how he needs to say everything. It seems connected, somehow, to his deafness.

We get to the circle. The cruiser has powerful high beams, they pick out the white specks of mica in the blacktop. For a second I think it has snowed.

Now, he says. Tell me where.

Where? I say. How do I know where? It was too dark to see. The cruiser's lights brighten everything, though. When I say this, it doesn't sound true.

Okay, he says. So. Charles O'Casey your boyfriend?

Who told you that?

Just a question I have to ask.

Why? I say. It's none of your business. No.

He writes something down, something that takes a long time considering what I have said. I look out at the houses. I can see the hopping white-and-gray lights of TVs; a person passing in front of a window. The voices from the police radio seem attached to the people, as though the woman across the street holding a salad bowl of popcorn is reporting: Light 27's out on the boardwalk.

Okay, Tony Packer says. What happened between you two? You and O'Casey.

Nothing, I say. Someone I can't see is throwing handfuls of popcorn at the woman.

Something, Tony Packer says. Or you'd know where he went.

We're friends, I say. Do you know everything your friends do?

Look, he says. The way I see it: he was driving you home, you had a fight, something. Am I right?

He sounds proud, deduction a skill like familiarity with local addresses.

Do they teach you that in Highway Patrol school?

Pardon? He leans in.

Nothing.

So, he says. That night. Did you have words?

Words, I think. I don't remember any words. Charlieo on me, his weight, his head thrown back, his long silvery neck. I hated him, I remember saying that, but I don't feel it now, the feelings have retracted: something happened. Nothing did. It was between Charlieo and me. It was private.

Look, I say. I can't help you. We didn't fight about anything. Talk to his family, I say.

Have done, Tony Packer says. They're the ones reported him missing. We all thought you might have some clue to . . .

Clue? I say. What is this, Sherlock Holmes? Why don't you go out there and take, I don't know, tire samples off the road. Then you can see if they match the tires of all the cars between here and . . .

No need, Tony Packer says. We found the car straight off. Car's found.

CHAPTER 35

....

Ida thinks at first it is the change of life, though she doesn't know how to tell and is shy about asking. She's neighborly with the other women who live in the pushed-together houses on her street. No fences separate the backyards which look, from the sky, like quilt squares loosely basted together. The women talked about cooking and gardens and about children or grandchildren, starting sentences – You know what that child did? – their voices juicy with pride or amazement or distaste. Some of the women talked about husbands, but Ida has never been one of those. There is a line, to Ida, of what you do and don't talk about.

Ida's next-door neighbor is Ella Finch, a woman older than she is by some, whose laugh is like a song with two notes and who pinches down her lips when she feels laughter coming, trying to hold it back. Ella Finch has a small crabbed peach tree growing in her backyard and sometimes Ella and Ida stand underneath it when their talking goes on for a while.

One Saturday, Ida is in her warm house looking out the side window to see if Ella Finch comes outside. Ida has her coat on so she won't waste time in case Ella's only ducking out for one minute.

You're not *boilin'* to death in that coat? Johnny asks her.

Ida says, I'm going out in a minute to bring in the wash and I don't care to be havin' to take my coat on and off every five minutes, and then she says in a sharp way, Johnny, you writin' a book? and then she goes out to the yard.

She's taking down white sheets and white pillow cases stiffened with cold so they make a near cracking sound when she folds them against her. I can talk to Ella next week, she says to herself, lips moving, steam coming off her lips and her teeth. Can't be any *hurry* to this, though now that she's decided to ask Ella, she does not want to wait, and then Ella's springless back door smacks into the side of her house and smacks shut.

How long you think I been asking that Sim to fix that door now? Ella calls to Ida. You know what he tells me? All in due time. Well, it's been gotta be fifteen years. I'd say that *over*due time, and she sputters with laughter. Ella's husband was always promising he'd get to things that he never did. Ella's been laughing at Sim's doings for going on thirty-five years.

How you feelin' today, Ella, Ida calls over.

Don't hear me complainin', Ella says. How's yourself?

I'm feelin' fine, Ida says and takes a few steps nearer to the peach tree. Ella, seeing this, takes some steps herself.

Seems like snow, Ella says. They look up at the sky: heavy white clouds are piled on top of each other like scoops of meringue. They appear to Ida to be moving and she is suddenly dizzy and she drops her head and puts her hand out towards the tree.

You all right? Ella says, ducking her own head to get a look into Ida's bent-over face. You want to sit down?

Ida shakes her head. I been missin' my monthlies, she says. It's probably that. It's the change, probably. And she is amazed at how easy this hard thing was to say.

Ella gives her a sideways look that makes Ida know she is talked about by the neighborhood women. That she is called cold or stuck-up or close-mouthed. The change? Ella says. You're too young, Ida, how old are you?

Thirty-nine, Ida says. Be forty.

That's all? You mean to tell me I'm fifteen years older than you? and Ella pinches her lips down so the skin between her nose and her mouth bubbles, mirth percolating behind it.

Whenever I'm feelin' too frisky, the Lord finds a way of takin' me down a peg, she says. I'll count that as my humblin' lesson for today.

Well, Ida says. You don't look it.

Ella's two-note laugh sings out in the cold air. No, she says. I sure don't. I look like your *grandmother's* what I look like, and she laughs again and shoos Ida off with her hands.

Ella does look like a grandmother, the way fat curves above and below the delicate bones of her elbow like two puffed sleeves; the way she gets breathless just walking a few feet; the milky blue-black coating over her eyes. Ida has never noticed before: Ella looks something like Ma'am.

That was a good one, Ella says, what she always said when she gave in to laughter. You too young for the change, Ida. You got any other symbols? Hot flushes?

Ida has to shake her head. She had not even been over-warm, wearing her coat in the house.

Now me, Ella says. I was closer on fifty. I don't think I heard of anyone startin' so young as you are. I'm not saying I got any scientific evidence, Ella says. I just don't think so. You get other symbols. Hot flushes and whatnot. You maybe just stalled. Take some hot baths and another thing, tea, sassafras. Speeds things along. Probably that might start you up again. Now unless you *can't* start, Ella says and presses her lips together again.

Ida's annoyed at the roundabout way of this speech. She says, Well, you just said it's not the change.

Ida, you married how many years and be as old as you are *and* as dumb as a chicken?

Oh, Ida says. I see what you're sayin'. It's been a long while since all those babies started and then refused to grow in her. Almost as long as since Ma'am and Solomon.

Forty's too young for one kind of change but it's sure not too *old* for the other! Ella says.

Ida looks away, into the other yards. No, she hears in her head. I am past the time in my life for carrying and losing children. The voice in her head is decided.

It's not that, Ida says. It's not a good time, is all.

It never is, Ella says. It never is a good time, and her lips press together again and Ida steps away from the tree, her back straight and formal. She is back to the Ida who never gets over-familiar.

I better get on inside, she says. 'Fore my sheets freeze. She's afraid Ella will go on, ask why she and Johnny didn't have children, did she ever try? and that she will have to answer, information the fee for this talk, and she stands stiff as the sheets she is holding. These sheets almost frozen, she says, forgetting she's already said that.

I hear you, Ella says. I hate that.

Ida takes her washing inside. The kitchen has the metallic, boiled smell of fresh coffee.

Hey baby, Johnny calls to her. He's sitting at the table. Come on in here. I did us some lunch.

Baby, Ida says, her lips pursed. I look like a baby to you?

Johnny looks at her, surprised. "Baby's" what he's always called her, one of his pleasure names.

There are boiled eggs on the table, sliced and sprinkled with pepper. There's a pile of bread on one plate and sliced pickles on another and the smells of the pickles and the warm eggs and even the coffee are rich, churning smells to Ida and she remembers how, other times she'd been pregnant, smells bothered her and she closes her eyes.

It's good, b . . . , Johnny says, he almost says baby again, stops himself and says Ida, instead. Ida. Let me fix you a sandwich, but she holds up her hand and says, I can't eat.

Pickles and eggs? Johnny says. Don't kid me! I know you love . . .

You goin' deaf, Johnny Lee? I'm not eating, and she feels a kind of freedom in the sharpness of her voice and in the words. She will not eat and she'll take hot baths and what was maybe growing inside her would shrink down and shrink down until it slid out with no trouble.

Johnny stops midway into making a sandwich – too old for somebody to start calling him Daddy, Ida thinks – the big mitt of his hand covering the pile of bread. Ida, he says, as if she's going someplace and he's calling her back. His brain sticks for a minute on how he said Ida, not baby, and how, for some reason, he's having to say goodbye to that favorite word.

What all's the matter with you today? You sick?

I'm fine, Ida says. I'm goin' upstairs to take me a bath.

A bath? Johnny says. It's twelve . . .

I have to do everything the same time every day? she says. I need your permission? Ida turns and goes out of the kitchen and up the stairs where she takes off her shoes so when she walks on the not-too-secure second floor, Johnny will have no idea where she is.

CHAPTER 36

....

I have my feet up on my kitchen table, the red-and-white plastic cloth pushed back, the rust-pitted sides and chrome legs of the table visible like thighs under a skirt.

It's Monday, my one day off, weekends were too busy. I loved the long hopeless slide from Tuesday forward, Monday a speck in the distance moving slowly closer. I liked sleeping until I woke myself up Monday mornings, panic catching like a stove burner, then subsiding. I liked walking around my apartment drinking instant coffee (light, sweet) out of a Joe mug. But then the liking of Monday receded. On Mondays, unless I asked for change in the laundermat or said, Fine. And you? to the checkout at the market, I did not speak at all.

I look at my legs up on the table. I could shave them. Maybe wash then cut my hair. I pull my hair up off my face but I'm too lazy to go into the bathroom and see what it looks like mock-short. I settle for the blurred and striated image of myself in the ribbed chrome edge of the table.

Leon called yesterday. At work: I do not have a phone here. He calls every other Sunday, a pattern I saw as random at first, before it resolved into regularity: the first and third Sundays, but not the second or fourth.

Are you free tomorrow? he asked. I'm always free, I wanted to tell him.

Why? I said.

He said, I thought we might have dinner. Ida made me a whole chicken! I'll have to eat it for weeks if you don't agree to help me!

I remembered the dinners Isabel used to fix: chickens, stuffing, pies, mashed yams. I don't know, I said. Maybe.

When I got off the phone I missed him. I sat at my desk in the office and the air around me raised and widened so there'd be room in it for loneliness.

Leon came home to an empty and silent house. His feet echoed on the front porch and made another, shut-in sound when he got inside. The house was dark except for the gloomy yellow light in the kitchen where Leon ate alone, his briefcase like a guest at the table.

I'll go for dinner, I think. In the wake of the thought, loneliness abated. The Leon I missed was not the Leon I got.

There is a knock at the door: Leon, I think, as I have been thinking of Leon. But it is a Monday; Leon teaches Mondays.

It could be my landlord who comes over to collect rent or on bogus maintenance missions. He's married though his wife is an invalid and invisible: lung problems, he told me when I first moved in, gesturing towards the air conditioner in his first floor back window. It ran all the time, even in winter.

Another knock. It's some man in a blue uniform: blue pants, blue shirt. Electricity, I think, or water or gas.

Yes? I say, opening the storm door. I'm just on my way out.

Joellen? He says, Jo and then Ellen, two names.

I think, Joe. I look more closely, Joe? and then I know who it is, I know and at the same moment read the red stitching over his shirt pocket: Gene. I check the hook-and-eye latch on the screen, making sure it is locked. I want the door in between us.

I . . . Look, can I come in? It's freezing out here. He shifts from one foot to the other.

Why? What for?

He turns his head, looks up the driveway. It's sunny out on the street but the sun takes a long time to get back here in winter. Back here it's dark.

He says, It's about Joe.

I try not to hear him. Outside the landlord's wife's air conditioner runs.

He presses his hand to the screen. The skin on his palm blisters up.

Let me in? he says.

He says the word body. I do not catch what words come after that. Body's enough. It is like gone.

I say, When? I mean, what time. I am thinking hours. I am thinking time zones.

He says, Oh. Weeks ago. Weeks ago now.

Impossible, false. Joe has been moving around in my head. I walked through the parts of his day. Dressed in fatigues and his helmet he paced the same limited clearing where he was standing in the photo he sent me, doing the things scouts do camping. He slept cocooned in a green sleeping bag. He cooked his meals over wood fires. There was a canteen on his web belt. He was safe.

Let me in, he says, but there's no way I'm opening this door.

Let me in, just for a minute. Okay? I won't bother you, I swear it. I won't stay.

What for?

Joe, he says.

Oh, see, I was confused. Joe! I've been making Joe stand outside all this time!

Joe! I say and unhook the lock and he steps in and then I look down at his steel-toed work boots. They look insubstantial, as though they are standing there empty on the dirty linoleum floor.

Liar! I say. Cheat.

We sit at the table. Gene gets the bottle of Old Grand-dad I have been keeping, unopened, on top of the refrigerator.

He gets two Joe mugs, but I get up and take the mugs and bring back two glasses and a tray of ice cubes. It's so noisy! The cracking of ice. The refrigerator humming.

Stop that! I say, and Gene says, Excuse me? and I say, Not you, and kick the refrigerator.

He pours shots.

I say, You *know* I need a chaser, and go to get a glass of water from the sink. The tap whines and protests. All *right*, I say, and bring the water glass back to the table and then I have to push it away, carry it back to the sink, but even at that distance I can still hear it.

The sun slides into the backyard, into the kitchen. Water sweats off the ice cube tray and the glasses and beads up on the red-and-white plastic cloth. I move my glass around, corralling the drops. My hand travels past Gene's hand over and over. Our hands graze. I feel the hairs move on the back of his hand.

He just stays.

We are in the bedroom, our clothes heaps on the floor. Gene's bigger than I expected, bigger than Joe, taller, fleshier, with more body hair. It seems unnecessary.

We do not talk. I hear the cloth of our clothes sifting, wind ticking the window.

We fuck and then drink and are quiet – sleep or do not sleep. I wake to his hands bounding over me, his mouth on my places.

I say, Make me feel more.

I say, Find me.

It is ten or eleven or twelve. The bottle is empty. He goes out for another.

I go into the kitchen for ice. I run water over the second ice tray, hoary with frost. It takes a while for the snow to melt off, for the handle of the tray to release and pulling it, my hand slips and the water glass knocks into the sink where it breaks.

There was broken glass on the tracks the day Martin Luther King died: brown, bottle green. I would have taken some, but it didn't belong to me.

I put the pieces into my fish bowl. The fish won't mind. I can turn them into beach glass. I can do more.

I take a bowl from the stack in the cabinet and hold it at the height of my shoulders and drop it into the sink. It breaks in three pieces; not enough, so I try another. I stand at the sink breaking dishes. I leave the shards. I push my hands down to see if the broken dishes will cut me.

What are you doing? Gene says, when he comes back, not knocking, just comes right in. I had forgotten about him. I say, Who are you? He pulls my hands out by the wrists but they are intact. I wouldn't bleed.

His hands touch my wrists, his thumbs tap the veins. I unzip his pants in the kitchen. He calls out Joe or Jo; he keeps calling, pumping my head in his hands – Jo, Joe, he says, and I slip in and out of the names so I am both of us. Joe and me.

It's three or four in the morning. Gene sits with his legs over the side of the bed rubbing his hair. My wife, he says.

He has three layers of stomach that kiss one another like rows of fleshy lips.

I told her I had a big job, an emergency, he says, and I know he called her when he went out for the bottle. I can picture him whining into the phone to his wife. I taste whiskey and come in the back of my throat. I want to spit.

What kind of emergency can a gas station have in the middle of the night? Or any time? I ask him. I'm just curious.

When he is gone I wait for sleep and for quiet.

I hear trucks from the highway.

Somebody stacking their dishes.

A rooster.

I hear electricity hum through the wires. I unplug my lamp and my clock.

Pieces of beach glass click.

Somebody calls. Jo, they are saying, or Joe.

The chime of whiskey in the neck of a bottle.

Hands that slide and slide over wet skin.

Sounds like slaps. Sounds like kisses.

I wake in the light and lie in the odored, disordered nest of blankets and sheets and hear my muscles stretch and the crack of my bones. I feel drugged. When I was younger this used to happen sometimes in the middle of the night: I woke up and had not one clue who I was or where and I lay there panting as if memory was tied to breath until I caught at some fact – Joellen Stein – and then other facts – Leon Stein and Isabel Stein – and I rebuilt myself out of names.

The stale whiskey smell brings me back.

How do I know it's true? Where's the proof? Maybe that fat flabby brother just wanted to jump me. That day in the ticket shack, the man (Gene, it was Gene) crowding the doorway, watching me hunkered down on the ticket shack floor. Maybe he's been waiting to get me since then.

I am late for work, though I don't know how late since the clock is un-plugged. I take a shower. My hair is still wet when I leave.

You gonna catch p-neumonia, Ida says.

I'm sorry I'm late, I'll tell Alice King. A personal tragedy.

Another one? This is getting a little tiresome.

I go to the diner where Joe and I used to go sometimes when it was cold. Eggs, I say. And Toast. And hot coffee. I am very hungry.

I leave money on the table before the food comes.

A bunch of men are hanging around across the road at Gene's Gas. Is this a bus stop? I ask them. They stop talking, they stop moving and look at me. I hear the squeaking sounds of their beards coming in.

The office is all glass. Jo! Gene says when I walk in, or Joe! and I look behind me.

Sorry I missed your Grand Opening party.

The Grand Opening banner, the plastic pennants are still up though what was it, a year ago now?

He says, Yeah. It was a good . . .

Why should I believe you? You lied. You're a liar. I can't even remember one true thing you said.

He sits down in a chair. The chair scoots back inches. I wouldn't lie, not about this.

About other things.

Some big job, I say. A big blow job!

I say, What's your wife's name?

Patty, he says in a forthright way, his face up: proof of manliness or veracity.

I say, Where is he? I say, I don't believe you. I think of last night, Gene's body and having it on me and I am flopping around in the office, knocking into the filing cabinet, this big desk.

I hated it, I say. I shudder, flopping around. What a mistake!

Here, he says. Stop. Here. He opens the filing cabinet and takes out a box. JO, it says in pencil and ELLEN in pen.

What is this?

Joe left it for you, he says. He said if he didn't come back. Gave it to me for safekeeping.

The box had been touched by them both. Like I had.

I undo the paper. Gene stands over me the way Mrs. O'Casey used to, at Christmas. Nightgowns, she told me.

Money, Gene says.

All the bills are used and creased, none of them are new though they had been carefully smoothed, carefully stacked, carefully rubber-banded. Joe's hand had been here. Joe's careful neatness.

For you, Gene says. From Joe.

The money weighs something in my hand.

I say, You're calling this proof? This is pathetic! Where is he?

I told you last night, Gene says. Buried. We buried him. He looked so peaceful. He . . .

We, I say. I wasn't there. Who's we? You and LuAnne?

I'm very sorry, Gene says. I just didn't remember. I wasn't thinking too straight at the time.

We, I say. You think I believe this? You think I believe you?

Believe me, Gene says. I can show you where he's buried.

So? I say. Like that proves anything.

I'll show you the grave! Gene yells. I'll show you the fuckin' bullets they took out of him! His face is red, there are parched crescents at the sides of his mouth, under his nose.

They were wrong then, I say. It must have been somebody else. Joe has been walking around in my head. If he wasn't alive, would I see him?

He's gone! He is dead! Gene yells, his mouth open. His teeth are yellow and rot-brown and filled with silver.

I'll show you the fuckin' grave. I'll show you the fuckin' headstone: Joseph Andrews Handy. Born . . .

Andrews? I say.

I didn't know Andrews was his name.

I bang into the file cabinet. It rocks underneath me.

I hate him, I hate him. I hate you, I say. I hate you, I say again.

He says, I heard you the first time.

He moves away from the desk, passes me, his arm touching. I don't hate his arm, so I touch that, hug it against me; or his shoulder, or his leg, and then my pants are half down and his are unzipped and he has his arm up on the filing cabinet, his big navy blue jacket that is orange inside spread like a curtain, and the filing cabinet rocks back and back underneath me and then I look over the jacket, at the glass front of the office. I look out and there are those men at the bus stop, bearing witness.

CHAPTER 37

....

I'm stopping. I tell Gene, Don't come here again. Do Not. We were in my kitchen, at night, the light on, our reflections clear in the window glass above the sink.

Don't come here again. Leave me alone. Don't ever come here.

But I was the one who stalked him. I went to the gas station, right into the office.

Don't *come* here, Gene said. I'll come to you. Here isn't good! He looked shifty. I only had to press up against him. I only had to touch my foot to his ankle.

We fucked in the office and in the gas station restroom and in the back seat of his gold car, banging the buckles of the child's car seat.

Here, he said, spreading a towel or something and I smiled and when he had his eyes closed, I pulled it from underneath me and dumped it on the floor of the car.

Patty! he said and swatted my hands when I scratched him. I let my nails grow, like Joe's Strike Anywhere thumb, for a purpose.

Mine, I said, running my nails down his side. Pink stripes appeared on his white skin, then faded.

Lust is transforming: an incubus, a balm. It feels like movement, change, resolution. It keeps you busy. It feels like a life well-lived.

Tony Packer came in on a Tuesday in February.

Joellen? he said, standing over my desk. I frowned: a person too busy to remember a face.

Tony Packer? he said. His hands patted his chest.

Who? I said. Charlieo? You found him?

He looked down, pained by the question or the answer. No, he said. I'm sorry to say. We did not.

He said, I'm here on personal business. I thought you might show me some houses. Since I was here that time I been thinking, maybe now's the right time to start looking?

You'll have to come back, I said. I'm alone. I can't just leave the office.

Alice King was not here. I was glad. I was suddenly afraid to be outside.

When Alice comes back I'm sure she'd be happy to . . .

I can wait till you have time to take me.

Look. I'm new at this. Somebody else, Alice . . .

He shrugged. I already started with you, he said. I don't like having to tell my life story over and over.

It's strange, walking through empty houses. Intimate. One of you says, Over here would be a good place for . . . , and one of you says, Come look at this fixture. You picture living a life in the house.

Some of the houses were occupied: potholders on hooks, stuff in the closets, people watching TV; some were empty.

We were in a house that had been vacant for months: Very Anxious Seller, Alice wrote on its page on the clipboard. It was the third or fourth time I'd taken Tony Packer out looking. I read out the addresses, he drove right to them.

This house was small, a living room, kitchen, bedroom, all on one floor. There were no domestic effects, no heat. The house had the echo and chill of an empty Mason jar.

I was in the bedroom. You could see the train tracks from the window. Hey! I called. Joe! Come look at this.

Tony Packer was examining baseboards, he didn't even look up.

I couldn't breathe. The cold punched at my lungs.

You take your time, I'll be outside, I said. I got myself out, down off the porch. The yard dirt was frozen into clots that bore my weight. It was misty, the trees tangled in mesh, as though they were all covered with gypsy moth nests.

I stood breathing in the visible exhalations of my own breath. I couldn't look back at the house. If Tony Packer wanted to come see it again, I couldn't bring him, though he had not so far asked to see a house more than once.

I couldn't tell what Tony Packer thought about any house. He gave each one his meticulous attention. Leaving each house, while I relocked the doors, he said some positive thing: So much space! or, Nice view! or, Solid! like he was being careful to let the houses hear these good things about themselves even though he wasn't going to come back.

Cold? he said, coming out behind me. He started the cruiser. The heat went right on. I could feel it even before I opened the door of the car.

I sat on my hands. I said, I don't think I'm cut out for this.

Winter?

Real estate, I said.

How long you been at it?

I had to think about that, back up and count out the time in my head. It was four months.

He said, Four months? Well, really, that's nothing.

It's temporary, I said. I'm not planning to do it forever.

You could though. I mean, if you wanted. You're good at it.

I said, You're better at it than I am.

He smiled. You think? I do know this and that about plumbing and heating and whatnot.

I said, You do, though that was not what I meant. He was impartial. He was unattached. Every house I went into was a house I could have lived in with Joe.

It was a bleak day, people's yards the same color as the road: dark powdered with sugar. After a while, Tony Packer pulled off.

Where're you going? I said, sitting up. I was afraid, although the fear was generic: a man, a road, a car. I was not afraid of Tony Packer.

I want to show you something. Here. This place. Who do you think lives here?

The car bumped over ground that had frozen into tire ruts. He stopped in front of an old humped trailer. Once it had been two-tone, white and some other color like a saddle shoe, but most of the paint was gone now, the sides scabbed with rust. It was the kind of trailer you can hitch to a car and take on most highways if you keep to the slow lane, only this one had no wheels. It was up on cinderblocks, its axles rusted out.

Pretty rusty, I said.

He nodded, but his eyes stayed on the trailer like it had fine qualities apparent only to him.

Yeah, he said. Rust comes off. She may not be pretty, but she's good to go.

You were in the service? I said. Marines? The O'Caseys said that: Good to go.

Army, he said. Then my eardrum got blown out. He tapped at the cartilage of his ear.

How come you didn't tell me that? I said. It seemed like something you'd say right off: Tony Packer. War wound.

But he didn't answer. That ear. When he drove his bad ear was to me. Sometimes he didn't hear what I said. It was its own kind of sweetness. Deep down.

Tony Packer calls me one Sunday after he's been in three Tuesdays in a row. He says, Joellen? Listen, I'm not coming this week. Better give you some time off for good behavior. Your boss, she probably thinks I'm just doggin' it, wastin' your time. Right?

When I was not with Tony Packer, I didn't much care for him: sniffing around after Charlieo, that limiting deafness. I did not want to see him between Tuesday and Tuesday, though when he did not come in this Tuesday, I noticed his absence.

Can't drive you home tonight, Alice King says as we were locking up. It was always the two of us, Vivian left early.

Hot date, Alice says. Anyway, where's your highway patrolman today? Give up his quest for new housing?

I shrug. Alice did think Tony Packer was dogging it. She'd said, He's just dating you on my time. The word "date" makes me feel slightly sick as do other words: "boyfriend," "sex," all soiled in the way of rutted sheets. In Italian, the word for vagina is figa, fig. I pictured the taut green exterior sides of the fruit and the interior: split, seeded, juicy, red.

He's not "*dating*" me, I said. I don't "date."

I follow Alice's taillights up the slope of the parking lot, wait for her to make a right onto the highway, my legs pink, then invisible. I am going in the direction opposite to where Alice is headed – hot date.

A car honks, and I hop back. It honks again. I look down, I'm already way back on the shoulder, and then I hear squawking, the tinny voices of two arguing men. It's the cruiser, Tony Packer leaning out the open window, his headlights on high.

I cross the highway. Off duty, I tell him.

Yeah I am. Well, you know. Off all day Tuesdays.

No, I say. I meant me. I'm done for the night.

Well I know that. Hop in, I'm here to drive you.

I almost do not. You know I might not be *going home*. I might have a . . . but I do not say date. I look down the highway: the red ribbons of taillights, the swallowing dark.

It's just a ride home, Joellen, his soft voice says. That's the extent of the offer.

I wait till he's gone; till the bronze-colored cruiser pulls away from the curb, into the frost of the streetlamp, back into the dark. There's a small pool of light from the back window of my landlord's house where his wife sits in the air conditioning, but the driveway, the rest of the yard, the long flight of stairs to my door, are dark.

I go up the stairs, my hand on the railing. My foot brushes something, then a hand closes over my ankle.

Hey! I yell, trying to shake the hand off. I think: Charlieo's back. I think: Charlieo.

Hey! I yell again. Get your hands off me!

You never said *that* before, the voice says, Gene's voice, oily, self-satisfied. "Hands off's" not in your repertoire.

Yeah, well, I'm saying it now. What the hell's wrong with you? You scared me to death. What are you doing here anyway?

Guess, he says, but he lets go of my ankle. I hear him stand, the wood step sighs as it gives up his weight. Then he's behind me, his boozy breath a wall at the side of my face, his body wedged into my back. He's hard, his prick pushing against me.

Hey, I say. Go home. I'm tired.

He wraps his arm around me, turning me: my back is against the door now.

Who was that? he says, the same voice as before, insinuating and oily.

Who was who?

The "boyfriend."

Spying on me?

He says, The guy in the car.

Nobody, not that it's your business. A client.

A client? In business? His hand goes down the front of my pants – Get out of here, I say, but I am moving, moving against it: date, fig, boyfriend, sex.

How many you do in one day? he says, his fingers walking between my legs.

Real estate, I say. My hips move. My voice is an exhalation. Inside, I whisper. Inside, but he doesn't stop. The doorknob butts the small of my back. I smell the cold dirty glass. My keys click in my palm.

His jacket's open. I hook his belt, claw at the zipper to his pants. He holds my wrist with his free hand, his other hand working. After I come he says, Keys.

No. Do it here.

No way! I'm not gettin' caught with my pants down. He looks at the small spill of light from my landlord's wife's window. He takes the keys from me and opens the door.

What a gentleman, I say.

Gentleman's not what you want from me. Is it?

I watch him undress in the dim silvered light in the bedroom, almost no light, it comes from flood lamps two houses away. He gets thinner and smaller: his jacket, his work boots, shirt, undershirt.

Now, I say, but he's taking his time.

I look out the window, I look back. His trisected belly winks at me as he lowers himself. He smells of dried sweat and of wet sweat and of car oil and, faintly, of shit and I cover my breasts with my hands.

He slides right in. Raises my hips, holds me at the waist with one arm, his other arm braced. The top of my body lolls back.

He sucks air in behind his teeth.

I count off the seconds in my head.

He is not Joe, a voice says, over or under the counting. He is not Joe. For one clear second I see that, in a way, I had believed he was.

Don't be mad, he says after, when his breathing has slowed and he has rolled off me. I gotta go. Only got time for a quickie! He sits on the side of the bed getting dressed. He still has his socks on.

Good, I say. Don't come back.

He goes on dressing, his head inside his undershirt. Hey, he says. Don't be like that.

Maybe Gene was my version of grief. Maybe he helped me keep Joe for a time, until I was ready to live in his absence. I'm finished, I say. That's all.

Listen, Gene says. I'm sorry. If I was too rough? I thought you'd like it. He is puppyish, coy. I have to look elsewhere.

It's not that, I say. I can't explain this to you. It's just over.

He smiles and nods, doesn't believe me, but it doesn't matter. I had loved Joe and lost him and lost Charlieo and I had lived through it. It was over. Grief passes.

I felt peaceful, and the peacefulness stayed after Gene left. I showered and put on something dry and clean, a nightgown I had not worn in a long time. It smelled only of the inside of the drawer.

I went into the kitchen, got the Joe mug – the one that would have been Joe's – and wrapped it in newspaper and looked for the right place to put it. Joe was gone, I was finished with Joe, the cup was the only Joe thing that I had.

In my landlord's backyard there was a redwood picnic table and benches and a statue of the Virgin, and though I knew Joe was not religious it seemed right to me, a place of quiet and protection. And I had been a virgin when we met. If he had not gone, I would have stuck to him: there was something virginal in that.

I took the cup out to the backyard and dug a hole with a spoon and laid the cup in it. And while I was showering again and digging at the yard dirt under my nails with a toothpick and then lying on my bed, on the sheets I tried to restore to cleanness and dryness, I thought of the quiet place where Joe's cup lay.

I could not sleep. The cup was buried in the backyard at the hem of the dress of the Virgin. I thought of the cup. Hours passed and I could not sleep – Under the ground, it was under the ground – and near dawn, with the ground, the air freezing, the grass frozen and brittle as I knelt, I dug it back up.

We sit in the cruiser outside my landlord's house, equidistant from the two streetlamps whose light falls just short of us, front and back. The cruiser's still running, the heat on, the dashboard lights ghastly and green.

Tony Packer had called me to ask me out – Really, he said (he did not say date) and I felt peaceful and calm and said yes. I knew who he was. Things seemed clear. Bad things happened, good things happened and they flowed together like hot and cold running water. This was life. You found someplace to live. You got up in the morning and boiled water for coffee and looked out your window and noticed how it was summer or winter and then you went to work. Grief happened, an acceptable loss, a hiatus. The other things went on and on.

The car hums, the police radio turned all the way down, its static distant.

I better go, I say.

Tony Packer continues to sit with his head down: he hasn't heard me. I touch him, the way you touch the deaf, to restore them to the world of the hearing. Think of the things, the words and phrases, over the course of a lifetime, he'll miss.

I'll see you later, I say and then, again, I better go.

He lifts his head, smiles.

And I kiss him. One hand on either side of his face, erasing the moony green light from his cheekbones. Tony Packer, Tony Packer, Tony Packer.

Come in? I say into the rake of stubble on his cheeks and his chin. Later tonight, tomorrow morning, the skin on my face will start to scab.

I run the side of my finger over his cheek. Joe's face was smooth.

I can't breathe. It is the heat of the car. That dryness.

Tony Packer says, What?

I'm okay. I say, It's the heat. I get out of the car.

Tony Packer follows me up the driveway, letting me keep two steps ahead as though he's leaving me room to change my mind.

Inside, he sits on the edge of my bed, mindful of neatness. He plants me before him.

His kisses are chaste and dry.

It goes on a long time, the dry kissing.

He unbuttons my shirt, kissing down. He kisses the boy-flat center of my chest.

I put both my hands on his shoulders.

Our kisses wet up.

Fierce is the word I am after.

His hands on my hips, two fingers: he means wait. I am not good at waiting.

I straddle him – he is wider than . . . my legs haven't been called before to this distance.

His fingertips are dry as powder.
He smiles.
Everything is different.
He is not Charlieo.
He is not Gene.
He is not Joe.

CHAPTER 38

....

T ony Packer and I spend most evenings at my house.
I've been in his trailer only once. It's wood panelled and shabby inside, it looks
like one of those birthday cards for men only – manly dens and pipe racks and
duck decoys and more than one dog.

He slept at my house, though he went back to his trailer mornings to change.
When he turned up at my door in the evenings it was empty-handed – no gym
bag, no change of clothing – like he wasn't presuming I'd ask him to stay.

We cooked most nights, or he did. Cooking defeats me: the alchemy is too
mysterious, the distance from raw to roasted or baked, too great. We shopped for
each dinner buying only what would make that one meal, nothing beyond, food
another thing he was not presumptuous about.

Our supermarket is huge: the aisles wide and long and high. It has its own
liquor store and pharmacy and a section of cards and gift wraps: a self-contained
city-state. The meat case runs the entire back width of the store coloring the air
with the pink and red of packaged meats and with the smell of frost and cold
blood.

I did not shop during the day, when women with families shopped. Like
Isabel, I liked things off-peak.

On a Monday morning, though, I needed eggs. I was baking a cake for Tony
Packer's birthday, a recipe Vivian wrote out for me in her neat, spidery hand. I'd
been enthusiastic about this cake last night, or about the picture of presenting a cake
I had baked to Tony Packer. But the directions were so long, so imprecise. What
exactly was "lemony-colored"? "Double sifting"? "Beat until light"?

I stand with my carton of eggs, trapped between women with full shopping
carts, their children kicking the metal belt of the checkout. The lights are fluores-
cent and harsh. The cart of the woman ahead does not seem to empty, though the
checkout girl prices and rings up and slides goods behind her: 49 cents, 52 cents,
33, 33, 33.

The bill in my hand is soggy and softened by sweat.

A child kicks at the counter. Fifty-seven cents, 1.49, 1.03. A child pulls magazines off a rack. They make a spilling sound when they fall. What if the cash register runs out of tape? The checkout girl runs out of nickels? I'll be right back, sorry, sorry, I'll be right with you.

Out of the store I open my jacket. The cold is a shock on my skin, pleasant, then less so. I walk the parking lot covering ground, giddy with the lack of restriction and aware that the liberty I feel is out of proportion to the liberty gained. Stray shopping carts drift, on their own, across the lot.

And then I am standing behind a familiar car, a familiar color, a sky blue Oldsmobile, and I think: Charlieo. I expect to see his head rise out of the opened trunk, blond, almost shaved, the knobs of his skull visible. I expect two legs.

But it is Mrs. O'Casey. She straightens, reaches for another bag from the piled cart behind her, then she sets that bag down on the floor of the trunk. This is the car Charlieo had been driving: abandoned, found, reclaimed. It seems wrong that it should be here, doing the shopping.

Mrs. O'Casey straightens again, sees me and startles and toddles backwards into a shopping cart which crashes into another parked car.

Joellen! she says.

I smile, my eyes on a wedge of rear fenders. They are like wings tipped red, silver, black.

She is nodding, as though the conversation we could be having now – How are you? Fine, fine. Still with the real estate? – we are in fact having. She has her hand on her groceries.

Can I help? I ask her.

Oh, I'm fine. Don't trouble. You've got your own, she says. I don't know which she means: my own groceries, my own trouble.

Baking, I say, lifting the bag with the eggs. A cake for a friend.

She is midway down to the trunk with a package, but she stops. She thinks I mean Charlieo, I can tell by the posture of her frozen back. "He has other friends," she had once told me. But it was not true. He did not. She thinks he is with me, the way, the night he took off, it is what Mr. O'Casey thought.

Vivian, I say. It's her birthday.

She raises her eyebrows and nods. Good! she says. Good for you!

Well, I don't know about good! We'll have to wait and see how it turns out! If it's even edible! I say.

Her groceries are loaded, she closes the trunk. I feel exposed suddenly; the vastness of space beyond the raised lid of the trunk a surprise.

Well, she says. Best of luck. With your cake. Her head is cocked, her face round and owlish. She says something else, her voice so low I don't hear it.

Pardon? I say and lean in. Before my head turns, my ear towards her mouth, I see her eyes. I have not really seen them till now – distance, her glasses, a trick of the light. The pain is so clear I take a step back.

What I said was, Nice to have seen you, she says, her voice normal and pleasant, as though she is used to provoking shock; as though the compassed, indelible lines visible on the skins of people who are receiving radiation are visible on her; as though she has mentioned disease.

I'll let you get on, she says. I'm sure you've loads to do. As do I. Errands and whatnot. She pats at her hair as though on her next errand, neatness counted.

I nod as I am backing away. She has on a black coat, too dressy for grocery shopping.

Wait, I say. Mrs. O'Casey? She's in the car now, leaning to pull the door shut. I crouch on the pavement, set my grocery bag down. Eggs crack.

No word? I say. Nothing? It is not really a question: Nothing, I am telling her. No word. I look up into the horizontal crease lines of her neck where there is also a residue of the overly pink powder she's always used. That powder was the smell of the O'Caseys' bathroom. That and a scouring detergent and the smell of boy-piss on the floor.

No, she says. Nothing. Her voice is lighter, relieved: There is nothing to know. I am keeping nothing from her. Not a word. She looks down at me. That pain has darkened the color of her eyes.

We say:

He'll turn up.

Could be any time now.

Time's what he needed.

Could turn out to be best, in the long run. Some time to himself.

Don't you think?

Don't you think?

NO BODY, we're waiting for someone to say.

PEOPLE DON'T JUST DISAPPEAR. But of course that's wrong. People do.

CHAPTER 39

....

I pictured the cake tall as a top hat, sober and solid, the way Vivian's cake must have looked, but it didn't turn out. Mine tilted. The icing – milk and confectioner's sugar – clotted. Lumps exploded in powdery drifts in our mouths. The cake was dense, it lacked a cake's lightness. I'd shorted on eggs: too many broken.

Oh, I'll dump it, I told Tony Packer, this was before we ate it.

Why? He said, NO! He *loved* it, he said. It was sitting on the counter. He went and looked at it, bending down, his hands held carefully behind his back.

I had no taste for the cake, or the dinner, whatever it was he had cooked, or for his kisses, his tongue like wet meat pressing into my mouth. I rolled it aside with my tongue but it kept coming back, a stupid, brainless thing.

We are still at the kitchen table, our elbows among dishes, the overhead light on. My gold real estate jacket's draped over a chair.

To kiss me, he dips his head down and then up.

Down and then up. The orange taste of the cake rides up in the back of my throat. I put my hands on his chest. I say, No more.

I say, I can't do this.

Do what? he says and looks around as though, while he's been sitting here kissing, I've been busy with some other, hard thing: electricity, plumbing.

I lean towards him. My elbow soaks up something wet. I can't do this. I need to be by myself. I need you to go, I tell him.

Now? Tonight? It's my birthday!

I swallow against the orange taste.

Tomorrow, he says. Okay?

Sorry, I say. I'm not putting out.

Oh Joellen, for Christ sakes, you know I didn't mean that!

I knew he didn't. He was too good, he didn't ask for payment, not even proof of affection: Let me kiss you, he'd say as, in bed, he said he got off on making me feel good. It was sometimes confining, all that goodness.

We'll just hang out, he says in his eager voice. Watch TV.

I feel clammy, sick. All those hours to go until morning.

He gets up, walks in a surefooted way from the kitchen into the living room. He knows where things are. The table and sink are full of dishes. He cooks, I clean up. It is the way we do things.

The TV goes on, a babble of voices and laughter as though there is suddenly a party.

I put my head down on the red-and-white plastic cloth, its sour rag smell. I can't do this, I say into the nest of my arms.

Things meant to be temporary were permanent. This apartment. My job. Absences.

The gold uniform jacket fit me now, its new, sized stiffness gone. It had picked up the curve of my shoulders, my elbow points. It didn't make any difference that the jacket was cheap and that this was why it had taken only months to conform to my shape. It was my jacket; nobody else could quite fit it.

Things are too normal, I say to Tony Packer in my head, but "normal" was not right. Things were distorted. The talk from the TV, the pauses for laughter.

I know this is how Isabel felt, that last morning with Leon. The steam rising off the pancakes. The weight of the hours ahead spent with him, alone. His presence pressed her. She went out for a walk. Pressed, she stepped into the street. A green car was going by.

My mother should not have married: a true thing. I imagine us – Isabel, me – at our kitchen table; I imagine her telling me this. She would have told me at some time or age chosen by her for its invisible rightness.

I should have been married to you, puss.

I am a real estate agent, a high school dropout. I will not go to college. I will not learn to drive.

Tony Packer has his shoes off, the toes of his big white wool socks pulled up so his feet look enormous, the paws of a gigantic rabbit.

I'm sorry, I say. I turn off the TV. The picture fades then there is the blank box. I go on watching it. I can't look at him. Those feet.

After a while I hear the whipping sounds of the laces of his shoes.

Walk me to the door? he says. I do. He says, I'll call you tomorrow.

I almost change my mind and say, Stay. He is that nice.

I say I'm sorry again.

It's okay. I understand. I do. Really.

I hold the door and watch him get into the cruiser. The police radio squawks into the dark. Yeah, a voice says. All quiet. Not a thing goin' on.

CHAPTER 40

....

Before he is even gone, up the driveway, out on the dim street, away, I have begun to rehearse his absence as I had not rehearsed Isabel's, Charlieo's, Joe's. I do not want to be taken by surprise.

Blood beats in the front of my face. My cheeks feel pinched. I think: that cake. Too much sugar. An allergic reaction.

How will I get to Mercy, two towns away? My landlord will have to drive me. I tear a piece from a grocery bag. Help, I write on it. Can't breathe!

I'll call Tony Packer, tell him to come back. I put coins for the pay phone in my pocket.

How long will it take him to get home? Ten minutes, maybe less. He knows all the shortcuts.

I look up at the clock.

But what if he does not go home? It is still his birthday. I think of the bars I have never been in, bennie bars, quieter now, available bar stools, available blonde girls, nurses winding down after hospital shifts and waitresses, triangles of pink showing at the necks of brown naugahyde coats. I see Tony Packer's big, solid self; heat from the skin at his open neck button flaring out at some waitress, some nurse.

Watch TV! Read! Turn on the radio! Bake! Clean the bathroom! Wash floors! Go to bed! This in the voice of some strident mother.

In bed I flop from my back to my side like a vigorous fish.

How Would You Rather Die: swallowed down whole or snagged and then hoisted up in a net, watching the water recede, knowing what was going on?

A lamp salesman.

Agriculture, botany.

Criminal tendencies.

Wrong, wrong, I'd been seeing the wrong thing! A husband, he'd been trying to tell me. A father. I turn on the light.

Quit it! I yell, loud, and hear, as my own voice fades from the air, the whir of the air conditioner outside. Quit it!

It's two, it's three, it's four. The bed is the only safe island. Do Not Let Your Feet Touch the Floor. I turn the light on, off, on.

Sculpt a pillow into the shape of a body.

Run my hand through the dust on the table next to the bed. J, I write, then erase it.

The clock dial's a phosphorescent jellyfish green.

That green photo Joe sent me, it was from basic training, North Carolina, had to be. Otherwise the numbers didn't add up. Things are not what I thought.

I get up – 4:00 or 4:10 or 4:20, my toes curling away from the cold floor, my fingers stiff as they button.

Outside, it's dark, the sky black, the black less intense towards the beach as though someone has rubbed against paper darkened with charcoal.

I go to the beach. The fried clam store is closed, all the boardwalk stores are, fronted by corrugated steel gates.

Those rubber clams, hot oil branding the tongue. I wish I had liked them!

The click of glass pieces against plastic; the quieter tap as they piled on top of themselves.

In the dark, I cannot even tell if the beach is empty; if there are humped blanketed bodies, humping.

I should have been married to you, puss.

Meaning: I was the one who liked clams!

I walk. The sky lightens: more charcoal rubbed off. It is the deep hollow core of the morning. Empty parked cars. One white high top, one black shoe scudded into the seam of the curb at the fake lake. In the floodlights from the houses the lawns look iced.

No one.

Downtown, the neon in Vinnie's Pizza fritters and winks, making a sound like moths against glass.

Carl's Diarrhea. Vinnie's what?

A car.

Another car.

The sound of tires. The tink of turn signals.

Another car.

Lighter, the sky now a cottony gray.

I keep walking. The air becomes blue, houses and trees casting blue shadows. This is the road to my old grammar school. The air raid drills, the intense, smelly dullness. I am afraid, suddenly, now.

The sun comes through. On the ground, the light's a dense gold.

I lean against the fence at the horse farm. It undulates around the fields. It gives with my weight. Only three horses are out. They are auburn in the sun, blue in the shadows.

Isabel's story comes back – fever and the swelled giant horses – and I turn so I am not seeing the horses, though I can still hear them. Their bits jangle like change in deep pockets.

The horses move into my sightline. Their skins shudder. They pull their lips back. Their forelocks hang into their eyes like bangs.

Missile and crisis and shot and lost and gone. Words rush like bugs smashing themselves on a windshield.

The horses canter away. My skin shudders, like the horses.

Tired. A fever.

Words are stampeding like bugs, like horses: friend, boyfriend, mother, click, glass. Rifle and nightscope and late model white Mustang. I see hands spearing pancakes, hands cupping breasts, knees with floating islands of blue. Green.

Quiet! somebody says. Quiet! Don't you hear me?

Even in school, even on radio shows, sometimes they asked for a moment of silence: a moment, I would be happy with that, a single round droplet of time when the world would just stop.

But there is sound everywhere. The jangle and puffed out air of the horses and underneath the sound of grass bending under the horses' hooves, the mechanical chop of flies' wings. Sounds float like dust motes, like pollen or light – crisis and missile and kiss and Yes and No and Stop! batting around like tossed balls, suspended on air.

The fog's gone, the light like cooked butter. You can't ever tell, in the morning, if it will be sunny or dim. All days start the same, the sky like a pitched awning swaying with wet. It has to be nine, it could be later. Work, I think. I see the interior of the office – phones, the sliding and sticking of file cabinets, the winking red eyes of the space heaters, Alice King in her fur coat, Vivian in her tidy skirts, her gold jacket. Aren't you freezing? I once asked. She leaned towards me over her desk, plucked at her sleeve and out came a sliver of what looked like batting. Long underwear, she whispered.

I head towards the office, but then I pass it as I have passed Beef-O-Rama and the swimming pool outlet and Caponegro Brothers Auto Parts, or maybe they're not there anymore. I go home, walk up the driveway, my feet chafing the concrete. A noise, a plane, I look up, but it doesn't pass, the sound continues: the air conditioner.

I hate the landlord's wife who I have never seen. I am not even sure she exists. There is only the air conditioner's endless hum.

I take off my jacket and shoes and get into bed; smell the rusty outdoor cold off my clothing, smell horses and, faintly, salt off my cuffs and I chew the salt out of one cuff, then the other.

But this bed is too noisy! How can a person sleep here? Gene's voice and Tony Packer's have sunk down into the mattress: Gene's piggy grunts and Tony Packer's solicitousness and I smell the sex smells that are and are not the same smells I remember from Joe.

I pick up the blankets, the pillows, one sheet and head into the living room, then to the kitchen. The blankets are a nest on the floor. I lie near the base of the hot water heater. Settle in.

Better.

CHAPTER 41

....

Tony Packer comes by on what Joellen thinks of as the next night, but it is not; is the night of the morning of the beach and the horse farm. She gets up and stands in the bathroom while he taps on the glass of the door and rattles the knob and wonders who she is out with. She cannot let him in. He would expect kisses. She cannot open her mouth. Words roll from the cruiser, parked in the driveway.

Alice King doesn't come. The first day, a Tuesday, was Alice's day off so she does not miss Joellen until Wednesday and then she is just angry.

Irresponsible, irresponsible, she walks around telling herself. I had a *feeling*, she says which makes her feel cozy inside her own angry skin. She pictures Joellen hung over, as she had been drinking herself the previous night and the lingering taste of tequila and the shifting headache that makes her sit at her desk pressing her fingers into her eyes, occupy her. She can picture no other reason for Joellen's absence.

The next day Joellen is also not in and has not called and Alice King is furious whenever she looks at Joellen's vacant desk, the fury redeemed only by the pleasure she anticipates in firing Joellen. She pictures this intermittently, between 9:10 and about eleven, when Vivian comes over to her desk.

I'm going on over, Vivian says, buttoning the buttons on her coat. They are silver and tick like muted bells.

She might be sick, Vivian says. She might be in some sort of trouble.

Alice King gets up, touches Vivian's coatsleeve and says, I'm just going. You stay here. I'll go, her anger suddenly gone, like all she had to do to shed it was stand up.

From her nest on the floor – pillows, books, the lamp from the bedroom – Joellen hears a car. She thinks it is Tony Packer. He came by again last night, parked on the street so she did not hear the voices he toted with him as though bickering relatives lived in the glove compartment of the cruiser.

It is Alice King, Joellen sees her through the window in the bedroom. She scoops the blankets and sheets off the floor and pushes back the books and the lamp, then opens the door. She does not know what will happen. She cannot speak.

You're all right? Alice King says. Are you sick? The white smell of outdoors and the smell of cold animal skins rush into the kitchen.

What is it? Alice King says. What's wrong? Vivian's concern would have been active and bustling; Alice King sounds only impatient.

Joellen puts her hand to her throat.

Laryngitis? Alice King says. Do you have a fever?

A mistake, letting Alice King in. Joellen cannot explain this. Even speaking she could not explain, but she cannot speak. Sounds crowd into her mouth, words butt at her teeth and her shut lips, hard and indelible and mean.

Look, Alice King says and picks up a cash register tape from the table. Get me a pencil, a pen. Write.

Can't, Joellen writes and then, Speak. Voice, she writes and then, Gone. The words, written on the tablecloth, are pebbly.

Joellen looks at what she has written and pushes the paper over to Alice. The sight of the words on the paper makes her feel nauseous and bruised.

Why? Alice King says and Since when? and Have you seen a doctor? She pushes the rectangle of paper back to Joellen. Joellen shakes her head.

Alice King says, *Shouldn't* you?

Joellen makes a rolling motion with her hand.

Well, Alice King says. I don't know what to say. If you're sick, you're sick. I guess, come back to work when you're okay.

Joellen nods, smiles: she thinks she is smiling. There is a pull in her cheeks. She holds her thumb and first finger an inch apart: Soon. A few days. Little word. At the moment this seems possible, though the rest of the time it does not. How can she do her job without speech? She has tried to think of some other job she could get, speech not required: a cashier, a tollbooth attendant, the person who sits in the kiosk outside the market and takes rolls of exposed film from people and hands out envelopes of pictures. But there is no job. There is always some irreducible point where speech is essential. Didn't cashiers have to say, Have a nice day? Come again? Thank you? And what if you got robbed? Didn't you have to yell, Stop! Thief!!

She cannot speak. She cannot eat or kiss. She cannot go to work. There is Joe's shoebox of money. She takes the right number of bills out of that and puts them into a white envelope. She writes the name of her landlord and RENT in letters too large and thick to be missed on the envelope and tapes it to the outside glass of her door.

CHAPTER 42

....

Ida lives alongside anger like it's a third being that has moved into her house. Sometimes it's the shape of a man, big hands batting and lifting her skirt, eyes with their red pilot lights hop-jumping. Sometimes it's a woman, lips a stitched line, kicking and kicking the leg of the table.

The man follows them upstairs, Ida and Johnny, so now there is the weight of three people on the not-that-strong second floor. He gets into bed with them, lies on one side of Ida or the other so sometimes she pushes her way to the very edge of the bed to get away from him, and sometimes she rolls nearly over on Johnny. Johnny's hands come out for her; even asleep, he is ready. He strokes the long slope of her spine, the rise of her behind, his fingers trailing down, whooping up.

Been touched enough for one lifetime! the angry woman says so Ida sometimes goes to the cold, unused room they'd meant for children. The man and the woman don't follow her there.

The first time she did it Johnny said to her in the kitchen the next morning – Where you went off to last night? Had you a date? – his voice teasing and bouncy and Ida said, I was kicking around, restless. Didn't want to be waking you up.

The next time, Ida told him he had snored, a big old bear sound, couldn't get you to stop for gold!, and the laughter that was under her words made Johnny feel the manliness of it and he laughed too, and said tonight she better bring clothespins.

Now it's been more times than they've counted. Johnny doesn't ask anymore, and Ida doesn't offer a reason. He looks at her when she hands him his plate of breakfast, then he looks away. Ida feels bad, and she almost tells him what's wrong: pregnant again, thought I was past this, too old, don't know if I can go through losing another one. She feels the words lining up to be spoken, but then the angry man gooses her and the angry woman kicks the leg of the table.

Ida is angry, too, when Leon comes hunting for her one Sunday morning, though at first she does not know that it's Leon. She's outside sweeping her front porch, the broom making sneezing sounds as she lifts and chops it over the gray painted surface. Looking up, she sees a white face at the corner, or not a face yet: a white-and-pink blur above a gray coat. Not too many white faces came poking themselves around here: the mailman, flocks of small white boys every once in a while, bold, like what they were doing was dangerous.

Ida watches the man's slow progress. He stops in front of each house, peers up at the front looking for numbers which most of the houses don't have. Ida goes back to sweeping. The next time she looks up, she sees it is Leon.

This is *Sunday*, she thinks, anger like straight pins pushing into her flesh. She feels some Godly clause has been violated though all that she's doing is sweeping. She leans the broom up against a corner of the house and slips inside. From the side of a window, she watches Leon: one house, stop. Another.

I'll run next door to Ella, Ida thinks. But she can hear the metallic ring of Johnny's spade on the hard frozen ground in the back – remulching his roses – and she does not want to pass him, see his face light up because he thinks she's coming out to be with him. I'll be to Ella's, she'd say, or not say: either way she'd have to watch the light in his face blink out.

What time do you have to be always explaining everything to that Johnny? the angry woman says.

There's a tap on the front door, a weak, tentative sound. Ida jumps anyhow.

I'm not answering, she tells herself – the man and the woman both nodding. She sits on a chair, her back straight, her hands like covers over her knees. She sets her lips in a thin line, like the angry woman's.

Tap, tap, and another sound, clearing his throat. Like somebody gonna be asking him to speak up, the angry woman says.

Ida does not move.

She hears him going away, his footsteps peppering the hollow porch floor. She hears the sandpaper of soles on the sidewalk. Then she hears, Yeah, Hey. How ya doin'! Johnny's voice, reverberant, loud. She can't tell if Leon spoke first or what he answered. Under the anger that's beating in her ears like winged bats, she can't hear Leon at all.

Ida stays put in the dark living room she keeps polished, waxed, although they hardly used it. Every so often she hears Johnny, the timbre of his company voice, no words. For a time, the voice shields her from Leon and then Ida thinks: He better not ask that man into this house! She stands, her chair skitters back across the waxed wood floor, but by the time she gets to the side door, Johnny's voice and then Leon's are inside.

Ida, Johnny calls, then drops his voice when he sees her. Look who all came by!

Ida, Leon says. He stands in the well at the side door, three steps down.

Well, come on in, Johnny says. He comes first, his face puckered with question as he passes Ida. Why didn't *she* say this, ask him in?

Coffee? Johnny says, looking at Ida.

Leon hesitates, seeing many implications in the offer and his response. He does not want it to seem like they're working for him in their own house, or like he is asking them to.

Don't go to any trouble, he finally says and is pleased with this choice, properly pleasant, properly neutral, leaving action up to them. He's at the top of the stairs now, inside the kitchen.

No trouble, Johnny tells him. He has waited a beat for Ida to say this too.

Ida stands near the side door, her arms tight-folded in front. She looks forbidding and chilly.

Leon is nervous. He asks technical questions about the roses while Johnny makes coffee. Johnny answers slowly, as though Leon is writing things down.

Like he cares about somebody's roses! the angry woman snaps.

Johnny puts three cups and three saucers out on the table. Ida turns one cup upside down, not too gently, although she is proud of these cups, white with green clovers, and worries about chips.

I'm sorry, Leon says. I know it's Sunday. To intrude. He is looking at Ida. He tastes the coffee, his eyebrows come up: it is so delicious! He wants to say this to Johnny; better than Ida's he could joke, but then he doesn't mention the coffee.

I wouldn't have, he says. Bothered you. But it's, it's . . . An emergency, he had been planning to say, but you can't sit in somebody's kitchen waiting for coffee to perk, then say that. "Emergency" is one word that has to come first.

It's Joellen, Leon says and something in Ida's chest clenches. Not Joellen, she thinks.

This man can't hold on to *no* women! the angry woman says.

What about Joellen? Ida says, she can't help it. Johnny and Leon both look at her: it's the first time she's spoken.

Ida clears her throat. Well? she says.

And Leon explains, going farther back than he has to. Says, I don't know if I told you . . . and describes the weekly phone calls between him and Joellen and the one visit he'd paid to her apartment.

He tells how Joellen still has no phone so that his calls are to the real estate office. Every Sunday, he says. She works Sundays. Monday's her day off.

Ida listens. It's the first news she's had of Joellen in months. She is surprised to find out how dry she's been for it, how thirsty.

Leon sips his coffee, raises the cup at Johnny thinking now's the time to tell him how good it is.

Go on, Ida says, her voice sharp.

Leon puts the cup down. She hasn't been there, he says. Not for weeks.

Ida shrugs. Took off again, she says. She is thinking: took off kind of family. She's always thought Isabel would have, if that car hadn't got her.

I went by her apartment, Leon says. The first two times she wasn't there. The last time? He stops. He swallows against what he has to tell. What does it say about him, the father?

She, he says. She . . . He swallows again. Curled up on the floor in the kitchen.

A frown pinches then smooths out between Ida's eyes. In it are all the questions she wants to ask, all the brushing aside she could do. It is the angry woman, shaking her head, saying, White people.

Where's she at? Where's she living? Ida asks.

Leon sits back in his chair; it is metal, the seats and backs are red plastic. Something eases in him. It is not that he's less concerned, he tells himself, only that someone competent, able, will take over now. He takes the folded piece of paper on which he has written Joellen's address from his pocket and he passes it over to Ida.

He come prepared! the angry woman says.

Ida opens the paper.

Johnny, Leon says. Tell me the secret of this coffee!

284

CHAPTER 43

··

After Leon goes, Ida looks around her kitchen thinking
what things she might take: sponges, a broom, a potholder, a lemon. She has no
idea what will be useful.

Here, Ida, Johnny says, coming at her. 'Case you need something. The green
and cream colors of money loom close, making her eyes cross.

What would I need? Ida says in a sharp voice, but she takes the money.
Probably be a good father, she thinks and the angry woman snaps out: We back
to that same old same old?

Johnny walks her outside, touches the sleeve of her black-and-white coat. For
a moment they stand facing each other, Ida looking out past his shoulder. Then
she goes down the porch steps, the heels of her black shoes like the blows of a
hammer. She knows Johnny is still there, the back of her neck feels him watching, but she doesn't look back.

Joellen thinks: this is me dreaming. So many times she has imagined Ida
coming to see her. She has imagined the smells of cooked meat and of a heat-
softened brown paper bag.

Still, when she gets up off the kitchen floor, looks out and sees it is Ida, she
hesitates. She does not like to be around talking, can feel the strain of the other
person's speech in her own vocal cords, the hum in her chest and her head.

She keeps things as quiet as possible. She does not speak, she does not eat.
Sometimes she flushes the toilet only at night as though she is Anne Frank in the
attic.

What's wrong with you? Ida's voice comes, grouchy, from the other side of
the door. Don't you know how cold out it is?

Joellen opens the door while Ida's still talking: "out it is" comes at her loud-
est and clearest. If she could speak now, Joellen would tell Ida: go home.

Ida is frowning and silent, her mouth one tight line, stitched brows another.
Even Leon's alarmism fell short of what she sees now. The girl is so skinny. She

can see the bones – ribs, clavicles, wrist bones – shivering and floating under Joellen's skin. Her neck is fluted as though gullies of flesh have been scraped out. Her lips look powdered, coated with the white rimy blush found on plums, and there are streaks under her eyes, slanting over her cheekbones, plum-colored too. Her hair is smooth in the front; the bangs that come to the crease of her eyelids give her eyes the dense feathered look of false lashes. But in back the hair is uncombed, a ratted nest.

What you *thinking* about! Ida says, toeing the heap of blankets and sheets on the floor. Your sense forsake you? She could take hold of this girl, shake her stick arms, but Joellen is too frail to be touched.

Ida puts up a kettle of water, though she is not thinking "tea" or even "hot water" as she does this, it is just something to do. The heating kettle makes a normal sound.

She looks out the window above the sink. If she closes her eyes she is not here, this is not some kitchen she's never been in. They are at Leon's, she and Joellen, back to the fighting they left off – over sandwiches, over milk.

When you last eat? she says.

Joellen has sat down at the table, her strength spent in standing, opening the door, listening to Ida. Her head rests on one hand. With the other she is drawing a capital G then an O over and over on the tablecloth, fitting the curve of the letters inside the red and white boxes.

I don't care if you talk to me or you don't, Ida says. I'm cookin', you're eatin', all's there is to it.

She opens the refrigerator in which there is nothing and the cabinets – cans of soup, some powdered hot chocolate that was here when Joellen moved in. When the kettle's boiled Ida makes a cup of that. Her movements are urgent – the way she digs a spoon into the mix, stirs – and precise, as though seconds counted.

She puts the cup down in front of Joellen. You *drink* that, she says. For starters.

Joellen shifts to the side of her chair so the chocolatey steam will not reach her. She would get sick even if she were able to part her lips and drink this. She allows herself only rationed Anne Frank–type sips of water. She has noticed how the texture of water has changed, thickened, first to witch hazel, then mineral oil. Now it is the consistency of mercury.

I don't want to see none of that when I get back, Ida says, her face level with Joellen's, nearness and firmness the same thing. There is a smell, like beauty shops, Ida thinks. Like nail polish remover.

I'm goin' shoppin'. Then I'm comin' back. Don't even think about not bein' here.

Joellen blinks. It is what she is thinking: slipping out. She does not think where she would go or how she would get there. The truth is her strength wouldn't carry her far, would not even carry her down the steps.

When Ida goes out and the quiet settles again like a lofted sheet, Joellen lies back down on the floor amid her blankets and sheets and she blocks out the sight of the cup on the table and the fresh cold smell that Ida's let in. The only smell: Ida had not come with food in a brown paper bag after all. Then she sleeps.

It's Sunday, the supermarket is closed. Ida lets herself be angry about this and the anger, which is normal to her and familiar, settles her down.

She does not know the part of town where Joellen lives now: the blank, neat-looking houses; the garages, some with apartments like Joellen's, added on. The lawns and driveways are identically neat. She does not know anyone here.

Ida walks in the cold, salty air, cold twisting around her ankles and lashing up under her skirt and tickling her neck like a scarf. It feels good after the closeness of Joellen's apartment; the beauty parlor smell.

She finds a delicatessen that is open. There are no aisles of food here; customers, when there are customers, stand at the counter and call out what they want. Ida waits a long time. When a man comes out from the back she calls out bread and milk, eggs, potatoes. Oatmeal and sugar – and let me get a sack of those apples.

She asks for one thing at a time, the way, if this was a regular market, she would shop. The man is impatient, huffing air out through his nose after each request, moving in a slow, put-upon way to where each item is stored.

He adds the things up on the back of a bag. It costs about four times what Ida's expecting. The man has a look on his face, a half smile, like he's daring her to say she's been cheated.

Seems high, Ida says.

The man says, You got a problem?

The angry woman says, *You* the cause of *my* grief!

Ida hands over the money. She leaves the store like a girl pushing out of a circle of bullies. There's a laundermat across the street with a phone in front and she crosses and calls Johnny.

It's me, she says, watching herself in the laundermat's plate glass window. It is large and clean. Shadowed shapes move on its other side like tree branches.

Ida? Johnny says, his voice loud.

I just told you it's me.

Where you at? How's the girl?

Bad, Ida says. I'm stayin'.

A pause, both of them thinking how first she moved out of the bedroom, now out of the house. Ida thinks it because she knows Johnny is.

How long you think it'll be? Johnny says, and Ida hears underneath, Are you coming back? and for the first time she thinks: maybe not.

She says, Long's I'm needed. I didn't know how bad things was . . . and under that Johnny hears: until this moment I never knew I could leave.

Anything you need? Johnny asks her.

Ida watches herself in the laundermat window. No, she says. Maybe in a few days you can bring me by some clothes. Johnny hears: I haven't made up my mind yet.

Sure, sure, he says, a good sport: he doesn't know how else to do this. Like what all?

Don't know. I'll call you, tell you later, Ida says. She means: I'm not gone yet, and that is what Johnny hears also.

Joellen wakes to the sound of Ida's shoes striking the wood steps and she gets up from the floor and sits back down at the table as though she has not moved since Ida went out. She is pleased that Ida will not know she has slept, her sleep will stay secret, though even the front of her hair's tumbled now; the fruit-colored streaks under her eyes are more vivid.

Ida makes oatmeal and applesauce out of the apples. The kitchen fills with a steamed juicy smell and Ida stands with her eyes downcast and her head lifted inside the sweet steam, to cover the nail polish remover smell that Joellen gives off.

She carries a bowl to the table, half oatmeal, half applesauce, the divided meals people serve to small children. The hot chocolate is still there, cooled and darkened.

Joellen moves away from the bowl of food.

Ida picks up a spoon, holds it over a napkin, moves it towards Joellen's mouth.

Joellen's head turns, her mouth a zipped line.

The spoon pursues her, it touches her lip and Joellen jerks her head back and the food, the oatmeal and applesauce, flies.

How do you know it's no good if you don't taste it? Ida says. She mops up the spill with the napkin. There's a spot of oatmeal on the floor that she misses. Joellen watches it.

I made this you know, Ida says, stabbing the applesauce. It's good, it's dee-licious. She touches the spoon to her own lip pretending to taste, though she does not want to eat either. It's true, though. The applesauce is good.

I can sit here all night, Ida says. I got another whole pot of these apples. I got no place to go either.

Joellen opens and closes her fists.

They sit for hours. Joellen is tired, has to work to keep her lips closed, to keep her jaw from falling open. The cold oatmeal gives off the smell of kindergarten paste.

It is ten, it is eleven, it is one in the morning.

Joellen is almost asleep. Sleep is the thing she likes best, the thing she is best at.

Her eyes close, flutter open, close.

She is dreaming. Something cool touches her lips. Something pebbly. Sand, she is thinking, but the touch is cool, not unpleasant. She puts her tongue out, touches the outside of her lips.

Good, a voice says, far off but she can still hear it.

Ma? she is thinking.

Cool again. Her lips.

And then she knows it is not sand and it is not Isabel. She stands, her chair tips then rocks back. She holds her lips away from each other. She feels it on her mouth, hands slap at her lips.

Stop! Stop it! Ida yells. You got to eat! You don't eat, you . . .

Joellen runs, is running into the bathroom, slapping and slapping her lips, and then she is gagging, throwing up. Bile and fumes and words stream out of her mouth.

No! she says. No, she is screaming and screaming, the scream echoing back from the scooped hollow shell of the toilet.

Ida's behind her; Ida's knees one on each side, Ida's hands stroking the wet hair back off her face.

Go on, Ida says. She says, Hush. She says, It's all right – sound far away, sound echoing off the porcelain.

There is no stopping. Now that she has started, she will never stop.

She screams and screams and screams and screams.

Words stab at her throat and climb over her teeth. She spits them, bloody, into the bowl.

Hate, she thinks once. There is not one word I don't hate.

Ida stays, a fixture, a sink. Her hands move, flowing like water.

And then it is quiet. No sounds at all.

Too much been livin' inside you, Ida says. That's no good.

They sit on the floor of the bathroom.

Ida's skin still has the creamy look of cake frosting. Joellen remembers, when she was small, wanting to lick it. This close, though, she can see the dryness, the gray ashiness in the corners of Ida's mouth.

Ida changes the sheets on Joellen's bed, shakes out the blankets, gets Joellen undressed. Joellen's eyes are closed, she is asleep standing up.

Ida takes off her own clothes – dress and stockings and underwear and her bra, unhooking it under the top of her full white cotton slip – and gets into bed with the slip on.

They sleep on opposite sides of the bed. In the night, or the morning – it's past four by the time they're in bed – their legs touch.

Ida thinks – Solomon.

Joellen thinks of no one, of nothing.

CHAPTER 44

....

It seems every fifteen minutes Ida asks, You hungry? and Joellen says Yes, or more often No, and Ida says, Eat anyway.

During the first weeks Ida is with her Joellen eats little, as she speaks little also. Words roll out of her one, two at a time, down her bruised throat and out her mouth where she delivers them, as surprised as if she is spitting out eggs. Her stomach won't hold much; her body's reluctant to go back to eating. Two spoonfuls, she's full or bound for the bathroom.

It'll come back. Take some time, that's all. We got time, am I right? Ida says.

Ida eats when Joellen does, she is always hungry, eats and eats making up for lost time, one hand on the mound of her belly. She has a taste for everything: foods she has always cooked, foods she has not eaten since childhood, foods she's never seen before or heard of. When her eyes fall on a candy bar in a child's hand or a picture on a magazine cover at the supermarket checkout, her mouth fills with water for that thing and she pushes past the people in line to go get it.

For a long time she had no taste for food and the food that she cooked but did not eat herself was tasteless. She got used to the sound of the salt shaker, belled with three grains of rice, as Johnny ate by himself at the table.

Ida gets bigger, it seems daily. At night she stands in her slip on top of the closed toilet seat and swings the medicine cabinet door out towards herself, the only way to see in the only mirror in Joellen's apartment. She pulls her slip in at the back to make her silhouette clear, though soon she does not need to do this: the loose white cotton becomes as tight as a stocking on a leg.

They have their routine, cooking and eating and washing and sleeping; the routine has its own slow pace. Their days are quiet and peaceful and not interrupted by men. Ida gives herself to it. She does not think, I have another life to get back to. There is no other life. Her house, her neighbors, Leon, Johnny seem clear but distant, like something she might have dreamed in detail but that did not exist.

During the day she does chores. She washes Joellen's hair and sits behind her and combs it. She used to wash Ma'am's hair outside in the summer: a bar of caramel soap, water in a pitcher. Bubbles the colors of prisms nested in the furry denseness of Ma'am's head.

Feel good? Ida says to Joellen.

Mmmm, Ma'am said, the sound like a hum.

Joellen nods, making the comb ride down her hair.

One afternoon, about four, it is late April, the light outside the kitchen is silver. Joellen is sleeping inside, Ida's got the water running in the kitchen, washing potatoes. Somebody knocks.

She sucks her teeth, thinking: that was me knocking at her, Ma'am'd be pullin' on somebody's ears. You can wait, she says, under her breath.

Knocking and knocking. Hello? a man's voice calls. Anybody in there? It's Johnny Lee Iron.

Johnny Lee Iron, Ida says to herself. What's he want? She shuts off the water and goes to the door. The man's old-looking, not the Johnny Lee Iron she's expecting. For a second she's tangled up someplace between her old life and this one, but the cool air on her wet hands brings her back.

Johnny! she says.

I brought you over some things, Johnny says. He holds up two dresses on hangers.

Ida nods. She wears the same clothes every day, the dress she wore here, the white slip. She washes them on alternate days, hanging them over a chair in front of the oven to dry.

Some things, Johnny says again. Figured, by now, you could use 'em. Ida hears what he is saying underneath: You've been gone a long time. Are you coming home?

Come in, Ida says, and has to flatten herself against the open door. With Johnny in it the small kitchen feels smaller.

Johnny hands over the dresses, holding them by the shoulders, the skirts draped over his arm the way he'd carry a woman who'd fainted. They are summerweight, though it's still mostly cool out.

It feel like a heat wave to you? Ida stops herself from saying.

You're looking fit, Johnny says.

Ida holds up the two dresses, screening her bigness. The rose-colored one might be all right, she thinks. The other was tight to begin with. She can feel it pressing against the place where her waist used to be. Her clothes are mostly form fitting, but she is the shape, now, of a filled bag of sugar.

Okay, Johnny says. I just stopped. Best be goin', let you get on with whatever . . . He makes a rolling gesture with one hand, then rescinds it. The kitchen is so small. He crosses his arms over his chest, trying to take up less space.

You stay to supper, Ida says. There's more than plenty. She can go hours, days, without feeling Johnny's absence, but his presence makes her lonely.

I been tryin' new recipes. "Spices tempt the appetite": I read that.

That's fine, Johnny says. I never say no to a little adventure.

Fine, Ida says. She turns Johnny towards the bathroom. Now go on and wash.

Johnny says, Bossy!

Ida carries the dresses into the bedroom. Joellen's just waking up. She still sleeps hours and hours; sleeps and eats, she has said, like an infant, and it is an infancy in other ways too. Staying home. Being taken care of.

Who is it? Joellen asks. Hearing a man's voice she'd thought Leon, who has stopped by several times to leave bottles of juice, his colleges' student newspapers. Joellen likes the editorials. They are about co-ed dormitories, the hamburgers in off-campus pubs, their concerns quaint and distracting like novels about teenagers from the fifties.

Say I'm asleep, Joellen tells Ida.

Not *for* you, Ida says, sucking her teeth. It's my Johnny.

Ida's in the kitchen, bent over one of the too-tight dresses Johnny brought, letting out the waist.

Take somethin' to eat, she says when Joellen comes in. Milk, and there's pie. What're you doing?

Looks to me like I'm lettin' the waist out of this dress, Ida says. The dress is embroidered at the waist and the short sleeves and collar with orange and brown and green daisies; inside out, Joellen sees only random, snipped threads.

Why? Joellen says. You gain all the weight I lost? She has never spoken to Ida this way before, but the past weeks have made her bold.

I always wondered about that, what happens to "lost" weight. Where does it go, outer space?

You tryin' to be funny, Joellen?

I thought that *was* funny, pretty funny. I didn't think I was trying.

Joellen sits down at the table. I did notice you're eating a lot, she says, then she's not sure if that's true. All those years, she never saw anything pass Ida's lips except swallows of sugarwater.

Well, that's what happens when a person's eating for two people, Ida says.

If you mean me, I'm holding my own.

Ida shakes her head. You always think everybody means you. I'm not talking about you. I'm talkin' about me and this child I'm carryin'.

Child? Joellen says. Baby?

Did I just say that? Anger strains across Ida's chest like a pulled thread, then it eases. She hasn't heard much from the angry woman in some time.

What'll you name it? What's Johnny say?

Be named what its name is, Ida says. My Ma'am said she knew soon's me and Solomon came out of our own mother Virginia what our names was. Children come with their names on them, Ma'am said. Lord names them. Lots of folks though, they don't listen. Ida looks at Joellen. She thinks: what was Joellen's God name?

Johnny, I'm tellin' him tonight, since you seem to gotta know.

He doesn't know?

Ida tucks her chin down, pops her eyes at Joellen. Somebody left the Seat of Judgment vacant I don't know about and asked you to step in?

I was surprised, that's all. I thought . . .

Well, you can stop thinkin'. I'll tell you something about me, Joellen, so's you'll know. I lost the two people meant most to me on this earth. Ever since, a part of me's been sittin' back in Ma'am's kitchen, not closin' her hands around nothin' for fear of losin' it. You understand what I'm saying?

The skirt Ida is sewing is spread over her lap; the needle is loose in her fingers. Other people hung on to her, or tried to. She never said yes.

But you're here! Joellen says. You've got Johnny! She remembers the night, years ago, watching Ida and Johnny through their window. They moved in a stately, gliding way like two people dancing.

This is *my* history, Joellen, Ida says. You let *me* tell it! The thread of anger tightens again, then subsides. She says, Things happen in their own ready time.

Then she goes back to sewing. She'll wear this dress tonight, when she sees Johnny. She had forgotten: the two dresses Johnny brought by are his favorites.

That evening, Ida puts on the newly let-out dress, and she waits outside for Johnny to come up the driveway, a worshipful, courting man. She remembers herself a girl, Johnny a younger man, but she does not remember this feeling of fluster, of fear that he will not come. When he walks up the driveway in the dusk, his shirt white as teeth, relief makes her grouchy.

Hey, Johnny says. Don't you look fetching this evening!

Hey, Ida says back. I'm fine. The baby is tumbling and drumming inside her; it steals her attention. This is a far-advanced baby, all this moving and it is not even five months.

Come on here and sit down, Ida says, pointing to the picnic table in the backyard. It's almost dark. Joellen's porch light is on, making their shadows long.

All right, Johnny says. I'm sitting. Now what is it? His voice is tense, almost angry. He thinks Ida's ready to tell him – I made my mind up. I'm leaving.

I'm carryin' a child, that's all, Ida says, a little haughty. She had planned to take her time telling this news, but Johnny rushed it out of her.

Johnny nods. I knew that. He does not think this is the thing she means to tell him.

You knew? Who . . . Ida slits her eyes, which Johnny does not see: it is dark, he is looking up at the porch light. Moths are clustered around it. He is surprised. It seems early in the season for moths.

No "who," he says. You think I been living with you all this time, your bein' pregnant's not something I'd notice? You think I don't see things?

Ida doesn't answer, no way to without insult. She did not remark changes in him; it took her months to notice he'd gotten eyeglasses.

Johnny Lee Iron, Ida says. I'm tellin' you you about to be a father and . . .

Ida. You asked me here, so here I am. Now you got something to tell me? You didn't just get enough something?

Ida, he says again, and she can hear the sudden weariness and care weighting his voice. It scares her.

If you're about to tell me you don't want this baby, "I'm too old to be somebody's father". . .

What? Johnny says. Who said that?

Ida's angry, which makes her feel peaceful, herself. She says, Fine. She says, Let's go in to supper. I guess that's enough good news for one evening.

....

CHAPTER 45

Ida watches Tony Packer get out of the cruiser. She does not know him, but he is wearing his uniform and the police radio's gabbling out from the car's open window. She stiffens out on Joellen's porch where she has been repeatedly drawn by the balmy May day, the day tainted now by the presence of the policeman. She's sure she has violated some white law or custom she knows nothing about. A strong homesickness overtakes her.

Tony Packer leans into the cruiser and turns off the police radio. In its absence the sounds of arguing birds, an air conditioner, a distant shout fill his good ear. He walks to the porch stairs, puts one foot on the bottom step before he says, Evening. Joellen here?

Ida looks at him. Her eyes are side-glancing and damp.

'Scuse me? Joellen here? Tony Packer says again, his inflection the same. He figures the woman didn't hear him. He is patient with deafness.

Do you know where I can find her? he says, his voice a little louder, a little more distinct.

Maybe I might, Ida says. Depends on who's askin'. What for.

Tony Packer starts up the porch steps; Ida shrinks back from him until she is stopped by the porch rail and even then she appears to keep moving back: her shoulders hunch, the top of her chest scoops out, her arms cross over her belly. Tony Packer stops, seeing now how Ida's afraid of him.

If you'd tell her "Tony Packer," he says. He holds up one empty palm the way he'd do to a horse or a dog, showing he's friendly.

The kitchen is dark after the light from outdoors and Ida puts her hand out for a chair back. She lets her eyes get adjusted to this light and lets herself settle down. Tired of white people, she thinks, and tugs at the dress she has on, too tight at the waist. She thinks: time for me to be home.

* * *

Joellen's in the bedroom with the TV on though there's no sound, just the hopping of light. She can face the pictures on the news: the helicopter blades parting and matting the leaves of the Southeast Asian trees, the dripping wet air. She can watch the newsmen's lips move, but she does not want to hear what they say.

Nice out, Ida says. You should go out, breathe some new air.

It is early May, the day warm, perfect, a perfection so transient you feel the loss of the day while you're still in it.

Joellen looks up. Shadows from the TV jump over Ida's belly. It looks like it's moving.

Boy outside, Ida says. Says he been looking for you.

Joellen closes her eyes. She waits to hear "Charlieo" in Ida's voice the way, a long time ago, she had closed her eyes and waited to hear "Joe."

Says Tony Someother, Ida says.

Joellen sits up, surprised. She has not thought of Tony Packer in how long? Nearly three months. She does not even think at first, Tony *Packer*, his last name momentarily gone from her head.

I used to see him, Joellen says, pleased, shy.

Go on out then, Ida says, you can see him again. He's standing right over there. Her voice is snappish. The fear Tony Packer called up in her outside is invisible to Joellen.

Joellen presses her feet to the floor, makes the muscles ride up in her thighs. Maybe they will not support her. Maybe she will not be able to stand. Maybe I can't, she says.

Well you got to find that out your own self. That thing that tells you – Go on.

Like what? Joellen says. What thing? She is suddenly lightened, hopeful: there is an answer. Ida knows it.

Like, I don't know what, Ida says. Different things for different people. For herself it was the acceptance of the child she's carrying, but Ida knows, there are certain good things you don't say.

Hey, Tony Packer says when Joellen comes out. He stands with his hip leaning into the hood of the cruiser. He was not sure she would see him.

How you doin'? Okay? You look fine, he says, though Joellen's thinner than any girl he's ever seen and he looks at the trees above and beyond where she is standing, giving himself time to adjust.

I'm better, she says.

He nods. Puts his foot up on the cruiser's front bumper. So, what're you up to? What'll you do now? Go back to real estate?

Joellen shrugs. Lifts her chin at the cruiser. I might learn how to drive, she says. Plan-wise, that's about it.

Well, get in, he says. I can teach you. He smiles. When he looks back at her again, she seems less altered.

Come on, Tony Packer says.

You mean now? I didn't mean now. I meant soon. Maybe. Maybe later.

Why not now? Tony Packer says. Now works for me.

Joellen thinks "now." An N word.

She comes slowly down the steps and walks to the cruiser, amazed that she is doing these things. They are ordinary things, Joellen, she tells herself: ordinary, an O word. Except they are not.

Tony Packer had backed the cruiser into the driveway, as if this driving lesson is part of an ongoing series of lessons; as if she is not up to "backing out of driveways"; as if she can drive only in straight lines, and Joellen looks up: Charlieo? Not Charlieo.

Joellen Stein, she says to herself. Isabel Stein. Leon Stein.

Tony Packer, Tony Packer, Tony Packer.

Tired, she says and leans her head against the curving chrome door strip.

It's okay. You're fine, Tony Packer says in a voice of professional calm, oddly soothing.

Joellen clears her throat, checking that she can still make sounds, then she gets in. The car's ready. All she has to do is put it in drive, touch her foot to the gas. Go.

That's it, Tony Packer says. Nice and easy.

The cruiser's a Dart, not too big, and rides smooth as a sailboat just skimming the water. The windows are open; air packs into the interior space of the car, into their ears; their hair blows straight back. Tony Packer's cream-in-coffee-colored uniform shirt billows around him.

You're not so bad, he says.

What? Joellen says. The air noise is too loud to hear him.

Your driving, he shouts. He taps the dashboard. He yells – Lessons.

Joellen shrugs, too hard to yell and drive both. A long time ago, she says. I didn't know I'd remember.

She remembers everything. Joe's hand vibrating the shift knob. The heated plastic smell in Leon's Rambler. Charlieo's father's car's wraparound windshield. Gene's gold car with the baby seat in back. The green car that hit Isabel.

The cruiser slows, her foot eases up on the gas.

Tony Packer leans over. Driving? he says. It's best to maintain steady speeds.

Oh, Joellen says. Sorry, and she presses her foot back down on the pedal. I can't do this, she thinks. Too much drag against forward motion.

They pass the Last Gas – crowded, Joellen's surprised. She hasn't been out much; didn't know they were this close to summer. At the tollbooths there are so many cars, she has to slow almost to stopping.

My best customers, Tony Packer says, sweeping his hand out the window.

Joellen sits hunched over the wheel. In the cessation of wind she can hear the dim knocking voices of the police radio, tuned low.

I hate this, she says. Bennies.

Cut out, Tony Packer says.

Joellen looks at him.

Cut out of the line. See the service road? Head over to that.

Joellen shrugs. You're the cop, she says. While she's looking behind and to the side of the cruiser noticing the cars she'll most likely bump into, the siren starts up. She jumps. What did I do? she says, thinking she's touched some wrong button.

Tony Packer grins. Not a thing. Just take her slow till we pass the service road.

I know. Safety. Caution.

Hell no, Tony Packer says. I want to check out their faces.

All around them rock-n-roll disappears from the air as car radios lower; sunburned feet get pulled inside car windows; in convertibles, butts drop back into seats.

Slow enough? Joellen asks.

Perfect. They are not looking at each other, but they are both grinning.

At the end of the service road, Joellen lets the cruiser shoot out onto the high-way. She is amazed at how pleasurable speed is, how easy. Your foot on the gas and that's all. Wind fills the cruiser again. They pass the "Now Leaving . . . " sign of the town and then the "Now Entering" sign of the next one, but Joellen's going too fast to read them.

They drive right into the lowering sun. Joellen looks up for a second; when she looks back at the road, round green balloons pulse on the highway and the speed and power and weight of the car are suddenly tangible to her. Her damp hands slip on the wheel.

The potential for loss is everywhere, scattered like dead animals hit by cars then piled along the side of the road.

How Would You Rather Die: Shot up? Hit by a green car? Of loss or of grief?

She feels the car under her, the forward-moving, heavy machine.

Again, her foot eases up on the gas; she does not know this is happening until she hears Tony Packer, realizes she is hearing him clearly because there is less wind, less interference. He has one hand on the wheel, keeping them steady. Joellen has drifted almost to the shoulder.

On the highway, he says, his voice calm and instructional. Maintain steady speeds. There is no hint, in his voice, that he has said this before.

Joellen nods, but for a second she does not want to go on, thinks: can't. The air sounds she hears now are made by other fast-moving cars rushing past. I don't know if I can do this, she says.

Tony Packer doesn't answer, maybe doesn't hear her, though with him riding shotgun she's got his good ear.

Can I turn around? she says. Maybe I've gone far enough for one day. She wants to be instantly home. To erase the distance she's gone. Not to be driving.

You can turn, Tony Packer says. But not here. He points straight ahead through the windshield at some hidden turnaround Joellen can't see but trusts is there because he knows or can see it. She does not know how far off the turn-around is, how long it will take her to get there. All she can see is the permanent horizon of the highway ahead, the sun a round red disk. She has no choice. She drops the sun visor and drives right into it.

* * *

Ida stands at the top of Joellen's porch steps, where she was standing before Tony Packer pulled in. Her arm's a half-circle at her center where there are daisies embroidered on her dress.

She watched Joellen walk towards the bronze-colored cruiser in a hunched, stiff-legged way as though her legs were reluctant to carry her. Ida's never driven a car herself; not all that often been in one. Except for the skip in the so-far-middle of her life when she and Johnny drove up here from home she has not ever been more than a walk from the places she needed to get to.

On that trip Johnny kept saying he'd teach her to drive once they got settled in. Ida looks through the screen door into the kitchen like she's meaning to finally hold him to it, then remembers Johnny's not here. This is Joellen's house, not her own.

First time I've been alone since I got here, Ida thinks. First time in longer than that. She has not been alone in her own house, hers and Johnny's, maybe ever. The thought is startling; she pushes away from then settles back on the porch rail. Johnny was there when she left for work in the mornings, home nights before she got home, sitting with a book or newspaper, looking at her through those eyeglasses she can't get used to, his eyes, through the lenses, the size of half dollars.

She sat alone in Ma'am's house for days or weeks or months, although she can't remember a sense of aloneness. She sat at the table in Ma'am's pink dress smelling the hot rain smell of that part of the South, that time of year, the wet heating as soon as it hit so puffs of steam and dust came up off the hot ground: a smell close to the smell, here, of the water from hoses.

Before that, between the time Ma'am died and Solomon did, was a different alone, Solomon gone from the bed they had shared their whole two lives. His leg, gone; his body heat. But that was not exactly like being alone either because she dreamed him, caught him in glimpses: his skin, a color between trees; his voice, though his words stayed just on the far side of hearing.

While she stands in the darkening backyard – it is not as late as it looks; the sun Joellen sees out on the highway is visible up the driveway, out front – Ida feels the baby stir inside her and thinks: Not alone now either.

She tips her head down to her stomach which ripples under the tighter and tighter skirt of her dress. The flowers stitched at the waist shift like real flowers in a small wind.

302

You in some kind of rush to get here? she says. Her belly ripples.

Ma'am said Solomon was that way – eyes open, sliding right out.

The baby pushes and kicks.

You in some rush, huh? Ida says again. I don't know why you so anxious to get out to this place. You gonna be one of those ones anxious to get on with everything, right?

The baby kicks, drumming against her and a sort of cramp shimmers across her belly and she hears or knows that the answer is yes.

ACKNOWLEDGMENTS

....

M y thanks to the New York Foundation for the Arts and the National Endowment for the Arts for financial support. And to Kathryn Lang for everything.

ABOUT THE AUTHOR

Mitchell Zykofsky

Edra Ziesk's fiction has appeared in anthologies, and in magazines and quarterlies including *Playgirl, Other Voices, Folio,* and *Turnstile.* She received fiction fellowships from the New York Foundation for the Arts in 1994 and from the National Endowment for the Arts in 1996. She lives in New York City in an apartment so small she has to sit on the steps outside to write when her daughter is home from school.